The Music Teacher

David Cato-Evans

Copyright © 2024 David Cato-Evans
Cover design © Jamie Ross Evans

The moral right of the author has been asserted.

Apart from any fair dealing for the purposes of research or private study, or criticism or review, as permitted under the Copyright, Designs and Patents Act 1988, this publication may only be reproduced, stored or transmitted, in any form or by any means, with the prior permission in writing of the publishers, or in the case of reprographic reproduction in accordance with the terms of licences issued by the Copyright Licensing Agency. Enquiries concerning reproduction outside those terms should be sent to the publishers.

This is a work of fiction. Names, characters, businesses, places, events and incidents are either the products of the author's imagination or used in a fictitious manner. Any resemblance to actual persons, living or dead, or actual events is purely coincidental.

Troubador Publishing Ltd
Unit E2 Airfield Business Park,
Harrison Road, Market Harborough,
Leicestershire. LE16 7UL
Tel: 0116 2792299
Email: books@troubador.co.uk
Web: www.troubador.co.uk

ISBN 978 1805142 737

British Library Cataloguing in Publication Data.
A catalogue record for this book is available from the British Library.

Printed and bound by CPI Group (UK) Ltd, Croydon, CR0 4YY
Typeset in 11pt Minion Pro by Troubador Publishing Ltd, Leicester, UK

For Vicky, with love and thanks for coping with it all.

Chapter 1

Monday, 14 August 2017

The woman tries to control her breathing as she sits on the floor of her bathroom, back against the wall, her head close to the hand basin. The bile rises. She thinks she's going to vomit, so twists to kneel with her head over the lavatory. The shadowy reflection of her eyes in the water fills her with disgust. The need to vomit passes and she sits back, finds she is weeping, sobbing uncontrollably, filled with self-pity, self-hatred.

She reaches up to tear a couple of sheets from the roll, wipes her eyes, blows her nose and drops the soggy tissue in the toilet bowl. She breathes deeply, slowly, remembers what she must do and leans sideways to squeeze the phone out of her jeans pocket, winces as the fabric presses into the dressing on her right leg. Her right hand is throbbing, shaking. She taps 999 – gets it right at the second attempt.

After two rings: 'Emergency. Which service?'

'Police,' she tries to whisper. The noise in her head makes it hard to gauge the volume. 'There's a man with a gun in my house.'

'Transferring you to the police service.' She hears some clicks. A few seconds pass. The police answer.

'Juliette Walker.' She gives her address. 'A man's been shot. I saw it. The other one – with the gun – wants to kill me. I'm locked in the bathroom.' She looks up to her right to check that she had bolted the door. 'I think he's dead. I just ran.'

'Emergency response team is on its way to you. Ambulance service notified,' she hears above the continuing racket in her head. 'Are there any other people in the house?'

'No. Please hurry.' Her voice rises. Another question. 'Yes, I am in danger. He could smash the door down.'

'How many shots were fired?'

Does it matter? 'Two. I was only there for the first one. I ran upstairs and was in the bathroom when I heard the second shot.'

BAM! No. Impossible. Another gunshot. A scream, loud, tortured. Not her. This can't be happening. It must be a dream. Reality has stopped.

She freezes, legs out straight. The phone is in her hand, but she can't do anything with it. It doesn't make sense. Her hand is clamped around the phone, throbbing painlessly. She closes her eyes, knows she must breathe. Relax. She listens to the tinnitus. As usual, it covers about two octaves, up high, no identifiable notes. Something like a woman screaming without having to draw breath, while using a powerful hand dryer. Or a vacuum cleaner. A rushing of air. Always loud at times of stress, but at least something she is familiar with. Almost a comfort. But that was a real scream.

She looks at her left hand. It's holding a tissue – two tissues – with blood stains. She twists to her right and drops them in the toilet bowl, then reaches up and pulls the flush handle. She closes her eyes, tries to get rid of the recurring images of blood spurting, the man's face, rolling eyes, lips moving as he tries to speak. Then it seems she's up high, looking down on herself – with disgust. How can this have happened? Surely she wasn't to blame, was she?

She's unaware of time having passed, when she hears the sirens above the noise in her head. It is then that she sees the drop of blood on one of her black trainers, and spots like dirty marks on the right leg of her skinny black jeans near the ankle. They must be the same blood. Think. Whose can it be? But what's that? A sound – sounds. A scrape. A gasp. A grunt. This can't be real. Another nightmare. She'll wake up before the demon gets into her. If only…

The sirens are getting louder. Thank God. But there's the thing, it must be the man. He's managed to get up the stairs. This is really happening. There's a louder grunt, then a bang on the door. She shudders, pulls her legs up. She's making herself as small as possible in behind the toilet, looking over it at the door. Her phone is on the tiled floor. Her hands are hurting, clasped together under her thighs. She can't take her eyes off the door handle. A tiny movement? Impossible. She's panting, gasping for air through clenched teeth. *Count to ten. Slow down.* But then another thump on the door. Can't be mistaken. She sees it shift slightly with the impact. She looks up at the bolt, holding, but only strong enough to keep children out.

BAM! The noise stabs her head. She brings her hands up and presses them against her ears. She opens her eyes, lifts her head just far enough, and sees a splintered hole in the door near the floor. The roar in her head is overwhelming. She turns and sees the mirror has shattered, shards of glass have fallen silently into the hand basin, and some onto the floor. She closes her eyes again, unable to move, plunging into darkness.

Chapter 2

Saturday, sixteen days before the shooting at the Walkers' house.

Juliette came into the kitchen through the back door, panting and sweating.

'Lovely morning for a run.' Steve was holding a plastic spoon of porridge for Lucy, who was in her highchair.

'Good morning, my darlings.' Juliette kissed the top of Lucy's blonde head, then walked round the table to give Jason a little cuddle. 'Almost too warm. The lawn's looking dry.'

'What are you lot up to today?' Steve was wearing a light blue shirt and a tie with a colourful abstract design.

'Jazzy's swimming club this morning. Lulu and I will watch. Then I'm taking them to Karen's. I've got a couple of flute lessons to do in town, and one here for piano this afternoon. Busy Saturday, as per.' She felt a small furry body push against her calf. 'Oh, Ziggy, no one fed you yet? Come on.' The cat led her into the utility room.

'What are we going to do at Karen's?' Jason called after her.

'Well,' she called back, scooping dry cat food into the bowl, 'if you're very good, there's just a chance, a remote possibility…'

'The beach, the beach,' he yelled.

'Eech, eech,' Lucy echoed.

Juliette came back into the kitchen. 'You might just be lucky, as her two love it as much as you both do. And, if I can squeeze it into my busy schedule, I might meet you there for half an hour and bring you home. And then there will be a short piano lesson for my most important student.'

'Me, me,' Jason said. '"Ode to Joy". I can play it, Daddy. Grown-up music.'

'We're still working on the left-hand part,' Juliette said. 'He's coming along well.'

'Will you play it for me when I get home?' Steve said. 'Something to look forward to if you're not too tired.'

'Lulu can't play any tunes. She just makes a noise.'

'That's how you started when you were two, Jazzy. Thumping the keys and discovering the different sounds they make.'

*

Juliette was in the kitchen again with the children, when her phone jingled and trembled. She held it to her left ear while using her right hand to stir a saucepan of scrambled egg.

'Hey, baby.' The still familiar nasal drawl she hadn't heard for years.

'What?' She pulled the phone away from her ear and stared at it for a second before hitting the red button. *Why the hell does he think I'll talk to him?* She turned to the children sitting at the kitchen table. Lucy was using her half of a banana to make a pattern on the plastic table fixed to her highchair. 'Lulu, don't do that. Jazzy, can you help her? Gently. Scrambled egg will be ready soon.' Her father, after three years – what could he possibly want?

Her phone beeped. A text: *Jules you've got to listen you and the kids are in danger I'll phone again in one minute you don't have to talk to me just listen.*

Her hand shook as she put the phone back on the worktop. Was it some kind of trick to get back into her life? Well, it wasn't going to work. She'd listen to him – then tell him to fuck off.

She was ready for it when the phone jingled again. She turned the gas off under the egg and perched on a bar stool, checked that the children weren't fighting. Jason was holding the half-banana for Lucy to break bits off.

'I'm listening,' she said, trying to keep her voice steady.

'Jules, this is the last thing I wanted, honest. I'm in a spot of bother.' It sounded to her like 'bovver'.

'Why should I care?' She inwardly cursed herself for asking the question. It was too much like entering into a conversation with him.

'Business. Deal's gone tits up. Where's Steve?'

She wasn't going to fall for that. She kept silent as she looked out through the steel bars of the open window. The lawn looked parched in the August sunshine. She'd get the sprinkler out later.

Eventually he spoke again. 'I get it. He'd be in the shop. Saturday. So you're on your own at home. Just you and the kids?'

'I'm not having a conversation with you. Say what you've got to say, then let me get on with my life.'

'I wish. You don't want to be on your own, Jules, you and the kids. Whatever you think, I care about you – all of you. You want someone with you, your mum. Or a friend?' His voice was tense.

'What's going on?' She couldn't stop herself from asking.

'Look, you don't need to panic. It'll be okay. Just take precautions. Stay close to the kids, and don't be on your own.' His voice wasn't as steady as usual.

She slipped down from the stool and walked out of the kitchen, crossed the hallway to the sitting room, out of the children's earshot. 'What the hell is this?'

'There's this bloke. Mean bastard. He's trying to find me, and I'm trying not to be found.'

'Should I wish him luck?' She walked across the sitting room, opened the French windows and walked out into the sunshine. She sat on one of the wrought iron patio chairs.

'This bloke. Been inside a long time. Kidnapping and extortion. Been out a few weeks. Putting himself about. Chip on his shoulder. Oh, and rape – that too.' He sounded out of breath, walking fast, or running.

She started listening properly. Maybe he was on the level.

'Your mum might remember him. She defended him. Thirty years ago. Johnny Frampton. Piece of shit. Got the drop on me while I was in Belgium. Bastard.'

She was pressing the phone against her ear to stop her hand shaking. 'So Mum could be in danger?'

'He's the sort of bastard who'll think of someone's weak spot. I'd get a message telling me to go and meet him or something'll happen to one of you. That sort of bastard.'

Juliette closed her eyes. The noise was starting. 'I'm phoning the police.'

'Jules. Fuck's sake, no cops. Listen, that'd get right up his nose. Nothing they'd do. They're not going to give you an armed guard on your say so, and certainly not on mine. But it'd up the ante. Push him into making a move. Promise me: no cops!'

She struggled to control her voice. 'You're scaring the shit out of me. This is your mess. If you really care about us, you'd come out of hiding so this man finds you and we'd be out of danger.' The anger had been festering for three years.

'Jules, we can win this. Trust me. We just need to take precautions. It's just him. He's not going to come at you with an army. If there's two of you with the kids at all times, you'll be safe. Believe me. Never turn your back on them, not for a second.'

'I'll never forgive you if anything happens to Jazzy or Lulu.' She felt tears running down her cheeks. 'And what the hell am I supposed to say to Mum, and Steve?'

'You can handle it – easy. Don't say anything that'll make either of them go to the cops. Best not to mention Frampton. Get your mum to come and stay with you. She thinks I'm on a business trip. She'll be happy to get out of the mansion and come to yours. Just tell her because of the summer holidays you need help with the kids. She'll jump at it. Same with Steve, when he's not busy in his shop. He's got that consignment from Belgium due Thursday.'

'For God's sake, we can't be together all the time. What about the music lessons, and my morning run, and when I meet Tim in the park?'

'It's not long term, baby.'

'Don't fucking well call me baby,' she yelled, needing to find some kind of release.

'Yeah, look, you need to keep calm. It'll all be sorted in a couple of weeks, probably sooner. I'm fixing things. You know me. I always come out on top. Best to cancel the lessons, except the ones you do at home. Don't go running, Jules, not on your own. The things with Tim – plenty of people in the park. You make sure you're not followed, don't you? You only do one a week, don't you? Risk is minimal. Johnny won't get wise to it. Just make sure the kids are shut up safe and cosy with your mum at your house, doors locked, CCTV on.'

'If this man comes near me, I'll do what I can to help him find you.' She knew her voice was unsteady but felt a little better for having got those words out.

'You'd better forget what happened years ago. Think of the kids. Just take sensible precautions. And don't worry. The Belton-Smart empire will be back in control very soon. I've got it all planned. I had to take some money. Your mum'll be pissed off about that too. Try to smooth—'

There was a high-pitched scream from the kitchen. Juliette sprang up and ran in, heart thumping. She found Jason allowing Lucy to chase him around the kitchen table. There was banana mush in her hair.

'She started it. It's her fault,' Jason said.

Juliette sighed. *Thank God.* 'Who's ready for scrambled egg?' She managed a reassuring smile for them, but her mind was still on the things her father had said. She looked at the screen on her phone. Dead. She tapped it a few times to reconnect, and held it to her ear. After several rings a synthetic voice told her the person was not available.

She tried to focus on the children – blue-eyed Lucy struggling to get egg on her little spoon and then into her mouth. She'd help her after a few more attempts – as long as she could hold her hand steady. She glanced at Jason, dark and with his father's brown eyes – a confident five-year-old; he'd already finished his bowl of egg and was munching a piece of wholemeal bread. But her father's words kept spinning in her head. How could even such a despicable man endanger his daughter and grandchildren? Then, through the hatred and rage, a part of her mind was telling her he must still care about them, or he wouldn't have made the phone call.

*

'Jewel, darling, that was a lovely meal.' Caroline relaxed into an early Victorian wing-back chair. She was wearing a terracotta-coloured blouse and matching culottes.

Juliette was rehearsing words in her head.

Her mother continued, 'I like this chair – good back support. Are you going to keep it?'

'It'll have to go back to the shop at some point.' Steve shrugged as he topped up the glass on the table beside her chair with white wine. He was still wearing the colourful tie, now loosened at the neck, with the top button of his shirt undone. He indicated the Edwardian couch that he and Juliette were sitting on. 'This is a real back-breaker without the cushions.'

'Mum, if you see or hear Steve behaving oddly, it's because he's rehearsing a role in the operatic society's new production.'

'Tell me about it?'

'I'm Arturo in *Lucia di Lammermoor* – not a huge part, but quite demanding.'

Juliette assumed her mother didn't know the story. 'He enters into a marriage contract with Lucia, who's in love with another man, drives her mad and gets murdered by her. It's a horrible story.'

'That's why it's such a great opera,' Steve said. 'Dressing it up in formal clothes makes it bearable – equips us to deal with the horror.'

Caroline said, 'Well, I look forward to the performance anyway.'

Steve had a glass of red wine. Juliette was drinking herbal tea. She glanced in turn at her mother and husband, feeling a pang of envy at their ability to drink alcohol without any fear of losing control – a thing she hadn't done for three years. But her mind kept going back to the phone call from her father. Was there some clue she hadn't picked up? There must be something he hadn't told her. Was he overstating the danger? Or understating it?

Steve was talking again. 'You're looking well, Cara. Your hair's very elegant.'

'Thank you.' Her medium-length blonde hair was tied in a loose knot with the ends spraying out at the back. 'I've decided to let the grey through. Can't be honey-blonde forever. You always look so smart. I didn't want to let you down. And I've always liked Jewel's shaggy look.'

'I thought Richard came back from Liège. The stock should be delivered on Thursday. I can't wait. Walker's Antiques is going to look completely different – attract new customers. Do you know how long he's going to be away?'

Juliette had lost patience with the small talk between her mother and husband. There had already been enough of it at dinner.

Caroline shook her head and sighed. 'God knows. He comes and goes as he pleases. He could be shacked up with that tart he calls his PA for all I know.'

'Why do you put up with it?' Juliette looked sharply at her mother.

Caroline sighed. 'I'd need psychoanalysis to work that out. Inertia, I suppose.' She sipped her wine. 'We each live our own lives. And… you'll think I'm naïve. I keep thinking of moving away, but I've got friends in the village, the centre's nearby, I keep busy…' She took another sip of wine.

Juliette didn't want to pursue that, and saw the opportunity. 'I should have told you earlier. He phoned this afternoon and told me he had to go away in a hurry. To be honest, I'm worried about him. I think we should try to find out where he's gone.'

Steve turned to her. 'You mean you actually spoke to him? At last.'

Caroline looked at her. 'Why didn't you tell me – and the sudden concern?'

'I didn't say more than I had to.'

'He hasn't laid a hand on me since that time. We're actually quite civilised with each other.' A shadow seemed to pass over Caroline's face.

'I've got a feeling. I think it's important that we find him. Steve, has he said anything to you about where he might have gone?'

She looked at him sideways. She had made the Edwardian couch as comfortable as possible with a pile of cushions. She was still smitten by her husband's profile. Mediterranean looks inherited from his mother: straight nose, well-defined cheekbones, firm jawline. She looked again. It wasn't just the light. There was a slight sag under his chin. Not yet thirty and beginning to show the signs of good living. She was holding his hand that was on her thigh.

'Not a thing,' Steve said. 'I assumed he'd be staying at home after he got back from Belgium. It was good of him to supervise the shipping of that stock. I can't wait to get it in the shop. I'm really glad you've broken your vow of silence; it's been so awkward. But what did he say to you? Why did he phone you?'

'Are you sure he hasn't dropped a hint? Nothing between the lines? Does he ever mention Vanessa?'

'We only talk about business, really. We don't socialise,' Steve said. 'He's really helpful, though – cheaper rates than any other carrier. I wish you could get on with him. It'd make things easier. Didn't you even ask him where he was?'

'Why don't we all go over to your house tomorrow, Mum? The children can play in the garden – at least while a couple of us are with them. We could have a look around the house to see if he left anything. Anything that might give us an idea where he's gone.'

'He keeps the office locked. I don't see why we need to really. He always comes back when he feels like it.'

Juliette realised she'd have to tell them a bit more. 'He told me he's in trouble. He's having to lie low. I definitely think we ought to try to find out where he is.'

'What sort of trouble, darling? Some of the people he does business with can be quite unpleasant.'

'He didn't say, but that's the point, isn't it? He did say he'd had to take some money. Mum, you'd better check. You use a joint account, don't you? Have you got the mobile app?'

Caroline looked flustered as she reached for her phone

in the handbag on the floor beside her. After several taps she gazed at the phone with an expression of disbelief. 'It's all gone.' She looked up at Juliette. 'Right down to the overdraft limit. I expect he's still refusing to answer.' She stabbed the keys on her phone and put it to her ear. 'Switched off,' she said after a few seconds, glaring with fury.

'I deleted him from my contacts long ago. This is the number he called me from.' Juliette held her phone for Caroline to see.

'So he's got a new phone.'

Juliette said, 'I've tried it several times since he called. Not available.'

'Yes, let's find him. He never touches that account. Now he's taken £30,000.' She gulped some wine and put the glass back on the table, missing the coaster.

Steve looked up and lifted a hand. 'Cara, don't worry, we can lend you what you need from the shop account. Oh, and if we're going to your house tomorrow, could we borrow some of your videos?'

'They're quite old.'

'We'll need to get into his office. Have you got a key?' Juliette asked.

'No, he's never let me in there.'

'Those are the ones we like,' Steve said. 'Seventies and eighties – and older. You've got *Wait Until Dark*, one of my favourites, and that Hitchcock collection.'

Chapter 3

'I didn't hear you go out.' Steve was spreading butter on to one of two warm croissants on the small plate in front of him. He was wearing a dark blue Armani polo shirt. The kitchen was filled with the aroma of freshly made coffee. A television cartoon, and frequent bursts of children's laughter, were audible from the sitting room.

'I didn't.' Juliette had come into the kitchen wearing running shorts and a white T-shirt. Her face was shining with sweat. 'Opted for half an hour on the exercise bike. Glad it's your free Sunday.' On the bike she had been thinking about the phone call and had decided she had to tell them both all about it.

'Nick's covering today – shouldn't be too busy.' Steve sipped a mug of coffee. 'Your mum seems to have found a way of coexisting with your dad.'

She went to the fridge and took out a carton of orange juice and a tub of zero-fat yoghurt. She put them on the table and examined her hands. They were steady. *He's going to suspect something if I'm not careful.* 'Steve, do we really have to go through this again? Zero tolerance means zero tolerance for me. Providing transport for the shop doesn't change the principle.' She poured some juice into a glass. 'Anyway, it's irrelevant as long as he's... out of touch. In your business dealings with him, has he ever mentioned a Johnny Frampton?'

'Frampton? Not that I remember. Why?'

'I'll tell you both when Mum comes down.'

Juliette was eating a bowl of granola and yoghurt when Caroline came into the kitchen wearing a colourful silk dressing gown, with red and blue flowers amongst green foliage. 'What are you having, Mum, toast and marmalade, croissant, granola?'

Caroline started with just a mug of coffee. When she was sitting at the kitchen table, next to Steve, Juliette said, 'There's something I ought to tell you both. Dad asked me not to, but, well, I think I should. Mum, has he ever mentioned one of his business friends to you – Johnny Frampton?'

Caroline jerked her head up, put the mug down, spilling some coffee. 'That's a name I was hoping never to hear again,' she said softly. 'He's serving a long sentence.'

'He's been released. When Dad phoned yesterday, he said he's hiding from this man Frampton. He told me you would recognise the name.'

'We must call the police.'

'That would be the worst possible thing. Dad said if we did that it'd make it more dangerous for us.'

'Dangerous? For us?' Steve, who was on his third mug of coffee, raised his free hand, palm open.

'Dad said he was the sort of man – mean bastard, he called him – who'd exploit his weaknesses. I think that meant us.'

Caroline was looking pale. 'Did he say why he's hiding from Frampton?'

'He said a deal had gone wrong. I think Frampton took advantage somehow while Dad was in Belgium. That's why he wants us to stay together. Frampton isn't likely to try anything if we're together.'

'What do you mean "try anything"?' Steve's dark eyes caught Juliette's.

'I know what he means,' Caroline said. 'Frampton was the defendant in a rape case. He'd be in his sixties now.'

Juliette stood up, gathering her bowl and mug with a clatter. 'Sorry, can we talk about this later? I've got to put a load of laundry on before we go. She dropped the crockery on the sideboard and rushed out of the kitchen and up the stairs. Two rapists – one chasing the other. What would happen if Frampton found her dad? Did she care? She sat on the edge of Jason's little bed with her head in her hands. They would all be safe. Problem solved. They'd all be safe – except her dad. He'd be beaten up, forced to do what? Hand over money he'd stolen? Something else? He'd sounded so scared. Scared for his life? She stood up, grabbed the children's laundry bag and went downstairs.

Steve and Caroline were still in the kitchen. He was telling her something about eighteenth-century French furniture. When Juliette had started the washer-dryer she came back to the table. 'Sorry to interrupt. I just needed to get that done. You were going to tell us the grisly details about this man Frampton?'

'Not if you don't want me to.'

'I think we should know what you know, okay?'

'It's horrible, but yes.' Caroline took a sip of coffee.

'Early eighties, not long before I quit the legal profession. John Frampton. I was defending him. The one rape case I lost. Some wretched man owed Frampton a lot of money.' Caroline's voice had gone quiet. Juliette was listening intently. She glanced at Steve, who was also giving Caroline his full attention. 'Frampton threatened that if he didn't pay up, he'd rape his daughter. The girl was only seventeen. Her father went to pick her up at school, knowing that that was the time of most risk. Three thugs jumped them both. Drove them to some isolated house. Jesus.'

Juliette wanted to block her ears. She didn't want to hear the rest of this story but needed to. She was feeling sick. 'Mum, are you sure you want to...' She saw her mother's eyeliner beginning to smudge.

Caroline looked up and said quickly, 'Frampton raped the girl, his thugs forcing the father to watch. Then they took it in turns. God. Then they drove them both several miles to some remote area in their own car, told them that if they went to the police, they'd do the same for his other daughter, who was twelve at the time. A few days later the father hanged himself and it was during the investigation into that, that the girl who had been raped told the police the whole story.' Caroline put her head in her hands, sniffed.

Juliette couldn't speak. She would do anything to stop such a man getting near her children. She passed her mother a box of tissues.

'What's this got to do with Richard?' Steve looked grim.

'God knows how he can have anything to do with a man like that,' Caroline said, carefully dabbing each eye with a tissue, then wiping her nose. 'You can see, can't you?' She looked at Steve. 'If Frampton really wants to find Richard, he's the sort of man who might abduct one of us to force him out of hiding.' Turning to Juliette she went on, 'Yes, I agree, Jewel, what you said. We must stay together. We could go away. Somewhere he can't find us. Take the children for a holiday.'

'Dad said we'd be safe as long as we keep together,' Juliette said slowly, not wanting them to become too alarmed. 'And we've got good security in the house. I think our best hope is to find my dad. And I don't want Jazzy and Lulu to know anything's wrong, so let's act as normally as possible.' Ziggy Stardust glided blackly into the kitchen and uttered a 'myah'. 'Starting with you, Ziggy. Let's go and get your breakfast.'

Juliette closed the utility room door behind her and put the cat's food bowl down. Ziggy attacked it. 'Simple life for you, isn't it, Zig,' Juliette whispered. 'Food, sleep and lots of cuddles. You don't know what it's like to be violated, do you. Well, just that time I took you to the vet. You didn't know, did you. No sense of indescribable hurt, loss, rage, disgust. Just woke up with a bare patch in your fur and a few stiches. She'd gone inside your body and sliced away the possibility of your becoming a mother. It was my fault. I'm sorry.' Juliette blinked away a tear as she looked at the cat, who was still crunching into dry food. 'You'd have been a great mother. Hardwired. Same reason you're a great killer of small creatures. One thing I know, Zig: motherhood – guaranteed to give you a purpose in life.'

*

On the drive, twenty minutes or so, to her parents' house, Juliette sat in the back seat of the Volvo with Jason on his booster seat in the middle, and Lucy strapped into her child seat on the other side of him. Caroline was in the front passenger seat, Steve driving.

Jason had his head down, a picture book on his lap. Lucy pointed out of the side window and said, 'Cow.'

Juliette turned her head. 'They're sheep, darling.'

Lucy said, 'Seep.'

Jason, without looking up from his book, said, 'You're thick.'

'That's not a nice thing to say, Jazzy. You didn't know the difference when you were two.'

'What noise does a sheep make?' Jason wasn't giving up.

'Mooo,' said Lucy.

'See? I told you.'

'Be nice, Jason,' Steve said, keeping his eyes on the road.

Juliette looked at Lucy, who smiled back, blue eyes sparkling. What had Jason's vocabulary been like at that age? Maybe Lucy was a bit slow. Jason was concentrating on his book again, a finger helping him follow the few lines of text on each page.

Steve slowed the car and steered it into the familiar driveway, then stopped to open the heavy steel gate with the remote control. After a second, the gate started sliding on its rails to the right. The two concrete heraldic lions looked down from the tops of the brick pillars on each side of the entrance. Juliette turned to look at Lucy, now asleep, head tilted forwards and to the right, and felt an urgent need to protect her, as Steve slid the car forwards.

'We're here! We're here!' cried Jason, smacking his book shut, causing Lucy to jerk awake and echo, 'Here.'

As the car twisted through the S-bend of the driveway,

leaving the gate to slide shut behind them, Juliette caught Lucy's eye, trying to imagine what was going on in her head. Steve stopped the Volvo in front of the three-car garage, which was fully open and empty except for a garden tractor in the right-hand bay.

'Do you always leave it open, Mum?'

'When we're not here and no cars here. The gardeners use that mower thing on Tuesdays.'

'Steve, can you entertain them for now? You know where the toy box is. We'll all go and play in the garden this afternoon.' As they walked across the gravel, Juliette was holding Lucy's hand as she was still drowsy. Steve was holding Jason's hand to stop him running around the house into the garden.

As Caroline went up the three stone steps to open the front door, she said, 'Anyone really intent on robbing us could drive across the field at the back and climb over that little wooden fence. The gate at the front's mainly for show. Richard's vanity, self-importance – wanted it to look like a fortress.'

'Goes with the fake columns,' Juliette said, waving at the light grey pillars on either side of the door, topped by a mock-classical portico. She closed her eyes as she went in. Entering his domain. *Don't let them see.* She hated this house because it was so redolent of him. And it was ugly. They followed Caroline into the house and saw her disable the alarm system.

Once inside, Steve took the children into the sitting room. Juliette went down the short corridor to the right of the hall and tested the door at the end. 'Have you never had a key, Mum?'

'Never been in there since it was converted. Never wanted to. I accepted that it was best for me not to know about his shady business deals. I've no idea if there's a spare key.' Caroline was keeping her head turned away from Juliette. 'I know what you're thinking.'

'What am I thinking?'

'Bloody hypocrite.'

'I'm not, actually. I'm thinking we all make compromises. Don't beat yourself up.' *Not thinking about you. Thinking about me – and him.*

'Compromises. No kidding.'

'Let's give ourselves half an hour looking for a key. If we don't find one, we'll call an emergency locksmith. If there's going to be a clue as to his whereabouts, it'll be in the office.'

'If we find an address for that tart, Vanessa, we'll have him.'

'I'll do upstairs. You do down, okay?'

At the top of the stairs, Juliette turned right down the corridor, passed the door on the left to the main guest bedroom with the ensuite, the bathroom on the right, then the next door. She paused in front of it. Her room. She tried to remember the last time she had been in the room. It must have been before Jazzy was born. She turned the handle and pushed. Still the same blue – the deep sky blue of summer evenings as the sun began to set, and which she had been allowed to choose as a reward for getting Grade 8 Piano at the age of thirteen. They must have repainted it the same colour. There was no sign of the marks left by the posters. Then she saw the makeup, the bottles and pots, a hairbrush on her white desk. A mirror on a dark blue plastic stand, with a lamp on each side, turning the desk into a dressing table. She looked at the bed. The duvet was turned back, the sheet creased. There was the indentation of a head on the pillow.

She sat on the edge of the bed and remembered the room with the Jonathan Brandis posters. Jonathan Brandis, adolescent heartthrob, who looked like a younger version of her dad and who committed suicide when she was thirteen.

There had been a knock on the door. It opened a crack.

'I heard you crying.' His voice.

She was sobbing, hadn't answered.

'Can I come in?'

Then he was sitting on the bed putting an arm around her. He handed her a tissue. 'Tell me about it.'

'Jonathan,' she managed. She rested her head on his shoulder and smelt the tobacco smoke. She liked it then.

'I heard it on the news,' he said. 'Are you going to take the posters down?'

She loved the sound of his voice, knew about his working-class roots, how he'd pulled himself up by his own effort – and now speaking so gently, caring about her grief.

'I'll keep them forever.'

*

'Jewel, darling, have you found anything yet?' Her mother's voice, calling from downstairs, jolted her back into the present.

'I think I'm ready for that drink now,' she called back, closing the door of her old bedroom behind her. 'Any water in the fridge?'

Juliette cradled a glass of water in both hands, her elbows

on the marble-topped kitchen table. 'Mum, I went into my old room.'

Caroline started, looked at Juliette. 'Didn't I tell you? That's been my bedroom for a few years now. I had it redecorated. Same colour – I like that blue.'

'I suppose I should have guessed. Do you know why you've stuck it for so long?'

Caroline looked down. 'You must think I'm a coward – and selfish. You've been really strong, supporting me, making him understand.' She sighed. 'I've been more practical, I suppose, but I've never slept with him after that – after what he did.'

Juliette felt tears forming, so stood up to take her empty glass to the sink. *After what he did. You'll never know.* She fought to control her voice. 'You've drawn a blank here, right? It won't be in your study. The den's a possibility, but the master bedroom or Dad's dressing room are probably the best bet. Let's go up there together. Then we can check the den… oh… and the garage. I'll just take some drinks in to Steve, check that all's well in there.'

Steve was helping Jason build a tower of wooden bricks; Lucy was bouncing a brown, knitted kangaroo on her knee. Steve looked up.

'One elderflower and two weak orange juices, okay?'

While they helped themselves, she felt a compulsion to go to the sofa on the far side of the room and sit on it. It was near the end of her last term at primary school. She had been sitting on this sofa, reading. Her dad had come into the room with a long parcel wrapped in purple and white striped paper with a gold bow.

She looked up. 'It isn't my birthday.'

25

'This is for a special girl,' he said. 'Miss Ireson says you're the best recorder player she's ever taught. And she's been letting you play her flute a few times. You're a natural talent, she says.' He handed the parcel to her. 'Open it.'

She tore off the wrapping paper, saw a brown case with a handle and YAMAHA in big letters. She knew what it was going to be, felt the tears of happiness, put the case down, and flung her arms round her dad's neck.

'Are you okay, Jules?' Steve's voice wrenched her back into the present. She felt a tear drip down one cheek and put a hand up quickly.

'Fine. It's fun seeing you playing together.'

*

Juliette and Caroline walked into the master bedroom. Stale tobacco. Juliette went straight to the window and pushed it open wide. 'Stifling in here,' she said, as she rested her hands on the windowsill and looked out across the expanse of green lawn and the professionally kept herbaceous border. That smell. It was in his clothes the last time she saw him, was with him, had leant into him and, barely awake, had rested her head on his shoulder. *No, no, no...*

The duvet was neatly laid on the king-size bed. There was nothing on the dressing table, no clothes on either of the upright chairs. 'Marjory must have tidied and cleaned since he left,' Caroline said. 'He usually leaves it like a tip.'

Juliette shuddered. She could feel his presence in the room. The father of her adulthood, not of her adolescence. *Take a grip. It was three years ago.* But it was like yesterday. She couldn't remember a thing about it. And no one knew.

So it didn't happen. *Hold on to that.* No one except him.

'Let's try the dressing room first,' she said. 'If he's going to keep a spare key, it could be in a drawer, maybe under a pile of clothes.'

They took the purple and gold bedspread off the bed, looked under the duvet, under the pillows, under the sheet, under the mattress cover, under the mattress, under the bed. Nothing. They took all the remaining clothes out of the drawers, shook them, looked under the lining paper, looked in the pockets of all the clothes left in the wardrobe, in the bedside cabinet, and under all the furniture.

'On top of the wardrobe?' Juliette suggested.

'I'll do it.' Caroline grabbed an upright chair, dragged it to the wardrobe and climbed up.

Juliette looked at the only picture hanging in the room, a print of racehorses jumping a fence. 'Maybe I watch too many films, but you never know.' She reached up and unhooked it, turned it round and looked at the back. 'Dah, dah!' she chanted. A small straight security key was taped to the back of the picture.

Chapter 4

The tobacco smell again, but Juliette had made herself ready for it this time. 'I remember it being a granny flat,' she said. They were in Richard's office. A large mahogany desk dominated the room, a black, thickly padded executive chair behind it. There was a smaller light wooden desk at right angles to it, with a computer and monitor on it, and a typist's chair behind it. Juliette walked past the large desk, pulled up the venetian blinds and pushed open the large window.

Caroline said, 'I persuaded him to have this flat included when he had the house built. I thought Grandpa could use it before he died. I think Richard was planning it as an office all along – just humoured me.'

Juliette went to the filing cabinet in a corner opposite the window and gave the top drawer a tug. Then the other three drawers in turn. 'Locked. Might be a key to this somewhere.' She opened the door next to the filing cabinet and went through and switched on the light. A light oak board table with three chairs down each side and one at either end nearly filled the room. There were garish abstract paintings on each side wall and heavy curtains closed at the end. The only other piece of furniture was a small table in the corner with an array of bottles and glasses.

'This was the bedroom.' Caroline had followed Juliette into the room. 'That door on the right was the bathroom.'

Juliette opened the door and looked in. 'Still is. Nothing here.'

*

After a quick snack lunch, Juliette sat in the executive chair and looked at the desk. There was something repulsive about sitting where he had sat, touching the things that he had touched, but she couldn't help being drawn to it. A cream-coloured landline phone, a couple of cheap ballpoint pens, a small jotting pad and a dirty marble ashtray with a few cigarette ends were the only things on the desk. Having overcome the initial disgust, being in his seat, at his desk, felt strangely good. He had gone. She was here, sitting in his seat of power. She looked at the phone on the desk. One of the quick-dial buttons was marked V. Worth a try.

It was answered after a few rings. 'My God, Richard, where have you been?' A light, high-pitched woman's voice.

'It's Jules, his daughter.'

'Oh, it's Vanessa. Do you remember me? Your dad's PA. You must be in his office. Is he there?'

Caroline came into the office and gave her a questioning look. Juliette put up her free hand to stop her from talking. 'No,' focusing back on Vanessa. 'Do you know where he is?'

'He sacked me last week and he owes me loads of money.' Vanessa sounded as if she were about to burst into tears. 'Isn't he there?'

'What? You mean... Sorry, I thought... My mum had the idea you'd be more likely to know where he is than us. He hasn't been in touch for a few days.' Juliette heard loud sobbing on the phone. 'Vanessa, what's happened?'

After a few seconds, Vanessa managed to speak again. 'He just gave me notice last week. Phoned me at the weekend. He said his working methods were changing, having to move with the times, bullshit like that, and he wouldn't be needing my services anymore. He said he'd transfer three months' pay to my account right away in lieu of notice and email me a glowing reference to help me find another job. But he hasn't transferred the money or sent the email. And he hasn't paid me for July yet. That's well overdue. He's not answering his mobile.'

'Look, I'm really sorry—'

Caroline hissed, 'Let me talk to that bitch. She knows—'

'No. She wants to help. Let me.' Juliette turned away and took her hand off the mouthpiece. 'Vanessa, sorry about that. Look, we're trying to track him down as well. Have you got office keys? The filing cabinet? The desks?'

'I've just got keys to my desk and the filing cabinet. He was very strict about leaving them locked. Very security conscious. Can you or your mother transfer the money to me? It's like a family business, isn't it? It's what I'm owed. I'm a good worker, and I've been loyal to your dad, your family, for nearly three years. He can't just drop me in it like this.' She started sobbing again.

'I'm sorry. We're all in it together. We need to find him too. Could you help us? Can you give me your contact details?'

Juliette scribbled the phone number and address on the small pad on the desk. 'When did you last see my father?'

'Not for a couple of weeks. He had that trip – Belgium, he said. He phoned me a few times – usual things, just passing on messages, checking everything was in order. Then last Sunday he phones and lands this bombshell – told me I mustn't even come to the mansion, he likes to call it, to get my things. He sounded nervy, like he was upset at having to let me go. That's what I thought…'

'So you've got absolutely no idea where he might have gone?'

'No. But there's something might help. It sort of happened by accident. It was in my first week, year before last, he was out and had left his laptop on his desk, and he phoned me saying he needed to check if someone had sent him an email. So he told me his email address and password and asked me to look in his laptop. He's never learned how to use his phone for emails – not very computer savvy, your dad. I already had my PC running so I opened the account in that without bothering to open his laptop.' Vanessa paused for breath. 'I didn't mean to be nosy, but, well, in case it happened again, I saved the password.'

'Do you remember the address and password?'

'No, except it's Gmail, so easy to open on the PC. He's always locked his laptop in his desk since then, or taken it with him. He must think it'd be the only way I could read his emails.'

Could Juliette trust this woman? Was she really trying to help? Or could her mother be right? Vanessa and Richard could be together, just trying to extract another few thousand pounds. Giving her access to her dad's emails – what was that about? She decided to play along for now.

Vanessa was speaking again. 'Oh, and there's a spare key to the filing cabinet in my top desk drawer.'

'Vanessa, tell me the log-on password to the PC?'

'Meredith007,' Vanessa said. 'It's my hamster's name.'

'Is there anything else on the PC that might indicate where he's gone?'

'I can't think of anything. He was buying a house in Nottingham, but I doubt if he's gone there. I didn't use it much; he does everything on the phone, or meeting people; he's out nearly all the time. It was my job to answer the phone, you know, make it seem like a proper office.'

'Are you sure there's nothing else that might help us find him?'

'Nothing I can think of. Is there any way you can help me with the money I'm owed? I'm skint.'

'The best I can do right now is send you a couple of thousand, which I'll have to borrow from the antique shop. Can you text me your bank details and the total amount he owes you? If he turns up, I'll make sure he pays you. If he doesn't, I'll see what we can do. This is on the understanding that you'll let me know immediately if he contacts you, or you think of anything that might help us find him. I'll text you my mobile number.'

Juliette put the phone back on its cradle and looked up at her mother.

Caroline said, 'I don't like the idea of sending her money if she's just going to share it with Richard.'

'I might be able to access Dad's emails via her computer. I wouldn't mind sending her a couple of thousand if it really keeps her on our side. No need to decide now.'

Steve poked his head round the office door. 'The children are getting restless. They really need some exercise.'

Juliette was still sitting at the big desk. 'Mum, can you go out with Steve? Stay near the house. He can get the cricket and football things from the car. Lulu loves playing French cricket with him. She stands on his feet and helps him to hold the bat. Use one of the foam balls. I'll carry on here.'

As soon as she was sure they were in the garden, Juliette ran up the stairs holding her shoulder bag. She needed to look in the shoe box on top of the wardrobe in the dressing room. The one her mother had been so quick to climb on the chair to search...

*

She remembered the shocked expression on her mother's face – it must have been twenty years ago – when she had lifted the gun out of the hat box. She had to hold it with both hands because of its weight, feeling the roughness of the cross-hatched metal butt.

'Is it real, Mummy?'

'I think it must be Grandpa's. Daddy will know what to do with it.'

Then when her mother had left the room holding the gun, Juliette had looked in the bottom of the hat box where the gun had come from and had found a small brown cardboard box with printing on the top. She had lifted it in her small hands and had been surprised by how heavy this was too. She had pulled the top off and had found what, even at the age of eight, or seven, she had known must be bullets for the gun. She had called out, 'Mummy, these must be the bullets. I found them. Look, there are ten, and two empty spaces in the box.'

'I'll give them to Daddy when he comes home from work. He'll deal with them. It must be our secret, darling.

You won't tell any of your friends, will you? Put the lid back on. I'll put them somewhere safe with the gun until Daddy comes home.'

Her memories were interrupted by whoops and childish squeals coming from the garden. She felt safe, and dragged the upright chair over to the wardrobe, as her mother had done earlier.

It must have been about five years after the discovery. Her bedroom door was open. Their voices were raised. She walked slowly to the top of the stairs and looked through the banisters.

'You told me you were going to hand it in to the police!'

'Honey, it's better this way. No one's ever going to find it on top of that wardrobe. I feel safer knowing it's there.'

'I found it. I was looking for a box of old photos. How can it be safer?'

'It's like deterrence.'

'That's ridiculous. Deterrence only works if the other side know you've got the weapon. Are you telling me you've got enemies who would come and kill us all if they thought you were unarmed?'

'Honey, you're getting it all out of proportion. It's just that if there was an intruder, say, all I'd need to do is point the gun and he'd surrender or run away. I wouldn't even need to load it.'

'So get rid of the bullets. Throw them into the river.'

'Come on, honey, who's being ridiculous now?'

Juliette remembered her adolescent confusion as she had crept quietly back to her room to continue with her homework. But she had been unable to concentrate. What kind of man was her dad? A rough diamond, a rule-bender, certainly not a man who would be bossed around by his wife. She had trusted him to keep them safe.

*

She climbed onto the chair and reached. There might not be another chance. Got her fingers on the corner of the box. Pulled it across the top of the wardrobe. It felt heavy enough. Dust fell into her eyes as she held the box in her hands. She blinked, shook her head. With her left hand under the box, she removed the lid with her right. Yes. There it was. Not as heavy as she remembered it. She could hold it in one hand now. The rough, cold, masculine feel of the metal butt was just as it had been. A reassuring texture that would help you to grip it firmly, not let it slip. The box of bullets too. Webley .455 x 12 in faded black print on the brown cardboard.

Sitting on the side of the bed, she put the gun into her shoulder bag and opened the small brown box. Brass cases with the copper centre – still ten of them, two spaces. She replaced the lid on the bullets and put the little box in the shoulder bag with the revolver, then covered both with one of the plastic shopping bags she kept there.

There was something different. What was it? Christ. No noise from the garden. She ran to the window. No one in sight. She turned. Her mother was coming through the door. She gasped. 'Mum, you scared me.' She grabbed the shoulder bag, holding the top closed with both hands.

'The little ones were thirsty. We've been ever so energetic. They're in the kitchen with Steve. I wondered where you had got to. Found any clues?'

'I thought we might have missed something up here.'

She followed her mother down the stairs, wishing she had brought the bag with the zipper top, and thinking, *Shit, I should have wiped the shoe box.* 'I'll just put my bag in the car, make sure I don't forget it when we go home.' She mustn't let any of them feel the weight of it.

When Juliette came back into the house, she found them in the sitting room. The children were on the floor, Jason trying to pick up some wooden bricks with a crane and Lucy stroking a fluffy toy dog.

The rhumba on Caroline's mobile announced an incoming call. She said, 'I'd better answer this. It's Jack at Smart Move. Sunday – it must be urgent.'

When Caroline had finished the call, Juliette said, 'What's wrong there? Anything to do with Dad?'

'I've agreed to cash £1,000 tomorrow so that he can pay the men for a job today. The business account was cleaned out on Thursday. It must be bloody Richard. I'll get it out of my savings account. We can go to the bank together tomorrow, if you've got time. Jack's got no idea where Richard is either.'

'The morning would be fine. I've cancelled all my lessons.'

'Is Richard on the Walker's Antiques mandate?' Caroline asked.

'No, thank goodness. I'd better check on the computer, though, as soon as we get home, in case he's fiddled it somehow. Can you help Steve keep the kids occupied? I'll have a go at the office again – get into the desks and the filing cabinet, and the computer.'

When the others had gone back into the garden, Juliette went out of the front door to the garage. On a shelf near the workbench she found an electric jigsaw with a fine-toothed metal-cutting blade. The blade slipped easily into the gap above the top drawer of the pedestal under the secretary's desk, and she cut quickly through the cheap latch. Two small keys on a wire ring were in a stationery tray. One of them fitted into the keyhole in the pedestal. She turned it, heard the mechanism shift, and found that she had unlocked all three drawers. The top drawer was of no interest: stationery items and Vanessa's oddments – nail polish, lipstick, tampons. The two other drawers were half-filled with papers. She would look at them later.

The big desk wasn't so easy. There were three drawers on each side. Each one needed to be opened separately and the gaps were narrow, so that the blade kept jamming. She gave up trying to saw through the lock, twisted the narrow blade to saw through the wood around the lock. After success with the first drawer, she used the same technique on the others. No one would be using that desk again. The first drawer was empty. And the second. *He's taken everything*, she thought. She turned out to be right, except for an unused jotter pad and two empty, unwashed spirit glasses.

Next, she went to the filing cabinet, inserted the other key from Vanessa's desk and breathed a sigh when the lock turned. She opened each drawer – hanging files filled with papers. She would need to spend hours going through this lot.

Just time to check the password Vanessa had given her for the PC. Success. She shut it down and unplugged the box and the monitor. She went out into the garden and found Steve, with Lucy on his shoulders, kicking the football towards Jason, who was keeping goal between two garden chairs. Caroline was sitting in another garden chair reading a magazine. 'Time to go home,' Juliette said. 'Steve, can you help me load all the office stuff into the back of the Volvo?'

'Found any clues, darling?' Caroline looked up from her magazine.

'Not yet, there's a lot of stuff to go through.' At least she might find out what he'd actually been doing for the last few years. Whether that would help them track him down was a different matter.

*

Juliette, sitting on the Edwardian couch piled with loose cushions, took a sip from her glass of elderflower cordial. 'Mum, do you mind having to work on Skype? It can't be quite the same as face to face.'

Caroline was sitting in the Victorian wing-back chair, with a glass of gin and tonic in her hand. 'We use it quite a lot now. Some of the women seem to prefer it – can open up more when they're talking to a screen rather than an actual person. And the staff are always on hand in case any of the residents needs a hug. Anyway, Steve obviously needs to go to the shop, so here I am.' Caroline shrugged.

Steve came downstairs and into the sitting room. 'Both sound asleep. I've put all that stuff in the end spare room. Computer's set up on the dressing table. Four filing cabinet drawers and two desk drawers on the bed. I'm ready for a drink.'

Juliette was still looking at her mother. 'Thanks, Steve. I'll just go and give them a kiss.' Juliette went up to the children's room. Jason was on his side, his cheek on the back of one hand. She leaned and kissed his head quietly. Lucy was lying on her back with her mouth open. *God, you're gorgeous.* Juliette gazed at her for several seconds. *Whatever it takes, Lulu, you very special person. You're going to have a good life.* She gave the blonde hair a gentle kiss before leaving the room.

Her new sandals with wedge heels had been chafing her bare feet. She went into the master bedroom and changed into her slippers. The shoe box was on the floor where she had left it. Just what she needed. Perfect.

*

After dinner, Steve poured some red wine into his glass, held up the bottle and looked sideways at Juliette. 'Are you still beyond temptation, Jules?'

'What do you think?' she said.

'It doesn't do any harm in moderation,' Caroline said, and finished her glass of white wine. 'You used to enjoy a drink.'

'Not since I was pregnant with Lulu. I didn't seem to feel a need to start again after she was born.' *They'll never know. It was before I knew I was pregnant. Just determined never to lose control again.*

'Have we got time for a film?' Steve said. 'One of the ones I brought from your house, Cara? How about *North by Northwest*? I haven't watched it for years.'

Juliette said, 'You're on your own, Steve. I've got work to do.'

Chapter 5

Juliette sat at the old dressing table with the cracked mirror, and logged on to the computer using the password Vanessa had given her. First, the emails. She opened Gmail. There was just one account listed: qrletty73m@gmail.com. *Obsessed with anonymity – but that must be it.* A row of stars appeared in the Password field. She clicked OK. Maybe Vanessa was on the level.

Property deal, buying a house in Nottingham, offering £500,000. *Must be a big one*, she thought. Arrangements for Jack to unload the container at Harwich. Subcontractor in Liège would need personal supervision by Richard – unlike him to be so hands-on, but maybe it was the first time he had used them. She was feeling tired, took a gulp of coffee. Debts to be chased – boring, boring. She skimmed through the inbox looking for something unusual.

An email from eq7lymp89@gmail caught her eye. 'Goods delivered per your instructions. £700 tomorrow. Usual place.' No signature. Then another from a similar anonymous sender: 'Services rendered. Outcome satisfactory. Pub Thursday 12.30.' And another: 'Happy boy. Got 2 grand. 15%

for me. Sweet.' Several more, all supposed to look innocent, but vague, generic terms, together suggesting something shady going on. Gmail. Google wouldn't help identify them. Probably couldn't.

Juliette drained the last of the coffee, which was now cold, and looked back at the screen. There were no names in the emails – except Mr Love. Mr Love, Christ's sake. Three mentions, definitely dodgy – and unpleasant. Two and a half years ago, an email copied to Richard: 'Fat man in the parlour is skimming. Instruction needed. Mr Love informed.' She switched to the Sent folder, and found, just over a year ago, an email Richard sent to 'Malteser': 'That Polish bitch is on about Mr Love again. Get it sorted now, or it'll be the other method.' Then only three weeks ago: 'Time to drop Mr Love. Too much talk. Bloody silly to start with.' And then all emails to and from Richard had stopped eight days ago. That was probably when he left for Belgium. She'd check the date with Steve.

*

The next morning, Juliette slipped out of bed without waking Steve. Monday – shop closed. The children were also asleep, safe. Not long before they'd need breakfast; maybe Steve would help. She went downstairs, used the toilet, went to the utility room and changed into her running gear that she kept there – shorts, vest – but put on trainers instead of the cross-country shoes. Then back upstairs to the room at the back where they kept the exercise bike and the rowing machine. Fifteen minutes on each, followed by granola, yoghurt and coffee, should set her up for more work going through papers and computer records. Not as good as the run through the wood and round by the estuary, but it would have to do. Getting the bank sorted out would have to come first. Bloody nuisance.

After starting pedalling, she thought about the business she did with Tim. Steve must genuinely think the shop was doing well. He kept thanking her for the work she did on the website, and the efficient management of their finances, that he left entirely to her. One day, maybe in forty years or so, when they had retired and sold the shop, she would tell him what she had been doing, how they had survived the recession and prospered.

But more urgent things – the emails she had read last night. Nothing concrete. No obvious contacts to follow up. Some seemed legitimate, or nearly so. The ones with anonymous addresses were more likely to reveal something. What the hell was her dad up to? Still no clue as to where he might be. He was sure to contact her again soon. She went back over the phone conversation last week. There was something else. It hadn't seemed important, compared to the thing about Frampton. He'd taken some money. Well, they knew that now. Surprising he'd thought it worth mentioning. Supporting her mum was the priority. She turned up the tension on the bike, simulating riding uphill. Uphill – seemed like it. Life. Needing to breathe faster, thigh muscles and calves beginning to feel it. Not too many music lessons to cancel. Slack time in the holidays. Wouldn't want it to go on too long, though. Switch soon to the erg machine – work her torso and upper body as well as her legs.

Coming downstairs she heard Steve singing in Italian. When she walked into the kitchen, he was pouring hot water into a cafetière, gesticulating with the other hand, still singing. He turned and smiled. 'Lord Arturo welcomes you to our humble table.'

'I thought you said you were singing it in English.'

'Sadly yes, but it's so much better in Italian.'

The children were at the table, Lucy in her highchair, both of them eating cereal. 'Good morning, gorgeous people.' She bent to kiss Jason, then snuggled into Lucy's neck, causing her to giggle and spit out some mush.

'Perfect timing,' she said, reaching for a tissue to wipe Lucy's face. 'Just time for a glass of blueberry juice while that's brewing.' She pointed to the cafetière.

A few minutes later Steve came back into the kitchen after installing the children in front of the television. 'What time did you get to bed?'

'About two. Just scratching the surface. I haven't started on the papers yet.'

Steve raised an eyebrow. 'Any clues?'

'Not really. Thank God it's Monday.' Juliette wiped some sweat from her face with a paper towel. 'Steve, can you just stay indoors with them till Mum and I get back from the bank?'

'Jason asked me why we have to stay inside so much in this weather.'

'He loves those fantasy games you play with him.'

'Yeah, he'll be the astronaut and I'll be the Martian. The trouble is, Lulu tends to get left out.' Steve looked at Juliette as if he wanted her to prompt him, but then continued, 'She doesn't seem to pick things up the way he did at that age.'

Juliette's mind whirled. *Don't you dare tell me I've given birth to a fucking retard.* She caught herself and said, 'You're great with them. We'll be as quick as we can.'

*

Juliette drove her small Peugeot, with Caroline in the passenger seat. 'Bloody stupid money-laundering regulations. Who goes around with their passport and utility bills?' Juliette said.

'Stupid of me not to think of it yesterday.'

'It's not far out of our way. It won't take a minute.'

'I think I'll move out anyway now,' Caroline said.

'Why, because you're scared of him? Dad, I mean.'

'I used to be. But not for several years now, after that time he hit me. That changed everything. We arrived at a new way of tolerating each other, living our own lives. He lost interest in me sexually, wanted younger flesh.' Caroline sighed.

'Mum, you still look great. You know you do.'

'He made me promise not to talk to you about his early life.'

'Go on.' They were on a straight bit of road, and Juliette glanced across quickly to see her mother dabbing her eyes with a tissue.

'It's a somewhat clichéd hard-luck story. He was an only child. Father disappeared. Mother took to sex working to support him. He was taken into care, had a succession of foster homes, was abused, ran away several times…'

'God.' Juliette kept her eyes on the road. Was this the father she had known? It might explain what had happened. 'So, when he told you all this, you wanted to look after him.'

'It's not as simple as that. He was exciting – a big change from my humdrum barrister's life.'

They were just approaching the turning into the driveway. Juliette saw it first. 'Have you seen that car before?' A large dark saloon was parked on the verge just beyond the entrance. It accelerated away round the corner. 'Mum?'

Caroline twisted her head to look at Juliette. The gate was sliding open. 'Do you think—?'

'Let's get in as quickly as possible. Make sure no one's tried to break in. Did you get the registration number? I was turning.'

'It was so quick. Who do you think that was?'

'I doubt if they were sightseers, birdwatchers, whatever.'

Caroline unlocked the front door and went to disable the alarm. Juliette felt the strange emptiness, that contrasted with the activity of the previous day. And now there was this feeling that the house was being watched. She said, 'There's something slightly spooky about this house when no one is here. Do you think Dad might have come back?'

'Not likely,' Caroline said. 'I changed the code on the alarm.' She turned the lights on, walked down the hall. 'Passport and just one utility bill?'

'Bring two just in case.'

Juliette was standing in the hallway when the landline phone rang. 'Hello?'

'Where is he?' The same nasal Essex drawl, but a richer timbre and deeper tone than her father's voice.

'Who is this?' She heard footsteps and caught her mother's eye. Caroline stiffened, staring at her, face frozen.

'Prince Charles. Where is he?'

'Well, Your Royal Highness, if I knew about whom you were enquiring, I'm sure I would be able to advise you as to his whereabouts.' She caught her mother's eye again, looking puzzled now.

'Games'll get you in trouble. The bullshit man, as you know. Where is he?'

Belton-Smart. BS. The bullshit man.

'How did you get this number?' Juliette steadied herself against the wall. This must be him. *Christ!* The psychopathic rapist who wants to find her dad, or kill him.

'It's not all I've got. I'm not going to go on asking. Just tell me – to avoid any unpleasantness.'

'I wish I knew.' Juliette was struggling to prevent her voice from shaking. She wanted to smack the phone back onto its cradle, but forced herself to go on talking. 'Look, he just took off – on a business trip. I'm with my mother now. Neither of us knows where he is.'

'You'd better tell me as soon as you do know.' The deep voice sounded relaxed and even, as if it were conducting a polite conversation.

'How do I contact you?'

'Send a smoke signal. Think I'm as stupid as he is?' There was a click followed by dialling tone.

Juliette looked at the phone, managed to get it back on the cradle, then looked up at her mother. 'Frampton. Do you remember what his voice was like?'

'Essex. Deeper than Richard.'

Juliette started as her mobile phone rang. She looked at it. No caller ID.

'Hello?' She tried to keep her voice steady.

'Surprise, surprise. It's your new boyfriend. Your old man told me you're a slut. We'll have some fun together if you don't find him. Keep your phone switched on and charged up.' The line went dead.

Juliette closed her eyes, put a hand against the wall to

steady herself. The noise in her head started. She gasped for air. *Breathe. Slow down. Control.*

'Jewel, darling?'

She opened her eyes and took a few more breaths. 'Same voice. That was him. Must be.' She looked at her mother. 'How the hell did he get my mobile number? Do you think he's got Dad's phone? He might know where I live.'

'Don't you think we ought to tell the police?'

'No.' Juliette tapped her phone. 'Steve? You okay?'

'Tom and Jerry. I'm reading a really interesting article about American antebellum furniture. Shaker – that sort of stuff—'

'Check all the doors are double-locked. Don't open them for anyone. Put the CCTV on constant if it isn't already. Watch the monitor. We're on our way.' She ran into the kitchen, then straight to the magnetic knife rack next to the fridge and took the biggest knife, the one she called the Psycho knife, wrapped it in a tea towel and put it in her shoulder bag. She had brought the one with the zipper this time. A back-up weapon, second line of defence in case the gun wasn't within reach. She rushed out to the Peugeot while Caroline set the alarm.

*

'Everything all right?' Steve turned in the office chair and looked up from the screen. 'Did you get the bank sorted?'

'Bank'll have to wait. Any visitors?' Juliette had come into the study after asking her mother to see to the children.

'Not a soul.'

'A man's trying to scare us. Probably the one we were talking about – Frampton.'

*

In the kitchen, Steve poured boiling water into a bowl of couscous. 'Jules, have you decided? If you find out where your dad is, will you tell Frampton?'

Juliette was slicing a lentil and sweet potato loaf she had taken out of the fridge. Did she hate her father enough? She caught Steve's eye. 'He had the decency to warn us about him. I'd feel like shit—' She felt the tears come, put the knife down and went to Steve and held him tight, her face on his shoulder, sobbing. He held her and she loved him for knowing not to say anything.

At last, she pulled back, held his head in both hands and kissed his mouth quickly. She reached for a tissue and sat on one of the kitchen chairs. 'Bottom line is, do I believe Frampton would do something to one of us to get at my dad? Yes, I do. There's something cold, heartless, dead in his voice. I'd do anything to protect you and the children. And me, when it comes to it.' She took another tissue, blew her nose. 'I don't want them to grow up without a mother.'

Steve sat on another chair across a corner of the table. She felt him squeeze her hand. 'The irony is that it wouldn't work. From what Mum said about him, he might kidnap any of us and hold us hostage. Make my dad come out of hiding? Fat chance.' She wiped her eyes with a tissue in her free hand. 'The children and I are probably his prime targets, but he could snatch you or Mum in order to get me. The thing is, to convince him that my dad wouldn't give himself up to save any of us.' Juliette looked up, felt the tears come again.

Steve looked down at their hands, clasped together. 'Do you actually think that?'

'There's a lot you don't know about him, Steve. You're so bloody trusting. Think well of everybody. The hard truth is my dad would do anything to save his own skin.'

*

'Do you think that man will contact us again?' Caroline was holding a mug of tea. They were in the kitchen, having returned from the trip to the bank, and then to take cash to the removals company.

'He must have Dad's mobile, or got access to his contacts somehow. He's almost certainly got Vanessa's contact details as well as mine. Dad must know that. He wouldn't be at her place because it'd be the first place Frampton would look. And one thing I'm sure about is that Dad is very scared of Frampton.'

'Does that mean Frampton might come and look for him here?'

'We had better assume so. I need to go up and carry on searching through the files.' Juliette saw her mother's eyes were glistening.

*

Up in the end bedroom, Juliette found Ziggy curled up on one of the files that she had left on the floor. 'Hi, Zig.' She scooped the cat up and settled her on her lap as she sat on the Victorian dining chair in the corner of the room. 'You're like them, aren't you.' Ziggy remained curled up, but turned her head and opened her eyes to look up at Juliette, who stroked the top of her head. 'That's right. Purr away.

No sense of danger. Of course, if Frampton was completely rational, he might not be that dangerous. But to me he sounded quite pissed off enough to want to do me some serious damage, just to get back at my dad.' Juliette leaned back and closed her eyes. Frampton's voice came back to her – so controlled, so lacking in any sort of feeling. She could imagine him enjoying gang-raping a teenage girl in front of her father, delighting in the suffering of both of them. She opened her eyes to try to get rid of the image. 'When did a cat kill another cat? Well, not often. You've got more sense, haven't you, Zig. Strategies for limiting violent conflict. All that bristling and growling. Doesn't always work, though. And then there's the matter of rape. That ceased to be a problem for you, though, didn't it. A little snip by the vet and tomcats just aren't interested in you. Lucky you. Come on, I've got to get to work.'

*

'Mum, you didn't tell me about this.' Juliette crossed the hall, a sheaf of papers in her hand. 'Can you come into the kitchen?' Juliette put the papers on the kitchen table. 'Mortgage. Look, your signature, at least it looks like yours.' She turned the papers for Caroline to read. 'It's only three weeks ago.'

'Oh God. Yes. It was late at night. He had to raise some money for a new project. It's going to make us millions...' Her voice faded. She looked at the table. 'Are the deeds among those papers? It's in my name, the mansion. For tax reasons, he said, but it's in my name.'

'So does that mean the money would have to be paid into

an account in your name? You didn't think to check with him? Seven hundred thousand pounds.'

'He'd get angry if I asked questions about his business affairs.'

'You've got a few phone calls to make. Find out what has happened to that money. Come on. I'll help you.'

On the way to the study, Juliette put her head round the sitting room door. Lucy was asleep on the sofa. Jason was trying to untangle the string on his crane. The television was off. Steve was sitting in one of the wing-back chairs silently mouthing at a large book on his lap. It must be the vocal score of *Lucia*. No need to disturb them.

Half an hour later, in the study, their worst fears had been realised. The £700,000 had been placed overnight in a joint deposit account in the names of Caroline and Richard Belton-Smart. It required only one signature of either party to transfer funds. The money had been transferred to a private bank in Jersey.

'He's stolen all that money. He must have been planning it. Manipulated me.' Caroline had her hands over her face. 'The bastard.'

'It must mean he never intended to come back. Ever. Absolutely no way the bank in Jersey is going to divulge anything, and there's no point anyway. The money's probably been transferred out of that bank by now, so they wouldn't be able to help us even if their rules allowed them to.' Juliette stood up. 'Maybe it explains why Frampton's so desperate to find Dad. And why Dad sounded so scared on the phone.'

Chapter 6

'Are you sure you'll be all right?' Steve took a bite of toast, eyebrows raised, scanning Juliette's face.

'Of course.' Hiding her feelings was becoming easy. 'We need to carry on normally as far as possible. Best for you to go and open the shop. Your only danger area is the service road. Keep your eyes open when you park the car; keep your phone on you, ready to hit 999.'

He swallowed. 'He's more likely to try to get you than me.'

She knew he was right. 'Just keep alert. I don't want to get one of his bloody phone calls telling me he's got you and he'll let you go if I go and meet him somewhere.'

Steve reached and gently took hold of her upper arm. 'Honestly, Jules, don't you think we should tell the police – leave it to them?'

She put her free hand on his and looked him in the eye. 'That'd make Frampton more desperate to find my dad before they do. So, no.'

Steve seemed to want a change of subject. 'Is your mum really going to put the mansion on the market? Seems a bit hasty to me.'

'You don't mind her staying here, do you? Till my dad's been found.'

'I'm very fond of her.'

After Steve had gone, Juliette, still in her T-shirt and shorts, went to the study to check the security monitor. Six views covering all possible entrances to the house. Not a movement. Then footsteps on the stairs.

"Morning, Jewel." Juliette saw her mother go to the sitting room. A minute later they were both sitting at the kitchen table.

'Do you think it's good for them to watch so much television?'

'Mum, I read to them. I play games with them. I take them to visit their friends, and I invite their friends here with their mothers. I teach them piano; Jazzy's showing signs of talent. I do creative play with them. I'm sure I'm not a perfect parent, but who the fuck is, so let's not go through all that again.'

'Darling, I didn't mean to start an argument.'

'I know.' She took a breath. 'This whole thing's getting to me. I lay in bed hoping Frampton would find Dad and get it all over with – and feeling terrible about it.'

'You can't mean… Darling, Frampton's completely ruthless. It's obvious prison hasn't changed him.'

'Yeah, well, I'd rather he was ruthless with Dad than with any of us. Sorry, if that's bad.' She felt tears coming and turned away from her mother.

'Are you sure you don't mind coming to the mansion this morning?'

Juliette turned back. 'Still left his mark, hasn't he. He's got us all calling it the mansion. It started as a sort of ironic joke. It's the least I can do. You're being really helpful here.'

'That's probably what the estate agents will call it, or a neo-Georgian villa – some nonsense. Marjorie will be there this morning. Thirty years. I'll give her a reference for the new owners, when the time comes.'

'Stay here as long as you want, Mum.'

'I need to sort some things out. Phone the agents. I certainly don't want to spend another night in that house.'

*

'I'm glad she took it so well.' Caroline was sitting with Juliette in the kitchen of the house they called the mansion. 'I'll have to come here to show the estate agents around – then never again. What memories…'

'I've known Marjorie all my life. She taught me how to make jam tarts and fairy cakes.'

'She's going to come in once a week to clean, until it's sold. I've got a few things to do upstairs. You might as well go and sit with the children. I won't be long.'

A few minutes later, Juliette was on the sofa with an arm around each child, watching *Tom and Jerry*. She saw her mother standing in the open doorway.

'Darling, can you come?' Caroline's eyes were staring, her face taut.

Juliette followed her mother into the kitchen. *Oh God, not another row about watching TV!*

'He used to keep a gun hidden upstairs. You found it in a hat box when you were tiny. You probably don't remember. It's gone.' Caroline waved an arm. 'He must have taken it.'

'Are you sure?'

'Who else?'

'You said you'd changed the security code, so he couldn't have come back.'

'He must have taken it when he left. Had it all planned.'

'Why did you go and look for it, just now?'

'I couldn't just leave it there. I was going to bury it in a flowerbed, along with the box of bullets.' Caroline sat heavily on a chair, put her elbows on the table, and seemed to try to grasp air with each hand.

'It doesn't really change anything. He isn't going to threaten any of us with the gun.'

Caroline pushed herself up from the table with both hands. 'This has gone far enough.' She went to her handbag on the worktop and took out her phone.

'Mum, what are you doing?'

'Dialling 101.'

'No!' Juliette yelled, as she dived at the phone in her mother's hand and tried to snatch it. Caroline was too quick, turned and got an elbow in the way.

'Don't be so stupid,' Caroline snarled as Juliette tried to grab the phone away from her ear.

'Mum, please don't!' Juliette stepped back, realising fighting her mum for the phone wouldn't solve the problem.

Caroline half turned, holding the phone to the ear that Juliette couldn't reach. 'This is my house, and I decide what's best.' She glared at Juliette. 'We shouldn't have let it go this far.'

Ideas flashed through Juliette's head. No way she could stop her mum making the call. She could run upstairs, get the shoe box and get her fingerprints all over it. But how good were forensics? Would they be able to tell that some of her prints were there before her mum's? They'd accuse her of tampering with evidence – and they'd be right. *Shit!*

Caroline was talking to the cops now. 'It's very old. It was my father's, in the war. It came here by accident. My husband promised to dispose of it, but I know he didn't.' She glanced down at Juliette who was sitting at the kitchen table. 'Belton-Smart. Richard Belton-Smart. Yes, all right.' She covered the phone with her hand and said to Juliette, 'They're transferring the call. I'm sure it's for the best, darling. They'll find Richard soon, and we'll all be out of danger.'

'Mum, please don't mention Frampton. If he finds out we told the police about those phone calls, it'll put us in much more danger – and the children. Please?' Juliette sniffed and put a tissue to her eye. Another part of her mind was trying to work out how to navigate a way through this.

Caroline pursed her lips and nodded as she uncovered the phone. 'Hello. Within the hour? We're about to go to my daughter's house in Little Eastham – with my grandchildren—' She looked down at the table. 'Oh, I see. All right then. We'll see you within the hour.'

'Do you really think this is going to help?'

'This isn't the Wild West. We're not to touch anything – not to go in the room where it was. When I told them his name, I was transferred to a detective sergeant. I wasn't expecting that. He's coming here with a forensics officer.'

Juliette closed her eyes, pressed her left hand to the side of her head. 'Do you really not understand? If Frampton finds out the police are looking for Dad, he'll want to find him first. He might do anything.'

'How would he find out?'

Juliette sighed. 'Any number of ways. Someone in the village sees a police car arrive here – gossip central.'

'We should give them Vanessa's phone number. I still think she knows more than she's telling us.'

'It could just be this detective sergeant was bored and fancied a drive in the countryside. I can't imagine them getting too excited. Missing person, antique revolver – it's not as if a crime's been committed.'

'Unlicensed firearm. We should find out more before too long.'

Juliette said, 'I'll go and check the children. They're probably getting hungry. Let's have lunch before the police arrive.'

Lucy was asleep in a corner of the sofa; Jason was watching a cartoon that Juliette didn't recognise. She sat back on the sofa with an arm around Jason and closed her eyes. Should she have told her mum she had taken the gun? No way. She would have had to tell Steve as well; neither of them would accept having a gun in the house, even for self-defence. She hadn't reckoned on police involvement, though. *Shit, shit, shit…* She needed to assess the situation rationally. *The gun – slow down, Jules, Mum assumes Dad took it. Good. That's the way it needs to stay. But will the cops just accept that? Unlikely. Forensics officer – fingerprints.* She bit her lower lip. *If that dusty old cardboard can carry fingerprints, they'll find two sets – Mum's over mine. They'll question us both. Mum knows she didn't take the gun. They've got to be made to think Dad's got it. And if they're serious about wanting to find Dad, they'll want Vanessa's computer and the files. Christ, how much time have I got?*

*

DS Cartwright introduced himself in a rasping Norfolk accent – with the voice of a man who smoked and drank too much. He was a big man with a ruddy complexion and short hair beginning to show signs of grey – *a man living under too much stress*, Juliette thought.

'And this is our SOCO, Louise.' Cartwright indicated a young woman, taller than himself, probably six foot, who had followed him into the house. She had black hair and cherry red lipstick.

'I have a Polish surname which is difficult to pronounce.' She spoke with an exaggerated upper-class English accent, and smiled. 'Call me Louise.'

Juliette said, 'There isn't really a crime scene here. Just a shoe box that apparently used to have an old gun in it.'

Although this was addressed to Louise, Cartwright answered, 'We take all such reports seriously. We've checked the firearms database and we can't have unlicensed firearms falling into the wrong hands.'

Caroline led the officers upstairs to show them where the gun had been hidden. When she came down a minute later, she said, 'They want us to stay downstairs. They won't say anything. I asked Cartwright if they knew where Richard was, and he just shrugged.'

Juliette said, 'Presumably they're looking for Dad's fingerprints on this shoe box – proof that he took the gun?'

'That presupposes that they've already got images of his fingerprints.'

Cartwright came down the stairs. 'Mrs Belton-Smart, while Louise is doing her work up there, could you show me your husband's office that you mentioned?'

Juliette quietly looked through the sitting room door.

Lucy was pretending to bottle-feed the knitted kangaroo, and Jason was arranging a set of cars in a neat row on the carpet. So far, he didn't seem to have cottoned on to the fact that the visitors were police officers. She went to the kitchen. *What would be the most normal, expected, thing to do?* She filled the kettle and switched it on.

'Mrs Walker, can you tell me how long you have been aware that a firearm has been secreted in this house?' Cartwright was hanging his grey jacket on the back of a kitchen chair, having declined the offer of a cup of tea.

'No time at all, really,' Juliette said brightly. 'I have this vague memory of finding it as a child. It had been hidden in a hat box that had been my grandmother's. When she died, a lot of her clothes were brought over here. I was allowed to play with them – dressing up. That's when I found it. My mother told me it was very dangerous and that my father would get rid of it. I assumed he had done that, and didn't think any more about it. That's really all I can tell you. Oh, there was a box of bullets.'

She was ready for the next question and could answer honestly.

'Have you any idea where your father might be?'

'Sorry, none at all. He took his car – a Mercedes. I can tell you the plate number.'

She saw the tiredness in his eyes as he said, 'We know that.'

Caroline came into the kitchen, followed by Louise, who was holding a device that looked like a large smartphone. 'I just need your fingerprints, if you don't mind, for elimination?' She smiled at Juliette, revealing large white teeth behind the full red lips. 'I have taken your mother's already. It's quick – one finger at a time.'

Juliette couldn't help smiling at the incongruously fruity English accent, while thinking urgently whether it would be better to tell them now that she had taken the gun. But there was still a chance they wouldn't find her fingerprints. And her mum would go ballistic. She'd need a story. She said, 'My mother said the gun had been in a shoe box. Did you find any fingerprints on it?'

'I think – maybe.' Louise busied herself with the scanner.

Juliette tried to interpret that, and didn't decide not to tell them, but the moment passed.

As Cartwright was putting his jacket on, he said to Juliette, 'We'll have an officer come to your house for the computer and documents tomorrow morning.'

'There's nothing on the computer – except access to my father's email account.'

Cartwright looked at her. 'Our techies up at Halesworth'll find anything that's been deleted.'

She saw a trace of a smile on his face as he turned and left.

*

Juliette was at the kitchen sink washing the tea things. 'They seem to be taking it seriously.'

Caroline was sitting at the table. 'Cartwright told me I'd committed a serious offence – concealing an unlicensed firearm. He wouldn't say whether they'd charge me. I could do without—' She got up and pulled open the drawer next to Juliette, with a rattle of cutlery.

Juliette turned. 'What is it?'

Caroline pulled open the next drawer. 'It's not here either.

That big knife. The one you used to call the Psycho knife. Look.' She pointed to the magnetic rack next to the fridge. 'I always keep it there.' There was an empty space among the kitchen knives. She sank back onto the kitchen chair.

'Marjorie might have put it somewhere.'

'She'd never do that. It must be bloody Richard...'

*

Back at home, after dinner that evening, Juliette went quickly to Vanessa's computer. She opened the emails she had seen the previous day – the ones she thought might contain clues. She took photos of the screen with her phone. *The cops'll see I've been making my own enquiries. That's innocent, isn't it? Natural for a daughter to want to know where her father is.* She looked in the Document folder to double-check. Then scanned the whole computer looking for document files. There was nothing. What the hell did Vanessa spend her time doing? Perhaps her mum was right. There was nothing more for her to do with the computer. No way she could retrieve deleted files even if the cops could. She needed to see the children.

She took the picture book, that Steve must have been reading, off the Victorian button-backed nursing chair beside Lucy's bed and sat down, leaning forward, looking into her daughter's face. The cheekbones weren't yet discernible through the chubbiness. The jawline was too rounded to resemble her father's. The turned-up nose could become narrow and straight as she grew up. She leaned back and closed her eyes. She could just hear Steve chatting to her mother downstairs, but couldn't make out the words. It was a good thing her mother was staying – a distraction, as well as helping with security. The main thing was to act naturally, not let anyone suspect what she'd done with the gun, or the Psycho knife.

She looked at Lucy again. So beautiful. She felt tears coming. Wiped her eyes with a tissue. Got up from the chair and went to look at Jason. *God, I love you both, but Lulu's going to need more from me – more support, more love.*

She went to the main bedroom, to the Victorian rolltop desk and opened it. She pressed the secret panel, slid it sideways, reached under into the narrow cavity. She touched the handle of the Psycho knife. She didn't take it out. Didn't need to see it. Just needed reassurance that it was there. Touch was enough. *A backup weapon.* Maybe she had watched too many films.

When she went into the sitting room, Steve looked up from the vocal score of *Lucia*. 'I hope nothing goes wrong with the delivery of pieces I bought in Liège,' he said. 'I had been hoping to talk to Richard about it. Still, Jack seems to know what he's doing.'

'For God's sake, there's no reason why anything should go wrong. The subcontractors they use would have been paid up front, so it shouldn't be affected by my dad taking money out of the firm's account.' She joined him on the Edwardian couch with the usual pile of cushions. 'How are you getting on with Arturo?'

'I know all the words. English makes it more difficult to get the phrasing right, so for now I'm practising in Italian. Any chance of running through the main aria before bed?'

'Yeah, anything to get my mind off this shit with my dad and Frampton – and now the police. In the music room – I should be able to sight-read the piano part.'

*

There was something moving in the corner. It was too dark to see. Then it wasn't. The creature was smiling, swaggering, a grotesque figure from the *commedia dell'arte* with a giant phallus curving up in front. She leapt up, pressed her back to the wall, but it was coming towards her. She had a knife – she was almost sure it was a knife – in her hand. She swung it. Slashed, but much too slow. It was the Psycho knife, much too heavy for her. She couldn't breathe. The massive penis was hard against her belly, the face was leering, gloating, and it was him, and the penis was a serpent sliming its way up between her breasts to her mouth, and she screamed.

'Jules, Jules, it's all right. A bad dream. I'm here. My love, my love.' He was holding her. She was panting.

'God, Steve.' She was still trying to dispel the images.

'Do you want a glass of water?'

'Just hold me.'

Chapter 7

The house was still quiet. Juliette was on the exercise bike. *How am I going to get through the day?* She turned up the tension, pedalling harder, faster. *None of them understand. How can they? They mustn't know.* She gave the tension knob another twist – steep uphill now. She felt the sweat, gasped for oxygen. She pushed the pedals harder, felt the pain in her thighs, but the good feeling wouldn't come. The effect of endorphins, wasn't it? They seemed to have deserted her today. She pushed harder again. The pain was extending from her legs, her heart was palpitating. *Harder, harder – faster, faster.* She closed her eyes keeping the sweat out. She could hear her gasps now, like muffled screams. And then it all stopped. Her legs had stopped working. She slumped over the handlebars, head on arms. *My dad, Frampton, the cops – and bloody Tim. I've got to do something about Tim. How am I going to get through this fucking day?*

Still in running vest and shorts, she walked into the kitchen and did a few stretching exercises, deep breaths. Steve, in his mauve and green striped silk dressing gown, looked up from his coffee mug. 'Enjoy the bike ride?'

Juliette sniffed theatrically. 'I love the smell of coffee in the morning.'

'Better than napalm.'

Caroline walked into the kitchen wearing a smart light blue blouse and navy slacks. 'Sometimes I don't understand what you young people are talking about.'

'You know he was called Kilgore – the Robert Duvall character. Bonkers. Here, Zig. Let's get your breakfast.'

Juliette's legs still ached as she helped her mother put the breakfast things in the dishwasher. But the extreme exercise seemed to have cleared her mind. Should she say anything about the fingerprints? Would the cops be able to get them off that dusty old shoe box? No idea. But hope for the best. Say nothing for now.

'I've got to go to the shop this afternoon. Banking.'

'Can't Steve do it? Or Roger?'

'They'd mess up the spreadsheet. I'd have hours of work to do to put it right. I think the risk is minimal. We don't even know that Frampton knows where I live. I'll be in a public place all the time except for the drive there and back. If I see that black car, or anything else suspicious, I'll dial 999 straight away. I'll only be a couple of hours, three at the most. Sorry it'll be boring for you, stuck with the little ones.'

'I love being with them. I've told the crisis centre I'm having to look after my grandchildren for a few days. They're quite happy. I'm available for Skype or telephone counselling if needed.' Caroline looked into Juliette's eyes. 'I can't persuade you to change your mind, can I?'

'I've got some work to do at home on the accounts this morning.'

*

Juliette opened the rolltop desk and took out her laptop. Sitting at her dressing table, she opened it and checked her emails. She was expecting one of Tim's transactions, and there it was – a purchase order from a special customer in Evesham. 'Goods as seen and agreed to the value of £8,000 plus VAT.' She opened the accounting software and generated the invoice, attached it to an email and sent it to the email address on the purchase order.

She looked at her phone and saw an incoming text. *P12*. She pulled open the drawer in the rolltop, scrabbled about among the pay-as-you-go phones and found the one marked 12. She took a battery out of another drawer, inserted it, switched the phone on and, as expected, saw a string of numbers. Back to the laptop, she opened the coding spreadsheet, checked the date – 2 August – and typed 2 into cell A1. Then she typed Tim's sequence of numbers from the phone into row 2. The usual absurd routine. She set a formula to divide each of these by the contents of cell A1, using an absolute cell reference, pasted in the alphabet in reverse QWERTY order, MNBVCX and so on, ending with Q, noted the month, August, signifying that M is assigned 8, N 9 and so on up to 26, starting again at U 1 and ending with Q 7. Matching resulting numbers and letters gave her this: EVESHAM J THREE THIRTY. The date – 2/8 – add the digits – 10 – add those digits – 1 – meant that the collection time would be one hour earlier. 2.30. No problem. She quickly opened the special map of Christchurch Park. Bench J was one of the ones by the Round Pond. Could be worse. Bloody stupid code, she had told Tim at the beginning. 'Alan

Turing would crack it in ten minutes.' 'He's dead, and it's good enough to mitigate the communications risk sufficiently,' was all he had said in reply. She shook her head as she took the battery out of the cheap phone and closed the laptop. Tim: saviour of Walker's Antiques, pain in the arse and rip-off merchant. The secret business had started four years ago…

*

At breakfast, she was trying to get Jason to eat some mashed banana. A half-chewed teething rusk lay on the plastic table of his highchair.

'You look tired,' Steve said.

Jason uttered a 'Pu!', ejecting a mixture of banana and saliva on to the plastic table.

'Of course I look tired. I am bloody tired.' She flicked a strand of hair back behind her right ear, accidently leaving a blob of mashed banana stuck in it.

'We could get a part-time nanny – take the pressure off.' He pushed the plunger down on the cafetière.

'How many times?' She rolled her eyes up to the ceiling. 'We're not making ends meet as it is. You know the answer. Export to the States. Simple. The Americans will pay twice as much as we can get in the domestic market, plus shipping costs, including Victoriana – and they buy online, goods unseen. It's obvious.' She poured some milk into her coffee mug, while trying to spoon some banana into Jason's mouth with the other hand, saying, 'Open wide, Jazzy.'

'Do you have to call him Jazzy? He's going to really resent it when he grows up.'

'He's a baby, for God's sake. It suits him.'

'I've got to get going. You know how I feel about exports to the States. Every item exported is a loss to the nation, and on top of that the Americans don't know how to look after precious old furniture. It's not in their culture. My dad would never forgive us.'

'There isn't enough money coming in. Don't you see? Even if I went back to teaching, the cost of childcare would only leave us with a hundred or so extra a week. At this rate, in a year's time we'll be having to sell the house.'

'We're still pulling out of the recession. Things'll get better. I'm sure they will.'

She didn't have the energy to go on arguing. 'Sell shitloads today.' She smiled, not wanting him to see how she felt, and kissed him on the mouth.

'I'll try.' He bent and kissed the top of Jason's head. At the kitchen door he turned and said, 'Check your hair before you go out. Banana.'

*

That afternoon she was in the kitchen, blending some soya protein and sweetcorn with yogurt for Jason's next meal. She could just hear the sound of her mobile phone ringing and switched the blender off. She looked at the phone – Dad.

'Hi, baby, can we meet?'

'I'm quite busy. How about Sunday?'

'I want you to meet a friend of mine – a business associate.'

'Can't it wait?'

'In town, this afternoon. It'll be worth your while.'

'Can you tell me more?'

'Not on the phone.'

What could this be about? Probably one of her dad's dodgy deals. For years he had bragged about being 'a rule-bender' and having 'a flexible approach to the law'. Part of her was drawn to his cavalier attitude. But she had never known anything specific about what he was up to. Maybe she was about to find out. So it was a mixture of curiosity and the possibility of some extra income that led her to agree to meet this 'business associate.'

*

An hour later she was sitting outside the café in Buttermarket, where they had arranged to meet, with a small pot of Earl Grey, breast-feeding Jason. The plastic jar of soya and sweetcorn was still in her bag. She looked at her watch. Her father was ten minutes late. Then she saw him walking towards her from the direction of the cartoon statue on the corner. There was a man with him, taller and wider.

'Hi, baby, this is my mate, Tim.' Richard turned to his mate, Tim, and said, 'You won't have to mind her doing that.' Tim flushed. Juliette looked at his slightly florid sun tan, the large but reasonably fit-looking frame. She guessed late fifties, a few years older than her father. He was wearing a yellow polo shirt and light grey chinos. She imagined him being a fast bowler at cricket. She extracted her right hand from under Jason and extended it, giving Tim no alternative but to shake it.

When the men had ordered two flat whites and sat down, Juliette said, 'Excuse me a second. He needs to change tits.'

Richard said, 'She's modern.' Tim turned his head to study the details of the carving on the ancient house further down the pedestrianised street, while Juliette turned Jason round, making discreet use of a muslin square.

None of them spoke for a minute, then Juliette said, 'I love it when we get days like this in September – a sort of bonus at the end of summer.'

Richard looked at Tim, who said, 'Yes, I agree. But we didn't ask you to come here to talk about the weather.'

'That was my point. I'm waiting.' She used her left hand, the only free one, to raise the teacup to her lips.

'It's a cash cow,' Richard said. 'Tell her, Tim.'

Tim looked around, making sure no one at the other tables could hear his lowered voice. 'This is a matter of absolute trust. Your father has told me I can trust you.' He spoke with a cultured voice, but seemed to lack the confidence that usually went with a public-school accent.

'It depends. Try confessing to rape or paedophilia.'

'We haven't got all day.' Richard shifted in his seat. He had nearly finished his coffee.

'It would fit your business exactly – antiques,' Tim said. 'Some high-value items – some transactions still conducted in cash. I'd like to do some buying and selling with your antique shop.'

Richard raised his eyes to the sky. 'What he means is, he buys goods from you for cash, then he sells them back to you at a discount and you pay by bank transfer.'

She saw Tim throw a stern glance at her dad, saying hurriedly, 'That's not it at all. I just act as an agent – a broker, if you like. I've got a lot of contacts, buyers and sellers; I match them up. The suppliers have bank accounts for your company to pay into. My customers tend to pay in cash, which I will pass on to you. It's a confidential business; absolute discretion is required.'

Juliette sensed there was something about this proposal

that she wasn't being told. She looked at her dad, then back at Tim. 'So it's some kind of tax fiddle?'

Tim had taken a sip of coffee and swallowed quickly. 'Oh no. No, no. It's all, um, kosher. My suppliers will send you VAT invoices, and you will issue VAT invoices to my customers. It all needs to go through the Walker's Antiques books; your profit would be subject to, er, corporation tax.'

Juliette was aware that Jason had fallen asleep. She deftly hitched her bra back and buttoned up her shirt. He'd need a secure future – a good start in life. And well, she needed something extra in her life – something interesting, or exciting. 'What's the percentage?'

'Negotiable. We can talk about that later when you've had time to think about it.'

Richard said, 'I've known Tim for fifteen years. He'll have you sending messages in code.'

Tim put his coffee cup down and raised the index finger of his right hand. 'It's a highly competitive business,' he said, speaking quietly still, but emphatically. 'There are issues of information security – confidentiality – and risk management. I carry out a risk assessment for everything I do.'

Juliette nodded to Tim, wanting him to continue.

'When I've worked out the downside impact and assessed the likelihood, I put in appropriate safeguards. Coded messages using non-contract phones are part of that. We won't ever see each other, except for cash handovers, when we'll act as strangers. All you have to do is issue invoices according to the information I give you, receive the cash, bank it and pay the invoice you receive shortly afterwards. We'll start gradually so as not to ring any alarm bells at your bank, but soon you'll be handling £40,000 or £50,000 a month. You'll make a decent return for doing very little, and it's safe.' Tim took a sip of coffee. He seemed to have gained in confidence while he'd been talking.

'My husband won't like it.' Was she deflecting her own doubts on to Steve? He'd certainly try to talk her out of it when she discussed it with him. Sometimes he seemed to treat pieces of furniture like pets that needed a good home.

Richard intervened. 'Jules, baby, Steve mustn't know about it. He'll carry on working in his little world of antiques. He leaves all the finance stuff to you. All he'll know is that business has picked up a bit. It'd get complicated if he got involved in this.'

'What about the auditors? They come every year.' Was she just trying to create obstacles? Was it really the thought of going behind Steve's back that was putting her off?

Tim put down his coffee cup. 'All the transactions will be properly documented. There'll be nothing to worry about on that score.'

Juliette's mind flipped to the many arguments she'd had with Steve about expanding the business by exporting – the latest being that morning. If he found out about this business with Tim, he'd want to know exactly who was buying these goods and where they were going. But maybe it was what she needed – an enterprise of her own that she could carry on in the family's best interests, but without Steve's approval. She could do it just for a year or two – till Jason went to school and she went back to teaching. Steve need never know.

*

She had been doing it for a year when she found herself issuing an invoice to a P McCartney in Liverpool. *Oh, come on*, she thought, *how many of them are there?* That afternoon, sitting on the park bench with Tim beside her, she said, 'Do they exist? These suppliers and customers of yours, are they real?'

'We don't speak.'

'We just have done. I asked you a question.' She continued to look straight ahead, following that part of the protocol.

'Are you accusing me of money laundering?'

'I just want to know if they're real or fake. Simple.'

'Of course they're real. If they weren't, and if there were some money laundering going on, which there isn't, but if there were, you'd be up to your neck in it – risking a long prison sentence. It's a legitimate business that requires a high degree of confidentiality and information security. Keep it that way.'

She sat there for a while after Tim had left. Furious. Angry with herself as well as with Tim, and her dad. How had she been so naïve? But there was something else. She couldn't deny it. A frisson. She was doing something a lot more exciting than being a mother, wife and part-time administrator in an antique business.

She phoned her dad that evening. 'I've figured out what Tim's doing.'

'Best not to know, baby.'

'You got me involved in this.'

'Yeah, and it's keeping the antique shop afloat. Where would that be without this little earner?'

'Money laundering is a crime.'

'It's only a crime if you get caught.'

She wouldn't try to argue with that kind of twisted morality. 'How safe is it?'

'Dead safe – but just in case, if the boys in blue were to come and ask you about it, have a story ready.'

'What do you mean?'

'Make up a story – in which you are innocent.'

*

Keeping it secret from Steve, and everyone else, had been exciting at first. A hint of danger, and her own business enterprise, that no one except Tim and her dad knew anything about. She had had a sense of pride in her achievement in making Walker's Antiques prosper. It had been so easy to slip into this world of minor criminality.

But now it was stressful. She felt guilty about keeping it secret from Steve – disloyal. Her clandestine meetings with Tim in the park, to collect the cash, were no longer exciting, just ridiculous, and potentially dangerous – even before this thing between her dad and Frampton. She wondered if the people at the other end of Tim's business – the people who handed him the cash, for what? – were as fed up with him as she was. Could there be a possibility of cutting out the middleman? What would happen if she suggested a partnership? Her first step should be to tell the pompous, paranoid fart she'd done a new risk assessment and that the mitigation of the risk had been evaluated at fifteen per cent, not five.

Chapter 8

Juliette put her head round the sitting room door. Caroline was reading a fairy story to Lucy, who was sitting on her lap, pointing at the pictures in the book. Jason was on the carpet, crashing cars into each other. 'You okay, Mum?' She felt her phone vibrate in her jeans pocket. Number withheld. Could it be? Surely this time it could be her dad. 'Sorry, I'd better answer this.' She walked across the hall to the kitchen as she tapped the phone. 'Hello.'

'Found him yet?' *Oh Christ.*

She slumped against the fridge, dislodging a couple of alphabet magnets with her elbow. 'We're doing everything we can.'

'Think the filth are going to find him?'

Oh God, he knows the cops are involved. 'Probably not. I think he'll make contact before long.'

'Make sure he does.'

'There's nothing I can—' The connection had been cut.

It vibrated again while it was still in her hand. 'Look, whoever you are, I'm just as keen to find him as you are.'

'I'm glad to hear it, Mrs Walker. I assume that's your father you're talking about. This is Detective Sergeant Cartwright. We'd like to ask you a few questions.'

For a moment she felt relieved. 'Ask away.'

'It's not as simple as that. We'd like you to come to the police station in Museum Street. This afternoon. We'll send a car to fetch you, about two o'clock.'

Shit, it must be the bloody fingerprints. 'I'm sorry, I won't be available. It's urgent. I'm needed at our shop, Walker's Antiques. You know the one?' She took a breath. *Mustn't seem to be obstructive.* Another breath. 'I could come in at about four o'clock. It's a ten-minute walk from the shop. Save you a trip? I really want to help you find my father.'

'It's a serious matter, Mrs Walker. Ask for DS Cartwright.'

*

Juliette drove into Ipswich with her mother's words echoing. 'Why on earth should they want to talk to *you*?' The emphasis on 'you'. *Almost as if she's envious of the attention I'm getting from the cops.* Juliette had agonised about whether to say anything about the possibility of her fingerprints being on the shoe box. She had handled the shoe box when they were looking for the office key? No, it wasn't plausible, even if she had had an opportunity. Or maybe it was just that they wanted to talk about stuff they'd found on the computer or in the documents. *Surely, surely, it can't be the business with Tim. Cartwright's handling the missing person case; there can't be a connection. Can there?*

She went straight to the multi-storey car park in the town centre, near the Buttermarket shopping centre. When she drew up at the barrier, she glanced in every direction.

No sign of the dark saloon. No one seemed to be paying any attention to her.

After parking the car, she set off in the direction of Sainsbury's, trying not to make it look as if she were looking at everyone who came near. She stopped a couple of times as if to look in shop windows. No one else stopped. She searched the reflections in the windows and persuaded herself there was no danger. She came out of Sainsbury's with a large orange carrier bag loaded with toilet paper and tissues. She set off on foot for Christchurch Park, then turned round and went back a short way as if she had forgotten something. Having satisfied herself it was safe, she headed back to the park, flipping the hood of her light grey hoody over her head. She reached the bench by the Round Pond with five minutes to spare and put the carrier bag on the ground. It was a warm, muggy day, mostly overcast with occasional patches of blue. *Fingerprints, fingerprints.* What was that her dad had said? Something about having a story ready. But that had been about the business with Tim.

He arrived on time and sat on the bench beside her, putting his identical orange carrier bag on the bench between them. She and Tim both sat for a minute, looking straight ahead – no communication, in accordance with Tim's rules. Then he spoke. 'Don't look at me. Do you know where your dad is?'

'Breach of the rules.'

'My rules. Do you know?'

'Everyone seems to want to find him. Me too.'

Two people looking straight ahead, talking to each other. Like something out of *Carry On Spying*. She was just feeding his paranoia.

'Let me know if you learn anything. Usual comms.' He left, taking the bag from the ground. She left, taking the bag from the bench. She was extra vigilant on the way back to the car park. She did not want anything to go wrong while she was carrying this bag.

Once she was back in the car, she looked under the newspaper on top of the carrier bag and checked the money. The usual combination of used twenties and tens. She flicked through one of the bundles of twenties. She knew it was £9,600. It felt right. It always was.

*

It was nearly three o'clock when she eased along the service road and parked the Peugeot next to the Volvo in their spaces at the back of the shop. No one in sight. She hadn't been followed – surely. She unlocked the rear door and immediately put the bulky orange carrier bag, along with her shoulder bag, under the desk in the office, before locking the rear door behind her. She opened the door to the storeroom and walked through to the shop. Steve and Roger were talking. No sign of a customer. Steve turned. 'Great news. Jack's just phoned. They're unloading the stock from Belgium at the depot as we speak. He'll be able to deliver the first batch tomorrow. Oh, and Roger spotted a little piece in the local rag – about Richard being missing.'

'Hi, Roger, can I have a look?'

'It doesn't say much.' He handed her the paper and pointed near the bottom of the page.

Local businessman Richard Belton-Smart, owner of the Smart Move removals and storage company, is missing from his luxury home in Hintlesham. We understand that Suffolk police are treating this as a routine missing person case.

'I see what you mean. Anyway, thanks for showing me.' She handed the paper back to him.

Steve ushered Juliette back to the storeroom and closed the door behind them. 'Any problems? You know, anything suspicious?'

'Nothing. And I'm being very careful and vigilant.' She caught his eye. 'I'd better crack on with the banking. Don't want to keep The Law waiting.'

She went back to the office, bolted the door to the storeroom and double-locked the external door. Routine security. *Why the hell does a local paper publish a little note like that?* She clicked her phone and searched East Anglian, found the news desk number and dialled it.

'Hello, would it be possible to talk to someone about the notice in today's edition saying Richard Belton-Smart is missing?'

'Do you have information about him?'

'I'm his daughter.'

'Can you give me a contact number? I'll ask someone to call you as soon as they're available.'

After putting her phone back in her bag, Juliette opened the safe, took out the clip of cheques, the bag of cash – over £1,000 since she did the banking the previous Friday. They were certainly in the right business – a lot of traditional customers still wanting to use cash. She combined this with the £9,600 from the carrier bag, completed the spreadsheet, completed the paying-in slip, zipped it all up in her shoulder bag, went through to the shop. The bank they used was only a couple of doors away from the shop. The chances of being mugged on the way there were just about zero.

*

Back in the shop, her phone jingled as she was walking through to the office. She checked the time as she tapped. Five to four. Unknown number.

'Hello.' Juliette sat in the office chair, desperate that it shouldn't be Frampton, longing for it to be her dad.

'Hello, my name's Lara Salisbury. I'm a reporter at the *East Anglian*. I think you phoned earlier?'

'Yes. It's about my father – being missing. It was in the paper today.'

'Pathetic, isn't it? Do you know where he is?'

'It's very important that he is found soon. Why did you say pathetic?'

'That's all my editor would print. I know all about the business in Harwich.'

'What business in Harwich?'

'The massage parlour.'

What the hell is all this about? 'I see. You think he's in Harwich?' Juliette looked at the wall clock. Nearly four. Only a ten-minute walk to Museum Street, but better not keep them waiting too long.

'Not anymore. He seems to have vanished again.'

'I'm really glad you phoned. I've got an urgent appointment right now. We should meet. Tomorrow? Is this the best number to contact you on? I've really got to dash now.'

*

'I've come to see DS Cartwright,' Juliette said through the glass partition. 'Juliette Walker. I'm sorry I'm a few minutes late.'

The community support officer behind the desk smiled efficiently and said, 'Take a seat please. I'll let him know you're here.'

Juliette sat on the wooden bench. *Worst case, they've caught Tim, or somehow got wind of what he's doing. But why would Cartwright be involved? And wouldn't the timing be too much of a coincidence? And if they know I'm involved wouldn't they have come and arrested me, instead of being reasonably relaxed about delaying the interview by a couple of hours? But if it were to ask about the contents of the computer, wouldn't they have been less formal? That left—*

The glass-panelled door into the entrance hall swung open, as the word 'fingerprints' echoed in Juliette's head.

'Mrs Walker.' Not really a question, and not giving Juliette time to apologise for being late. 'Thank you very much for coming in. I'm sorry to have kept you waiting. DS Cartwright is available now. I am DC Gillespie.' She was a few years younger than Juliette, maybe mid-twenties, and a few inches shorter, maybe five foot seven. Her blonde hair was tied back in a short ponytail, making her face look quite round. 'Please follow me,' DC Gillespie said, with a smile that seemed genuinely welcoming. *She's trying to put me at my ease. This might turn out to be difficult.*

Following the young detective constable down a bleak but brightly lit corridor with insipid sage green walls, Juliette couldn't help noticing the slightly slack buttocks under cream-coloured linen trousers. *She could do with a few sessions in the gym.* 'Here we are.' Gillespie turned as she opened a door on the left. 'Nothing to worry about, but we do need to conduct a formal interview under caution.' She smiled again. 'Just procedure.'

A spotlight was shining down on a bare wooden table. The walls were the same sage green. DS Cartwright was wearing a dark suit, white shirt and no tie. He was sitting on the other side of the table. 'Hello, Mr Cartwright, I'm sorry I was late.' She felt her nerves – something like the feeling she used to have before going on stage with her flute.

'Let's get started then, DC Gillespie,' he said, with his eyes on Juliette.

Juliette glanced at Gillespie. *Good cop, bad cop*, went through her mind. The police interview room looked strangely familiar, from TV programmes. Gillespie sat next to Cartwright and started the recording machine. Cartwright said his and Gillespie's names, the time and date, and recited the stuff about the sky falling in on Juliette if she failed to say something she later relied on in court.

'Mrs Walker.' His brown eyes were fixed on hers. She decided to maintain eye contact for a few more seconds. 'Our technical officers up at Halesworth inform me that your father's computer was accessed as recently as yesterday morning, when it was in your possession.'

She tried not to look relieved. Lowered her eyes. 'Yes. That was me. But you need to understand it isn't my father's computer. He uses a laptop. His secretary used that PC. I didn't delete anything, if that's what you're suggesting. She'd used it to access his email account. That's what I did.' She raised her head and looked at Cartwright and Gillespie in turn. 'I thought there might be a clue, some indication as to where he's gone.'

'And was there?'

'Not that I could see. But his secretary would know more about it than me. Vanessa Drysdale.'

Cartwright shifted his chair back, reached under the table, and produced the shoe box, in a clear, sealed plastic bag, and Juliette clasped her hands together, trying not to shake. Clever bastard. He wasn't in the least interested in the computer. That was just to wrong-foot her.

'Mrs Walker, can you explain how your fingerprints came to be on this box?'

Juliette looked at him and moved her lips, without any sound emerging. She clenched her eyes shut. Maybe she could force a tear? Anyone would be upset in this situation. She reached down and fetched a small packet of tissues from her bag. She extracted one and wiped her eyes.

'For the recording, Mrs Walker is showing signs of distress. Do you want me to repeat the question, Mrs Walker?'

'No. It isn't fair.'

'What isn't fair?' Cartwright was insistent, without sounding aggressive.

Juliette turned to Gillespie, and said, 'You would have done the same.'

'Do you recognise this shoe box, Mrs Walker?'

Juliette let her shoulders slump, then looked at each of the officers in turn. 'I did the right thing.' She shook her head slightly, wiped her eyes again. 'My mother has fits of depression.'

'I'm sorry about that, but please can you answer the question?'

Juliette steeled herself, looked forlorn but resolute, she

hoped. 'I removed a Webley .455 service revolver and a box of ammunition from that shoe box on Sunday, on a visit to my parents' house.'

She heard a small gasp come from Gillespie. Cartwright's face relaxed. He said quietly, 'It would be a good idea for you to tell us the whole story, including the current whereabouts of the firearm in question.'

'May I have a glass of water, please?'

Gillespie looked at Cartwright, who nodded. She said, 'DC Gillespie leaving the room to get the interviewee a drink of water.' She switched the recording machine off.

'Get three,' Cartwright said, as she left the room. 'You've been a silly girl,' he said to Juliette. She kept her eyes down. *Don't react to the sexist insult; don't recite, improvise; let it come out naturally.*

When they were each provided with a plastic beaker of water and Gillespie had switched the machine back on, Cartwright looked at his wristwatch and said, 'Interview resumed at 16.23. Mrs Walker, please give us a full account of why you took the weapon, and what you did with it. I remind you that you are under caution.'

'Should I have someone with me – a solicitor or someone?'

Cartwright sighed loudly. 'That is your choice. Getting a solicitor, either one of your choice or a duty solicitor, will delay us by several hours. Your choice.'

'Let's get it over with.' It was Juliette's turn to sigh, not too theatrically. 'On Saturday, I received a phone call from my father. He had been away for several days. He told me his trip was complicated and he might be away for several weeks. For reasons it was important for me not to know, he said my mother must not know where he was or what he was doing.

He said he had told her he was going on a business trip, but it would soon become obvious that it was more complicated than that. He thought she would worry – become anxious.'

She caught Gillespie's eye. The young officer seemed to be studying her, without showing her own feelings.

Cartwright was breathing heavily, so she pressed on. 'He told me there was a handgun in a shoe box on top of the wardrobe in his dressing room. My mother knew it was there, and it was vitally important that I should remove it. She drinks far too much and has bouts of depression. I didn't need much convincing from my dad, that we shouldn't leave her in the house with something that would make it so easy for her. So when we were at my parents' house on Sunday, I took it, without any of them knowing. I took it home in my bag – this one.' She leaned down and lifted the bag from the floor and held it for a few seconds at shoulder height.

'For the recording, Mrs Walker has held up a grey suede leather or similar lady's bag with shoulder straps,' Cartwright said. 'Please continue.'

'When we got home, at the first opportunity I hid it where my father had suggested. He had said I shouldn't keep it in the house but in our garden shed, which is always locked. He said I should stick it with tape under an old pool table we keep in there. That's where it is – and the box of bullets. We keep the shed locked as my husband has some expensive tools.'

It was her father's earlier words that were echoing in her head – have a story ready, one in which you are innocent.

'But your mother is staying at your house.'

'Yes, but I don't know how long for. And she often has

things to do at her house. It must be quite depressing for her.'

'Mrs Walker, we need to find your father. Where is he?'

'I really don't know.'

'Why was his absence going to become complicated, as you say he told you?'

'He took a lot of money. My mother probably told you that. It could be about three-quarters of a million. My mother has the details.'

Cartwright looked at her with a barely perceptible nod. 'Is there anything else you want to tell us? In case it later becomes apparent that you've been hiding something?' His expression darkened, making the threat obvious.

She paused, looking thoughtful. 'Nothing that I can think of.'

'I see. Right, that's all for now. We might need to talk to you again if further information comes to light. Interview terminated at,' Cartwright looked at his wristwatch, '16.41.' Gillespie turned off the recording machine. 'Did it occur to you to hand it in to us?' Cartwright said.

'That would have got them both in trouble.'

'They *are* both in trouble, and so are you – wasting police time, possession of an unlicensed firearm for starters.'

'I've tried to explain that I did what any decent person would do in the circumstances. My car's at the back of our shop. Do I get a copy of the recording?'

Cartwright looked at Juliette and let out a breath. 'You've been watching the wrong TV programmes. One is secured as evidence. The other is our working copy. Dizzy, you go with Mrs Walker. Take some evidence bags. We'll meet at Mrs Walker's house.' As they were getting ready to leave the interview room, he said, 'You know the old saying: when you're in a hole, stop digging. Mrs Walker, the next time you get a word, a whisper, an idea, a thought, anything, concerning the whereabouts of your father, make sure I'm the first person to know about it.'

*

'Can I ask a question?' Juliette was driving, with the young detective sitting in the passenger seat. 'It seems a bit disproportionate. Formal interview, under caution. This interest in an antique pistol. It's not as if it's been used in a crime or anything.'

'I can't really say, well, except that it's part of a wider investigation. We need to find your father. He's a person of interest. DS Cartwright wants to make sure he doesn't get the gun. We try to prevent crimes as well as catch criminals. It's really important you don't do anything to help him, you know, avoid us.'

'Believe me, I want you to find him too.' *If Frampton doesn't find him first. Anything to make my children safe.*

When Juliette pulled into her driveway, DS Cartwright was getting out of a dark blue Vauxhall parked in the turning area. She led the officers through the house and across the lawn, down to the shed at the end of the garden.

'Some shed,' Cartwright said, as they reached it. It was about twenty feet by fifteen, surrounded by trees. 'What's the combination?'

'I'll do it,' Juliette said. 'My husband is very security conscious.' She opened the door.

'You stay there, Mrs Walker. Come on, Dizzy. Ah, the pool table in the corner.'

Juliette stood outside the door, preparing herself to look shocked. She heard a grunt and looked through the door. Gillespie was crouching on the ground examining the underside of the pool table with a flashlight. Cartwright was kneeling near her, with one elbow on the edge of the table. His face was red, perhaps from having to bend down. After a few seconds, he lurched towards the door. 'It's gone. Loose tape hanging under the table. Explain that.'

'Oh God! Are you sure? It must be...' *They're more likely to believe the story if they work it out for themselves. Just drop a clue.* 'No one else knew it was there.'

Gillespie followed Cartwright out of the shed. He said, 'Dizzy, lock that door and stick some crime scene tape across it. Get forensics here asap. If they can come this afternoon, stay here and show them what we want. Mrs Walker, you must keep your family out of the garden until our people have finished their work. Not a blade of grass to be broken. Do you understand? I take it your father knows the combination?'

'He might have remembered it. He needed to borrow our chainsaw last year. But he wouldn't... Oh God.'

'Who else knows the combination apart from your husband?'

'No one... I'm sure, but...' She shook her head. 'I was so sure it would be safe there.'

Juliette walked back to the house trying to assess whether Cartwright believed the story, or might suspect her of lying. He'd be weighing up the options. How much suspicion would it take for him to get a warrant to search the house?

Chapter 9

'I've just made a fresh pot. The children are watching television. Let's sit in the kitchen. You can tell me what on earth is going on.' Caroline had the severe look that Juliette remembered from her teenage years.

'Not much to tell,' Juliette said. Then, sitting at the kitchen table, occasionally sipping a mug of tea, she said, 'It was horrible. They just went over and over, what exact words did my father say on the phone? Was there any background noise? God, you'd think they watch too many detective thrillers. That went on for about half an hour. I told them what I could. They wanted to know everything about his businesses.' She paused, knowing she was putting it off. She would have to tell her mother the story about the gun.

'Why would they ask you about that, and not me?' Caroline didn't pause for an answer. 'And what are the police doing here?'

Juliette looked at her, caught her eye and decided to get it over with. 'Another thing he said on the phone. He said it wouldn't be safe for you to be in the mansion with that gun. He asked me to take it and hide it in our shed where it'd be secure.'

'You mean he was saying I might shoot myself if the gun was left there?'

'He said you knew where it was. You'd been very depressed. He thought you'd be upset about him going off with the money. You might do anything when you'd, well, when you'd had a few drinks. He convinced me it'd be dangerous to leave the gun there. God, I feel so stupid.' She didn't feel bad about lying to her mother. It wasn't harming her in any way – and it was necessary. 'They found my fingerprints on the shoe box.'

'And he told you to hide it in your garden shed?'

'He just used me, Mum.' Juliette started up the sobbing again. 'He made me think it would be safer to have the gun here. I told the police it was there in the shed. Once they knew I'd taken it from that shoe box, I thought it best to tell the truth even though it'd get me in a bit of trouble.' She put her hands over her face. She could almost believe it herself. The lie now seemed more plausible than the real truth. 'And it was just so that he could get his hands on it. He must have come in the night and taken it.'

'Well, you've done the right thing telling them, but have you not thought how serious this might be? Let's hope to God he doesn't use it, but, darling, if he does, if he shoots someone, you could be charged as an accessory.'

Juliette took her hands away. It wasn't difficult to look shocked. She longed to ask her mother what would happen if she shot someone who was trying to abduct her children. The police would find out she'd taken the gun and deliberately deceived them. Was that proof of premeditation? She struggled to put this out of her mind and focus on the story – the one she had prepared. 'Cartwright told me I could be charged with handling an unlicensed firearm. And wasting police time – they could do me for that even if Dad doesn't do anything with it.'

'Let's hope the police find him and he doesn't do anything stupid. God knows what might happen if Frampton finds him.' Caroline looked at her fingernails, seeming to examine the pink polish. Then she went to the worktop and came back to the table holding a tin of biscuits, which she put on the table, opened it, took one and said, 'We might be able to establish coercion if it goes to court.'

'It sounds so stupid now, but I thought it was for the best.' Juliette was beginning to relax. Her mother believed the story.

'The cunning bastard got you to hide it somewhere outside the range of the security system, and it's easy to get into and out of that shed without being seen, because of the trees.'

Juliette tried to conceal her pleasure. Her mother was so convinced by the story, that she was filling in gaps and adding her own details. Juliette decided she could afford to insert a complication. 'I'd forgotten he knew the combination. It doesn't explain the knife.'

'He must have it. His trickery over the revolver means he wants to be armed for some ghastly reason. He could have easily taken the knife when he decided to run off.'

'But why wouldn't he have taken the pistol at the same time?'

'He might have been in a desperate rush or might only have thought of it afterwards. Who knows?'

The front doorbell rang. Juliette looked at the entry-phone screen – Gillespie. She pulled open the heavy door.

'We've finished now, Mrs Walker,' Gillespie said. 'Fortunately, the forensics officer was available, so we've got it all done. We won't have to come back just yet.'

Juliette became aware of her mother coming up behind her. 'This is my mother. She's staying here for a while.'

'Ah, Mrs Belton-Smart, good afternoon. Just the obvious really, for both of you: let us know if anything happens or anything you think of. It's really important. Oh, and it's possible the local press might start asking questions. Please don't tell them anything. If other people are looking for Mr Belton-Smart, we don't want to help them.'

'Who else might be looking for him?'

'Sorry – the wider inquiry. I can't really say.' Gillespie pursed her lips.

'Of course we'll contact you.' Juliette held the detective's gaze, raised her eyebrows to emphasise her words – all innocence. 'Look, I'm sorry about the gun. I really thought I was doing the right thing.'

'Yes, well, goodbye for now.' Gillespie turned and walked towards a police car parked in the drive.

*

Later, when Steve had come down from reading to Jason, Juliette came and joined them in the sitting room. She had told Steve an abbreviated version of how she had taken the gun and hidden it in the shed. Caroline said, 'Do you think the police know Frampton's involved? Do they realise we're in danger?'

'I think Dad's going to turn up quite soon. If we carry on taking precautions as we are doing, that's as safe as we can be.'

'Darling, we should tell the police we're being threatened by Frampton and get them to provide us with protection.'

'Ready for a G&T, Cara?'

'Mum, be real. You know the state of police budgets. You don't think they're going to post an armed guard around the house, do you?'

'Thanks, Steve. That would be lovely.' There was silence while Steve went to the drinks cabinet and, a minute later, returned with a glass clinking with ice cubes, which he handed to Caroline. She gave him a smile and turned to Juliette. 'The wider inquiry the young officer mentioned. For all we know they're already looking for Frampton as part of it.'

'I doubt it. We don't even know what the connection between Dad and Frampton is. All the police know about Frampton is the rape and extortion convictions he got years ago. We're agreed, aren't we, that Dad had nothing to do with that?' She knew it was weak. Refusing to tell the police about Frampton had made some sort of sense at the beginning. She couldn't tell them in a way they'd understand. They didn't know what her dad had done to her three years ago. She had to find him first, if Frampton didn't, and that meant keeping the police as far off the track as possible.

'Well, we know there's a connection between them. There's no reason to assume the police don't know.' Caroline sipped her gin and tonic.

There was one usable reason not to tell the police. 'Mum, has Frampton made any threatening calls to you?'

'Not yet – one thing to be thankful for. He probably hasn't got my mobile number.'

'There's a more likely reason he hasn't phoned you. You'd recognise his voice.'

'Yes?'

'We're calling the man Frampton, but it's little more than an informed guess. Don't you see?' Juliette wanted her mother to think it through.

'You mean he'd just deny it was him?'

'Of course. They bring him in for questioning. He denies he's got anything to do with it. All we've achieved is to make him extremely angry, and you've told us how ruthless and brutal he is.' That part was true. She was genuinely frightened of Frampton.

'You'd need to tell the police that Richard told you he's hiding from Frampton, and that Frampton's been threatening you to get information about Richard.'

'Honestly, Mum, it's probably my fault, but the police don't see me as their most reliable witness right now. All we'd be doing is putting ourselves in more danger – and the children.' The children – she closed her eyes. She had used them. Surely the direct risk to them from Frampton was slight. She herself must be his prime target. But she had used them to make a point – and hated herself for it.

Caroline sighed and reached for her glass. 'If Richard had an ounce of decency left in him, he'd go to the police station and hand himself in.'

Steve was looking puzzled. 'Cara, are you suggesting Richard must have done something serious enough to be held in custody?'

Caroline shrugged, making it clear she didn't want to continue the conversation.

Juliette's own words, 'I'm not their most reliable witness', started echoing in her head – and Gillespie's closed expression as she had left. What had the forensics woman found? No trace of anyone coming to the shed through the trees? Were the police considering right now that she might be hiding the gun, and were getting a warrant to search the house?

*

It was another warm night. *Christ, why does it have to be Lucia di Lammermoor?* A woman is manipulated by men, tragic misunderstanding, goes mad, commits murder, dies. And Steve was playing the murder victim. They had rehearsed his main aria after supper. Now they were naked under a sheet. She could hear Steve's steady breathing. As usual, it only took him a minute after putting his head on the pillow. As Arturo, he only appeared in one scene. His role cut short. They joked about it. And Lucia, the tragic heroine – Lucy, Lulu. What was wrong with her? What went wrong?

Chapter 10

After breakfast the next day, Juliette parked the children in front of the television. 'Just a little while, then we'll go and play in the garden.' She went upstairs. It was time to take a closer look at the gun. Steve at the shop, her mother volunteering at the rape crisis centre. Three whole hours for herself – and the children. Space at last, but she had to make it safe.

She dragged an upright chair over to the Jacobean wardrobe, feeling pleased at having replicated the hiding place that had been used in the mansion. She climbed on the chair, reached up and brought down the shoe box. Sitting on the bed with it on her lap, she removed the lid. The gun had some strange, unreal, mythical quality. A memory buried in her childhood, maybe not so big now, but harder. She left it where it was while she opened her laptop and googled, 'Webley revolver'. Ten minutes later she knew everything she needed to about the weapon. The names of many of the parts were already familiar to her, from watching so many films.

She grasped the butt and lifted the gun out of the shoe box, feeling the rough texture of the cross-hatching. She rested the barrel on her open left hand. The weight of it was reassuring. She pressed the hammer with her thumb. It came back. The cylinder rotated slightly as the hammer moved back and clicked into place. Cocked. There was a spike on the hammer. She saw how it worked. The spike would hit the end of the cartridge to fire the bullet. So old, but somehow immaculate.

Ziggy jumped on the bed and pushed her nose into Juliette's thigh. 'What do you think of this, Zig? Lethal weapon. You're lucky, aren't you. You can kill your little enemies without the need for anything like this.' She raised the gun and pointed it at the window, finger on the trigger. CLICK. Ziggy flew off the bed and out of the door. Juliette looked at the side of the gun. Pulled the hammer back again. It seemed easier this time. Aimed at the dressing table. CLICK. She pressed the small lever on the left side. The cylinder flipped out. She lifted the small brown carboard box out of the shoe box. Took its lid off. Ten cartridges. She took one out. Dull lead, discoloured brass and that small copper disc at the flat end. She slid it into a chamber. A perfect fit. Five more in the other chambers. Then she pushed the cylinder back into place. It would be possible to jerk the cylinder back with a rightward flick of the wrist, Butch and Sundance style. She might practise that later. The gun was heavier now.

She stood and looked in the full-length mirror. Held the gun up diagonally between her breasts. Imagined a beret on her head – Bonnie Parker. Then pointed the gun at the mirror. 'Who you lookin' at, Travis Bickle?' out loud. 'Seriously though, Jules,' she interrogated her mirror image, 'if someone threatened your children would you be prepared to shoot?' The question went unanswered as she slipped the loaded gun into her shoulder bag. She stripped, put on her yellow and blue bikini and matching smock.

*

She tilted up the back of the sun lounger. Sky blue – *azzurro*, Steve had called it. She loved hearing him and his mother speaking Italian – Stefano, the name on his birth certificate. She would need to be vigilant. Ready to reach for the gun. She looked at the children in the paddling pool, naked except for sun cream and hats: Lulu sitting waist deep, giggling, playing with a plastic boat; Jazzy squealing as he repeatedly slid down the short plastic slide, landing with a splash that made Lulu giggle even more. Juliette leaned back, facing the corner of the house that was the only possible access from the front. They would need to break down the gate between the house and the garage. It wouldn't take long. The black iron bars on all the downstairs windows, insisted on by the insurance company when they started keeping valuable stock in the house, increased their safety in the house now, but made it feel like a prison. She opened the zip on the shoulder bag by her right hand and lay back. She told herself she was exaggerating the danger, feeling now the need to have a loaded gun within reach. Tim would call it mitigating a risk. Or she was acting out a dramatic fantasy. Or it was paranoia.

The azzurro sun lounger. They had bought it about six years ago. She closed her eyes.

*

A hot summer day, soon after they had moved into the lovely old house, given to them by Steve's father when he retired. No bars on the windows then. She was alone. She dragged the new azzurro sun lounger out on to the lawn, draped a towel over it, took all her clothes off, gave herself a good covering of factor 40 and lay on her back. She kept her sunglasses on to help her eyelids keep out the glare of the sun.

What did Dad think of Steve? Polar opposites, but they seemed to have a good working relationship, the removals firm providing a collection and delivery service for the shop. But strangely formal, having little to talk about other than business. Steve and Mum were another matter; she had adopted him like a son. From childhood she had been called Cara by her family, short for Caroline, but coming from him it seemed to carry the Italian meaning. *La mia cara...* They both had similar values – concerns for fairness and justice. Mum was longing for a grandchild. But how would Dad feel? *Twenty-two's too young. You should live, while you've got the chance.* Something like that. Was he jealous of Steve? Having to share her with him?

She loved them both in completely different ways. Dad for his freewheeling independence, his disregard for rules; Steve for… should she make a list of all the things she loved him for? His consistency and reliability, his ability to understand her changing moods and support her regardless, his tenor voice that he put to good use in the local amateur operatic society, and – maybe this should have come first – his body. There were several times each day, like now, when all she could think of was getting back into bed with him – the unhurried exploration of each other's bodies…

She must have drifted off. She was lying on her back and was shocked awake by a concerned voice from the outside world. 'Jules, you haven't got anything on.'

She opened her eyes. 'Hi, Steve. Get the other lounger. Come and join me.'

'The Oakwoods – they can see you.'

'Yeah, I bet the old man's in his upstairs bedroom with his binoculars trained on me.' She sprang up from the sun lounger, arms high in the air, shook, got some movement in her breasts. 'Hello, Mr Oakwood. Like my tits?' She put one foot up on the sun lounger, legs apart, and thrust her pelvis forward. 'And how about my pussy?'

'Jules, for God's sake.' Steve reached down for the towel, nearly caused her to fall over as he grabbed it from under her foot, held it in front of her.

She took the towel, put it over her shoulders, pulled him to her, enveloped them both. She felt his muscular chest through his white cotton shirt with her breasts, the beginnings of some hardening in his smart chinos. 'Steve, your mother's a Catholic, right? Obedience – difficult to shake off. Have you never wanted to do something you're not supposed to do? Break a rule? Transgress a little?'

He smiled. 'I might just surprise you one day.'

'I'm pregnant.'

*

A splash of water on her shoulder jolted her back into the present. 'Why are you laughing, Mummy?'

'Oh, aren't you big – and wet. It's time we went in. We don't want you and Lulu to get sunburnt.' On the way to the

French doors, she looked round the corner of the house. The bolt was in place, the gate was intact, but it was only six feet high. The sudden return to present reality had been shocking, but reassuring. Things were normal – or seemed so.

*

Juliette drove the familiar route into Ipswich feeling grateful towards her ever-reliable mother, who had worked a shift at the rape crisis centre and got back to the house as arranged at twelve-thirty to look after the children. The reporter hadn't given her any more information on the phone – just an invitation to meet for a snack lunch at the café in Buttermarket.

Lara Salisbury fitted the description she had given: slim, with black hair cut in a bob. She wore a pink blouse, glasses with large round lenses in green plastic frames, and looked as if she might only recently have left school. She was holding up a copy of the *East Anglian* and smiled as Juliette approached. They introduced themselves and Lara ordered drinks and salads. Lara said, 'With your dad missing, it must be a bit worrying?'

'It's worse for my mother, but thanks. Obviously, we're keen to have him back.'

'When did you last see him?'

'Oh, I can't remember.' Juliette paused as if trying to remember a date. The reporter was just after a story, obviously. 'On the phone you said something about Harwich. And a massage parlour?' She smiled to maintain the friendly atmosphere.

'I thought you'd be able to tell me more about that.' Lara returned the smile.

'Sorry. I had no idea he'd gone to Harwich.'

'Okay.' Lara sighed. 'I'll be upfront with you. I've been doing this job for a couple of months – just out of uni, my first job. A 2:1 in English Literature with Creative Writing and they've got me working on weddings and car crashes. So I'm trying to work my way up, right? This lunch is on my expenses, which means it's a working lunch. I'm supposed to have something to show for it.'

'You sound ambitious. That's good.'

A waiter put a beetroot and goat's cheese salad and elderflower pressé in front of Juliette, and what looked like a salmon salad and Coke in front of Lara.

'So, can you tell me anything about your dad?'

'It's got to be off the record. Perhaps I should pay for the lunch?'

'Look, Juliette—'

'Jules, please, I hate Juliette.'

'Well, Jules, they're letting me work on crime. It's what I want to do. I had a chat with the senior crime correspondent, who spoke to the editor, and they're letting me work on this story about your dad, as long as it doesn't interfere with my other duties.'

Juliette swallowed. 'What's my dad got to do with crime?' *Please don't let it be anything to do with money laundering.*

'We both want the same thing, don't we? You obviously want him back, and if I get information that leads to him being found, it could be a big story that'll boost my promotion. I've been trying to get hold of your mother too, but there's no answer from her house.'

'I'm pretty sure my mother won't talk to you. Look, Lara, I absolutely see what you want, and I want to help you in any way I can. You're right about us both wanting the same thing. If we share all the information each of us has got?'

Lara reached into the rucksack beside her and took out a slim laptop. 'That ridiculous little note in the paper yesterday. I wrote a whole story, which the editor spiked. So if you give me the names of some of his friends and business associates, I'll let you read the story.' She opened the laptop and started pressing keys.

Juliette quickly dismissed the idea of mentioning Frampton. Tim didn't even need considering. There was just one possibility which she could offer in exchange, that would appeal to Lara. 'Sorry, Lara, I just need the loo. Won't be long.'

In the women's room, Juliette clicked her phone and sent a text: *Hi Vanessa, I've just found out something I wanted to warn you about. A local reporter has got hold of your name from somewhere. She's been asking me about you, but obviously I'm playing dumb. It's important nothing about Richard appears in the press. The police are very emphatic about that. If any reporters contact you, please don't tell them anything, just hang up. Did you get the money OK? Thanks, Jules.*

As Juliette sat back at the table opposite Lara, she said, 'I've been racking my brains. My dad's very private about his business affairs. You know about Smart Move. You could try speaking to Jack. He's the manager. I never met or heard my dad mention anyone else he works with, except for one – his PA. In the media, you've got this thing about not revealing your sources, haven't you?' She saw Lara nod and continued. 'She's called Vanessa Drysdale. I'm afraid I don't have a contact number for her, but I know she lives in Ipswich and there can't be that many Vanessa Drysdales here. You really must not tell her that I gave you her name.' Juliette leaned forward. 'Okay?'

Lara nodded. 'Agreed. There are two versions of the story. I showed it to the senior crime correspondent. He told me to cut out the superfluous descriptions, the Keystone Cops, and all names. Apparently, we don't print anything that makes the police look incompetent. It might make them less co-operative. And naming people in a story like this might be defamatory. Not like weddings where the idea is to name as many people as possible. So, I did as I was told, just like junior school, and cut it down to about half the length. Complete waste of time as it got spiked anyway. You'll find the original draft more interesting,' she said, as she turned the laptop for Juliette to read from the screen.

Docklands Brothel Raided

A light drizzle was falling in Osterley Road. One of the orange streetlamps had failed, enabling the blinking red and blue lights of the Sunshine Massage Parlour to stand out more clearly. Under this sign was a stark yellow unblinking MASSAGE on a sign attached to the door. Across the road, four or five men were smoking outside the Mason's Bolster, apparently unconcerned about the drizzle. The noise of seventies music, loud conversation and occasional laughter could be heard coming from the pub behind them. Two of the men were arguing about whether to cross the road to the massage parlour.

This scene was being surveyed by Sergeant Renfrew of the Suffolk Constabulary from a corner about fifty yards away. He saw one of the men cross the road and go into the massage parlour. Turning to PC Hendricks, behind him, he said, 'They've got at least one punter. Let's give it another five minutes.'

Hendricks turned to the five uniformed men behind him and said, 'Ready to go in a couple of minutes, lads.' A minute later, Renfrew saw two more men walk down the street from the opposite end and enter the massage parlour. He said, 'Time to go – nice and easy.' As the seven men, five of them in police uniform, walked round the corner into Osterley Road, there was suddenly no one outside the pub. Cigarettes sizzled on the damp pavement as the door swung shut. When they reached the massage parlour, the five uniformed men stood with their backs to the betting shop next to it, while Renfrew opened the door and went in, followed by PC Robinson, also in civilian clothes.

Adjusting his eyes to the low light, Renfrew took in the shabby entrance lobby. To the left, a couple of upholstered chairs with slightly threadbare arms stood each side of a small round table, on which stood a purple china vase with a bunch of pink plastic flowers.

'Evening, gents.' The tired greeting came from a middle-aged woman behind a chest-high counter on the right. Her face was lit from the side, accentuating the patch of bronze rouge on her cheek and a slightly displaced black eyebrow.

'Me and my friend, we'd like the full service,' Renfrew said.

'Read, can you?' The cigarette in the corner of the woman's mouth hardly moved as she spoke. She nodded to a price list on the wall.

'Yes, but we'd like the full service.' Renfrew tried to smile and actually winked at her as he said this.

She sighed. 'As you will see, we can offer you the topless full body with oil. Anything else is a matter between you and your professional *masseuse*.' She enunciated the last two words as if she were projecting to the back of a large auditorium. At that moment, the pink door at the back of the lobby opened and a large middle-aged man wearing a light grey tracksuit came out. He said, 'See you next—' before he saw Renfrew and immediately made a dash for the front door. The first thing he hit was PC Robinson, who fell back against the door. The signal for the five uniformed men to enter in force was to have been a knock on the door from the inside by PC Robinson, but the impact of his body against the door served the same purpose. As they made their entrance, led by PC Hendricks, pushing PC Robinson into the counter, the man who had had his exit obstructed turned and ran back through the pink door. As this opened, a tinkling of bells could be heard throughout the building, caused by the woman behind the counter pressing a button under it.

Renfrew said to Robinson, 'Stay here. Don't let her move. Lock the front door.' The building had come to life. Renfrew said, 'Follow me,' and rushed through the pink door. The patter of feet on the carpeted stairs stopped as the officers positioned themselves at the bottom of the staircase, then started again. Renfrew yelled, 'You two – back door, see no one leaves. Hendricks, check these two rooms. Parsons and you, other one, follow me.' He started up the stairs two at a *time. On the first landing, he heard a shout from the back of the building. 'Sarge, they're coming down the fire escape.' He yelled back, 'Stop them. Stop them.'*

Having checked that the four rooms upstairs were unoccupied, Renfrew glanced at the trapdoor in the ceiling above the top landing and made a mental note to check it later. 'Right, lads, let's see what we've got downstairs.'

The two uniforms who had checked the downstairs rooms reported that they had found no one. 'Right, out back, all of you.' In the service area at the back of the building, next to three unpleasant-smelling wheelie bins, Parsons and his colleague had corralled five young women wearing various degrees of improvised clothing – sheets, towels – except for one. She was standing on the bottom step of the fire escape, naked to the waist, hands above her head, smiling with her mouth, making eye contact, swaying seductively, showing off her skinny body, her tiny breasts.

'Nice catch, eh, Sarge.' Parsons beamed.

'Where are the men? And it's Sergeant,' Renfrew shouted.

'What? The punters? We didn't want to hold them, did we?'

'Get them wrapped up and inside.' Renfrew could barely contain his rage, and muttered, 'F***ing Specials,' under his breath in an effort to do so.

Back in the entrance lobby, he found PC Robinson, still preventing the woman from leaving her position behind the counter. A man was sitting back in one of the worn-out armchairs, legs crossed at the knee, smoking a cigarette. This man has been identified as Mr Eric Scannel. The woman behind the counter gave her name as Mrs Dorothy Leviticus. Sergeant Renfrew discovered in the loft a very basic living space. It had been vacated recently, and in a hurry. There were scraps of food on a plate, a half-full can of beer, and the skylight was open. There was a crawl ladder across the roof and a short drop on to the platform at the top of the fire escape. Renfrew formed the opinion that this was designed for a quick getaway in emergencies. Forensic examination the following morning revealed fingerprints in the loft which have now been matched to Mr Richard Belton-Smart, the managing director of the removals firm, Smart Move. Mr Belton-Smart has been reported missing by his wife, Mrs Caroline Belton-Smart.

Juliette looked up. 'If you don't mind my saying so, I can see why they didn't want to print all that.'

'Yeah, well, I'm just learning. It's different to the stories we had to write at uni.'

'You must know someone in the police.'

'To be honest it's sort of third hand, but the thing is, your dad was there. He must have been one of the men that came down the fire escape and got away.'

'What else do you know?'

'Nothing. That's why I'm trying to find out – get a proper story.' Lara folded the laptop and put it back in her bag. 'What sort of man is he? What does he do apart from running the removal company?'

Juliette shrugged. 'He's my dad. That's about it. He's kind

– very supportive. But quite private. He never talks about business, so I can't tell you anything about that.'

'It looks as if he was hiding in a massage parlour – the sleazy sort, a brothel really. And now he's disappeared again.'

'I don't know what to say. I can't believe that he's the sort of man who'd go to a place like that. Are you absolutely sure?' Juliette was thinking he'd feel right at home in a brothel.

'Sorry. My source says there was a tip-off. The police carried out the raid in order to... well, because they had information that he was there. Then they found proof that he had been there.'

'You mean he's wanted in connection with what was going on at the massage parlour?'

'Some of the women are underage. Hardly a word of English between them.' Lara looked up, and anticipated the question that Juliette was about to ask. 'From Eastern Europe mostly, a few from North Africa. There's suspicion of people-trafficking, which the police are investigating.' Lara drained her glass.

'And you think my dad is... involved?' Juliette felt her heart accelerating. Prostitution, people-trafficking. The wider investigation Gillespie had mentioned. Could that be it? And could that be where the money came from that paid for the mansion, expensive cars, her school fees, music tuition...

'Maybe he's got a friend who agreed to put him up in his loft. Like if your mum had thrown him out and he didn't have anywhere else to go.'

'Give me some credit.' Juliette forced a smile so that Lara wouldn't think she was being aggressive. 'It'd be great for your career if you can expose my dad as a pimp and people-smuggler.'

109

The two women paused as a waiter cleared the table and suggested coffee, which they both declined.

Lara leaned forward. 'No. Absolutely not. I simply want to find out who's behind the racket. I can see where you're coming from. I'd be gutted if my dad did anything like that. Look, Jules,' Lara tapped the table with an index finger, 'face it, your dad was there. Someone allowed him to use that loft. He must know who.'

'Yeah.' Juliette felt tears rising. She needed to bring this to an end. 'Those two who were caught. The man and woman in reception. Presumably they've been arrested and are being questioned.' She looked at her phone. 'God, is that the time? My kids are at home with my... oh... with the babysitter. I promised to be back by now.' She stood up. 'Thanks for the lunch, Lara. Good luck with Vanessa, if you find her. Let me know anything you find out. And I will, of course, if I find out anything. Let's keep in touch.'

Chapter 11

Caroline was holding a glass of whisky but hadn't drunk any of it. Steve had gone to bed, telling them he would need to make an early start in the morning.

'The website designer has got some interesting ideas.' Juliette was trying to jog her mother out of an apparent reverie. 'The one I had lunch with – I told you.'

Caroline looked up. 'That's good.' Then silence again.

'You've been very quiet. Are you frightened?'

'I can't bear the thought of Frampton getting his hands on you. I think I've stopped being frightened of Richard. As long as we just carried on as we were. Conditioning, I suppose. He hasn't laid a hand on me since that time three years ago.'

Juliette's mind flipped. Three years ago. 'They were horrible bruises.'

'There's so much I need to tell you. God. I'm so sorry.' Caroline put her hands over her face, sobbing. 'I've been a lousy mother.'

Juliette could just make out the words among her mother's convulsions. She went to her mother and knelt beside the chair. She dreaded an emotional scene, but couldn't ignore her mum's distress. 'Mum, has something happened?'

Caroline lowered her hands. Juliette reached over to the coffee table and put a box of tissues on her mother's lap. She'd heard enough about men abusing women at lunch. But now she needed to hear this, really concerned for her mother.

'Being here – in your house…' Caroline wiped her eyes and blew her nose. 'Jewel, darling, you've been so kind – and Steve. I've had time to think. It's my bloody husband causing this trouble…'

'You aren't responsible for Dad's actions.'

Caroline raised her head, looking resolute, dry-eyed. 'I think he's gone now, forever. With all that money. There's something I should have told you years ago.' She was speaking with a new calmness and determination. 'It's been on my mind the last few days. I'm going to tell you now. I don't know if you'll forgive me. Can we sit in the kitchen? Have some tea?'

A minute later the glass of whisky had been left and they were sitting across a corner of the refectory table in the kitchen. The kettle was coming to the boil noisily.

'I never told you how I met him. Defending him in court.'

'What?' Juliette looked sharply into her mother's eyes, but Caroline looked away. 'You met through a mutual friend. That's what you said. You both said. You must have agreed.'

'Darling, you must understand—'

'What I understand is that you and he made up a story and both lied to me about how you met. So what terrible crime were you defending him for?'

Caroline seemed to shrink back into her chair. 'Extortion and grievous bodily harm. He was found not guilty.'

'So why the big cover-up? Jesus, people like to know how their parents met. If he didn't do it, why do you both have to lie to me?' Juliette was trying to understand her own anger. Should she have realised it must have been something like this? How likely was it that such different people would have a mutual friend? She was angry with herself for not having questioned that story.

Caroline sat up straighter and seemed to stiffen. 'He got off because the key witness, the man who owed him money and who had been beaten up, changed his testimony. Case dismissed. It didn't even go to the jury. Richard told me it was impossible to exist in the financial services industry without making enemies. I, well, I gave him the benefit of the doubt. He had this strange, rough charm, and when he asked me out to dinner to thank me for representing him, I just said yes. Things just went on from there. I can't really explain it. I remember asking him if he minded having a reputation as a loan shark. He just smiled and said, "The Great White, that's what they call me. The Great White." It was just after the *Jaws* film had first come out. It wasn't till years later, when I'd got to know him better, that I realised the witness in that case must have been got at, by Richard or someone working for him.'

'So why have you decided to tell me this now?' Juliette put two mugs of steaming tea on the table and sat down again, seething.

'I'm trying to explain our relationship—'

'Your relationship's crap. We know that – since the time he hit you.'

'It's more complicated. You're going to think I'm a terrible coward...' Caroline seemed to sink back into her own thoughts.

'Take your time, Mum.'

Caroline looked at her mug. 'When I met Richard, I had a boyfriend called Adrian. Adrian. He was gentle and sensitive. A thoughtful, intelligent man. A bit left-wing. I'd been seeing him for years. So when Richard started showing an interest in me, I had a choice to make. I'd never actually lived with Adrian. He seemed to want to carry on as we had been, spending two or three nights a week together, doing things together at weekends. He was very knowledgeable about art, theatre, classical music – so we'd go to concerts, art exhibitions and so on. Richard was about as different to that as you could imagine. I was in my thirties by then, working hard, really committed to my career, but, well, wanting to settle down. Adrian was a couple of years older than me, stuck in his ways, and to be honest, I was beginning to find him a bit boring. Richard was so dynamic, so ambitious. Things were changing. Margaret Thatcher came to power. I was fascinated by her.' Caroline reached for a tissue from the box on the table.

'So I chose.' She looked across at Juliette. 'Adrian was heartbroken. He said he loved me and if only he had known that I wanted to get married he would have proposed to me.' She wiped her eyes with another tissue. 'It was a terrible mistake.'

'Well, you can't turn the clock back.' Juliette realised that sounded harsher than she had meant, softened her voice. 'You've got me. That's not so terrible, is it?'

Caroline dabbed her eyes with a tissue. 'Richard and I had been married about three years. He was going on and on at me about having children. Needed to perpetuate his genes, he'd say. All about him, as usual. By that time, I'd realised he was a monster. He was sleeping around, would demand sex with me only for reasons of procreation. I was absolutely determined that I would not bear a child of his, so I made damn sure I didn't.' Caroline managed a defiant smile. 'I saw there was a law conference in London. Organised by Adrian's firm, I knew he'd be there.' She closed her eyes.

'Mum?'

'God, I'm so sorry. I didn't have the guts to tell you.' Caroline jerked her head up. 'You've got his eyes. I've always known.'

Juliette reached across the table to grasp Caroline's hand. She saw her mother's tears and felt her own. Was this what her mum was telling her – her dad wasn't…? Her mind wouldn't take it in.

'Mum, you are telling me what I think you're telling me?'

'You can have a DNA test, if you like. But I know. I'm so sorry.'

'He isn't my father. This man Adrian is.' Juliette laughed wildly. *The man who… he isn't…* Her world was upside down. The idea was repellent – too much. She needed her mum to spell it out – but dreaded hearing it. At last, she controlled the laugh and looked at her mother, waiting.

Caroline lifted her mug, looked at it and put it back on the table. 'After you were born, Richard was desperate to have a son. I don't really know what was in my head. I had you. And I had this secret. You were so special, my precious Jewel. I stopped taking precautions. You were only a few months old. It's hard to believe now – for me to believe. You were mine. If I became pregnant again and had a son, he would be Richard's. Crazy.' Caroline sipped her tea.

Juliette looked her mother in the eye. Had she been

having some kind of breakdown? 'Mum, it doesn't… I don't really understand.'

Caroline looked forlorn but still resolute, and the tears had stopped. 'Looking back now, I know it doesn't seem rational. I had this belief that if I bore him a son, he'd leave me alone. I loved you so much. That was enough.' Caroline lifted her mug, saw there was nothing in it and carried on. 'Time went by and nothing happened. He'd check my cycles and demand sex at the best times for conceiving. Nothing. I was terrified of getting AIDS. Then after a few years it just stopped. I'd passed forty by then. Nothing was said. He spent more and more nights out. I didn't want to discourage him if it meant he didn't need to have sex with me.'

'Was that when you started sleeping in my old room?' Juliette had been listening to every word, but another part of her brain was processing the idea that Richard Belton-Smart was not her father. It could explain…

'Stupid. I daren't. I was still playing the role of wife. Right up until the time…' Caroline looked at Juliette. 'The last time I came to stay here.'

'You said you'd fallen over in the kitchen. I believed that for about ten seconds – until I saw the bruises.' But she had been too absorbed in what had happened to her.

'He found out. He came home drunk. Just came in and slapped me and called me a bitch. It had happened a few times before. But then he punched me in the face. That was a first. The impact, the shock – I can't describe it. I fell over and he kicked me and started calling me a fucking whore. He demanded to know who your father was. I could barely speak. I tried to ask him what he was talking about. He kicked me a few more times and yelled more abuse. So I told him I'd had too much to drink and had a one-night stand in a hotel with a man I hadn't met before and had no means of contacting. Richard just stormed out and I heard him drive off. I thought I had a couple of broken ribs to start with. I thought about running away, trying to disappear, but he would have found me and it would have been worse. So I just went to bed, probably had a glass of Scotch. Thank God, he didn't come back that night. He must have been busy with some tart.'

Juliette shuddered, stood up and looked out of the window into the darkness. *Not a tart, Mum.* She felt the anger rising. 'Why the hell didn't you leave him?' She hissed, to prevent herself from shouting. 'I tried to persuade you at the time. I do not understand how you can live with a man who did that to you.'

'Well, you live in a nice sanitised world where everyone is considerate and polite, kind even.' A defiant look came on to Caroline's face. 'Just listen, will you? In the morning, I wanted to phone you, but I felt so bad. It took me until the afternoon to make up my mind to tell you I had had a fall. I left a note on the hall table telling him where I was. I didn't want him to have an excuse to hit me again. At the time, I just couldn't tell you.'

'How had he found out?'

'I'm coming to that. He'd say, "What's sauce for the goose, eh, honey," or something like that, and be out for the night. It wasn't actually much different to how it had been before, but he was more blatant about it. He genuinely seemed to think that my spending one night with another man twenty-five years earlier was justification for total disloyalty. That's when I moved my things into your room. Never slept in the same bed with him again. God, I hate being called honey.'

'I don't understand how you can even live under the same roof as a man who's done that to you.'

'You know I'm not proud of that. I'm still trying to tell you what happened. He came back a couple of days after the night he hit me, all calm and self-righteous. What I'd done was such a shocking betrayal. Finding out was a terrible emotional shock for him. He'd just reacted the way any man would. Then he calmly asked me again who your father was. I told him I couldn't remember after such a long time, and the man couldn't know I'd become pregnant because we didn't exchange contact details, and I'd been completely faithful to him since then in spite of his cheating.' Caroline shook her head and looked again at her empty mug. 'He seemed to believe me. He asked me if you knew he wasn't your father, and I told him you didn't. He said he'd do horrible things to me if you found out – too disgusting. And he seemed to lose interest in who your biological father was. The most important thing for him was that you should continue to believe it was him.'

'You still haven't told me how he found out.' Juliette focused on this one issue. Was her mum trying to dodge the question? Maybe it wasn't important, but how could a secret like this lie buried for twenty-five years and then come out?

'I didn't know until about a year later. A woman came to the house, mid-thirties I'd guess. Her name was Cynthia, or Sybil, something like that. She was upset. She was looking for Richard, but when I told her he was out, she asked to come in. I sat her down with a cup of coffee and she poured out this whole sad story. She was childless and desperate to have a baby. Richard had said he was too. He needed a son to perpetuate his genes, same old twaddle. They started having sex on a regular basis. Usual bloody thing: he told her he was getting divorced and as soon as that was over, he'd marry her. After no success for about six months, he'd said she ought to have a test to see if she was capable. She had said, in effect, "I will if you will," and the outcome was that he was found to be sterile. "He'd been firing blanks all his life," was the way she put it. I told her there had never been any suggestion that Richard and I were getting a divorce. She said if she were married to a bastard like him, she'd be looking for a divorce double-quick. I've no idea if she caught up with him. I didn't see her again and didn't mention her to him.'

Juliette was looking straight ahead, mind whirling. 'You mean he's incapable of becoming a father?'

'He always has been. Why are you smiling?'

'I'll just go up and check the children. I'll just be a minute.' She stumbled up the stairs – sheer joy now finding a place among the confusion of shock and anger in her head.

When she reached the children's bedroom, she went to sit in the nursing chair beside Lucy's bed. The child's face was visible in the warm glow of the night light in the corner of the room. Juliette looked into her daughter's face in wonder. How could she ever have thought that Richard was her father? She leaned forward and put the flat of her hand gently against Lulu's cheek. The child stirred slightly. A tear landed on the edge of the duvet. Juliette whispered, 'Sleep well, gorgeous,' then stood up and went back downstairs.

Caroline was still sitting at the kitchen table. Should she, could she, tell her? *Mum, after beating you up, he didn't go and spend the night with a tart. No, no, no, as long as no one knows, it didn't happen.*

She sat at the table and looked at her mother, trying to grasp the real feelings amongst the confusion.

'I'm so sorry, darling.'

That was it. Juliette took a deep breath. 'For fuck's sake, stop apologising. It's a bit late for that. Twenty-seven years too late.' She stood up, intending to walk out of the room, then decided to go back and sit down. 'You should have left him. I don't mean three years ago. Before I was born. You didn't love him. He was being a complete bastard. I just don't understand. How the hell could you demean yourself by living like that? A fucking doormat...' Juliette was sobbing by now and reached for a tissue. But she hadn't finished. She looked at her mother and was surprised to see defiance in her eyes. 'And lying to me, lying to your only daughter about who her father is, for all these years – living a lie.' She blew her nose and added, 'That's unforgivable.' But she wasn't sure if it had been audible.

Caroline stood up, went to a cupboard, took out two tumblers, filled them both at the sink, put one in front of Juliette, and sat down. 'You're right. I owe you a debt I can't repay. I've been dreading telling you.' She shook her head slowly. 'I've longed to – and kept putting it off. Cowardice, I suppose. But you haven't seen his nasty side.'

That's what you think. She looked at her mum, hating her, wanting to hold her, seeing the misery. How had a successful, intelligent woman allowed this to happen? All because of a man. Men. 'And this poor man Adrian. I bet you've never told him he's got a daughter. How could you...?' Her mind was racing ahead. She'd get her mum to tell her his surname. She'd turn up on his doorstep. *I think you're my father...*

Caroline gave a gentle shake of her head. 'It was a

wonderful night, the night you were conceived. My last experience of real love-making.' She smiled through the tears. 'How could I tell him?'

Chapter 12

'Were you up late?' Steve was tipping chopped banana and strawberries into the children's cereal bowls. Juliette had just walked into the kitchen wearing her blue and white striped dressing gown.

'Morning, you lot. I love you.' She kissed each child on the head. 'I'll have my workout later if there's time. And I love you too.' She wrapped her arms round Steve and kissed him on the mouth.

'That's one way to get a mug of coffee,' he said. 'I can't hang about. The stock from Belgium.'

Ten minutes later she was on her own in the kitchen, having settled the children in the sitting room with the television. She sat at the table, on the chair she had sat on talking to Caroline the previous evening. Now she had a bowl of muesli with yoghurt, and a steaming mug of coffee. Ziggy landed softly on her lap. Juliette held the knuckles of her left hand for the cat to press her face against and stroked her back with her right hand. The purring started instantly.

'Lucky you, Zig. We humans decided you'd remain a virgin forever. It's a bit more complicated for the rest of us. Blissful ignorance. Different matter when your father turns out not to be your father. Just some piece of shit—' Ziggy squawked, and Juliette realised she was gripping her back too tightly, so relaxed her hand. 'Sorry, Zig.' Ziggy resumed her purring. 'The thing is… well, he isn't my father, but he was. Till I met Steve, he was the most important man in my life. And it must mean something to him too. He phoned me to warn us about Frampton. He didn't have to do that. Even though he knows I'll never forgive him. I need so much to tell him, ask him, get him to admit it. You understand, don't you, deep in there.' She put her fist against the cat's forehead and pressed. Ziggy pushed back, purring like a machine, her pupils reduced to narrow slits in the August morning sunlight.

Juliette tested the coffee, decided it was cool enough, gulped some down. Had she expected more from Steve? That he was half Italian had attracted her at the beginning. Did it lead her to expect something more romantic, fiery – unpredictable? 'Stereotypes, Ziggy – you can never rely on them, but I can rely on Steve. If I'd had a dull, conventional dad, like my mum did, I might have chosen a wild man like she did. Just as well I didn't. Glad I've got someone safe, who isn't going to betray me like that bastard did.' She drank some more coffee and turned her mind to more practical matters.

'It's a mad world we live in, Zig. You know what? I might have a problem with the police. No way of knowing if they fell for that trick with the gun. You don't know what risk management is, do you, with your little hardwired brain. It's a thing Tim does. And it's time I did some too. Any moment they might arrive with a search warrant.'

'Is Steve still here?' Caroline came into the kitchen wearing her floral dressing gown. *Christ, did she hear any of that?*

Juliette gathered herself. 'He went a bit early. The new stock he keeps going on about.'

'I thought I heard talking.'

'Just me and Ziggy.' Juliette eased the cat off her lap, stood up, went to Caroline and held her. 'Talking nonsense.'

'You'll set me off again.'

'I haven't slept much.'

'Nor me.' Caroline sat on the same chair as the previous evening.

'Mum, do you think about Adrian? I mean over the years.' She poured some coffee into her mother's mug.

Caroline helped herself to milk, then took a sip of coffee. 'As a former lover. I've managed to avoid thinking of him as your father, until last night. Telling you made it real.' She took another sip. 'I lay awake wondering what sort of father he might have been.'

'Dad – Richard, I mean – wasn't a bad father… until… what happened. I used to love him. I had no idea what he was putting you through.'

'It was best that way.'

'He exploits weaker people.'

'I'm not going to be weak anymore.' Caroline looked into her coffee.

'Sorry, I didn't mean… I still don't understand why you didn't leave him. He's a bully, uses people. That's what weak people do.'

'Did you tell Steve?'

'I'm still trying to get my own head round it. It's a lot to take in. Steve's so wrapped up in his delivery of Belgian antiques. I don't want the children to know, until they're a bit older.'

'Best not say anything for now.'

'I'll have to pick the right moment.'

'I'm really sorry, darling.'

Juliette sighed. 'Yes, well, I think you can understand why I'm angry. I'm also confused and actually quite relieved. I hated the thought of having such a piece of shit as a father.'

Caroline looked Juliette in the eye, clenched and unclenched her fists. 'I wouldn't have left without you. If I had taken you, he would have tracked us down and probably done what he had threatened.' Caroline shrugged. 'We can't turn the clock back. Some daughters would actually be grateful.'

'So if it hadn't been for me, you would have left him?' Juliette closed her eyes. She longed to wrap her arms round her mum and have a long tearful hug, but something stopped her. 'You could have told me, say ten or fifteen years ago. Trusted me.'

Caroline shook her head. 'I longed to – so much. You were close to him. I thought you wouldn't believe me. You'd go and ask him if it were true.'

'What about three years ago, then? I would have believed you if you'd been honest for once and told me why he'd beaten you up.'

'That would have been practically suicidal.' Caroline took a deep breath. 'I'm not really hungry. I'll just pop up and have a shower, get dressed…'

Juliette stayed sitting at the kitchen table. What would she have done? Not been stupid enough to marry him in the first place? Who knows? She knew how loving he could be, when she was a child and a teenager – before Steve. That was when their relationship had started to cool. She jolted at the sound of her mobile. She looked at the screen. No caller ID. *Please, please, let it be Richard.* She tapped it. 'Yes?'

'Found him yet?' The deep Essex voice.

Juliette flinched, swallowed and hunched forward over the table. 'We're getting closer. He was in Harwich a couple of days ago.'

'Thinks he can skip the country, does he?'

She forced her mind to change gear, to focus on this other detestable man. 'I don't think so. I think he's got a friend there, who was helping him. I want to find him. We can help each other.' She had to stop to think. Needed more time. Better try to convince him she was getting somewhere. Options rushed through her head. Should she ask him? Yes. 'What do you know about the Sunshine Massage Parlour?'

'Was it you tipped off the filth?'

So he does know about that. 'I didn't know anything about it. I'm doing everything I can. I'm finding out where he went from there.'

'You've got till the end of the week. You can't hide from me. You can't stop me.'

'Look, you need to know—' The line went dead. *You need to know he, the BS man, he isn't my father. He wouldn't lift a finger to save me or my children. He's only interested in his own skin.* She'd tell him next time. Get it in first.

She hadn't spoken to Jack since giving him the cash to pay the men. Maybe he'd heard something. She tapped her phone. 'Hi, Jack, have you heard anything about my dad?'

'Not really. Do you know anything?' Jack sounded evasive.

'Not a lot. Jack, you wouldn't hold out on me?'

'He told me not to tell you.'

'You know, anything you tell me won't go further.'

'I think he's skint. I got him a motor.'

'Have you got the Merc?'

'The Merc's long gone. Everyone's looking for it. They won't find it. He wanted a runabout. I got him an old Fiesta. Said he owed me one and not to tell a soul, including you.'

'Anything else, Jack?'

'Nothing I can't handle. The cops came asking. They know nothing. No need to tell them. It'll take them months to link the Fiesta to Richie. I didn't tell that newspaper woman nothing neither.'

'What newspaper woman?'

'Young one. She'll be poking her nose in with you soon. Seems to think she's hot on the trail of some master criminal.'

Juliette was still adjusting her thinking. Surely Frampton must know about Smart Move and would have contacted Jack. She decided not to ask, or to mention the brothel in Harwich. 'Right. Thanks for the heads-up. Let's both stay dumb with the police and media. How was he? Richard. When he picked up the Fiesta.'

'Didn't see him. Had to leave it in a lay-by on the A12 just south of Woodbridge. Saturday night. It was gone Sunday morning. No cameras there.'

'Anything else you know?'

'Not a thing. Steve's like a kid with a new toy. I left the shop half-hour ago. Left a couple of lads shifting things for him. Nice stuff.'

'Thanks, Jack. Take care.' She ended the call.

*

Juliette was still sitting at the table nursing a cold mug of coffee, when Caroline came down, wearing a light blue blouse and linen culottes. 'Mum, do you really hate Richard?'

Caroline sighed. 'There have been times. Oh, I don't know. I hate what he is, what he became. Not quite the same as hating him personally. Does that make sense?'

'I'll need to think about it.' Juliette was thinking how much she did hate him – personally.

'Abused by his foster father. He made me promise never to tell you. Same old story.'

Juliette looked at her mother and waited.

'Ran away when he was sixteen. The way he told it, his so-called brother, which meant his foster parents' natural son, caught him stealing cash from a pot in the kitchen, so Richard stabbed him in the thigh with a pencil, then knocked him out with a frying pan. That was in Walthamstow. He stole as much as he could carry and hitched to Harlow. Stayed in a squat with a friend he'd known from approved school. He never said how he survived, started making money. I didn't really want to know. He told me this when we first started going out. He had never been loved. I thought...' Caroline looked at Juliette and shrugged. 'I don't really know what I thought, but I was drawn to him – that energy and drive.'

Juliette looked at her mum. She was still angry with her, but the bond was still there. And in current circumstances they needed to get on with each other. This story about Richard's early life? It could be the truth. Or it could be a sob story he made up to get her sympathy – one of his many lies. It didn't make any difference. 'Mum, I've got a few things to do upstairs. Can you sit with the kids for a bit? How about us both taking them to that beach funfair in the park, then all of us go and look at the famous Belgian furniture?'

'That would be lovely,' Caroline said. 'Are you sure it's safe?'

'We're safer now than we will be next week, if he still hasn't been found.'

*

Ziggy was asleep on the bed. 'Hi, Zig. Time to implement Plan B. It's all a matter of risk management. Tim'd be proud.' She went into the ensuite bathroom and came back with a packet of baby wipes. She opened the rolltop desk, took out the laptop, opened it, wiped it carefully – keys, screen, every surface, inside and out – stuck a dongle into a USB port, then slid it into a rucksack. Then the phones. Each one got a thorough wipe before being dropped into the rucksack. Next came the Psycho knife – out of its secret compartment. After wiping it and wrapping toilet paper round the blade, she put it into a black tote bag. With the help of a chair, she removed the service revolver and box of ammunition from the shoe box on top of the wardrobe. She was especially careful wiping the gun, opening the chamber and cleaning all the parts she could have touched. The gun and ammo joined the knife in the tote bag.

'You see, Zig, something's got to happen. That dastardly Mr Bullshit, my erstwhile father, is going to come a cropper one way or another. Seems he escaped by a whisker from that dump in Harwich. Won't be so lucky next time. Or Frampton'll catch up with him. Either way the cops'll get heavy. My hands have got to be clean. You know, the safest place to put all this stuff would be in the garage at the mansion. A tad inconvenient, though. So it's got to be our shed. All the gear Mr Bullshit uses for communications with Tim – and his armoury. Regular visitor to our shed is Mr Bullshit. Big professional search of the house, where they draw a blank. There's a good chance they won't bother with the shed, as they've just searched it. If they do, then I lose this stuff, but I'm still in the clear because it all belongs to Mr Bullshit. My God, he's so devious, and clever. Tim'd be pissed off. He'd probably make me pay for the new laptop and set of burners. The gun and the knife would go, but that was a stupid idea in the first place. Can you imagine me shooting or stabbing anyone?'

Ziggy didn't stir.

Juliette put the rucksack and tote bag on the floor in the utility room, then went back and put her head round the sitting room door. The television was off. Caroline was on the sofa with Lucy, trying to get her to join in singing 'Humpty Dumpty'. Jason was unfolding a square board on the coffee table in front of them.

'Nearly ready, Mum. I forgot to check the shed yesterday. Make sure the police didn't make too much of a mess and locked it properly.'

*

In the shed, Juliette slid the rucksack and tote bag into the narrow gap under Steve's workbench. She looked at the bench from different angles. Steve would never find the stuff under it. If the police searched, they'd find it all. She had her story ready. Better there, for so many reasons. Steve was the only other person who knew about the secret compartment in the rolltop desk. He'd probably tell the police about it if they asked. Now, she could too. Better that way – maintain their trust, or try to regain it. There was nothing in the house that could incriminate her – surely. She came out of the shed, satisfied. She could still carry on the business with Tim. She'd just need to wipe the phones and laptop every time she used them. And the gun and knife were still available in emergencies.

The French windows were open. When she reached the patio, she could hear some whooping and laughter coming from the sitting room. She went in. Lucy was kneeling at the coffee table, drawing red patterns on the cover of an antiques catalogue with a wax crayon. Her mum was with Jason on the carpet playing a boardgame.

'Granny's just gone down a snake and me gone up a ladder,' Jason squealed.

'Who wants to go to the beach?'

'Yeah, me, me,' Jason yelled, with an echo from Lucy.

*

'What a lovely day.' Caroline sat back in the wing-back chair and raised her glass of gin and tonic. Juliette had just come downstairs from putting the children to bed.

'They're both knackered. They love that funfair. Steve should be home soon. Can you give me a hand with the supper?'

'The Belgian furniture has made so much difference to the shop. I'm sure it should improve sales.' Caroline pushed herself up from the chair and followed Juliette to the kitchen, glass in hand.

Juliette's phone jingled – Steve.

'Jules, I've found something.'

'I'm just with my mum getting the supper ready. Are you coming home soon?'

'It's white powder. Well, it's sort of off-white – light grey, a bit beige, ivory, well, off-white.'

She turned away from Caroline, walked out of the kitchen. 'What the fuck are you talking about?'

'It was hidden in the Belgian commode. That one near the middle of the shop.'

Her mind raced. Drugs imported from Belgium. It had to be Richard. 'Did you touch it?'

'Just to look at it. It's stuck to the back of a drawer with tape. Do you think it's… You know?'

'Jesus.' Juliette went into the downstairs lavatory and locked the door. Was this why Richard had to go to Belgium to supervise the transport of the antiques? Drug smuggling as a new side-line? Or was it new?

'I thought you should know first.'

'How much is there?'

'Six bags. Might be a kilo each.'

'Has anyone else seen it?'

'No. I'd closed the shop. Roger had already gone.'

'Can anyone have seen it through the window?'

'I doubt it. It's too far back. You have to have your face right up to the window to cut the reflection. Sorry, I'll be home late. I'll phone the police now.'

'For God's sake, they'll know Rich… my dad was in Belgium. They'll link it to him. Intensify the search for him. That'll make Frampton even more desperate to find him first. And imagine the hassle. You'd spend hours being questioned.

They'd want to close the shop. There'd be forensics all over you. Where is it now?'

'I pushed the drawer back. It's out of sight, like it was before.'

'Leave it there. It means you can plead ignorance, and innocence. If you move it, and it turns out to be what we think it is, you could be charged with handling controlled substances.'

'I'm really not happy having it in the shop.'

'Just make sure the drawer is closed – exactly how you found it. Lock up and come home. We'll decide what to do this evening. Steve, vitally important, not a word to my mum, okay? She's tired, so she won't stay up long after supper. Do you understand that telling the police would increase the danger to all of us, including the children?'

'Then we should talk to your mum about it. She'd know the legal aspects.'

'Let's discuss that this evening. Don't spoil our supper. We'll tell her in the morning, if that's what we decide.'

'It's a bit of a shock. Are you sure your dad's responsible for it?'

'I don't know. Just stay calm and come home. We can make a sensible decision this evening.'

Chapter 13

After Caroline had gone upstairs with the usual glass of Scotch, Juliette said, 'Let's go to the kitchen. I'll make some espresso.'

Steve sat at the kitchen table, refilled his glass with red wine and said, 'As things stand, we've got seven of the Belgian items on display in the shop, ten in the storeroom at the back and another twelve in store at Smart Move. It wasn't till I was driving home, that I realised that what I found could be the tip of an iceberg. There could be more packets hidden in the other pieces.'

Juliette sat at the corner of the table near him, angled so that she could see when the red light on the coffee machine came on. 'Exactly where were these bags of powder?' She raised an eyebrow, looked him in the eye.

'Taped to the back of a drawer in the commode. It was sticking out a couple of millimetres and wouldn't go right in. So I pulled it right out to see if there was something – and there they were.'

'Just a sec.' Juliette stood and took two espresso cups to the machine, pressed the button.

Steve waited till the hissing had subsided and she had returned to the table with the two small cups. 'I had talked to Roger about whether we should use the word commode when trying to sell it, or whether to play safe and call it a chest, or something similar. It's not a commode in the modern sense. There's no potty in it or anything like that. Roger was against dumbing down, as he called it. You should refer to things by the correct name, regardless of whether people think it means a portable toilet. You should educate them. That's his opinion.' Steve looked as if he was retreating into his world of antiques, so Juliette gave him the raised eyebrow treatment again, silently this time.

'Sorry. Six polythene bags of whitish powder, secured with black gaffer tape. That's when I phoned you.'

'My dad insisted on going personally to Liège to supervise the packing, and then to Antwerp for it to be loaded into a container. It's got to be him. He's got some questions to answer.' *My dad, not my dad, the BS man.*

'He wouldn't do that to me,' Steve said.

'He's always thinking of ways of using people. That's the way he works. Be real.'

'It could be any of the Smart Move men.'

'I know those guys. They wouldn't have the cash to buy it, even if they had the balls. It's got to be my dad, he's got the resources, and it's got to be linked to his disappearance. He must have been planning to remove the stuff at the Smart Move depot, before it got to Walker's. Then something happened.'

'We should report it to the police.'

'Let's not go over that again. Do you want to increase the danger to Jazzy and Lulu?'

'We should tell your mum. Ask for her advice.'

'You know what she'd say. Absolutely no way. Let me deal with it.'

*

'You'd better get there before Roger goes and sells that commode.' Juliette was still sweating after a spell on the exercise bike.

'Yes.' He swallowed the last of his toast, looking thoughtful, then gulped down the remains of his coffee and went upstairs.

Ten minutes later he was downstairs, clean-shaven, looking immaculate in his linen jacket over a light blue shirt. 'Steve.' She put her arms around him and looked into his eyes. She was about the same height as him, even in her slippers. 'If you absolutely can't bear the thought of it being in the commode, just hide it somewhere safe in the back room. For God's sake, don't let Roger see it. I'll pick it up when I'm in later, and I'll get rid of it. I'll bury it among the trees behind the shed. Deep.'

He kissed her. 'See you later.'

Juliette cleared away the mess of the children's breakfast, feeling irritated by the new text she had received that morning. She'd have to go to the shed to decode the message. Tim's been busy. Jesus, it would be a full day: settle the kids with her mum, half an hour with sweet little Anna still trying to play 'Twinkle Twinkle Little Star' on the piano, Sainsbury's, bench in Christchurch Park, Walker's to deal with the packets of powder and do the banking, bank, Waitrose – it would have to be ready meals this evening – and home. Why hadn't she told Steve yet? Told him about Richard not being her father, not being Jazzy and Lulu's grandfather. How would he react? Yes, but, Jules, he's been like a father to you, hasn't he? Would she pretend to be upset? Not let him see the relief she felt – or the hatred, or the rage?

'Mum, I've got a really full-on day, can you stay with the children?'

Caroline had come into the kitchen in her dressing gown. 'Do you think it would be safe to go out? They loved that funfair yesterday. Or I could drive them down to Colchester Zoo.'

'The zoo's a great idea. I'm sure Frampton won't—' As if on cue her phone rang. Unidentified caller. *Surely, this time it could be...*

'Hello.'

'Give me some news. Good news.' The deep Essex drawl.

'The first thing you need to understand is that he is not my father. He doesn't care about me or my children. You'd be making a terrible mistake.'

'What do you take me for?'

'He's incapable, infertile, firing blanks. Anyway, I'm really close now. Just give me a few more days.'

'End of the week, I said. That's today.'

'No, tomorrow,' she found herself yelling into the phone, but it was dead. She felt the sweat on her forehead, ripped a piece of kitchen towel off the roll and wiped her face.

Caroline looked up from the kitchen table. 'Frampton, presumably.'

'Mum, I think you'd better keep them at home today. You've been brilliant. I'll have them tomorrow. Let you have a free day. I'm sure Richard will turn up soon, so next week we'll all be able to go to the zoo.'

'Better safe, I suppose. You were talking to Steve late last night. Did you tell him about, you know, our conversation the night before? Your father.'

'We had urgent things to talk about to do with the business – plans for the new stock. I must remember to take the camera in today. Get some images for the website. He can hardly think about anything else at the moment. I've got some shop work to do on the computer upstairs then a piano lesson here at eleven. One of the little ones.'

She left Caroline, taking her coffee and toast through to the sitting room to be with the children. She went round the back of the vegetable patch and through the trees to the shed; her mother might see her if she went straight across the lawn. Just an invoice to generate in the accounting system – to a special customer in Newcastle for £6,000 plus VAT. Next, work out what to do with little Anna, whose mother was showing signs of disappointment with the lack of progress. Maybe try her on 'The Grand Old Duke of York' and hope for improvement – then get away as soon as possible.

*

After doing the necessary shopping at Sainsbury's, Juliette took a baseball cap from her shoulder bag, put it on, and headed on foot up to Christchurch Park, orange carrier bag in hand. Her mobile rang – Steve.

'Jules, you're going to be angry with me.'

'Yes?'

'I told your mum. She'd know the legal aspects. I thought it was too big a risk not to. She told me there would be big trouble if I didn't report it to the police. They're here. They're dealing with it.'

She had just reached the entrance to the park. Stopped and closed her eyes for a moment, gathered herself, opened her eyes again, tried not to shout. 'We agreed!'

'No, we didn't!'

'Have you told them where it came from?'

'Well… I couldn't lie. I told her Liège.'

'My dad. Did you tell them he's involved?'

'That's the odd thing. It was a direct question. So, Mr Belton-Smart was dealing with it? She must have known he was there.'

'Got to go. Talk later.' She tapped the red circle to end the call, after missing it at the first attempt, and slipped the phone back in her jeans pocket, shaking. She started walking again. She knew the bench, near the wilderness pond. The cops'd be intensifying the search for Richard. *Shit! Just as things were quietening down, the cat's among the fucking pigeons again.* She reached the bench, sat down, put the carrier bag on the bench beside her, hand shaking, kept the shoulder bag on her lap and did some diaphragmatic breathing. She'd need to go along with it – not get too angry with Steve. She'd check that the cops had left, before going into the shop.

She was sweating. It must be the heat. Shit – her phone again. Lara. Christ.

'You'd better answer it. Act normal.' He was there, on the bench, putting an orange carrier bag on the ground between them. She didn't turn.

'Hello?'

'Hi, it's me, Lara.' Sounding cheerful, upbeat. 'Just wanted to catch up with you. Any news?'

'How lovely to hear from you!' *Make it sound like a friend.* Juliette moved the phone to her left ear, away from Tim. 'Look, I'm a bit tied up at the moment. Let's chat when there's a spare minute. I need to hang up. Sorry. Talk soon.'

'I've got a name. Someone the police are looking for – connected to your dad. I'll call you back – or call me when you're free.'

She closed the call.

'Complications.' He had actually spoken. 'Extra security. Comms equipment to be kept off-site.'

She turned. Tim was walking away with an orange carrier bag. *We've been watching too many films*, she thought, as she picked up the carrier bag from the ground, hoisted her shoulder bag and turned the other way, heading for Sainsbury's car park.

When she got into her car, she put the baseball cap back in her shoulder bag and put both bags on the passenger seat. She looked in the carrier bag for the first time. On top, there was a sliced white loaf and a box of tissues. Kind of him. She took them out, revealing a brown paper bag. She unfolded the top of the paper bag without taking it out of the carrier bag, to reveal the bundles of twenties and tens. It looked about right. As usual she would count it when she got to the shop. Before driving off, she tapped her phone. 'Hi, Lara, it's Jules.'

'Hi. Yes. Have you got a minute? That name I've picked up. Probably doesn't help, but I promised I'd let you know anything I found out. Huntingdon. Thomas Huntingdon. Mean anything to you?'

'No. Doesn't ring any bells. I don't suppose you can tell me…'

'Sorry, have to protect my sources.'

'What's he got to do with my dad?'

'Not sure yet. Known associate – seems he's got form for drugs offences. So what have you got for me?'

'Just a sec.' Juliette's mind was buzzing. Lara would find out about the police visit to the shop. Should she tell her now to gain more trust? Better to pretend not to know about it yet. 'Well, thanks. Nothing new at my end, I'm afraid.'

She tapped her phone again. 'Hi, Steve. Have you been able to open the shop yet?'

'In about half an hour. Police have gone. The forensics woman is still here, but she reckons she'll be gone in a few minutes. We'll open as soon as Roger and I have cleared up, wiped all this powdery stuff off the stock.'

*

At the shop, in the privacy of the back room. 'You do see, don't you? It's all for the best.' Steve was looking apologetic.

'What's done is done,' she said.

'It might help in the hunt for your dad.'

'I need to get on with the banking. Can you get the stuff out of the safe?'

'The police have been and gone. It was that same one, Gillespie; she told me to call her Andrea. I must be in their good books – and the tall fingerprint woman with the lipstick.'

When he was back in the shop, she bolted the two doors as usual. She checked the cash he had handed to her with the records, then took the much larger amount of cash from the orange carrier bag. It was in bands of £1,000. She counted one. It was correct. She flicked through the other six, compared the thickness of each, all correct. Some tens in an elastic band. £7,200. The bank would put it through the counting machine anyway. She put it back in the carrier bag, added the cash from the safe. Having listed the cheques and completed the paying-in slip, she added them to the carrier bag, then opened the door to the shop.

When she returned from the bank, she checked her emails on the computer in the back room. As expected, there was an invoice attached to one of them from a special supplier for £5,700 plus VAT. They were in a town she had not heard of in Dorset. Terms were seven days. She would pay it next week. She logged on to the banking system and paid the invoices that were due, including one for £7,600 plus VAT from a special supplier in Oswestry, for goods supplied to the special customer in Evesham. She was glad that Steve focused on the antiques, on buying and selling them, and did not take any interest in the financial side of the business, which he left to her. He had once said that Walker's Antiques would not survive without her. He had no idea how true that was. As she was closing her emails, Steve came into the back room, smiling. He said, 'We've had several expressions of interest in the commode. Do you think it'd sell better if we call it a chiffonier?' Juliette didn't answer. She was thinking, *Five per cent isn't enough.*

*

Juliette and Steve were on the small Edwardian couch with the pile of cushions. An espresso cup and a tea mug were on the coffee table in front of them.

'Your mum's being very tactful – keeping out of the way, going up to her room after supper,' Steve said.

'She wanted to avoid talking about the police involvement. I wish you hadn't gone behind my back.'

'You should be kinder to her.'

'I'm very fond of her. She'd be embarrassed if I got all demonstrative, like you Italians. I just wish she had left that piece of shit long ago.'

'Jules, he is your father.'

No, he isn't. Would now be the right time to tell him? 'She was a brilliant barrister. Highly intelligent and knowledgeable. Now: sort of defeated – passive. All because of him.'

'But it's good, that work she does with rape victims.'

'Survivors, Steve, not victims.' She shook her head slowly, trying to think what to say. 'Do you understand, telling the police isn't going to help?'

'It's sad when a woman's husband disappears with all their money and she seems almost glad about it.'

'She's got the mansion.'

'And a hefty mortgage.'

'Still more than half a million quid net equity. Plus her flat in London – must be a decent rent. She'll never have to work. Apart from his little scam over the mortgage, it looks as if my dad'd go down for drug smuggling too now. Frampton's going to be very pissed off if the cops get him before he does. I'm guessing my dad has got something that Frampton thinks should be his.' *My dad, I must tell him. Not my dad.*

'Thieves falling out. But you can't want your dad to be caught by Frampton. At least he'd be safe in prison.'

Juliette nestled into his side, putting an arm around his neck, her head on his shoulder, and said, 'I should be kinder to you too.' *I don't want a sadistic psychopath to be angry with me*, she wanted to add, but didn't. 'There's something I need to tell you. About Richard.'

'I'm sorry, you know, about the police.' He was holding her other hand in his lap, with both of his.

'Should I be counting?' She squeezed his fingers and looked up into his face with a big smile. He looked puzzled. 'The number of times you've apologised,' she said.

'Sorry.'

She laughed and kicked his leg quite hard.

'There's no need for red-hot pokers. Hell is other people.'

She drew back slightly to look into his eyes. 'So erudite. Sartre.'

'*No Exit*,' he said, and smiled back at her.

'*Huis Clos*,' she said.

'Smart arse. How much trouble are you in about the gun?' His face was serious again.

'I don't think they'll be locking me up for that. Since you want to be serious,' she reached for her mug and took a sip of camomile tea, 'can you have another dredge of those great big grey cells, and come up with names that my dad might have mentioned?'

'I keep thinking about it. I can't remember him mentioning any names. He keeps things very close to his chest. He did say something about property deals in Ipswich, but he was always doing that, and I'm sure he didn't specify an address, or even a street. There is the man your mum talked about.'

'Frampton. He's a tosser – someone Dad would keep a million miles away from.'

'Have you tried the people at Smart Move?'

'I know them all. I know they'd help if they could. They're keen that Dad's found, obviously. I drew a blank with all of them. Vanessa says she doesn't know anything. I believe her; she must want him to be found so she can get her money.' *Dad, Dad, Dad, but, Steve, he isn't my dad. I don't give a shit about him. I'd quite like it if Frampton tortured him and killed him.* There must be a way of telling him. Just tell him about Richard firing blanks, and a man called Adrian. *I don't really want Frampton to catch him, do I? Is it him that changed, or me? Better ask Ziggy.*

Steve was saying something. 'Do you think your mum wants to stay here?'

'We need her here.'

'She's great with Jason and Lulu. I think it's the least we can do for her. Presumably the police will have reactivated the hunt for your dad. Now that he's suspected of drug smuggling.'

'Let's not go over that again.'

'They don't tell us anything.'

'Jack told me they've talked to all the people at Smart Move. They've checked all the other pieces – nothing.'

'They had a dog in the shop – sniffing.'

Juliette's phone jingled, to her relief. She wanted something different to think about. Lara. She turned away from Steve, trying not to make it obvious that she didn't want him to know who it was. 'Hello.'

'Hi. I'm sorry to phone so late. Time doesn't stop in our business. Just a quickie. Does the name John Frampton mean anything to you?'

Chapter 14

Lara was wearing dark glasses with circular lenses and wire frames, also a sleeveless black top exposing tattoos on both her upper arms. Juliette could make out a couple of dolphins on the right arm and a large owl in dark foliage on the left.

'Sorry, I haven't got long,' Lara said. They were sitting at an outdoor table in the Buttermarket café, the buildings shading them from the morning sun. Juliette had bought lattes for both of them.

'Did you track Vanessa down?'

'Yeah, dead loss. Either she doesn't know anything, or she's been got at. I still haven't been able to contact your mother.'

'You'd be wasting your time. She has no idea where he is.'

'Yeah, but background, to build up a picture.' Lara took a sip of coffee.

'You'd be up against a brick wall there. You mentioned someone called Frampton on the phone.' Juliette tried to make it sound casual, not wanting Lara to know how keen she was to find out more about this man.

'Yeah. Have you found out anything? Anything that'd help find your dad?'

'I've tried everything. The guys at the removals firm don't know. The police took all the files and the computer before I had time for a proper look. Do you think this man Frampton knows something?'

'He's a proper bad guy. Just come out of prison after a long sentence for multiple rape, extortion, God knows. Thing is, I've looked up the court records. His trial.' She took another sip of coffee.

'And?' Juliette guessed what was coming and started preparing her reaction.

'It's really tricky. I'm sorry. The thing is, your mother was his lawyer. Counsel for the defence. She was on his side.'

'Goodness! Quite a coincidence.' She hoped she'd sounded suitably surprised.

'Well, is it? Something smells. Do you think she's avoiding me on purpose? And my editor doesn't want me spending time on this story. Some higher-up in the police must have had a word with him. He said there's no way he's going to print anything more about it unless it's really solid, corroborated. I'm supposed to be at a farm near Bury in half an hour, where they've had a couple of tractors stolen. Sorry, I can see why you're looking puzzled. They've linked Frampton to the brothel in Harwich. Some kind of business partner of your father's. And your mother—'

'Who's linked Frampton to the brothel?'

'The police. Sorry, I'd better not tell you how I know. But, anyway, it's obvious I've got a friend in the… you know. Sorry I'm in such a rush. It only came up last night. I just thought you should know.' Lara looked at a chunky black watch on her left wrist. 'Christ, I must be moving, my editor'll have my bollocks, as he's ever so fond of saying, if I don't get my arse to that farm, pronto. But there's more. I know how they've linked your father to the brothel. I've got a note of all this, but just in outline, the premises are owned by a property company which might or might not be legit. It's leased to a company registered in the British Virgin Islands which is owned by a trust, the sole beneficiary of which is another company, and it goes on like this. There's a whole trail I've got written down. Half a dozen further steps back, we find, hiding in the shadows, another company registered where it doesn't have to disclose anything, whose one hundred shares are all owned by a certain Mr Richard Lee Belton-Smart.'

Juliette absorbed every word, almost enjoying the way this information added to her hatred of the man. 'I've given up being surprised by anything I find out about him.'

'Frampton's name crops up in the trail too. Co-director of one of the shell companies. Sorry, I've got to rush. The other thing is it used to be here, in Ipswich. Moved to Harwich eleven years ago.'

Eleven years ago. Juliette's mind was buzzing. *Christ.*

'By the way, the man arrested in the massage parlour. Cool as you like, silly prat tried to make out he was a punter, innocent of all offences, unlucky to be in the wrong place at the wrong time. Name's Eric Scannel. They found a stash of heroin under the floorboards in one of the rooms. His fingerprints all over it. Seems his job included giving the girls just enough, keeping them desperate, willing to do anything to get the next fix. Nasty bit of work. He won't say anything. Seems he's scared shitless. I really must push off now.' She slid sideways off the chair and stood up. 'Jules, I'm not telling you all this for fun.'

'I get it. I owe you. Thanks anyway. I really will let you know anything I find out.' Juliette looked Lara in the eye, trying to impress her with her sincerity.

*

When Juliette reached her car, she closed her eyes and took some deep breaths. One thing at a time. Next stop, the mansion. Deposit the rucksack and its electronic contents in the garage. Hide it under the workbench. Difficult to find, but not too difficult if there were a proper search.

Next decision: how much to tell her mother? *She'll be furious if she knows I've spoken to the reporter. So I can't say anything about Richard being in the brothel.*

*

'Did the lesson go well, darling?'

'Lily. Very talented. On Grade 5. Could go all the way. How've you and the little ones been?'

'Let's get them out in the garden now that we're both here.'

Juliette checked that the side gate was bolted on the inside, while Caroline applied sun cream to the children. Minutes later the two women were sitting in the shade with cool drinks, while the children played in the paddling pool.

'Mum, do you remember the Ipswich prostitute murders?'

'God, do I not. 2006. Five of them in a few months. That was when Richard had that long trip to the Far East – Hong

Kong, Thailand and Singapore. He sent me an email nearly every day. What made you think of that?'

'Might be just gossip. Lily's mother said that she'd heard from her friend who's married to a policeman that there was a raid on a massage parlour in Harwich a few days ago. The sleazy sort – a brothel, really. She said the people running it came from Ipswich, had been running a brothel in town and moved it to Harwich eleven years ago. So, five prostitutes get murdered in quick succession in Ipswich, and this brothel owner decides to move his business to Harwich.'

Caroline shrugged. 'So you're suggesting the brothel owner decided it was too dangerous here, and moved his prostitutes to Harwich. Can't we talk about something else?'

'I can hardly bear to think about it. Young women completely trapped. Modern slavery.' Juliette looked at Caroline, who held her eye.

'Raped fifteen or more times a day. We sometimes get women who've escaped from that at the centre. The sort of thing John Frampton would be up to his neck in…' There was silence as Caroline leaned back in the patio chair and closed her eyes.

Juliette examined the screen on her phone. 'There's lots of stuff about the prostitute murders in Wiki. The man who was convicted of all the murders went on protesting his innocence. He could have been set up as the fall guy.'

Caroline opened her eyes. 'Are you trying to suggest it's got something to do with Richard?'

'How do you know he was in the Far East?'

*

'I suppose I'd better sing it in English.'

'Not a bad idea to sing it in the language you're going to perform it in.'

'I know it in both. It's more natural in Italian.'

'Okay, English then.'

Juliette was sitting at the piano in the music room. Steve was standing beside her. She had read through the piano part for Arturo's aria and duet in *Lucia di Lammermoor*. There were no snags. She played; Steve sang, leaving gaps where Enrico would sing. They went through to the end.

'You sound smug – self-satisfied.'

'That's the way she wants it, Janet, the director. You know, feminist interpretation. He's a powerful politician, pompous, narcissistic.'

'Are you sure you're right for Arturo?'

'She offered me Edgardo. Huge part. I said I was too busy, so I accepted Arturo who's just got the one scene.'

'So he's about to get married.'

'He thinks of it as acquiring a beautiful chattel.'

'So he gets what's coming to him. Do you get killed on stage?'

'I don't have to be there. We're doing it in silhouette, behind a sheet. She stabs him multiple times in a frenzy, blood everywhere including splashed against the sheet. Then she appears on stage, dagger in hand, blood splattered all over her white wedding dress, face and arms.'

'So she was mad before she committed murder?'

'She's a strong woman, but unstable because of the way she's been treated by men. She's deeply in love with Edgardo, but believes he's betrayed her, so gets manipulated by her brother, Enrico, into agreeing to marry Arturo. Then she decides the only way out of that mess is to kill him so that she'll be free to marry Edgardo.'

'Then she goes completely bonkers. What does she actually die of?'

'Her death is symbolic, Janet says – the death of every woman who is owned by a man. But her spirit lives on.'

'Let's do the aria and duet once more, then go to bed.'

*

Juliette lay under the sheet, unable to sleep. *Madness and murder. Why the fuck does he have to be in such a ridiculous opera? Women don't just go mad and kill people. And why does she have to be called Lucia, like my little Lulu? Get a grip, Jules...*

Chapter 15

The landline phone rang in the darkness. Juliette nudged Steve. The phone was on his bedside table. He switched on the light and lifted the receiver. 'Hello... Yes, Steve Walker... Any sign of damage?... Right... Yes, of course... About half an hour.'

Juliette half opened her eyes. 'What is it? What's the time?'

'There's been a break-in at the shop. It triggered the alarm. The police are there. Three-twenty.'

'Oh God. Has a lot been taken?'

'They need me there so I can tell them. Time is of the essence.' He was already out of bed and getting dressed.

There was a knock on the bedroom door. It opened a crack, and Caroline's voice said, 'I heard the phone. Is it Rich—?'

'No, Mum. It's something at the shop. Steve's got to go. Go back to bed.'

'It's a break-in,' Steve said. 'I've been lucky. It's the first one I've had for about five years. It doesn't sound too serious. The thieves were probably frightened off by the alarm. But I need to check what's missing. A couple of ormolu clocks and some porcelain vases are the most likely things. I doubt if they would have had time to move any furniture. With a bit of luck, we'll have some video footage.'

'Presumably you're insured.'

'Don't worry, Cara. I hope I won't be more than an hour or two. With luck I'll get a bit more sleep before breakfast. I'll see you later.'

Five minutes later, Steve had left the house and the two women were in the kitchen with only the lights under the wall cupboards switched on. Caroline was sitting at the kitchen table and Juliette was watching over a saucepan of milk heating on the hob.

'I'd like to meet Adrian.'

'It's so long ago.'

'You should have told me earlier – like, ten years ago at least.'

Caroline seemed to examine the grain in the kitchen table. 'I know. But you were so close to Richard, growing up. The way you used to sit on his lap, have cuddles.'

Juliette cringed at the thought of those cuddles. 'That adolescent thing I had about Jonathan Brandis – remember? Some of those posters could have been of Richard as a teenager. My dad, so I thought. I used to idolise him. He could have used his rough charm to attract almost any woman he wanted. You must have meant something special to him.' Juliette poured steaming milk into two mugs and stirred in chocolate granules.

'When he proposed to me, I was smitten in a way, needing to break out. I think I realised I was a sort of status symbol for him. Married to a barrister – he enjoyed that. I just went along with it. In fact, I rather enjoyed it. I soon gave up thinking I could reform him – smooth off the rough edges.'

'My life would have been different if I'd known.' Juliette flashed a look at her mother as she felt the anger coming back.

'We would have had to run away.'

'Mum, come on. That's a bit over the top, isn't it?'

'He would have sensed it, would have realised I'd told you.' She took a last gulp of cocoa. 'A sort of numbness came over me – the only way I could live with the fear. At least I'll never have to live under the same roof as Richard again, so even with this bloody man Frampton to worry about now, it still feels as if a weight has been lifted.'

Juliette couldn't help feeling some sympathy, as well as anger, towards her mother, and was frustrated that she had deflected her question about meeting Adrian, but didn't have the energy to pursue it. 'Let's get back to bed. I'm knackered.'

*

When she was woken by the alarm at seven o'clock, Juliette found Steve lying beside her. 'How's the shop?'

'Dead lucky,' he said. 'The thief must have been scared off. Nothing missing, just a smashed front window. It's boarded up now. I'll go straight in and organise a glazier.'

'Anything on the CCTV?'

'Just one person, probably a man, well covered, not identifiable.'

At about ten to eight, Steve, having rushed a bowl of cornflakes, said, 'Short day, Sunday. Just as well. I'd better be off.'

'Steve, there's something I need to tell you. About Richard.'

'What? Has he been found?'

'No, not that.' She hesitated, couldn't find the words. 'It can wait.'

He was heading towards the front door with his briefcase. 'Tell me this afternoon, when you come to the shop.'

*

She was looking through the bars of the kitchen window, down the garden, seeing the pattern of morning sunlight on the trees, trying to analyse her feelings towards her mother. Angry, certainly, for not doing something. For being so passive, for tolerating such a man for so long. And for preventing her own daughter from knowing her real father. And deceiving this man Adrian, keeping him in the dark. So unfair. But… But, needing to be loved, and deserving it.

Caroline came down at about half past eight in her dressing gown. 'I feel terrible,' she said. The sound of a children's television cartoon was audible through the kitchen door.

'Well, don't.' Juliette hugged her and showed her what was available for breakfast. 'I'm sorry I was unsympathetic last night. I would have probably done the same.' Juliette took a sip of coffee, fully aware that she would have done nothing like it. 'We were lucky about the shop. Steve thinks they didn't take anything. Mum?' Juliette saw that her mother wasn't listening.

'I keep thinking he might come here.' Caroline had her elbows on the kitchen table and was holding a mug of coffee in both hands, near her chin. 'Just ring the doorbell and ask to come in.'

'Richard? Extremely unlikely. I haven't had any contact with him since he disappeared.'

'Except when he told you about Frampton and asked you to hide the gun.' Caroline took a sip of coffee.

'Oh yes,' Juliette said. 'Except for that.' She scooped a spoonful of granola into her mouth. They ate in silence for a minute, Caroline tearing bits off a buttered croissant.

'Are you sure you don't mind me staying?'

'Mum, I want you to, really.' Juliette looked her mother in the eye, to make sure she was listening. 'It feels as if we're making a fresh start. Thank you for telling me about Adrian. I understand why you didn't before, really. It was quite a shock. It must have been painful for you, keeping the secret. You understand why I want to meet—'

Juliette's mobile emitted its jingle. She looked at the screen, then at her mother's anxious face. 'Unknown caller. Let's hope.' She picked it up from the table.

'Hello.'

That voice. 'So your man's gone for the day.'

She froze, closed her eyes.

'Stuck for words, are you? Your mam's with you, seeing as her Beamer's in your driveway.'

'If you touch a hair—' She couldn't stop her voice shaking.

'I expect you're wondering why I'm being so patient.'

He sounded so relaxed. She pictured him sitting back in a comfortable chair.

'I'm getting information all the time. Really. It'll only be a day or two.'

'Oh yeah. The girl from the paper. Useful informant she'd be. I reckon she's told you all she knows, and a bit more besides.'

Juliette turned and looked out of the window. A cloud had turned the trees an opaque grey-green. She steadied herself against the worktop. *He's watching us. He knows where we live.* She regained control of herself, assessed the risk. *I need to give him something, tell him something he doesn't know already.* 'Was that you in our shop last night? Thought you'd find him hiding there?'

It took him a full two seconds to speak again. 'I don't work Sundays, which means you've got till tomorrow.' The line was cut.

They ate in silence for a few minutes. Juliette was trying to think calmly, balancing risks. The police might come and search at any moment, so the gun needed to be in the shed, where she could say Richard must have put it. But what if she needed it in a hurry to defend them? She decided not to risk panicking her mother by telling her that Frampton was watching them, so simply said, 'Frampton.'

Caroline swallowed some coffee. 'Do you think we ought to go away somewhere for a while? All of us. Shut the shop. Somewhere safe, just until Richard's found. It might only be a few days.'

'If only.' She sighed. 'If only there were somewhere safe.' She turned to her mother, feeling an urge to tell her about that night, what Richard had done. But how could she, when she couldn't confront it herself? *If no one knows, it didn't happen.* Her mind flipped to Lucia. *Why does that have to be the one Steve is rehearsing? Woman commits murder, goes mad, dies.* Was that the right order? Or was it, *Woman goes mad, commits murder, dies?*

Juliette snapped back into the present reality as her phone came to life on the table beside her. She so wanted to tell her mother about that night, but knew she couldn't. It'd make it too real. 'It's Steve.' As she put the phone to her ear, Caroline signalled that she was going through to the sitting room. She mimed something that could have been switching off a television.

'Hi, how's the shop?'

'There's a note.' Steve seemed to be struggling for words. 'Jules, it was your dad. It was him.'

'What do you mean?' Juliette put her mug down and turned towards the window, giving Steve her full attention. 'What note?'

'I'm sure it wasn't here yesterday. It was in my in-tray, under a couple of bills. I took them out to put them in your pile. There it was, scrawled in pencil on a scrap of paper.'

'Just tell me what it says.'

'*Urgent. Tell no one. Bring the stuff to...* then there's just TM and a string of numbers. Then it says: *After dark tonight. Come alone. My life depends on it.*'

'My dad would send a text.'

'I know, but who else could it be?'

'Has anyone else seen it?'

'No. Roger's in the front with the glaziers. We can't open till they've finished.'

'Just hide it, Steve. Lock it in your desk or something. I've got a full day. I'll get there as soon as I can, but it's not going to be much before three. The numbers must be a grid reference. We'll decide what to do then. And, Steve,' she turned and closed the kitchen door, but still kept her voice down, 'for fuck's sake do not tell the police, and do not tell my mother.'

'Wouldn't it be for the best? The police could just go there and—'

'Steve, listen.' She was desperately thinking of a reason not to tell them, that Steve might accept. 'There's no need to rush. It'd be much better if my dad hands himself in. I could persuade him to confess to the drugs offences. He'd be safe from Frampton and get a shorter sentence. We'll talk about it this afternoon. Just don't do anything till then, okay? I want to hear you agree.'

'All right. We'll talk about it this afternoon.'

After ending the call, Juliette sat down again on one of the kitchen chairs. Yes, it would be simple. Just get them to go and arrest him – Richard in custody, the threat from Frampton goes away. No, not simple. *I want justice. I need to see him, get him to admit what he did.* She heard herself sigh. 'Right. First things first,' she said just audibly. She poked her head round the sitting-room door. 'You okay, Mum?'

'Fine, darling.' It looked as if another game of snakes and ladders was starting. 'Try not to be too long.'

Not too long – just an extra twenty minutes to go to the mansion to raise a special invoice. Bloody risk management.

*

The collection was the same as usual, until Tim was sitting beside her on the park bench. She spoke, looking straight ahead. 'Sunday collections need to cost more. Extra risk from having to keep the cash in the safe overnight. Ten per cent.'

'Talking to yourself, are you?' He got up and walked away with the bag of screwed-up newspaper and a few cheap groceries on top.

'Fuck him,' she said, just loud enough to draw a snigger from a young woman walking past with a pushchair.

*

At about ten to three she went into the shop by the back door into the office, carrying her shoulder bag and a Tesco carrier bag containing a box of tissues, a packet of falafels (was that one of Tim's attempts at humour?), yesterday's *Daily Mail* (that certainly must be) and £8,400 in used notes. She left the bags in a corner of the room and went through the storeroom to the shop. Steve and Roger were looking at the front window. Steve saw her and came back with her into the office. 'It's in the desk,' he whispered.

'I'll go,' she said, after reading it several times and turning it over in her hands.

'It might not be safe. Don't you think it would be more sensible to… you know.'

'Take it to the police? No, I do not think that would be more sensible. Knowing him, he's got an escape route planned. They'd come after him mob-handed, and he'd be off. It'd just make Frampton more desperate. I think it would be extremely dangerous, for my dad and for us.' She knew it was weak, so followed up quickly. 'And he's got that gun. He might do something really stupid. Anyway, I want to see him. With luck I can persuade him to come with me. I'll drive down to Museum Street and we can go in together. It's in his best interests.'

'Why didn't he just send a text?'

'I'll ask him. Maybe he's lost his phone. He must have been hoping to find the drugs where he'd hidden them.

I promised my mum I'd be home by four.' She opened her phone and logged on to Google Maps. 'Yeah, grid reference. Looks like the middle of those woods the other side of Woodbridge.'

Chapter 16

Juliette set the alarm for midnight. She had complained of a headache after dinner and gone up, even before her mother. The time had come. She was going to see him, she hoped, for the first time since that night. She had to retrieve that memory, as much as she could. The memory she had succeeded in blocking for so long. She lay under the sheet and forced it back into her mind. It started the evening before…

*

What was it? The intensity of her love for two-year-old Jason clashing with the drudgery of looking after him all the time. The loneliness during the day. The feeling that it was all a mistake – married at twenty-one, a mother at twenty-two, now twenty-four and worn out, run down already. The obligation to get a meal on the table every evening for Steve, when he came home, often late, always tired. Her thwarted ambition to improve as a flautist. Longing to get back to teaching, but still finding the pressure too great. The stress of the transactions with Tim and keeping them secret from

Steve. And wine – until recently she hadn't started till Steve got home. Then she thought a glass with her lunch would help her through the day. Before long she was buying extra bottles at the supermarket and hiding the empties under other recycling rubbish.

She had talked to Steve about all of these things, except the business with Tim and the wine. Details of the conversation were now a blur, but somehow they had agreed that Steve would take Jason to his mother's for a couple of days so that Juliette could 'chill out'. She remembered his using that phrase.

It must have been a Sunday. After waving her husband and son off for their two-day break in a village about twenty minutes' drive away, she felt a sense of loss. It was the first time she had been separated from Jazzy, after two years of bonding, exasperation and depression – and love. So she opened a bottle of reasonable Rioja, before going into the garden to work. She thought about the rows between her parents, the sullen silences, the stifling atmosphere, her need to escape. She had made the right choice: marriage and motherhood, her only means of escape from what had gone before.

Just over two hours later, having mown the lawn, weeded most of the border, and decided that the hedge could wait another few weeks before its annual trim, she washed her hands, refilled her glass and sat at the grand piano in the music room. A clumsy attempt at some simple exercises reminded her that she had never been able to play properly after even a small amount of alcohol. Still sitting at the piano, she took out her flute and tried that. She had trouble getting the embouchure right, let alone the problem of disobedient fingers. She giggled to herself, took another sip of wine. She would do her music practice straight after breakfast the next day. When the bottle of Rioja was finished, she felt like a change, so opened a bottle of Muscadet.

The kitchen phone rang. Shit. Better answer it in case it's to do with Jazzy.

'Oh, hello, Dad. Fancy hearing your voice at this time of the… thing… night.'

'Yeah, baby, well it is nearly nine o'clock. Is your other half there? Is that singing? Are you having a party?'

'I'm just happily. I'm having a holliway – just a couple of delays, though, they're coming back tomorrow, the dogs of war will be released once more, cry havoc, the four horsemen of the apolkadots…'

'Sounds like you're having a good time. Are you on your own? How about if I come over? I could be there in twenty minutes.'

'Good time, that's me, good time girl. Not a parent, but myself. Me. Just today, or tomorrow.'

'So I'll come over.'

'I'm on myself, dear Father. About to climb to the upstairs to my rest, perchance to dream.' She was sitting on a hard wooden chair, too heavy to get off it. Her eyelids fell.

The doorbell rang. She must have opened the front door. He was holding up a bottle of light brown liquid.

'Single malt, baby. You look as if you're ready for some.' It was her father. His voice. The blond hair and light blue eyes occasionally shifting into focus.

'I don't like wishky.'

He was at the drinks table, facing the wall. She heard a pouring sound. Then he was facing her, getting bigger. She tried to focus. She became aware of him in front of her, holding out a glass.

'Try this, babe. It's not like any whisky you've tasted before.' She decided that not drinking spirits was a rule that ought to be broken – cast aside. Break rules, that was it. Make full use of her freedom while she could. She was sitting in a semi-upholstered chair, gripping the arms to try to stop the room moving. Several times she managed to let go with her right hand for long enough to lift the glass from the table to her lips. Then she saw that the glass, which she was sure had been nearly empty a moment ago, was full again. He had just said something, so she said, 'Wha'as that d'you say?'

'Come and sit with me on the sofa, baby.' She staggered over to him, slopping some liquid from her glass on to the table at the side of the sofa. 'You aren't who you think you are.' There was a hardness in his voice.

'Oops, I've properly had too much…' She tried to focus on his face. Grim, unsmiling. She wanted him to be happy, like her.

'It's good for you, once in a while. Have some more. Do you remember the way you used to put your head on my shoulder? Yeah, like that. I'm going to teach you who you are. Bastard spawn…' She felt herself rising into the air, being carried across the room, up the stairs.

*

The noise came first – a rushing of air with something high-pitched, perhaps a scream, struggling to be heard above it. Then came the light – a dim red glow that made her aware of something outside, something that might become visible if she opened her eyes. But she didn't want to open them, sensing that to do so might increase the throbbing in her head. At last she forced herself to twist her legs out from under the duvet and push her feet into the thick rug, pressing the heels of her hands against her eyelids to protect them from something she couldn't identify.

Still sitting on the side of the bed, she slowly removed her hands from her eyes and opened them a crack. She gave herself a minute to adjust, before trying to stand up. A sour taste and furry sensation in her mouth and throat now competed with the threatening noise, the throbbing headache and the aggressive light. Shielding her eyes, she squinted at the bedside clock. God, ten-fifteen. Steve hadn't woken her up before going to work. Jazzy! She half ran, crashed her left shoulder into the door, realised she was naked, staggered across the landing to Jazzy's bedroom. His cot was empty. The moment of panic passed. She remembered; she was having a break from motherhood. It was Monday. The shop didn't open today. She could do what she liked until teatime.

But her head, God, the noise, the throbbing and the bitter, constricted feeling in her mouth and throat; she had to make an effort to balance, and her limbs didn't seem to function or co-ordinate properly. She went to the bathroom and took a couple of paracetamols, looked at herself in the mirror. God, what a mess – dark shadows under her eyes as if she had been crying. There was a small bruise on her left breast. She put her hand on it. Her nipple was sore. She sat on the edge of the bath. *What? How?* She walked unsteadily back to the bedroom and pulled back the duvet. The greyish patch was there, still slightly damp in the middle. She sat on the edge of the bed. *What the hell?* She went back to the bathroom, filled the toothmug with water and drank it in one. *Christ!* There was a sickening ache between her legs. It was never like this after sex with Steve. She looked in the mirror, looked away quickly. *It was... It couldn't have been... He was here.* Her legs gave way. She grabbed the edge of the handbasin to break her fall. She let out a piercing wail. Sitting on the bathroom floor, she hugged her knees, bent over, sobbing. *How could he?* It was her fault. She'd been pissed. She led him on. She desperately wanted a shower, to clean herself, but couldn't bring herself to move from the floor.

Then she was in the shower with the water too hot. Punishing herself, her body. It was while she was drying herself that her self-hatred became mixed with anger. How could he? Her own father. A man she trusted – and loved, but not like that.

In the kitchen, her head was beginning to clear. After drinking more water, coffee became the next priority. While the kettle was boiling, she took her phone out of her jeans pocket. She would phone him, get him to admit it, tell him what she thought. She closed her eyes, trying to rehearse the words. Nothing made sense. She would phone the police. All women should do that – report a rape. The questions they would ask: had you been drinking? Yes? How much? He had spiked her drink. That was it. It wasn't just wine. He had brought a bottle. If only she could remember. Then she started thinking about the things he would say about her when they questioned him. And Steve would have to know, and her mother. She sat, looking at the phone in her hand, then slipped it back into her pocket.

There were two people who knew what had happened. She could be sure her dad wouldn't tell anyone, so if she didn't... *If no one knows, it didn't happen.* While the coffee was brewing, she went upstairs, tore the sheet off the bed and took it down to the washer-dryer.

After some coffee and toast she had another shower – longer and more leisurely. The noise in her head had abated.

The two whisky glasses were upturned on the drainer, washed and left to dry. *He wouldn't have done that unless he had spiked my drink.* She went into the sitting room and found a half-empty bottle of Côtes du Rhône that she didn't remember having opened. She tipped it down the kitchen sink. *Never again, no more alcohol – ever.* She took that bottle and two others out to the recycling bin. Back in the sitting room, she tried to wipe a cloudy mark off the demilune table, but couldn't. Steve was always saying how important it was to use coasters on these antique pieces. He'd know what to do. She set about vacuum cleaning all the carpets, then dusting and polishing the furniture, making everything clean, removing every invisible trace of him. The man she would never speak to again.

She was sitting on the sofa, trying alternately to make sense of her feelings and feeling emotionally numb, unable to deal with it, to feel anything, when her phone jingled. 'Hello, Mum, you sound... have you got a cold or something?'

'I've had a little accident. It's nothing really – just a few bruises. I wasn't going to tell you, except Richie's away on a business trip, and this house gets to me sometimes when I'm alone.' She paused.

Juliette's mind flipped. *Away on a business trip!*

Her mother was talking again, 'Are you there, darling?'

'Sorry, Mum. The house – on your own. Me too. Steve's taken Jazzy to his mother's, but they'll be back soon. Did you say accident? Are you okay?'

'A few bruises. I really want to get out of the house. Could I bring a bag? Just a night or two. I'll do lots of cooking. Take the pressure off you a bit.'

'Well, putting it like that, how could I say no? Any chance of you going to a supermarket on the way here? I'll text you a list.'

'Of course, darling. You know I like to help.'

*

The mad woman in a blood-spattered white dress was standing in front of her, up close, singing coloratura, while violins screeched the shower murder discords from *Psycho*. The woman waved a bloody dagger with blood spraying from the end of it. Juliette was a young girl. She shouted, 'Lucia, I'll look after you. I'll help you.' Then the blood had gone and the woman was her mother, opening her blouse showing a diagonal row of bruises across her ribs and belly. 'I fell over in the kitchen.' Her voice was muffled by a swollen, split lower lip. There was a bell ringing in the distance.

Juliette awoke with a start, reached for her phone and shut off the alarm. She lay back for a moment, working out what had happened. The memory – that was real; that night, the following day – that was real. She must have fallen asleep. She heard Steve breathing beside her, the warmth of his body. Why did it have to be *Lucia di Lammermoor*? But not him being murdered. Not him, just the character he was playing. It was only an opera. A ridiculous story.

She slipped off the bed, put on the baggy jeans and prepared herself, remembering the bruises on her mother's face and body, and her unbelievable story about falling over in the kitchen.

Chapter 17

Her heart was beating faster than normal as she drove along the small country road in the dark. She felt bad about having to be brief with her mother that evening. 'But, darling, we've got so much to talk about,' was still echoing in her head. She had had to promise to spend more time with her the following day – a lovely pub lunch overlooking the estuary. Juliette was looking forward to it.

She had spent some of the evening finding out as much as she could about the location she was now driving to. Remote. It looked like a cottage or perhaps a barn, but Google Maps wouldn't give her a clear picture as it wasn't near a road. She had tried to work out a route staying on small country roads where there were no surveillance cameras, but having discovered that that would take her an extra two and a half hours for the round trip, she had decided to drive through Woodbridge, and then on the small roads as she headed east. She was occasionally reminded of the tape on her right leg below the knee. It tugged slightly when she flexed her ankle to operate the accelerator or brake. She was wearing her black hoody, the baggy jeans she usually wore for gardening and comfortable old sandals with flat soles. Another glance at the phone. About half a mile, slow, lights dipped. She came to the turning on to the farm track, stopped the Peugeot and got out. She walked to the track and shone her torch on the ground. There was grass up the middle and the sides were dry and dusty. Good – the rain a couple of days ago hadn't been enough to dampen the ground. She got back in the car and drove slowly up the track. Checked the phone again. About 200 yards, but with dipped headlights she couldn't see more than about thirty yards into the pitch blackness. There was a gate into a field on her left. She turned the car round and parked it in the gateway. She heaved her shoulder bag out on the passenger side.

She had the old feeling, the one she used to get waiting to go on stage with her flute. She felt the sweat, tore off the hoody and stuffed it in the bag. As she locked the car, she winced at the loudness of the bleep and the brightness of the briefly blinking orange lights. She slipped the keys into her jeans pocket, smiling at the thought that this would be impossible in the jeans she usually wore. She double-checked the contents of her shoulder bag using the flashlight on her phone before setting off on foot, using the same light to avoid stumbling on the rough surface of the track.

Soon, she became aware of a denseness in the dark ahead of her. The group of trees she was expecting. She continued, once more aware of the pumping of her heart, the tugging of the tape on her leg as she walked. She was still feeling sweat under the cotton T-shirt, even as the chill night air sent a shiver through her body. The trees crowded around her now. Occasional rustling sounds signalled the presence of small nocturnal animals, hunting their prey – or trying to escape?

A light. Faint. Curtains drawn closed. Now she could see light coming from two windows. She shut off the phone light. She was at the front door. A horseshoe hung loosely by one end on a nail – not a lucky charm, a doorknocker. She took several deep breaths, then knocked. His voice: 'It's open.'

'Hello.' She heard her voice waver, realised she came so close to saying, 'Hello, Dad.' God, the stink: stale urine, body odour, rotting food…

'Hey, baby.' The Essex drawl she hadn't heard for a couple of weeks. 'I was expecting Steve. This is man's work.' He came towards her, arms wide.

She put an arm up, ready to push him away. 'Don't.' She saw the light stubble and remembered him hating being unshaven, because his beard was light and patchy. The sight of him disgusted her as much as the smell. The rapist who pretended to be her father.

'Yeah, sorry. I'll keep my distance. The bathing facilities here aren't quite what we're used to. Welcome to my humble abode. No kidding, eh?' He laughed. 'It's a temporary necessity while I get a few things fixed.'

The room had yellow walls turning brown, a naked bulb hanging in the middle over a small rectangular pine table. There were two windows on the left as Juliette saw the room. They were covered by what looked like pieces of old sheet, nailed up. Below them there was a mattress on the floor with a stained grey sleeping bag. This seemed to be as much a source of the smell as the man was. The far wall had a panelled door with dark blue paint peeling off it. On the other side of the room there was one window, curtained like the others, above a counter bearing a microwave, a kettle and a toaster, all of which looked new. There was a pile of food and drink cans, and other packaging beside them – ready meals.

While she was taking all this in, Richard had sat down on a straight-backed chair on the other side of the table, and was saying, 'The toilet's over there by the door.' He pointed past her left side. She half turned and saw an old spade leaning against the wall. A toilet roll hung on the handle. 'I've got a good system with a couple of stakes in the ground – move 'em each day so I don't dig up yesterday's shit. Concession to civilisation is the generator out the back.' He nodded at the bulb hanging over the table. 'Light runs on the battery for a couple of hours.' He smiled. She wondered if he wanted her to think he enjoyed living like this. 'You should see the other room.' He pointed behind him with a thumb. 'They kept sheep in there. And upstairs is where the pigeons live.' He laughed and took a gulp from an open can of lager. 'Have a beer. Make yourself at home.' He smiled and pointed in turn at the box at the far end of the counter and the chair opposite him, on Juliette's side of the table. 'Unfortunately, my refrigeration facilities are about on a par with my hygiene facilities, but it's drinkable. There's Scotch if you'd rather.'

The irony of it flashed across her mind – this man who enjoyed ostentatious luxury, trying to make out he was doing all right in this filth. 'What's going on?' she managed to say, as she pulled the chair back, checked that the seat was clean and sat on it, putting the heavy bag on the floor beside her.

'Business first,' he said, pointing round the side of the table at the bag.

'What the hell is going on? You owe me that.' She held his gaze, didn't blink, remembering what he had done that night, but keeping control. Questions to answer first.

'I've been too generous. You know me. All heart.' He took another swig of beer from the can. 'Gave 'em too much rope. Bastard so-called business associates of mine decided on a double-cross.' He shook his head sadly. 'It ruins your faith in human nature.' He glared and pointed at her with his index finger. She flinched; he was about to blame her. 'The fuckers – excuse my French – set me up. Big project – import.' He pointed at her bag again. 'Different scale. Needs organisation, seed money, investment. Three million quid each, that was the deal.' He glared at her again. She looked back, filled with contempt as well as revulsion. 'We shook on it. You know me and paperwork. I don't do fucking paperwork.' This time he glared at the light bulb. She saw a couple of moths flitting around it.

'"Bad news, Richie-boy" – the fuckers. "We've had to cancel the project." Yeah, yeah.' Richard found the beer can was empty and hurled it at the wall above the counter, where it bounced back on to the pile of packaging trash. He got up and fetched another can from the box in the corner. On his way back to his chair he gesticulated with the can. 'And watch that fucker with the cash. Are you still working in his laundry? That business is worth fifteen per cent. Don't accept a penny less. If Tom's only giving you ten, tell him it's got to be fifteen. What's he giving you?'

Bloody Tim. I knew it, fucking cheat. 'Fifteen,' she said, trying to hide her anger, but not wanting to be distracted. It was none of his bloody business what Tim was paying her. 'Tim.'

'Tim today, Tom tomorrow, what do I know? Good girl. I always knew you'd be good at business.'

Christ. Tom – Lara mentioned a Thomas. Best not to pursue that now. 'Steve's very pissed off with you – about the powder.'

'He was never supposed to know about it.' Richard was speaking in a tone as if he was the injured party. 'It was just a small quantity, so that I could pick it up in the depot. Lovely furniture imported from Belgium, for all those who value such things. No one knows a thing about it. No one gets hurt. No one gets pissed off. Then these wankers pull this other stunt on me, and I'm fucked. So I tell them what I'm going to do if they don't give me my money back, and they tell me what they're going to do, and as there's more of them than there are of me, and what with discretion being the better part of valour, here I am. Rather less luxurious than the penthouse suite in Harwich, where I resided last week.' Richard pulled the ring on the beer can, which sprayed over his hand. 'Shit.' He wiped his hand on the sleeve of his other arm. 'Which brings me to the subject of my get-out-of-gaol card which you have kindly brought me.'

'Is Tim one of them?'

'Good question. Not up front. Maybe in the shadows. He likes shadows – skulking in them. Below the radar. For all I know, it could be him that put them up to it.' He took a gulp of beer. 'That'll be one of my questions.' He took his right hand off the beer can and patted the back pocket of his jeans. 'I've got a little list. I'll be paying a few visits, using my enhanced interrogation techniques, making 'em offers they can't refuse. The white powder'll get me started – out of here.' He held out his hands, open.

Juliette decided the time had come. She pushed the chair back. It scraped on the old, dry floorboards. She stood, lifted the bag on to the chair, reached in and brought out the service revolver that had been resting on a dozen paperbacks.

Chapter 18

'What the fuck?' he says.

Juliette points the old gun at his chest. She reinforces her right-handed grip with her left hand, pulls the hammer back with both thumbs, stands behind the chair, arms nearly straight, without locking her elbows, feet apart, left ahead of right, like a boxer.

'Hey, baby, what is this?' he says, just failing to keep the shock out of his voice and out of his face, raises his arms sideways.

'Don't fucking-well call me baby!' she yells.

'Hey, look at me. Flesh and blood,' he says.

'Did you fuck me?'

His face shifts, the features sag. He places his hands flat on the table, arms out, fingers spread. 'I didn't think it'd be you. I knew they'd send someone. I thought I'd have a bit longer.'

She raises the gun to his face, the midpoint between his eyes. 'Did you fuck me?'

The beer can crunches under his grip. 'Is that your grandad's old revolver? Put it down, for Christ's sake. What're you talking about?'

She lowers the gun to point at his chest, feeling extra disgust if he's going to try denying it. 'You know bloody well. The night you found out I wasn't your daughter. Why I haven't spoken to you for three years.'

He looks to the side, as if trying to make a mental picture of the pile of detritus on the counter. He turns back to face her and speaks slowly, quietly, but with a new harshness. 'I went crazy, Jules. That bitch, that shitty parasite who's been sponging off me for thirty years. Can you imagine being betrayed like that? A man can't take that. Shouldn't take it. Not a real man. Yeah, I came over to yours a few years back. You said you wanted it, really wanted it, needed it. Bespectacled office-boy furniture salesman had gone off somewhere. You were desperate, rules, rules, you said, who cares about rules, you said.' He pauses. 'I was doing you a favour. You were all over me, really wanted it. How could a man resist?'

She feels the gun shaking in her hands. *He must be lying. He's got to be lying.* Her vision is blurred with anger. 'Fucking typical. Blame the victim. I suppose you blame those poor girls in Harwich for being trafficked.' She knows her voice is too loud.

'You're talking like a kid. Business.' His eyes are wide open, as if he's surprised by her accusations. 'I do deals, okay. It's called earning a living. Paying the bills – school fees.' He points at her again.

'You're sick. I was out cold. What did you put in my drink?' She grips the gun more tightly, tries to stop it shaking, desperately tries to look calm. 'Tell me that,' she says, realises she said it too quietly, and says again, 'Tell me what you put in my drink.'

He looks straight back at her, grabs the beer can, puts it to his mouth, throws his head back, pours, rights himself, belches, and smacks the can back on the table, causing some of the remaining liquid to slop out of it. She realises too late that he might have thrown the can at her face, but now he is talking again. 'Penis envy, is that what this is? You need a dick, because all the real people, the people who matter in this world, they've all got one. So you wave that old thing; it ought to be in that little shop of yours, fucking antique. Try firing it. Go on. Chances are it'll blow up in your face. It's a hundred years old, for fuck's sake, First World War.'

'You raped me. I want to hear you admit it,' she yelled.

He looks down, shakes his head, looks up again defiantly. 'You've known all along, haven't you, that I'm not your dad. Shitty little parasite. Sponging off me just like that dried-up bitch—'

The gun explodes in her hands. The hard noise shocks her, momentarily freezes her. There is smoke, just wisps of smoke through which she sees him staring at her. There is a wound in his right cheek, a trickle of blood. Without taking his eyes off her he puts his right hand to his face and plucks something out of his cheek. He holds it for her to see. Her hands are hurting, gripping the gun hard. She tries to make sense of what she is seeing. It's as if she is watching a film. He drops the thing he has removed from his face on the table. It is a splinter of wood about two inches long, half an inch thick. She looks at it as if it has some magical power. Just beside it there is a rough hole in the table. Juliette's brain tells her that she didn't shoot the man, she shot the table. She raises the gun again, terrified now.

'Urggh.' A strange guttural sound comes out of his mouth. *At least that stopped him talking*, she thinks. Then his mouth opens wider and utters an inhuman roar, his eyes bulging. He surges up, taking his end of the table into the air and thrusts it forward. The chair that she was sitting on earlier falls back, pressed down by the up-ended table, and lands on her right foot; she tumbles backwards, feeling a sudden pain as her left shoulder blade hits the handle on the door she had come in through. At the same time, her hands go up releasing the gun, which flies across the room in a leftwards arc and lands soundlessly on the filthy sleeping bag. She is now struggling forwards and to her left in the direction that she saw the gun fly. She knows she's on a level with it. She crawls. Standing up would take her further away from it. The noise is echoing in her head. He's standing. She sees him. Red stuff is pouring out of his groin. He sees her and tries to pounce, falls short. But his hands grab her ankles, one each. His grip is like steel, and he lets out another animal roar.

She remembers the knife and reaches down. What the hell was that film? Black and white. 'Always carry a back-up weapon,' one gangster had said to another, pulling up a trouser leg to show the knife taped by the blade upside down to the outside of his calf. 'One yank on the handle and the blade cuts the tape and the shiv's in your hand.' Why is this going through her head? She must escape. The man's grip on her ankles tightens. Her right hand is on the handle of the knife. Just one tug. But he sees it. Then their eyes meet. She thinks he is saying, 'Smar.' He must have let go with one hand. She kicks at his face. He ducks. The sole of her sandal hits the top of his head. Shit! Why isn't she wearing her DMs? It's his hand, not hers, on the handle of the knife. The blade, which Marjorie keeps so sharp, is slicing into her leg. Why is she thinking about Marjorie? She kicks with her left foot. Better

– a gurgling sound. It must be him. She must get the hand off her other ankle. Her left elbow is working automatically, levering her inch by inch across the floor towards the bed. She feels the mattress against her head. She thinks her leg is hurting. Her left shoulder is on the mattress. She reaches back with her left hand. Something hard. It's it! She can touch it. It slides away on the smooth surface of the sleeping bag.

She sees the man raise the knife above his head, with triumph in his face, and she thinks of Norman Bates. She twists her body with all her strength and feels the knife nick her leg as it bangs into the floor. Somehow, he's still got a firm grip on her left ankle and he's pulling on the knife, which is firmly stuck in the floor and giving him more purchase. But that twist has shifted her nearer to the gun on the sleeping bag, whose foul smell is now making her feel faint. She looks at the man again. It's impossible. He can't be trying to kill her, but… He's leering, pulling on the knife; he's Alan Arkin crawling towards her and she's the blind woman played by Audrey Hepburn, and now she's got the gun in her right hand and she's pointing it at his head, but she knows her feet are there. She tries to say, 'I don't want to shoot myself in the foot,' and thinks that's funny, but nothing comes out and she points it at part of his body that is clear of hers, and pulls the trigger, but nothing happens. He's watching her now. He's trying to push the knife back and forth to get it out of the floor. He's smiling at her, or to himself; his lips aren't moving, but she sees, 'Typical woman, forgot to cock it,' on his face.

She pulls the hammer back, aims at part of him which is clear of her feet and pulls the trigger. This second explosion shocks her again, but she sees something fly off him, and the grip on her left ankle slackens. She pulls her legs up and sees his face between her knees. No smile now, but something like a nod, as she pulls the hammer back and shoots. She doesn't hear the explosion, or feel the recoil, because she is watching part of his right cheekbone detach itself from his face and fly in a graceful arc, chased by a comet tail of shiny red dust, all of which disappear in an instant. From nowhere there is a splotch of wet red with grey flecks spreading back from the man's body over the upturned table, across the floor and just reaching the cupboard door under the counter in the far corner of the room.

She drops the heavy metal thing she has been holding, curls up, head between her knees, eyes closed. She's panting, struggling for breath. She tries to scream, but no sound comes. She opens her eyes. More red liquid, coming towards her across the floor from the head. It's reaching her feet. A malignant essence flowing from his body, coming to avenge him, to put right the wrong she has done. She must escape, leaps up, over the body, falls down, crawls to the toilet roll on the spade by the door. Left leg no problem, just a nick where the knife came down, just below her knee. Lucky. Pulls the loose jeans up, smacks some tissue on the cut. Hopes it will stick, like a shaving nick. Small cut in her jeans, easy to mend – or she could enlarge it and fray the edges, make a matching one on the other leg. Right leg, Jesus, two-inch gash on the outer side of her calf between the two severed bands of duct tape. Gaffer tape, duck tape (that's American, isn't it?), the names zip through her mind as she sees the blood pulsing from the wound and feels the pain, serious pain for the first time. She focuses on the leg, to shut out everything else. She presses the edges of the wound with her fingers, stops the bleeding as well as she can. Big swab of tissue – holds it in place with her left hand, unpeels duct tape with her right. Good thing she used plenty. *Christ, it hurts.* Wraps the tape as tight as she can over the wound – more tape over the lower part of the tissue swab. That has stopped the bleeding – hopes it holds long enough to get home. Some of her blood on the floor – wipes it with a tissue; some of it has dried.

She looks around, steps over the body, falls over again. Her right leg isn't working properly. She staggers up, avoiding the red pool by the head and the red mess behind it, gets to the worktop, the sink, turns the single tap. Nothing. Shit. The kettle. She doesn't need the kettle because there's a large clear plastic bottle of water behind it. She uses the water and toilet tissues to clean up every patch of blood that could possibly be hers. She knows she must have been bleeding when she was on the floor, but that whole area has been covered by the blood that came out of the man's body. Shouldn't be a problem; there's so much of it. Her left shoulder blade is hurting. She doesn't know why. Never mind, she can move her arms so she can deal with whatever happened to her shoulder blade later.

For the first time, she sees the hole in the back of the head that is face down on the floor – about an inch wide, not quite round, low, not far from its neck, and a bit to the right. She thinks it would have been neater if it had been a bit higher up and in the middle. Stupid. Concentrate. Focus. She has stuffed all the damp and bloody tissues in her large jeans pockets. She sits near the door and takes her sandals off, cleans them, cleans her feet. No sign of more bleeding from her wounds. She examines her jeans. There's a lot of blood on the right leg, but it's drying in the absorbent material. Good. Blood done, now fingerprints. She conjures an image of the tall young fingerprint woman with red lipstick working this scene. 'By golly, jolly hockey sticks, what a lot of gore,' she says out loud and laughs. A moment of dizziness, must focus on now, work to do. Fresh, clean tissue, she wipes everything she could have touched: the back of the chair, now partly under the upturned table, tap, kettle, water bottle. That's it; she'll do the door handles on the way out. She examines her shoulder bag, sees a tiny sprinkle of blood on one side, cleans it with a damp tissue. She takes one last look around the room to make sure she hasn't forgotten anything.

She's done everything she can and feels in control, so is taken by surprise when she involuntarily doubles over at the waist and vomits. Her head swims, her mouth fills with the bitter taste of bile, she sways, looks at the pile of vomit and throws up more, some of it over the body's left foot. She steps back, checks the floor and sits. Now it's the room swaying. It's natural, she says to herself, a physical reaction – the body readying itself for flight. The room looks okay. They'll see there's been a fight, think the killer must be one of the man's fellow crooks. They'll think the dead man had the gun because of her clever charade in the garden shed. The other man must have wrestled it from him in the fight.

She stands up, steadier now, hefts the shoulder bag, ouch – her back hurts nearly as much as her right leg – holds some tissue in her hand, goes to the door and opens it, wiping the door handle as she does so. The gun! She shudders, puts her bag down in the doorway, gets some more tissue, avoids the vomit, goes to the gun, has to lean awkwardly to avoid stepping in the blood. Wipes the butt, the trigger, the hammer, the cylinder, leaves the barrel as there's so much blood on it. She stands up, conscious again of the pain in her back. Sees the knife, still sticking in the floor with one of the man's hands curled loosely round the blade. She bends unsteadily at the knees and says 'Excalibur' as she pulls it out of the floor.

Chapter 19

The fresh night air was on her face and the noise was in her head. The noise – a roaring continuation of the gunshots. She closed the door carefully with a tissue in her hand, giving the handle a wipe. Satisfied that she had removed all traces of her having been there, she started walking to her car, gingerly, trying not to dislodge the makeshift dressing on her right leg. The moon had come out. She didn't need any additional light. She was clutching the straps of her shoulder bag in her right hand and the Psycho knife in her left. When she reached the car, she put an arm against it to steady herself, tried to find an explanation for the pain in her leg. She had fallen in the darkness on something sharp. No. She forced herself to turn and look back. The little house was still there, the light dimly shining through the windows. Undeniable proof. It had really happened. Her head was flooded. She beat her fists on the car roof and howled into the night. Both legs gave way, and she was on the ground, gasping, screaming, weeping, then yelling at herself to regain control.

The shoulder bag and Psycho knife were on the ground beside her. She reached and used the car door handle to pull herself up. Taking care not to spill any bloody tissues on the ground, she took her car keys out of her jeans pocket.

In the boot, she found a couple of carrier bags, put the knife in one and piled the tissues from her pockets in the other. She sat in the car and checked the dressings. As she expected, the one on her left leg was hardly more than a nick. The blood had clotted, and she was happy there would be no more bleeding. The small hole in the left leg of her jeans could have been the result of any kind of accident. The cut on her right leg was throbbing, but the pain was tolerable. But she couldn't control her right foot or apply any pressure. She put both hands under her right thigh, near her knee, and lifted, to bring her foot back out of the way. She'd need to use her left foot on the brake and accelerator. She could drive. She was focused. It had happened. It was in the past. Now she was in control. As long as she didn't think about what had happened in the disgusting cottage, she'd be able to get home, safe. She turned on the engine, put the gear lever in Drive, released the handbrake, pressed the accelerator with her left foot. She'd need to drive slowly, getting used to the unaccustomed use of her left foot, but she could do it. A new euphoria swept over her. The clock on the dashboard read 2.13.

Just after she turned left off the farm track, on to the small country road, she put her foot on the brake and pulled in to the side. Vomit! Vomit, vomit, vomit. Shit, her saliva would be in it. *Think. I'll never be able to clean it all up. So I can't deny having been there.* She drove forward slowly until she found a place to turn the car round. Then she drove back up the farm track, this time right to the little cottage. She saw in the headlights a small, dark-coloured car near the trees on the other side of the tiny building. A Ford Fiesta. *I bet he hadn't driven anything like that for a few years*, she smiled to herself. She parked on the area of rough ground in front of the cottage, looked at the door. It became impossible. She couldn't go back in there. But she had to. Or spend a long time in prison. Deprive Jazzy and Lulu of their mother.

At last, she got out of her car leaving the driver's door open, forced herself not to hesitate, opened the front door of the cottage and went in. God – the smell of the place. On top of the body odour and stale urine, there was now the powerful stink of vomit. She looked at it. *Too much*. Dozens of flies had woken up and were buzzing or crawling over the body and blood. *Right. New story. I found the body.* She stood near the vomit, put her left arm up and pressed her bare hand against the wall, as if she needed to steady herself. Stomach retching, but empty, she took a last look. The gun didn't look right. Too clean. Wiping the fingerprints off, she had also wiped off the blood. What would a killer do? A professional would leave it, knowing the bullets could be matched. A lowlife at the bottom of the criminal food chain would be more likely to take it. She reached carefully over the body and grabbed it by the butt. Near the door she took a piece of toilet paper to wipe the barrel of the gun. It was sticky. She'd clean it properly at home. She stuffed the tissue in her jeans pocket, then turned and left, turning the doorknob with her bare hand. Back at her car, she opened the boot and put the gun in the carrier bag with the Psycho knife. In the car, she sat and tried to think through what was going to happen. *Think like Tim. Maybe risk management isn't so stupid.*

She needed a story for the police. They'd get her DNA from the saliva in the vomit, so she couldn't deny having been there. So she got there and saw he'd been shot. She should have phoned them immediately. She clicked her phone and looked at the screen – no signal. Good. So she should have just driven to where there was a signal, then phoned. But she was in shock, so she drove home and meant to phone them, but was still in shock, and exhausted, so she left it till morning. The big problem was the wound in her leg. Could she cover it up? Would it heal without treatment?

Now his face was right in front of her, up close, just as the hole happened and the cheekbone shattered. She closed her eyes, but it was still there. Opened them, but still could not get rid of it. She reached down and rubbed her ankle. It stung as she touched it. What a mess – still, nothing that wouldn't heal. She reached down again. It wasn't the wound under the dressing that was irritating her now. She put the interior light on. She still couldn't see it. She used the light on her phone, shone it down on her leg. A raw-looking scratch on her ankle. She'd put some antiseptic cream on it when she got home. Christ! He must have scratched her. Another story – self-defence. The scratch was proof that he was attacking her. But, but… The final time she shot him, he was no danger to her. Defenceless. It had happened too quickly. After the second shot she could have got up and gone to phone for an ambulance. But at the time she didn't see a choice. No time to think, she just pulled the trigger. Now she had to go back again.

She flung the car door open and staggered, lopsided, nearly hopping, to the cottage, opened the door. She stumbled and nearly fell as a wave of nausea came over her. She fought to regain control, becoming aware of something sickly and metallic in the already foul air. Where the hell did she leave the bog roll? Back on the spade. She grabbed it, went quickly to the body, the hands. Blood all over them. First place they'd look, under fingernails. She tried not to disturb the position of the hands, the natural pattern of the blood which was beginning to coagulate. The position of the scratch meant it must have been his left hand. She removed as best she could any material under the fingernails of that hand, using the nail of her index finger with a tissue wrapped around it. Then the fingers looked too clean. She pushed them into some wet blood on the floor. Should cover any traces. She hoped. Done, tissue in pocket, get out. No. She saw the bulge of the wallet in the back pocket, remembered the snigger as he had said 'little list'. It came out of the pocket easily. Holding the wallet in a tissue, she took the cash, credit cards, a few scraps of paper, something like a driving licence, stuffed them in a pocket. The room started swaying. She bent and retched convulsively; acrid bile came into her mouth. She steadied herself again with a hand on the wall, threw the open wallet on to the back of the body, pocketed the tissue, hobbled to the front door, forced herself to turn and look over the room. Was there anything else she needed to change? Think. Think. It must be all right. She was feeling weaker. It would be all she could do to drive home.

*

She must have driven a couple of miles when she became aware that the car was swaying across the dark country road. She was only doing about twenty. She slowed the car further. Decided to stop. She just needed a rest to regain her strength. It couldn't have been a dream. The pain in her leg was proof.

It all came back: the guttural noises as he struggled, the stink, the look on his face just before it shattered, the red thing that flew off, the violent confusion. Then, somehow, rational thought kicking in. The need to clean up the scene. Some kind of gangland killing. She put her hands to her head. It was impossible. She could phone the police now. Tell them what happened. They seemed to have swallowed the idea that he had the gun. So, in his anger he pulled it on her. He was drunk, no need to make that up. She managed to get the gun off him, there was a violent struggle, the gun went off accidentally... Problem with that was that guns don't go off accidentally three times in quick succession. And by the time he received the fatal shot, he had already been wounded badly, twice. But it was self-defence. He really had been trying to kill her. Hadn't he? But then she had cleaned up the scene. Removed all trace of her having been there. Why did she do that? If only she hadn't thrown up... Could they prove she had taken the gun there? But it would have been for her own protection, to make sure he didn't attack her. Surely they'd understand that. And she had always known she couldn't ask Steve to lie to the police. He'd tell them she had gone to meet her father. That's why she'd driven through Woodbridge – no attempt to keep to the country roads avoiding the surveillance cameras. And the wound in her leg – if she couldn't hide it, she'd need a story for that.

Amidst all the confusion, some sort of clarity emerged. She banged the steering wheel with her right hand. It hurt, must have been bruised by the recoil of the gun. Stupid, stupid mistake taking the gun and the knife. For credibility she'd need to phone the police first thing in the morning. Assume she'd be prime suspect. They'd come with a search warrant. She'd need to hide the gun back in the shed as soon as she got home, might as well put the knife with it. God, no. *Think, Jules, think.* The story behind the gun being in the shed the second time was that Richard put it there. But he had just been shot with it...

Where was she? She took out her phone. Google Maps told her she was still about two miles short of Woodbridge. There was a copse of trees up ahead. She knew the spot – well away from the road, but surely far enough away from the crime scene to be outside the search area. She drove slowly towards the copse.

*

She slowed the car to a crawl as she pulled into the driveway. The house was in darkness. Her right leg was numb and stiff. There was a stab of pain as she pulled herself out of the car. She flinched as the motion-sensitive porch light flicked on. After closing the car door as quietly as she could, she limped to the big front door, turned the key and shouldered it open. She closed it as quietly as possible behind her. The last thing she wanted was for her mother or Steve to come downstairs.

She felt her way in the semi-darkness through the hall to the kitchen, closed the door behind her and switched on the light. She made straight for the high corner cupboard. A moment later she was gulping down two each of paracetamols and ibuprofens with water from the tap cupped in her hand. Ziggy's bed was empty. She'd be out, having one of her nocturnal adventures.

Juliette was tempted to slump onto a kitchen chair, but thought she might fall asleep there, so kept moving. She walked carefully back through the kitchen to the utility room. Took the jeans off, looked at her leg. The seeping had nearly stopped – not too bad. Some of it had dripped down over her ankle.

A bulge in the pocket of the jeans. She took out a few pieces of dirty tissue and a crumpled scrap of paper. The tissues were the ones she had used to wipe his fingernails – his blood, her DNA. She smoothed out the scrap of paper – the list. She scanned the names: John Frampton, Kenneth Almer, Glynis Swanning with a series of numbers, Eric Scannel (who had a flat diagonal line through his name), then a space, The Malteser, then another space and ???Timothy Harrington??? Just two of them were new to her. She could remember them. The numbers – a bank account? She copied the numbers on to the shopping list jotter on the worktop. They might be important. The list had to be destroyed along with the tissues. She didn't want to help the police track down potential suspects and find that they had alibis. She went to a kitchen drawer and took out a box of matches. She then went to the wood-burning stove in the hallway, put the tissues and paper in and set them alight. She watched the flames flare up and die. Then she took the poker from the stand and used it to stir the ashes of the tissues into those left in the stove from the winter. *Over the top. Thinking like Tim again. How likely are they to search the wood-burner?*

She examined the jeans and the T-shirt, took the pink plastic bottle off the shelf and sprayed the bloodstains – the big one on the right leg, a spot near the small cut on the left leg and the smears in the pocket where she had stuffed the tissues, barely visible patches and spatters on the maroon T-shirt, that she hadn't seen in the dim light of the cottage.

She put the clothes in the machine, turned the knob to a long cycle, and reached for the liquid detergent. Something stopped her. *There could be some of his blood there. It might not all come out.* She pulled the clothes out of the machine. They'd have to go in the wood-burner too – with a firelighter. She added a handful of kindling from the utility room in case the cotton fabric didn't catch too well.

After satisfying herself that the blaze in the wood-burner would destroy the two garments, she checked the blood on her foot was dry and would not stain the carpets. She made it up the stairs one step at a time, half hauling herself up the banister. Looked at herself in the bathroom mirror – grey, chalky complexion, strands of hair stuck to her forehead. *I didn't mean to. Really. I just wanted to confront him, get him to admit…*

She leaned over the toilet thinking she would throw up again. Nothing came up except the bitter taste into her mouth. She sat on the toilet and smeared some antiseptic cream on the nick on her left leg and covered it with a plaster. No problem. The scratch on her right ankle was only a problem if there was still some skin left under the dead man's fingernails. Risk: there were still traces of her DNA under those fingernails. She just had to hope the blood would cover it, make it impossible to detect. She thought of Tim. *Some risks are locked in place. Nothing can be done to mitigate them.*

She remembered how filthy those hands had been and dabbed some antiseptic cream on the scratch. One more thing to do. She looked at the makeshift dressing covering her right leg below the knee. Didn't want to see what was under it. Forced herself. Unpeeled the duct tape and removed the bloody toilet paper, hands shaking. Dropped it all in the handbasin. The sight of the wound, even in the cold light of the bathroom, brought it all back. The man tugging at her ankle, grabbing the knife, twisting and slicing, then somehow his face coming apart and the blood.

Then the present was clear, and she knew she had to work out what to do about the wound. It was about two inches long following the line of her leg on the outside of her calf and opened in a red pulsating gash. Fragments of tissue stuck to the edges where the blood had dried. A numbness had set in over the throbbing. She decided against superglue – didn't know the proper way to use it on a wound, probably couldn't have found any anyway – so squeezed some antiseptic cream straight out of the tube, could not spread it with her finger, folded a piece of lint into three thicknesses, pressed it down gently, then used several lengths of sticking plaster to hold it in place securely. Then she wrapped a bandage round and round, starting at the bottom below the sticking plaster, working up to just above the wound. She cut the bandage off with scissors, then used them to cut down the middle of the bandage about a foot down its length to make ties, which she tied in a bow, not too tight, the way she had been taught in First Aid at school. It looked neat. She would have to get through this somehow. If only she hadn't thrown up in that shitty place. She'd have to phone the police in the morning, tell them how she found the body. Such a shock. Vomiting was a normal reaction. She dropped the bloody tissues and duct tape into the toilet and flushed it all away.

She thought about waking Steve up, to tell him how she had found Richard's body. She was simply too tired, and the story needed more time. She wouldn't be able to hide the wound in her leg from him. So she eased herself under the duvet, aware of his breathing. Its rhythm broke as she tried to get comfortable, then resumed regularly. *Thank God he's a deep sleeper.* She lay in bed trying to think of the word at the edge of her consciousness, that she couldn't quite get hold of. The throbbing pain in her leg kept getting in the way. *Accept it. Don't fight it. Let it become part of me.*

More tired than she could remember having ever been, but unable to sleep, she forced herself to mentally run through the names on the list that she had stuffed into her pocket, before burying the other contents of the wallet, with the gun and the knife. She was trying to distract herself from the image of that smashed face, the blood and brain fragments. Five names. Two new ones: a man and a woman. What the hell did The Malteser mean? There was an echo, a memory she couldn't get hold of. Was it a person, a nickname for another suspect? She guessed that the question marks surrounding Tim's name meant Richard had not known whether Tim should be on the list of double-crossers or not. And he was also known as Tom. Scannel was the man arrested at the massage parlour. The line through his name must be because he had been remanded in custody, likely to be convicted and sent to prison for several years.

It was when she was turning these names over, conjuring images, especially of the woman, that the elusive word arrived in her conscious brain: Luminol – a word from films and TV. The chemical they use to detect microscopic traces of blood using ultraviolet light.

Chapter 20

Someone touched her shoulder. She twisted violently to get away.

'Jules. Jules. It's me, Steve. I didn't mean to startle you.'

She blinked in the light. 'Oh, it's you.'

'The kids are having cereal in the kitchen. Your mum's still in bed. How did it go? How is he?'

'He's dead.' She was fully awake now, aware of the dull ache in her right leg.

'What?'

'He was dead. When I got there.' The story was coming back to her. It had to explain the wound.

'Jules.' He sat on the bed and gently held her forearm. 'God. I'm so sorry. You should have woken me up.'

'Yes. I was exhausted.' She looked up at him, watery-eyed, then moved her arm to bring his hand against her cheek. 'I haven't had much sleep.'

'Do you know what he died of?'

Juliette paused for a moment. 'He was shot. I need to phone the police.'

Steve said, 'God.' He squeezed her arm. 'Shouldn't you have – straight away?'

'That hurts.'

'Sorry.' He slackened his grip. 'Lucky it's Monday. Shop closed. You stay there. I'll bring some coffee.'

She smiled weakly. 'Thanks.' While he was out of the room, she looked at the bedside clock – 8.43. Her leg was hurting now. It was her only proof that what had happened in that filthy cottage, what she had done, was real. Without the pain, it would seem like a strange fantasy, or a faint memory of something that happened long ago. But for now, the disgust she felt repelled her from the memory and anchored her in the real present moment, and the things she needed to do.

She remembered the bundle of bloody tissues that was still in the boot of the Peugeot. Steve had a key, but he was unlikely to use it. She'd deal with that later. First priority was to decide how to handle Cartwright. They'd find her blood. How could they not? Luminol. How did it get there if he was dead when she found him?

When Steve came in with a steaming mug of coffee, she said, 'Thanks, love. I've got to phone the police now. Do you mind giving me space? I'll find it easier on my own.' She became aware of her right leg throbbing. Luminol, Luminol, Luminol was beating the same rhythm in her head.

He smiled sympathetically. 'I'm here for you. Call me when you want me.' He closed the bedroom door behind him.

She moved to sit on the side of the bed and looked down at her leg. *Jesus Christ.* The bandage was soaked in blood. She pushed back the duvet – blood all over the sheet, and some on the duvet cover. The filthy room flashed back – the spray, the puddle, the shattered face. Fearful that a hand would reach out from under the bed and grab her ankle, she twisted her legs back onto the safety of the blood-soaked bed. She exhaled and took control of her breathing. After a minute she shook her head to get rid of the images, dragged herself back to the present moment and opened her mobile. Nine per cent battery – better plug it in. Her hands shook as she connected the phone to the charger. She retrieved the scrap of paper with the grid reference from her bag, then tapped the contact number she had entered from the card Cartwright had given her.

The phone was answered after about six rings, by a female voice. 'DS Cartwright's desk.'

'Can I speak to him, please.'

'He's busy. Your name and contact number, please?'

'This is Juliette Walker. I need to speak to him urgently.'

'That's the Belton-Smart investigation, isn't it?'

'Richard Belton-Smart has been shot dead. My father.'

'I'll transfer you, one second.'

The next voice she heard was his. 'Mrs Walker, good morning. Did I hear correctly?'

'Good morning, Mr Cartwright. I saw his body. It's in a ruined cottage in the woods the other side of Woodbridge. I can give you a grid reference.'

'That would be helpful.'

She read the numbers to him, and said, 'I was there last night. I saw the body.'

'We'll need to interview you. Formally.'

'There's something else I should tell you. You should get your forensics people to examine the floor between the body and the door. They should find traces of blood. It's mine. I vomited too. I'm sorry.'

'I see. We'll need to know how the blood got there.'

'Look. My husband's about to drive me to A&E. I've got a wound in my leg. That's where the blood came from. It's not life-threatening, but it probably needs cleaning up and a couple of stitches. I'll tell you what, why don't you come and see me in the A&E waiting room in the general hospital? I'll probably be there several hours.'

'I need to know how you got the wound.'

'It was an accident.'

'And when did this accident occur?'

'Last night in the old cottage in the wood. I can explain everything.'

'Did you see your father alive?'

'Yes, when I was there the first time. There was an accident.'

'Mrs Walker, who else is in your house now?'

'My husband, our two children… oh… and my mother.'

'You told my colleague your father had been shot?'

'Yes.'

'And you have a gunshot wound in the leg?'

'No – a knife wound.'

'Mrs Walker, can you stay right where you are? An officer will be there within thirty minutes. You are not to touch anything pertinent to the incident: the clothing you were wearing, the car you were driving, anything. The officer will escort you to the general hospital; your husband is welcome to accompany you. When your wound has been attended to, the officer will ask you to accompany her to the police station for an interview. Do you understand?'

Can I go through with this? Can I sell them the story? Would it be better just to tell the truth, and accept whatever happens?

'Are you there, Mrs Walker?'

'Sorry. I've got to break the news to my mother now. I've had a very difficult experience. I want to know who killed my father more than anyone. Then I've got to find a way of telling my children – their grandfather… I will co-operate in every way I can, but it's quite difficult for me right now.' She was struggling to control her voice.

'Mrs Walker, I appreciate your concerns. The position is this: a team will shortly be going to the location you have indicated. If there is evidence that a serious crime has been committed, it will be one of our priorities to eliminate you as a suspect. That is why I require your full co-operation. Anything that may become material evidence must not be tampered with. Do I make myself clear?'

'Yes, Mr Cartwright. I'll co-operate in every way I can. I'll wait here. There's something I should tell you. I didn't mean to tamper with evidence, but when I got home last night, I couldn't stand the sight of the clothes I'd been wearing. I'd fallen in the blood. I burned them. I must have been in shock. I'm really sorry.'

After closing the call, Juliette hobbled as quickly as she could to the ensuite bathroom and wrapped her leg in a towel. Came back into the bedroom, checked the carpet for bloodstains. There weren't any. She looked at her iPhone and thought about contacting Tim to say she'd be unable to do the collection today. Golden rule of risk mitigation: only use designated burner for all communications. No way she could get to the mansion today. In the circumstances it was a definite risk. The police would probably be taking her iPhone.

Then she shouted, 'Steve.'

He came into the bedroom a few seconds later. She said, 'Can you phone Janet for me and tell her I can't do Emily's flute lesson at eleven this morning. The number's in my diary, here.'

'Your mum's come down. She's in the kitchen. I didn't know if I should tell her, so I didn't. I just said she should prepare herself for bad news.' He saw Juliette's raised eyebrows. 'I can tell her if you want me to. Why have you got that on your leg?'

'I'll tell her. I've got a cut. The bed's a bit of a mess unfortunately.'

Steve looked at the bed, put one hand to his mouth and the other on the back of a chair to stop himself falling over. Then he looked at Juliette, and said, 'God.'

*

Juliette was sitting in the A&E waiting room, with her right foot on a stool. She was wearing a smart summer dress with a delicate floral pattern on a light blue background. The leg was covered with a fresh bandage that her mother had helped her with. Her hair was still damp from the hurried, but thorough, shower – her bandaged leg wrapped in a large plastic bag.

A nurse had told her to keep it elevated. DC Gillespie was sitting on one side of her, Steve on the other, holding her hand. She looked around the waiting room. A young man in cycling lycra nursing a crushed hand. A fat man holding a handkerchief to one eye. A child sobbing on a woman's lap. Ordinary people with ordinary accidents.

The image of the face with the jagged red-black hole in its cheek wouldn't go away. 'How about you, DC Gillespie? Do you get to see people who've been shot or stabbed to death in your line of work?'

'I'm quite new. There's a counselling service for people who go through that. Good support. It must be horrible.'

Juliette's and Steve's phones chimed simultaneously. Juliette looked at hers. WhatsApp from Caroline to the Walkers' group. *Police have arrived with a search warrant. I've checked it's all legal. They're copying what's on your computer. They're being quite decent and respectful, not making a mess or breaking things. Thought I should let you know. And they're impounding your little Peugeot. Such a nuisance.*

Steve said, 'Have you read that? Nuisance is a bit of an understatement.'

'Nothing to worry about, Steve. It's in our interests really, if it helps them find out who killed my dad,' she said, loudly enough for Gillespie to hear. Then she turned to the young detective. 'Will your colleagues need to search our shed?'

'Yes. Does your mother know the combination?'

'I'll text it to her.' Juliette tapped her phone: *Thanks for letting us know, Mum. I'm sure you'll be as helpful to them as you can be. Thanks. I'm sorry about the way I told you about Richard. There was just too much going on in my head. I know that although things went badly wrong, neither of us would wish him dead. We'll talk more when we can be more relaxed about it. Jxx PS still stuck in the A&E waiting room!! Police will need to look in the shed. Combination 736518.*

Juliette closed her phone and said, 'You know, all I want to do now is to be with Jazzy and Lulu. Just spend the rest of the day with them. And tomorrow. And the next day, as far as I can think into the future. Keep them safe.'

Gillespie said, 'I hope you don't have to spend too long at Museum Street.'

Juliette's mind was on the duct tape, still hanging under the old pool table.

*

The doctor said they had to complete a form where there was a possibility of knife crime. Juliette said it was an accident, and anyway DS Cartwright at the Museum Street nick knew all about it, and there was a detective constable in the waiting room, who was going to drive her to the police station to make a statement as soon as she'd finished here. The doctor asked why the police were involved if it had been an accident. 'Because it was followed shortly by a murder,' Juliette said. The doctor didn't pursue the matter. He asked if she knew how much blood she had lost. She said she hadn't measured it, but maybe a pint. They measured her blood pressure, which was low, but satisfactory.

She asked the doctor to have a look at her back, telling him she had bumped her left shoulder blade by falling over when she had the accident with the knife. With her dress unbuttoned and peeled down to her waist, he asked her to stretch up with her left hand, reach sideways, forwards, down. He pressed his fingers on and around the shoulder blade, asking her if it hurt. She said it did, and he told her it was a bruise that should go after a few days, but she should tell her GP if it didn't. To distract herself from the pain in her leg, and the recurring image of Richard's face, she tried to focus on the list of names. The Malteser? There was a connection. Richard had sent an email to Malteser. That was it. What the hell was it about?

She left hospital with a crutch on her right arm, and instructions not to put more weight on her right leg than she felt comfortable with; about half, to start with, would probably be about right. The fifteen stitches were the kind that would dissolve. She was advised to make an appointment with the nurse at her GP surgery to change the dressing and check that the wound was healing properly.

*

Sitting in the passenger seat of the police car, DC Gillespie driving, Juliette said, 'Will your colleagues need to take my phone?' as she took it out of her bag.

'They should be able to give it back before you leave. They might copy everything.'

'So I'd better not delete anything before we get there.' Juliette tried to make it sound light-hearted, thinking desperately if there could be anything incriminating on the phone.

'Better not,' Gillespie confirmed. They were approaching the police car park.

Juliette looked at the photos saved on her phone. She could explain the emails she had copied. It wouldn't matter if Gillespie saw. She found the shot of the email Richard had sent to Malteser. The Polish bitch and Mr Love – the other method. Was Malteser some kind of enforcer working for Richard? Thank God she had complied with Tim's instructions to delete each P text as soon as she had read it.

'I'm just texting my mum,' she said to Gillespie, who was steering the car into the police car park. *Mum, my leg's fine. A few stitches and some painkillers. I'll be hobbling for a few days, but recovery is expected to be quite quick. Steve's on his way home in a cab. I imagine I'll be a while with the police. Don't worry. Kiss Jazzy and Lulu for me. Jxx*

She turned to Gillespie. 'Am I a suspect?'

Gillespie reddened slightly. 'Person of interest is the term we use. Ideally, we'll be able to eliminate you as a suspect quite quickly and gather evidence that will help us find the killer.'

'Do you think I killed him?'

Gillespie reddened further and brought the car to a stop in a parking space. 'We're trained to deal in facts, evidence, not express opinions. Sorry. I'm sure if you co-operate fully, it'll all be fine.'

Chapter 21

DS Cartwright led Juliette into the interview room. 'Mrs Walker, this is DI Wentworth who is the SIO leading the investigation into the death of your father.' Wentworth was a lean man, late forties, dark-haired, clean-shaven. Juliette thought he'd be a good marathon runner. Both men wore grey suits, white shirts and conservative ties. Wentworth stood up and shook Juliette's hand. She slipped the crutch off her forearm.

'Thank you for coming to the station, Mrs Walker. Before we start the interview, may I offer my condolences on the death of your father.'

'Thank you. It's a shock.'

'And I trust your injury is not too serious.'

'It'll mend.' She looked into the steel of his eyes. 'Thank you.'

'Please take a seat, Mrs Walker.' Wentworth indicated a chair on the other side of the table from him and Cartwright. The two men sat, Cartwright near the wall and the recording device. She leaned the crutch against the wall and pressed her hands on the table as she sat down.

Wentworth continued, 'Given the circumstances, you understand that this is a formal interview under caution and, further, that you have the legal right at any time to be accompanied by a solicitor.'

'My mother has texted me with the number of a solicitor who can be here within fifteen minutes of a call. But I don't foresee any problems that would make that necessary, and I would like to help you as much as I can to find my father's killer, so I'm happy to answer your questions without a solicitor.' She was gabbling. *Stop. Be concise. Just answer the questions.*

'Let's get started then. Micky, can you start the machine and do the formalities?'

Cartwright pressed a switch, said the date, his rank and name, and Wentworth's, recited the statement about Juliette needing to mention everything she might later rely on in court, asked her to state her full name.

Then Wentworth took over. 'Mrs Walker, so that we can understand the background, please could you tell us something about your relationship to the deceased, your father? Would you say it was a close father-daughter relationship?'

'We loved each other, if that's what you mean. We became less close when I moved out and got married. My parents started having a difficult time with each other a few years ago. I tried not to take sides.'

'And more recently?'

Juliette had her answer ready. They shouldn't know that she knew about the people-trafficking and pimping. 'Drug dealing – that's crossing a line for me. But he had always been a very good father. Then, him disappearing like that, tricking me about that gun and taking a lot of money from my mother. I was angry about that. He'd obviously got mixed up in something bad.' She closed her eyes. *Don't say too much. Just answer the questions.*

Wentworth said, 'Mrs Walker, we will need an account of the events of last night, but before that, could you just explain the circumstances leading up to it. Your father had been reported as a missing person, so perhaps you could start by telling us what you know about the circumstances in which he went missing.'

'Of course. I'll tell you as much as I can, but it isn't much. He phoned me. I'm not sure of the date, but it was on my mobile, so I imagine the phone records can be checked. It was a week or two ago. Can I just say, I had a horrible, upsetting experience last night, I've got a knife wound in my leg, I've had about two hours' sleep, and I'm on prescribed medication for the pain. My mind isn't as sharp as usual, but I'll help you as much as I can.' She looked at the recording machine, then at each man in turn.

Wentworth said, 'You started telling us about a phone call. If you can remember anything about that, it would be helpful.'

'You've got all this from my previous interview – about the old gun.'

'In the light of these new developments, we want you to tell us about it again.'

'He told me he needed to go into hiding. He'd taken some money from family and business accounts, which we later confirmed to be true. He said it would all be sorted out soon and he would be able to return in a few weeks. He was worried my mother might do something stupid, so I should take the gun – make sure she couldn't find it.'

'I've listened to that interview. You didn't say anything about your father going into hiding.' Wentworth's eyes were fixed on her.

'I don't remember saying anything about why he was away from home.' She glanced at Cartwright. 'I wasn't asked. I was answering questions about the gun.'

'Hiding from whom?' Wentworth didn't shift his gaze.

She hadn't prepared for this. 'He didn't say.' *Stupid – they know about the connection with Frampton, the brothel.* Her mind really was working slowly, but she decided to tell them. 'Sorry, yes, I think he did. Johnny Frampton. Someone my mother unsuccessfully defended on rape and extortion charges thirty or so years ago.' Should she mention the phone calls? They'd want to know why she hadn't reported them, so she'd only tell them if they asked directly.

Juliette wanted to move things on. 'Then a note turned up in the shop after it had been broken into. Must have been my father, looking for the drugs he had smuggled in from Belgium in a commode, which we had handed in to the police as soon as we found them.' She looked at Cartwright, who conceded a slight nod. She reached into her bag and retrieved the small scrap of paper. 'Here it is, with the grid reference I gave you.' She passed it across the table. 'I went there to try to persuade him to turn himself in, on grounds that being in police custody would be better than being found by Frampton.'

'So you went to the specified location very late at night. Why so late?'

'It's what he wrote on the note. Look. After dark. I left it till about midnight. I think he didn't want me to be followed, but I suppose I must have been.'

'Why do you think that?'

'Well, it'd be rather a coincidence for me and the killer to turn up in the middle of that wood within an hour of each other.' She maintained eye contact with Wentworth.

'What happened when you arrived at the old cottage?'

'He was pleased to see me. But he was in a disgusting state. Must have been drinking a lot. It was fine until I told him I hadn't brought the packages of drugs, and that we'd handed them to the police. He got upset and said that stuff was what he needed to get him out of there and back on his feet. I told him I'd brought him £50 for anything he needed urgently – food or whatever. He got up from his chair and started yelling at me, "Fifty quid! What effing use is that to me?" and carrying on like that. I tried to reason with him, to calm him down.' She reached down for her shoulder bag. 'Sorry I need to take a couple of painkillers.' She tried not to look hurried as she popped the tablets out of the blister pack and unscrewed the top of her small flask of water.

'You were trying to calm him down,' Wentworth said.

'I should have mentioned there was that army revolver, the one you know about,' she risked a glance at Cartwright, 'or at least one just like it. It must have been the same one. It was on the worktop near the sink. I told him it'd be much better for him if he turned himself in. He'd be safe from Frampton and could get his sentence reduced. And he sort of lost it for a bit, was gesticulating and yelling again, effing this and that, you know, pigs, that sort of thing and then I saw there was this knife in his hand and he was coming towards me.' The thought of it shocked her. She could really see it like this.

'Mrs Walker, are you able to continue?'

'He was quite wild, you know, with the drink. I'm sure he didn't mean to attack me, but he was coming towards me, and the knife was in his hand. I backed off towards the door, but he kept coming, and I must have panicked and tried to kick it out of his hand. The knife. And that's when it happened. It just felt like a sort of bump. Then he dropped the knife, and I looked down and saw the blood, which he must have seen as well. He, like, collapsed and started crying and saying how sorry he was and he didn't mean to hurt me.' She struggled to get the words out, then put her hands over her face.

'How do you know he didn't mean to hurt you?'

She bent down over the table still covering her face. 'He was my father. He loved me.'

'But he was angry, drunk, aggressive.'

She could feel his hands gripping her ankles again, then grasping for the knife. She started sobbing, still with her head in her hands, on the table.

'We realise this is distressing for you, let's have a short break. DS Cartwright, could you pause the recording?'

A few minutes later, Juliette said she wanted to continue, and Cartwright switched the recording machine on again.

Wentworth resumed the questioning. 'You were going to tell us why you thought he didn't mean to hurt you.'

'Because he was sorry afterwards. When he was coming towards me, I was scared, which is why I tried to kick the knife out of his hand.'

'You were bleeding from the leg wound.'

She had used the break to conjure the image she wanted – her story. There was a calculated risk she had decided to take. 'The A&E doctor can confirm that my wound could have been caused the way I have said. I've forgotten his name, but I expect DC Gillespie made a note of it.'

Wentworth affected to look hurt. 'Why do you think we would doubt your story?'

'You keep asking me about it.'

'What happened next?'

'I was on the floor. He was over me with a roll of toilet paper saying he was sorry he didn't have a proper bandage. But he had some sticky tape which he used to hold wads of toilet paper on my leg, and it stopped the bleeding for a while. Then he said we must wipe up the blood, he couldn't tolerate having it on the floor with him. I helped a bit, with more toilet paper, and he poured some water from a big bottle and got the floor reasonably clean. I was just wanting to get out of there in case his mood flipped again. He said I must take the bloody toilet tissue, which we'd put in an old carrier bag. I found I could walk, just, so I wished him luck and got out of there as quickly as I could.'

'What was he doing when you last saw him, alive?'

'He was sitting on his chair at that old table with a beer can in his hand. He said I should get my leg seen to, told me to take care. He looked sort of… resigned. I said, "Bye, Dad," and went out the door. Closed it behind me.'

Cartwright intervened. 'Taking the £50 with you?'

'£50?' She recovered quickly. 'Oh, yes. No, I'd put that on the table when I offered it to him – before the… the accident. It must have still been there.'

'What did you do then?'

'Got in my car. Rested for a few minutes. Then started driving. I went very slowly because I needed to use my left foot on the pedals – it's an automatic – and I was still going down that track when I heard a bang, so stopped the car. My first thought was that it was a gunshot and came from the old cottage. And I was thinking, no he wouldn't, he'd never do that, and then there was another one, so I knew he hadn't. So I was sitting in the car deciding what to do, when I heard a third one. I thought maybe he's just shooting things, like beer cans, he's gone a bit wild after our conversation, and the blood. Or it's more like a gunfight, and he might be lying there wounded. It couldn't have been a car back-firing, not out there. It could've been poachers, but I didn't think of that at the time. After a few minutes and no more shooting, I decided to go back, to see what had happened.'

'Wasn't that very dangerous?'

'I wouldn't do it now, not in the cold light of day. It must have been the heat of the moment, adrenaline or something. I decided I couldn't just walk away, drive away, and just leave him there, not knowing what had happened. So, I turned the car round, drove back and looked through the window, in a corner past those raggy curtains and saw it.' She covered her face with her hands. She was seeing it.

'Take your time, Mrs Walker.'

'God. I knew he couldn't be alive, but I had to check. In case I could save him. So I went in. Sorry.' She removed her hands and closed her eyes.

'Take your time, Mrs Walker,' Wentworth repeated.

'I've never seen a dead body before. Not even one that had died naturally. And there was all this... horrible stuff...' She took a tissue out of her bag and wiped her eyes. 'I got my phone and dialled 999. Nothing happened – no service.' She looked up into Wentworth's eyes. Letting the tears run. 'Right then, I didn't even think I might be in danger, you know, if the killer had seen me come back and might have thought I'd seen him. At some point I must have thrown up. It was all too much for me. I'd completely forgotten about the wound in my leg. Then I just fell over and got blood all over me, and for a while I just lay there screaming. Then I realised all I wanted was to go home and get into bed next to my husband and lie down and go to sleep.'

Cartwright spoke. 'Where is the bag of soiled tissue?'

'God, I'd forgotten about that. I think it must still be in the boot of my car.'

'Thank you,' Wentworth intervened. 'You may be aware, we have your car.'

'It's just bloody toilet paper. I can't think...'

Cartwright again. 'We want to know if it's all your blood.'

Wentworth turned his head to look at Cartwright and shook it slightly. Then he turned back to Juliette. 'We'll return your car as soon as our examination has been finished. Mrs Walker, can you describe anything else you saw when you went back into the building?'

'The table had been upended, and the chairs knocked over. I didn't think about it then, but I realise now there must have been a fight.'

Wentworth's steely eyes were on her again. 'Mrs Walker, going back to when your husband gave you the note that he had found in the shop. Did it not occur to you that the best thing to do would be to give it to us? Let us deal with it?'

'Of course it did. I thought about it carefully. If I'd done that, he'd still be alive, I know.' She sighed. 'I wanted him to explain, including what he'd done with my mother's money. And if he couldn't, I wanted to tell him what I thought – what he'd been doing. Get him to understand. And I wanted him to turn himself in, either way. Then he might have been able to help you catch the people he was hiding from, and if he was guilty at least get his sentence reduced. Win-win.' *I'd never be safe if I grassed him up.*

Cartwright said, 'Mrs Walker.' She guessed he'd be trying to recover some kudos with his boss. 'Mrs Walker, who are you protecting?'

She looked at him. *Some kind of trick?* 'What do you mean?'

'Just supposing, someone was with you. Indulge me for a moment. You are going to visit your father in an isolated spot in the middle of the night. You suspect that he has been engaged in serious criminal activities. You want to have things out with him. You know he is armed. You know he is going to be angry when he discovers you have not brought the drugs he has taken the trouble to smuggle into this country. Would you go alone? I think not. So you go there accompanied by a man, I think. The sensible thing to do. You start by trying to persuade your father to hand himself in to the police. You try to be reasonable, but he becomes argumentative. As you say, he is drunk. He threatens you. He has a knife. Your companion sees the gun and grabs it, uses it to prevent him from killing you, but is too late to prevent you from being wounded in the leg. He has saved your life, and maybe saved his own too, by shooting this crazed, violent, drunken man. Mrs Walker, you are entirely innocent. Perhaps, even, you tried to intervene to stop the two men fighting, and that is how you sustained the wound. Your companion might face a charge of manslaughter, but with the lack of intent to kill and other mitigating circumstances, the sentence would be a light one. So, tell me, Mrs Walker, doesn't the story I have just told sound rather more plausible than the one you have told us?'

'Yes.'

Cartwright shifted in his seat, glanced across to Wentworth as if seeking approval.

Juliette found herself back in the hovel, on the floor, feeling Richard's grip on her ankles. She shook her head to try to get rid of the image. 'If I were having to make up a story to explain the killing, I'd probably come up with some fiction like that. But it isn't true. What I have said is true. You have to believe me.' She felt tears come and made no effort to stop them. 'Look at the note. "Come alone." It would have upset him a lot more if I'd gone with someone.'

Wentworth looked at her and waited a few seconds. 'Mrs Walker, you said your father helped you make a temporary dressing for your leg with toilet paper and sticky tape. Can you describe the sticky tape?'

The duct tape could be a weak spot in the story. 'Wide and black. Duct tape, I think. I took it off when I got home, to put a better dressing on the wound, with some antiseptic cream.'

'And where would it be now?'

'I flushed it with the toilet paper that'd been on my leg. There was blood all over it.'

'No roll of duct tape was found at the scene. Can you explain that?'

An image formed in her mind of a forensics officer carefully peeling the tape off the bottom of the pool table and putting it in an evidence bag.

'Mrs Walker – the roll of duct tape?'

'I'm trying to think. There might not have been a roll. I didn't examine everything in that horrible place. It might have just been a few strips that he pulled off something else. Or maybe there was a roll, and the killer took it.' She struggled not to sound sarcastic. 'And what about the £50 I left on the table? The table had been tipped over. I've no idea if the killer took that money too.'

Wentworth wasn't being deflected. 'The duct tape, Mrs Walker, would you say it was similar to the tape you used to attach the service revolver to the underside of your pool table?'

Her worst fear: they had found scraps in the hovel and were trying to get a match. She used it in her shed; he had it in the hovel. If they could prove it came off the same roll… 'Quite similar – possibly the same. It might be a common brand. I didn't examine it carefully.'

There was more. Was the revolver still on the worktop when she went back after the shooting? She didn't look. Description of the knife: a kitchen knife, not found at the scene. The killer must have taken it.

'Mrs Walker,' Wentworth again, 'I just want to understand more clearly. You are driving away, with a deep gash in your leg, and you hear shots. Surely, the sensible thing to do would be to dial 999 and keep at a safe distance from the shooting. Can you tell us again, why you drive back to the scene of a gunfight? One that might not have finished?'

'I wish I could. I wasn't thinking straight. I'd lost a lot of blood. I'd tried to dial 999 earlier and there was no signal. But I was as careful as I could be. Waited several minutes before going back. Looked through the window to make sure no one else was there. Listened for a sound of someone moving in the wood. It was just, like, automatic. I didn't think I was being brave or anything.'

Wentworth seemed to be trying to penetrate her with his eyes. 'And when you went back in there and saw the body, did you touch anything?'

'I think I might have passed out for a moment. The shock. I threw up. Couldn't help it.'

'Did you touch the body, perhaps to feel for a pulse?'

'Did you see it?' Her voice rose. 'A great bloody hole in his head.' She controlled her voice. 'No need to feel for a pulse. I couldn't have touched him anyway.'

'Can you describe the position of the body?'

'Face down. You must have photos.'

Wentworth spoke again. 'I realise this is difficult for you, Mrs Walker. It is useful for us to know if the killer might have returned to the scene after you had left – to clean up, remove evidence. Any discrepancies between what you saw and what our team found today, we need to know about.'

'Sorry.' Juliette closed her eyes again. 'I can't get rid of the image. I threw up. I fell over. That stuff was all over me. I just had to escape. The horror of it. Then as soon as I got out of there, I was very frightened. Put yourself in my place.' She made eye contact with each of them. 'Woman on her own in the dark. A murderer probably not far away. I just got to my car as quickly as I could and drove off.'

Wentworth nodded slightly. 'Before you left the cottage, did you see anything on the body? Anything unusual, that seemed out of place?'

'I don't think so.' She closed her eyes. 'No, wait. There might have been something on his back. Like a wallet or something. Open.'

'Did you see a vehicle near the cottage?'

'Oh my God!' She had been expecting this earlier and

looked wide-eyed, shocked. 'There was a small car parked right there, by the trees. Do you think it was the killer's? He was hiding in it?'

'It's being investigated,' Wentworth said.

Cartwright spoke again. 'And when you got home, your first thought was to destroy the clothes you had been wearing?'

'I wasn't thinking straight. I'd lost some blood. They were covered in my father's blood as well as mine from when I'd fallen over. I didn't think I'd be able to wash it out. On an impulse I got a firelighter and some kindling and stuffed them in our wood-burning stove. I wish I'd kept them. It would have helped prove my story – that the blood was from my wound and then falling in the blood on the floor.'

'What else could it be from?'

'I've watched TV shows where they do spatter analysis.' She looked up, feeling more confident now.

Wentworth fixed her with his eyes. 'Do you always carry a bag – like the one you have with you?'

'Yes, not having big pockets. A habit, really.'

'Were you carrying a bag when you went to see your father?'

'This one.' She pointed to it on the floor.

Cartwright's eyes lit up. 'We need you to leave it with us – for examination.'

'Yes, of course.' She managed not to hesitate. It was another thing she had planned for. 'If I could borrow a carrier bag. Actually, I left it in there. The first time. I was so confused… loss of blood… in pain. I just wanted to get out of there. Saw it when I went back and took it. When I got home, I saw some spots of what might have been blood on it and wiped them off. There might still be a trace. I didn't think. I just wanted to get it clean, didn't mean to destroy evidence.'

Eventually it ended.

'Thank you, Mrs Walker. That is sufficient for now. We might need to ask you further questions as our inquiries proceed,' Wentworth said, after Cartwright had switched the recorder off. 'Just one more thing now: we'd like to take a sample of your DNA, a swab from your mouth. If you have no objection, DS Cartwright will escort you to where a female officer will carry out the procedure. It's quick and painless, I assure you.'

Cartwright said, 'And I'll return your mobile phone. The records we need will have been copied, and we might have questions regarding them when our analysis is complete.'

Chapter 22

'I'll have to drop in and have a few minutes with your mother,' Gillespie said. She was driving Juliette home. 'I've been appointed family liaison officer.'

Juliette was sitting next to her in the unmarked car. 'Does that mean you're not part of the investigation?'

'Not really. Anything I find out that might lead us to the killer, I feed back to the team. Primary role is support for victims. You'll be hearing from Victim Support. I'll be liaising with them too.'

Juliette took her phone out of the carrier bag that now held her belongings. Three missed calls and a text, all from Lara: *So sorry about your dad. Can we talk asap?* Twenty minutes ago. After the police check? Surely they would have mentioned it if they had seen these. 'News travels fast,' she said, as she dropped the phone back in the bag. Lara would have to wait. They were approaching her house.

Caroline came out of the front door. 'Darling, let me help you.'

'Mum, I'm fine with the crutch.' Juliette held the carrier bag in her left hand. 'This is DC Gillespie.'

'How do you do, Mrs Belton-Smart. Andrea Gillespie. We met briefly before. I'm so sorry for your loss.'

After shaking hands with Gillespie, Caroline turned to Juliette. 'Steve's in the garden with the little ones. How did it go? Where's your shoulder bag?'

'They need to examine it. I'll tell you about it later. I think DC Gillespie wants to have a quick word.' She looked and saw her mother's puffy cheeks and watery eyes.

'Just a couple of minutes,' Gillespie said. 'To explain my role as family liaison officer.'

As they walked towards the front door, Juliette said, 'I can't wait to see the kids. Have you told them about their grandad?'

'Lulu's too young to understand. Jazzy hardly knew him. It won't mean much.' Caroline turned and led Gillespie into the house.

When they saw her come through the French windows, the two children started running. 'Careful with Mummy's leg!' Steve yelled, just before Jason reached her, wrapped his arms around her hips and pressed the side of his head against her stomach, in his usual greeting. Lucy arrived a few seconds later and Juliette bent to scoop her up as well as she could, letting the crutch dangle from her forearm.

'Can I have a go with your stick, Mummy? I hurt my leg playing cricket.'

'It's called a crutch. Wait till I'm sitting down, Jazzy. Steve, could you take them in and supervise hand-washing. My mum's talking to the so-called family liaison officer – your friend Andrea. Then maybe you could get some tea ready?'

As soon as her family were in the house, Juliette struggled as quickly as she could across the lawn, to the shed. She tapped the combination and went in. She bent with difficulty to look under the pool table, using the light on her phone. It had gone. No strips of tape dangling where she had made it look as if the gun had been hidden. There must have been some left in the hovel. They'd get a match. *God, I'm paranoid. As bad as Tim.* She locked the shed door and made her way back to the house.

'How did you get on with her?' Juliette said as Caroline came towards her carrying a teapot.

'She just explained what she'd be doing. Briefing someone in Victim Support. She asked me how the identification went, then advised me strongly not to say anything to the press if they approach me. She was perfectly pleasant and gave me her card saying I should contact her any time, if I needed support or thought of something relevant to the investigation.'

Identification – they would have to talk about that later. The children were rushing out, followed by Steve, carrying a tray.

'I've got an idea,' Juliette said, when they were sitting at the patio table, the children eating slices of Swiss roll and drinking beakers of milk. 'Beach funfair tomorrow, anyone?' Cries of 'Yeah' from both children.

Lucy slid down from her little chair and came and leaned against Juliette's thigh. She reached with both arms and said, 'Up.' Juliette grasped her under her armpits and pulled her up onto her lap.

'Let's just deal with your sticky bits,' Juliette said, using a baby wipe to remove jam and crumbs from Lucy's hands and face. Once this was done, she held the child close and kissed her forehead. 'Love you.' She looked into the sharp blue eyes and then felt the softness of her skin as Lucy nuzzled into her neck, hugging as much as she could with her little arms.

'What about me?' Jason said.

'Come here.' She freed her right arm from Lucy and wrapped it around Jason. She glanced at Caroline, whose eyes were brimming. 'So how about you two going and watching the TV? Steve, can you install them? Then come back.'

When Steve and the children had gone into the house, she looked at Caroline. 'A lot to take in.'

'Yes. They formally notified me – next of kin. A man believed to be Richard Belton-Smart. I had to go and identify the body.'

'That must have been horrible.'

'Part of his face was covered. He could have been asleep.'

'I should have come with you.'

Their eyes met. Caroline's were moist. Juliette broke the silence. 'It'll take time.'

'I can't believe he attacked you with a knife.'

Steve came out through the French windows. 'How's your leg, Jules?'

'Not too bad. Steve, sit down.' She looked at Caroline. 'Mum, do you want us to talk about it?'

'I don't understand why you went there.'

She closed her eyes and saw the piece of cheekbone splitting off from his face and all the red stuff, and the noise was back, the roaring wind in her head. She kept her eyes closed. 'He was very drunk, sort of gesticulating wildly with the knife. He was very sorry when he saw what had happened to my leg.'

'Steve told me about the note he found in the shop. Why the hell didn't you just take it to the police?' Caroline's voice was shaking.

Juliette opened her eyes and looked her mother in the eye. 'Because, because…'

'He'd still be alive, and you wouldn't have that wound.'

'Cara, this might not be the time.'

The noise in Juliette's head rose to a crescendo. She wanted to yell: *Because he raped me, the night he beat you up.* The secret that had tortured her for three years. Now it had to remain secret forever, because it gave her a motive. Her anger had to come out. 'Yes, that's right. It was really stupid of me. I actually thought I was doing the right thing, okay?' She was keeping her voice down. 'Steve, could you close the French doors? Little ears. And it's my stupid fault that fucking Frampton followed me and did what he did, and it's my stupid fault for having some residual sense of family loyalty in spite of everything and wanting him to see sense and hand himself in and co-operate with the police. Fucking naïve of me, I know, but that's what I did.' Tears were running. She couldn't stop her voice rising. 'And, incidentally, I wanted to tell him what I thought of him for the way he had treated you and being a drug dealer and God knows what else and for abusing Steve's trust by using Walker's Antiques for importing his stuff. Jesus, I'm so sorry and also very tired and not feeling well so I'm going upstairs to lie down.' She hoisted herself out of the chair with the crutch and headed unsteadily towards the French windows.

'Jules, can I help? Bring you anything?' Steve was on his feet.

'That carrier bag – it's got my stuff in it – and a glass of water. I need more painkillers.'

*

Ziggy Stardust was on the bed. Juliette wiped her eyes and blew her nose, then waited till Steve had left the room. She knew she had been unfair to her mum. Her anger had been real, but should have been aimed at herself. She looked in the full-length mirror. *What have you done, Jules? What have you become?* She turned away. Too many things had been happening. That bloody face came back. She tried to expel it, but then decided to examine it, to try to understand the reality of what she had done, to absorb it. Had she meant to do it? Had she gone there to kill him? She sat on the bed. Ziggy stirred.

'You know what it's like, don't you, Zig? Not being able to say what you really think, tell anyone what you've done. Well, you're lucky, because I can tell you.' Ziggy was on her back, rhythmically pawing the air and purring as Juliette stroked her chest and belly. Juliette looked at the door, even though she knew Steve had already shut it. She whispered, 'The man I went to see. There was the small matter of what he did, raped me, three years ago. I needed to talk to him about that. Oh yes. And that'd be a conversation begging for unintended consequences. You only see that afterwards. Jesus, Ziggy, when you play with a little bird, or a mouse, and mutilate it to death, do you get images of it in your head? Does it go away after a while?' Ziggy went on purring. 'One other thing, Zig: that thing about him not being my real father – better keep that secret, don't you think? Makes it less likely that I'd kill him.'

Ziggy had gone to sleep. Juliette started thinking about the police interview, while the image of the shattered face kept reminding her of that other reality. A hint of an idea came to her: the story for the police, she had started constructing it after killing him and made it up that morning, in a rush. If she had gone there in order to kill Richard, she would have planned it, had the story ready before doing it. Her mind snapped back to the present, to what she needed to do now.

She took her phone out of the carrier bag and looked at the messages. What to do about Lara? Ignore her? Cut her off, she's only going to be a nuisance, a possible danger? But she's got a contact in the police; she might have information about the police investigation. Juliette tapped the phone. 'Hi, Lara.' She was still sitting on the bed, next to Ziggy.

'Hi. Look, I'm so sorry about your dad.'

'We both know he's not a great loss to civilisation.'

'Still, it's a horrible shock. And you've got a wound in your leg, how is it?'

'A bit sore. It'll mend.'

'I heard you had a long session in Museum Street. How did it go?'

'Okay. But... last person to see him alive, family member, automatic suspect, you never know. They don't give much away. Do you know more?'

'Just what you'd expect. They're checking all known associates. Frampton's at the top of the list, but they haven't found him yet.'

'My father had a talent for making enemies. Frampton isn't the only one.'

'Scannel's got a cast-iron alibi – remanded in custody.'

'Do you know what evidence they've got against me?'

'Opportunity, obviously. Forensics were still being analysed, last I heard. They're working on motive.'

Juliette sipped some water. All those questions about her relationship with her father. Would they find out she hadn't spoken to him for three years? That he had beaten up her mother? That he wasn't her natural father? At least they wouldn't find out what he had done to her. 'Sorry, Lara, just trying to think what possible motive they might imagine I could have.'

'I like talking to you, but I'm not doing it for fun. How about a human-interest story? What it's like being the daughter of a gangster, your mother's involvement with the main suspect, finding his mutilated body.'

At last, the real reason for Lara contacting her. Juliette made a quick decision to play along. She needed to know as much as possible about every development in the police investigation. 'Lara, can we meet? How about the café in Buttermarket? Pat Val. Eleven tomorrow?'

'Eleven. Good, I'll be there.'

'Okay. I'll text you if I have to cancel.'

Juliette cut the call. Her leg was throbbing, so she pulled it up on the bed and sat, propped up on pillows, legs outstretched. Ziggy murmured and settled on Juliette's lap. The number on Richard's list had been nagging at her. She opened her wallet and took out the slip of paper she had written it on. Six digits. It had to be a phone number, probably a landline. She wanted to call it, just to find out who answered. Why? Might it lead her to the money Richard had taken? To find a way of getting that back would make a huge difference, especially to her mum. Or was it her longing to know more about what Richard had been up to, and the people he was involved with? And there was a chance, a long shot, that one of these people hated him and didn't have an alibi for that night. Someone she might be able to throw suspicion on and get some of the heat off herself. How dangerous could it be?

While this was going on in her head, and still unsure as to why she was doing it, she tapped the Ipswich dialling code followed by the six digits.

After half a minute, ''ello?' A woman's voice. Slightly hoarse. Then breathing. Sounded like a heavy smoker.

'Hello,' Juliette replied, sounding as friendly as she could. 'I hope you don't mind my calling. It's about Richard Belton-Smart. I'm contacting all the people who knew him. I'm very sorry to have to tell you—'

''e's gone. Someone got 'im.' A slight rasp in the woman's throat.

'Yes. I hope you don't mind my asking. Did you know him well?'

'Who are you?'

Juliette decided it was safe enough. 'Oh, sorry. My name's Jules. I'm his daughter.'

'I see.'

Juliette waited for some token expression of sympathy, but it wasn't coming, so she spoke. 'Do you mind if I ask who you are?'

'I need to talk to someone.'

'It's important not to be alone at a time like this.'

'Oh, I'm not mourning. No cause for that. I need to talk to someone about you.' The woman sounded matter-of-fact, as if she were explaining something to a child.

'Can I call you back later?'

'Tomorrow. Call me back in the afternoon. Goodbye.'

Ziggy stirred as Juliette put the phone back in the carrier bag. 'What do you think, Zig? Think that was Glynis Swanning? At least it wasn't a total brush-off. And Lara, do you think she could be useful? Problem if they catch

Frampton. He's bound to have an alibi. Just have to hope they don't find him. Come on. Time for your supper. Let's go down. Try to make peace.'

*

Juliette went to her mother in the kitchen. Steve was still reading to Jason. Caroline was taking a pasta bake out of the oven. 'That looks and smells delicious, Mum. I just can't eat at the moment. I'll probably get my appetite back tomorrow. And I'm feeling bad about the way I was earlier. I'm really sorry. I made a bad decision, going there to talk to him, and I'll regret it forever. I still think I made it for the right reasons.'

Caroline put the dish on the marble worktop. 'We both need to try to understand each other's feelings.'

'Let's talk in the morning. I'm really too tired now. I'll just get more water and go up.'

*

Lying under the sheet, she thought hard about motive. It was good that she had told the cops that she was angry with him about leaving her mother and taking the money, and about the drugs in the commode. Did that anger amount to motive? Surely not. They'd be questioning Steve and her mum before long. Should she ask them not to mention the rift between her and Richard? No. That'd make her mum even more angry. So the cops would find out that she hadn't spoken to him for three years. She should have told them. That was a mistake. And she should have told them about him beating up her mother three years ago. Would they find out that she knew about the people-trafficking and pimping? Lara. Would she tell her police contact that she, Jules, knew about the brothel in Harwich? More reason to keep Lara close. They'd question her again and challenge her about these things, accuse her of covering up the true nature of the relationship. She'd need to be ready. She concentrated on these problems to try to stop the image of that smashed face and the blood coming back, as she drifted off.

Chapter 23

'Bloody nuisance. At last it's safe to go for a run, and I'm stuck with this leg.' Juliette was having breakfast in the kitchen. Caroline had just walked in wearing a light green blouse and loose linen trousers.

'Darling, I'm sorry I upset you yesterday. I really didn't mean to accuse you.'

'I understand, Mum, I really do. It was a terrible mistake, to go there.'

'A few years in prison… He might have come out a better man.'

Juliette wanted to tell her about the trafficking of young girls, forced prostitution, modern slavery. Her mum had no idea what a truly horrible man Richard had been. But it would lead to so many questions she didn't want to deal with. And she wanted to suggest that her mum should feel relieved that she would never have to see Richard again, but knew she wouldn't react well to that. She said, 'Bereavement is complicated when you don't really love the person who's died.'

'I knew him better than anyone else – for more than thirty years…'

Juliette wanted to move the conversation on. 'We're safe from Frampton now. Get back to living normally. You can stay as long as you want, obviously.'

'Are you sure it's safe? Supposing he thinks you saw him? You'd be at risk.'

How could she tell her there was absolutely no risk of that? 'Well, the children are safe. Whoever killed Richard, they'd know I'm a suspect, so I'm quite useful to them. And I was driving in the opposite direction. They can't possibly think I saw them.'

'I still can't picture it. What was Richard like before… you know?'

Before. Yes, before. Before I shot him in the face. 'Angry with the people who had betrayed him, forced him to go into hiding. Pleased to see me, though.' Juliette sighed. 'So at least the last time I saw him, alive, he was being kind, in a drunken sort of way. Helping me, saying how sorry he was about the cut on my leg. He didn't even say it was my fault for trying to kick the knife out of his hand.' *Might as well try to make it easier for her.*

'It's been a shock for both of us.'

'I shouldn't have blown my top like that. Sorry.'

'It's only a matter of time before they release the body. I'll organise a funeral. You don't have to come. It'll give me some sort of closure.'

'I'll be there to support you. I wonder who else will turn up.' Juliette thought for an instant of the gangland funerals in films, where there's a police officer hiding behind a tree taking photos of all the attendees.

'Do you think we've heard the last of Frampton?' Caroline picked at half of a grapefruit with a teaspoon.

Juliette was about to answer when her phone vibrated on the table in front of her. No caller ID.

'Hello.'

That voice. 'What do you know?'

She gathered herself, registered the look of alarm in her mother's face. 'What do you mean? What do I know about what?'

'Take a guess, girlie.'

'I know he was shot and killed in a ruined old cottage in the woods the other side of Woodbridge.'

'Who by, and who's got the money?'

Juliette started to stand up, remembered she'd need the crutch, and sat down again. 'I have no idea. How could I? I was driving away when it happened.'

'Think.'

'He took about £700,000 out of family and business accounts. That was already being investigated by the police and the banks, and now the police are investigating his death, obviously.'

'You talked to him. What did he tell you?'

'Nothing. Personal stuff – to do with the family, the way he'd treated me, and my mother. And he'd tried to use our shop as a conduit for drug imports.'

'Slippery little bugger.' Click.

'That was him presumably.' Caroline was scraping at a few remaining bits of grapefruit flesh.

'Yeah, beat that for timing. Sounds as if it's come down to a question of money. Richard can't have had the money he took, otherwise he wouldn't have been living in that dump. Museum Street leaks like a sieve. He knows I talked to Richard.' Juliette reached for the crutch and stood up.

'One of his crooked deals must have gone wrong.'

The money. Maybe she should ask that woman about it, when she phoned her this afternoon. 'Mum, let's get back to normal. Starting now. Frampton's no danger to us, because there's nothing he can gain from harming or abducting any of us.' Juliette topped up her mug from the cafetière and added some milk. 'I've got a big favour to ask. The police are going to let me have my car back tomorrow. I've got a meeting with the web designer this morning – then the shop.'

Hauling herself upstairs she noticed that she was moving more easily. The pain was tolerable, and she had only taken one codeine that morning. In the bedroom she checked her phone. Just P7 in a text message. She looked at the rolltop desk, violated by the police only yesterday. No clue as to whether they had found the secret compartment.

After token resistance to Juliette driving with her injured leg, Caroline helped her put the children's seats in the back of the BMW. She dropped the children at the house of their usual babysitter, Karen, then drove to the mansion. No sign of a search. The rucksack was where she had left it. She picked out burner number 7. The decoding routine had become automatic. She entered the string of numbers in the template on the laptop and adjusted the time. 'Meet H 11.0. No shopping.' After wiping the burner and laptop, and putting them back in the rucksack, she sent a text to Lara: *Sorry can't do 11.00. How about 12.00. Early lunch.*

*

She reached the Tower Ramparts shopping centre and parked the BMW in the multi-storey. Getting about with the crutch wasn't too bad. She used it to take some of the weight off her right leg when walking. She could stand without using it, as long as she kept her weight distributed between both legs. She went into her favourite shop and bought a new pair of baggy jeans, putting the skirt she had been wearing in her bag. By five to eleven she was sitting on the bench in Christchurch Park, with her right leg resting on the crutch, keeping her foot about six inches off the ground. There had been rain overnight, giving the grass and trees a sharp freshness. There were clouds in the sky now, with some patches of blue allowing occasional bursts of sunshine. A woman with a child in a buggy passed along the footpath in front of her. Then another – no, this one was a girl, maybe a sister, or an au pair. Juliette noticed the rubber was missing off one of the front wheels of the buggy; the teenager was wearing a faded Sex Pistols T-shirt that was several sizes too big. Not an au pair. Someone wearing orange shorts and knee pads passed the other way on roller skates. Ordinary people, Juliette said to herself, trying to concentrate on what she needed to say to Tim.

Then he was sitting on the bench two feet away from her. 'My condolences,' he said. 'Fifteen minutes.' The usual rule: look straight ahead. Don't let a casual observer see they are communicating.

'Thank you. Do you know who did it?' she asked. She needed to make sure Tim didn't suspect her. The clouds parted, warming them with sunlight.

'That is a subject on which I was hoping you might elucidate. I hope the injury to your leg isn't causing too much trouble.'

'The people who dumped him. Who he was hiding from. They must have found him.'

'Our information seems to be at variance. He was the dumper, I can assure you, not the dumpee.'

'That doesn't make any sense.'

'He stole a lot of money. Money always makes sense. Do you have names?'

'The only one I know is John Frampton, the man he told me he was hiding from.'

'Who else?'

'He didn't mention anyone else. I've asked my mother. She doesn't know either.'

'Do you happen to know where the money is?'

'He must have lost it, or it's somewhere he couldn't get to it. He was desperate. Living in shit. He told me he'd invested three million in the import/export business, which they folded, and kept it.'

'And you believed him?'

'I don't know what to believe. Was I followed there? Is that how they found him?' A line she had practised, needing to sound innocent.

'We can only surmise. I take it our friends in blue didn't find our communications devices?'

'Off site, like you said. Safe. That's why I couldn't contact you yesterday.'

'Where?'

'You don't need to know. The police are taking a close look at me. We need to change the way we work.'

'The investigation into your father's death is more of a distraction for them. You're not under surveillance.'

So, he hides and watches me come into the park. I always thought so. 'You need to pay me more. Five per cent. It's worth fifteen.'

'Nonsense. The business practices I adopt make it a very good return. What I offer is unique. The risk mitigation techniques I use place me in a different category to other currency transfer operations.'

'Bollocks. I've been accepting five per cent because I take the long view. Now the risk's a lot higher. Dead men don't issue invoices.'

There were several seconds during which she could feel the thought processes going on in his head. 'My goodness, what a clever young lady you are. All our special transactions on a computer with an IP address traceable to your dear departed parent.'

'Something like that. I'm simply acting for him in banking the cash and paying the special suppliers. Now that he's gone, I've got to create a business partner of his, who's carrying on this business on the side. It's another layer that helps to protect you as well as me. Purchase invoices are processed on the shop computer, so they're not affected. They know me at the bank.' She was still looking straight ahead at the trees. 'In my world, your phoney customers are agents for American buyers who like to use cash for reasons we are not obliged to enquire into. Steve can't be told, because he's got a thing against European antiques going to the USA. That's the story if the police or HMRC ever ask questions. I've got to continue to be the innocent administrator of a legitimate business. Without my father, it's more complicated. More risk.'

'My business plan is based on a similar principle of compartmentalisation. A little more sophisticated, perhaps. I'm sure you could find someone offering a higher percentage, if you know where to look. You'd have to ask yourself if it was worth it. The greater the return, the greater the risk. Ask any investor.'

'Why don't we use WhatsApp – end-to-end encryption?'

'Time's up. Collection tomorrow. Will you be able to carry the bag with that leg?'

'I can always use a rucksack.'

Chapter 24

Juliette took a second to recognise Lara. She was sitting at an outside table – orange sleeveless top with Latitude in big black letters, denim cut-off shorts, flip-flops – but what threw Juliette to start with was the absence of glasses and the dark hair now swept back from her face. Lara half stood and they made an awkward attempt at a hug, partly obstructed by Juliette's crutch.

Juliette said, 'New look? I nearly didn't recognise you.'

'I'll take that as a compliment. I have a change every few weeks when I get bored. The contacts are new, though. How's your leg?'

'I need to put it up. It's throbbing a bit.' Juliette arranged her right leg on an extra chair, while Lara went in to order the salads and cold drinks. Juliette put her head back, eyes closed in the sun, breathed deeply trying to calm her leg after the walk.

When Lara came back, she put two tall glasses on the table, clinking with ice, and slid one over to Juliette. She said, 'Have you thought about my idea of a personal interest story? It wouldn't take long. I could record an interview at your house, write it up and get your approval.'

Juliette said, 'I think you'd be better off doing the investigative stuff. Speaking of which, what's the latest from your informant in Museum Street?'

'I can't imagine what it must have been like.'

'It keeps recurring in my head. The sight of him, I mean. The body, all that blood.'

'So, tell me everything.'

'It was horrible. You can print that if you like.' Juliette smiled.

'You're teasing me. I heard you got the wound trying to kick a knife out of his hand.'

'Any other suspects apart from Frampton?'

'They're still working on the brothel connection in Harwich. A Mr Love gets mentioned in the emails, a pseudonym probably; they don't think that's Frampton. Probably others, but I haven't got names. And technically you're still a suspect. Sorry about that.' Lara took a sip of Cola.

'What's it like at the paper? Starting your career. Trying to find a big story that'll make your name?'

'A bit frustrating. Being a crime reporter isn't that romantic. I'm still at the bottom of the pile, just a step up from weddings and car crashes. Trying to work my way up the greasy pole.'

'Did you go to people's houses? After a crash. Newly bereaved people, asked them how they felt?'

A waitress put a plate of salad in front of each of them, and cutlery wrapped in a paper napkin.

'We have to be very sensitive about that.'

'So can you try being sensitive now?' Juliette kept her voice low.

'Oh God. Sorry. No, it's not like that.' Lara put her glass down and looked at Juliette. 'That's not what I'm doing. I meant a story about what it's like being brought up by a professional criminal. Jules, please, I'm sorry if you thought I—'

'I'm still a bit raw.' She took a sip of sparkling mineral water, registering the anxious look on Lara's face. 'Can I make things clear? Eventually my father's killer is going to be caught, and at the trial a lot of information about my father, that we both know about, is going to come out. Can you imagine what that's going to be like for my mother? The truth is that they lived separate lives and she had no idea what he was doing. Nor did I. And my mum still doesn't know about the racket in Harwich. I don't want to lose clients, especially the schools I work with during termtime. We don't want anything printed that links us with my father's criminal activities. Surely you understand that?'

'So I'm wasting my time talking to you?'

'Not at all. I can help you.' Juliette tried to think of something she could tell Lara that would appear to be helpful. 'I told you about Vanessa Drysdale. I accept that it didn't come to anything, but I didn't know that at the time. Now, you've got the idea that somehow my mother is in league with Frampton. I can tell you, that is completely the opposite of the truth. At the time, thirty years ago, she was a recognised specialist in defending rape cases. It was a job she happened to be good at. She took the correct legal view that everyone is entitled to a fair trial, regardless of what they're accused of.'

'I want to be friends, but, like we agreed at the beginning, we need to share what we know. I tell you things, you tell me things, yeah?' There was silence for a while; both women sipped their drinks and nibbled at their salads.

Juliette was thinking of the two names: Kenneth Almer and Glynis Swanning. Should she take a risk and tell Lara? Maybe one of them?

'I like your jeans.' Lara broke the silence.

'I just bought them this morning. I need them loose like this because of my leg. Somehow I'm never comfortable in skirts.'

'It's amazing what they can do with fibres these days – the forensics people.'

Juliette swallowed some quinoa and grated beetroot. 'Go on.'

'Sorry, I was thinking you didn't want to talk about it. It's just that they think there must have been a fight.'

Fibres. Left at the scene? That could prove that she had been in a fight? 'Is this official or from your anonymous source?' She sounded as calm as she could.

'There are these fibres, too small to see with the naked eye. They think your father must have grabbed the other person's clothing. The team working on it had a briefing from the forensics guy. They think the left hand had been cleaned, but there were fibres under the right-hand fingernails – some kind of denim apparently, could be a jacket, or jeans. They're still doing the analysis to narrow it down. It's fascinating what they can do.'

Juliette's mind was on the contents of the wood-burner. Would it all have been destroyed?

'Do you get flashbacks?' Lara's voice.

'What?'

'Sorry, you were looking worried. Try to think about something else.'

'I was thinking about my children. They're at the

babysitter's. I need to pick them up soon. About the fibre, though, the cops aren't going to scour the countryside checking every piece of denim they see, so it's not really going to help in the search for the killer.'

'Detective work doesn't usually work like that. If they suspect someone, they gather evidence. What they'll need to get a conviction. Is there anything else you know that might help me build a story? I'll keep you and your mum out of it. Like any other names? I told you about the fibre.' Lara raised an eyebrow at Juliette, keeping it light. 'Your turn.'

'Look, Lara, if I knew anything like that I would have told you, just as I would have told the police. The sooner the killer is caught, the sooner I get eliminated as a suspect. That thing about the fibres. That's probably the sort of thing the police were looking for when they searched my house.' Juliette looked at her phone and checked the time. 'I've got to get to the shop. You know I do the book-keeping and a few other things that Steve hates and is rubbish at. I'm only just going to squeeze it in before collecting my kids, then I've got a flute lesson at my house at three-thirty. I've got to run, well, hobble.'

Juliette stood up, partly supporting herself with the crutch. When she was on her feet, she reached and held Lara for a few seconds. 'Keep in touch. Anything you find out. Can you send me a text straight away? It might jog my memory about something, and I'll be able to help you. Thanks for the lunch.'

'I'll text you,' Lara said. 'Bye for now, Jules.'

When Juliette reached the BMW in the multi-storey car park, she sat and tapped her phone. 'Steve, what's the banking like? Is there anything that can't wait till tomorrow?

The thing is, I really need to rest my leg. I'll be fine to collect the kids. My mum and I are taking them to the beach this afternoon. I could do with a couple of hours' rest at home before then.'

'The banking can wait, no problem. Are you sure you're okay to drive? I could pick you up and give you a lift. Roger could manage on his own for an hour.' She declined the offer, saying she was quite well enough to drive safely.

The bloody jeans. Fibres. Would they have burned completely? Any remaining fragments they could use to match? Why hadn't she checked before going to the hospital? Would they have searched in the wood-burner? All in good time. Next priority, while she was assured of privacy, was to phone the mystery woman and see if she could get any more out of her.

'Hello, this is Jules. I'm phoning back like we agreed.'

'Yes. I can meet you. I suggest 12.00 tomorrow in that big pub on Crown Street. Would that be suitable?' The same hoarse voice, sounding as if it were a line she had been practising.

A great barn of a place, plenty of people. Safe. 'The Spoons? I know the one. As you've agreed to meet, perhaps you could tell me your name?'

'Glynis, and please could you tell me your mobile phone number?'

They exchanged mobile numbers.

'How will I recognise you?' Juliette said.

'Table 22. It's near the middle. If it's occupied, I'll text you at 12.00.'

'You'll be on your own, won't you?'

'Just you and me – a private chat about your father.'

Juliette agreed, thinking she ought to do a risk assessment. Glynis had previously said she needed to talk to someone. So, she had been advised, or instructed, to arrange a meeting. Juliette could decide not to turn up if the risk outweighed the possible benefit.

*

When she got home, she opened the heavy front door as quietly as she could, and closed it behind her, turning the knob to minimise the sound. She did a quick tour of the downstairs and looked in the garden. Good. Her mother must be resting in her bedroom. She'd have to take a chance. She went straight to the wood-burner, propped herself awkwardly on the crutch as she bent to open the small door. Shit. No ash. It couldn't all have fallen through. She inserted the iron handle and pulled out the drawer at the bottom of the stove. Cleaned out. Jesus. They weren't just going through the motions, following procedure. They were really after her – that expression Lara had used, 'gathering evidence'. Even if all the denim had burned, the zip would have survived the fire, and the metal rivets – and buttons. Could they identify the manufacturer from those? Check the fabric they used? Match the fibres?

'Is that you, darling?' she heard from above. *Shit!*

'Hello, Mum. There's no need for you to come down. Sorry if I disturbed your rest. Why don't you stay up there for a while?' The metal drawer screeched as she pushed it back. She twisted. Trousered legs were appearing on the stairs. Too late.

'What are you doing with that? It's the middle of summer.'

'I thought I smelled something. Probably my imagination. I'm glad you're here. I just need to rest my leg a bit, before we go out.'

'One of the police officers cleaned out the ash and put it in a bag. I don't know what they expected to find.'

'It must have been ash from last winter.' *If only.*

'I'll put the kettle on. I told you, you shouldn't be driving. You should be relaxing, giving that horrible wound time to heal. How did you get on with the web designer?'

'Fine. We had a long chat. She's going to put together some ideas. Steve didn't need me at the shop, so we had a quick lunch and I had time to buy these jeans.'

Juliette glanced through the kitchen door and saw Caroline quickly putting a wine glass in the dishwasher. A few minutes later she was sitting back with her leg up on a pouffe. Her mother came into the sitting room with two steaming mugs.

'Just one day,' Caroline said. 'Somehow it feels as if he's been dead a lot longer. It's in the paper, and on the radio. Richard's murder. Police appeal for information and so on. They describe him as a businessman.'

'I'll be avoiding the news for a while.'

'They'll be digging for dirt, the media. It won't be long before they track me down. Expect me to play the part of the grieving widow. I'll just ask them to respect my privacy at this sad time. Act all innocent about what a vicious little shit he was.'

Juliette stirred milk into her tea. 'Does the name Glynis Swanning mean anything to you?'

'I don't think so, why?'

'Probably nothing. It popped into my mind. Richard

mentioned her a while ago. I think she worked for him at one point. I'm sure it's nothing. Forget it.'

A few minutes passed before Caroline said, 'I wish I hadn't been so frightened of him.'

Juliette picked up a biscuit. 'You don't have to be, now.'

Caroline closed her eyes. 'I told you how bloody good I was at defending rape cases. It sort of became my specialism. It seems impossible now. The culture was so different then. I've wanted to talk to you about it, get it off my chest; then the shame kicks in, and guilt, I suppose. There weren't that many female barristers in the seventies – even the eighties. I just got drawn into defending rape cases, because it was felt that having a man cross-examining the witness ran the risk of making the jury sympathise with her.'

'For witness read victim?'

'Nearly always. I could tie them in knots. Get the jury to believe they led the man on, then felt bad afterwards and decided to cry rape. I still can't forgive myself.'

'All the work you've done helping rape survivors. You've more than made up for it.'

'The culture was different then. At least society's moved on.'

'Not enough.'

'At the beginning, I was pleased to get Richard's approval. I was blind. I saw myself upholding the law, giving men the legal defence they were entitled to. It took me a while to see that Richard saw what I was doing as some sort of moral crusade on behalf of men to exert power over women. I realise now, I've hated him for twenty-five years. Hated what he became.'

'And now he's gone.'

'So it's too late. I can't challenge him, tell him what I think.' Caroline drained the last of her tea.

Juliette shifted her leg off the pouffe. It started throbbing. She said, 'Time to go. Jazzy and Lulu are at Karen's. It's on the way. You can drive.'

Chapter 25

The next day, Juliette looked at the other customers as she entered the pub. The collection with Tim had seemed normal. She had come into town with Steve and had picked up her car at the police station. They had returned her shoulder bag. There were what looked like acid marks on part of it. No explanation had been offered. The carrier bag with the cash was in the boot of her car.

She walked past a couple of families with young children having an early lunch. A man with a shaved head, sitting alone with a pint of lager, looked at her. She caught his eye and looked away quickly. There were a few solitary old men looking into their pints at the smaller tables. A man with dark hair and glasses looked up from his newspaper. She felt him examining her, but forced herself not to look at him. Just men looking at her, she tried to tell herself, like they often did. She still used the crutch, but her leg could take more weight now without causing undue pain. At this rate of progress, she might be able to dispense with the crutch in a few more days. She checked her phone – ten minutes early, just as she had planned.

She walked towards the middle of the pub slowly, exaggerating her limp. There was a low partition breaking up the space. In front of it, a woman was at a table for four, sitting alone in the corner of the partition, on a bench seat, turning to face her, watching her progress. She looked about fifty, dark hair with visible grey roots, thin eyebrows, dark but delicate eye makeup that you would expect on a younger woman, sensible lipstick, a natural red. Her pale face was thin, but slightly puffy, a probable legacy of too many cigarettes and too much booze. She saw Juliette and raised a hand with a hint of a smile.

'Hello, I'm guessing you're Glynis.'

'That's right. Keep your voice down, please. Have a seat. You're early.' The woman had a worn-out voice that went with her face. There was a large glass of white wine in front of her.

'Not as early as you.' Juliette put her shoulder bag on the chair opposite the woman and propped the crutch against it. She sat on the chair next to it.

'I came early to secure the table. Condolences in regard to your father. Can I get you a drink?'

'Something soft, please. Elderflower pressé if they've got it.'

When Glynis returned with the drink, Juliette said, 'Thanks. Can you tell me how you knew my father?'

'That's of no importance. How did you get my number?'

Juliette was ready for this. 'He'd written it in a notepad on his desk. I've been trying to contact everyone he knew.'

'To tell them he's dead?'

'Yes.' Juliette had planned this part of the conversation too. 'There's another reason. He took a lot of money from my mother.'

Glynis seemed to be thinking how to respond to this. She sipped her wine, then said, 'So you're phoning round to see who's got this money?'

'Or any ideas where it might be. I'm still a suspect. Any information that might lead to my father's killer would get the cops off my back.'

'So you want to know if I topped 'im?'

'Of course not. It's just that you might know something, or someone – anything that might help, even if you don't know it would.'

'I don't know nothing.'

Juliette leaned forward. 'Can I ask why you agreed to meet me?'

'Let's just say I've got a personal interest in finding out who did it. You have too, haven't you? The cops won't do much, just another villain out of the way, far as they're concerned.'

Juliette wished that were true. 'Is it to do with money? Did he owe you?'

'He owed me more than money. If we know what happened to the money he took, we'll know who topped him most likely.' A shadow passed across Glynis's face.

Juliette wanted to know how closely Glynis was connected to Richard's criminal friends, but decided a direct question would be counterproductive. 'Are you sure it's safe? We could be dealing with ruthless criminals.'

'I just want to know what you know.' An aggressive look came into her eyes. 'We know you was working with him. Still are – in his business. You should know what he did with the money.' Glynis raised the wine glass to her lips without taking her eyes off Juliette.

'His removals firm worked with our antiques shop. Deliveries, transport, that's all.' Juliette wanted to shift the focus of the conversation. 'You invited me here. It's a sensible place. Open, light, plenty of witnesses to make it safe, and no music so we can hear ourselves speak. Obviously, I'm curious. Can you tell me how well you knew my father? How long you've known him.' Juliette took a sip of her drink.

'I wouldn't want to be friends with a bloke like that.' Glynis took a sip of wine, as if mirroring Juliette, then dabbed her lips with a paper napkin.

'He had enemies. Were you one of them?'

'Like to see things black and white, do you? Friends and enemies. We know you work in the business. Up to your neck in it, aren't you.' Glynis's voice had risen in volume, but not in pitch. It wasn't a question.

Juliette looked around at the nearest tables. A woman with two young children, stuffing themselves with chips covered in ketchup. An old man who could be asleep, a pint glass with an inch or so of lager in front of him. 'Your turn to keep your voice down. I only worked with him in connection with our antique business. He was very secretive about everything else.'

'You know more than you're trying to make out.' Glynis had lowered her voice again.

'You're not telling me what you know.'

'Done in by his associates, or at least one of them. That's what we think.'

'That's the third time you've said "we". How many of you are there?'

'I've got a friend. It don't matter. It's just me that wants to know.'

'But you've come here on your own?'

'Yes.'

Juliette took another sip of elderflower. 'It would be helpful if you told me why you're so eager to find out who did it.'

'Personal reasons.'

'I think you're an undercover reporter, just out for a story.' She knew this wasn't true, but thought it might provoke Glynis into saying more.

'Nothing of the sort.' Glynis gulped at her wine, dabbed her lips again, leaving a plum-coloured smudge on the napkin.

Juliette took another sip of her drink, waiting to see if Glynis wanted to say more.

Glynis half rose from the bench, then sat back. 'Have you thought what them poor girls go through?'

Juliette looked into the woman's dark eyes. Was that it? Did this woman think that she, Jules, was involved in the brothel? 'I didn't know anything about that till last week. It came as a shock.'

'I want justice. You was helping him.'

Juliette wanted to calm things down and get this woman to trust her. She obviously knew more about Richard. 'When my father disappeared a couple of weeks ago, he took a lot of money, as you know. I have no idea where it is. The police have been all over us. They are saying he was involved in trafficking girls and forcing them into prostitution. I believe the removals firm is basically legit. There might be a bit of pilfering – strictly small-scale. My father used it to try to import some drugs. That was a shock too. I had no idea he'd do anything like that. He was extremely secretive. I didn't have access to any of his records, or communications, or to the people he worked with. That's all I know.' Juliette was aware that her voice was becoming unsteady now, but managed to continue, maintaining eye contact with Glynis. 'I didn't know about the brothel in Harwich till after it was raided. If I had done, I would have reported it to the police and got it stopped.'

Glynis, eyes brimming, said, 'Remember the prostitute murders?'

Juliette said, 'Of course,' before the shock hit her. The conversation with Lara. Brothel moved from Ipswich to Harwich eleven years ago. Everyone in and near Ipswich, who was old enough, remembered. Her thoughts were tumbling. 'I was a teenager. It must be at least ten years ago. Why did you mention that?'

Glynis looked at her. A tear ran down one cheek. 'Seems a lot you don't know.' Her voice was cracking. She wiped her eyes with the paper napkin, smudging mascara.

'I'm sorry you're upset. I'm being completely honest with you. Do you want to tell me the connection?'

A group of men in suits were seating themselves in the booth behind Glynis. She said in a hoarse whisper, 'We'll talk again.' She got up and left, leaving Juliette sitting there. She remained staring at the partition in front of her, without seeing it, then turned to make sure the woman left the pub. She saw her give a slight nod to a short, olive-skinned man with greasy black hair tied in a ponytail, who had been sitting at a table on the other side of the room, and saw the man nod in return and follow her out of the door.

Juliette finished her drink slowly, trying to think. Glynis had lied about being alone. It seemed as if she had been put forward; her chubby friend with the ponytail might have been sent to keep an eye on things. There could be a whole gang of them. The Ipswich prostitute murders. The Suffolk Strangler. 2006. Five women in a couple of months. What the hell was that about? Was Glynis on some kind of crusade to avenge the women who had been killed? Her mother had said Richard had been in the Far East at the time. Was it really possible that he'd had something to do with that? Juliette pushed herself up from the chair and hobbled laboriously, in case they were watching her, out of the pub and to her car. The walk helped. She could move at something like normal speed, punting herself along with the crutch.

*

She got her breath back sitting in her car. Was Glynis a mad woman trying to rid the world of all pimps and people traffickers? Had she threatened Richard, thus getting herself on his list? If she had called him using her landline, it could explain how he got that number. These questions would have to wait. The next priority was Lara.

She tapped her phone. 'Hi, Lara, this is Jules. How are things? Any news?'

'I was just about to phone you.' Lara had lowered her voice to a conspiratorial semi-whisper. 'I'm pissed off with the editor here. He's spiking every fucking thing I write. I don't think I'm cut out for this job. Anyway, what have you got for me?'

'I wish. Nothing new, I'm afraid. Your contact in the police is a more likely source. That was really interesting what you told me about the fibres. I was wondering if there have been any more developments on that?'

'Nope. Lots of stuff on ballistics, blood spatter analysis, fingerprints, DNA, you name it. They're putting together a detailed picture of exactly what happened in that cottage.'

The face was in front of her. Up close, the piece of bone and blood flying off.

'Jules?'

Juliette gripped the phone. 'Signal broke up. You've got details?'

'You haven't given me anything, Jules.'

'I would if I could.'

'Have you thought more about the personal interest story?'

'You know I can't. People trust me with their children.'

'You'd be able to approve the copy before I submitted it.'

'People would make their own assumptions. It wouldn't matter if you included a glowing character reference for me. And it would ruin my mother's reputation.'

'When they catch the killer, you'll be called as a witness at the trial. You can't help being linked. People will know it's not your fault.'

'You'll be able to write about it when that happens.' She heard Lara let out a breath.

'Stay in touch, yeah? I can't change the system. You give me something and I'll give you something, and I'm not talking about money.'

'Bye for now, Lara.' Juliette cut the call. She needed to stop worrying about the fibres. A risk locked in place, as Tim would say. She needed to think more positively about any risks she could mitigate. Anything she could still do to cover her tracks. And was there now a more serious threat? Glynis wasn't acting alone. If she, and whoever was with her, were serious about finding out who killed Richard, they might just succeed. They could be a lot more dangerous than the police. They weren't tied by the legal system.

She tried to dispel all this from her mind as she drove to the shop, concentrating on the banking, including the bag of cash in the boot.

*

She arrived home with the children, after picking them up at Karen's house. Her mother's car wasn't there. After settling Jazzy and Lulu in front of the television, she started to relax. Her phone beeped – incoming text. *P9*. Christ. The ultimate emergency phone, the one Tim called the nuclear option.

'Hey, you two!' She went into the sitting room. 'We're going to have an adventure – explore in the mansion, see if you can find some treasure.' She gathered Lucy up. Jason followed her with a puzzled expression.

Twenty minutes later they were at the mansion. 'We're not going in the house. See if you can find a rabbit in the garden.' She went into the garage and reached under the bench. She put a battery in phone 9, booted up the laptop. Inserted the string of numbers into the template. The usual absurd routine. Eventually she got this: MUST TERMINATE CAN UDO ONE LAST LOT ONE ZERO FIVE K THURSDAY MIDDAY DELAY TOO DANGEROUS. Shit. End of the money-laundering business. She thumped her fist on the workbench. The last word, 'dangerous'. Was it dangerous anyway? Even with no delay? And they would have to cope with the loss of income. How could they? And how would she explain it to Steve? Still, £105,000 in one lot to end it was better than nothing. *See what I can squeeze out of the old bugger.* She wrote the message: *OK risk so high return fifteen per cent required*, and typed the individual letters into the cells of the spreadsheet, used the coding process to produce the string of numbers to send to Tim.

She went into the garden with the burner in her hand. Lucy saw her and came trotting across the lawn. Juliette scooped her up. Jason was peering into some shrubs in the border. The burner vibrated. 'Let's go and look in the garage,' she said to Lucy.

With the sleepy child on her lap, she keyed the numbers from the burner into the laptop and decoded them to: *Ten per cent maximum. I am emigrating Thurs pm.*

A hundred and five thousand pounds. Tim emigrating. Sounded as if he was going into hiding. Knowing him, he would have had an escape route planned for years. How dangerous would it be for her? If Tim was quitting because the police were getting close to his dodgy operation, she would just have to brazen it out with her story. They wouldn't be able to establish a link between the money laundering and Richard's death, because there wasn't one. But – the big but – supposing Tim had fallen out with the people whose money he was handling, and was running for his life... She didn't let her thoughts go any further. She'd assess the risk later and decide whether or not to turn up at the appointed time in the park.

What would happen if she kept all the money? Ignored the special supplier's invoice. The idea was dismissed as soon as it occurred to her. She was in enough danger already. She encoded *Accept ten pc* and sent it. £10,500 would tide them over for a while.

'Are you coming to play, Mummy?' Jason was silhouetted in the garage entrance.

'Any rabbits?'

'No.'

'Let's go home, then.'

Chapter 26

Juliette was sitting up on the bed. Caroline had insisted on cooking the supper so that Juliette could rest her leg. She had relived it so many times, that last second. That moment when he had stopped trying to get the knife out of the floor and had loosened his grip on her ankle. The scratch on his cheek from the splinter of wood, the look on his face that she couldn't read – was it a grimace from the physical pain, or a snarl of anger? And that last gesture – did he nod, or was he just losing strength from the wounds, the loss of blood, letting his head drop? And in that instant, she had no choice but to pull the trigger. But he was already helpless. She could have wriggled away from him, driven off and phoned for an ambulance as soon as she could get a signal. The story would have been easier than the one she was stuck with now. He was drunk and threatened her. She fired the gun into the table to warn him, not meaning to hit him, then just had to defend herself. Ziggy jumped up and butted Juliette's hip before climbing onto her lap.

'You don't think I'm a bad person, do you, Zig? It could make anyone bad, that's what my mum said. Neglect and abuse could make anyone bad. I don't think being raped could be the same. Who knows? It could explain why I feel so shit now. Don't know anything about love, do you, Zig. Or affection. It's all about sensual pleasure for you.' Ziggy set up the purring and rolled over to get the chest and belly treatment. Juliette stroked her gently then lay back, her head on the pillows, her hand still on Ziggy's chest, feeling the vibrations.

How dangerous would it be? Going to the park to collect £105,000. If Tim was running from the police, she could handle it. The worst that could happen would be that she'd be charged with tax evasion, something like that. If it was a bunch of criminals? Tim was so risk-averse that he'd take steps to avoid being followed into the park. If they knew he had that much money, surely they'd find a way of getting it off him before he got near the park where there would be a lot of witnesses. Would they wait for her to have the money, as she'd be an easier target? But they couldn't know about her. They wouldn't know where he was taking the money. Surely. So the risk was high impact but low likelihood. Worth it for ten grand. She'd go.

Tim would have done his risk assessments. He'd know she couldn't try to cheat him by keeping the money. She couldn't take it all to the bank in one go, though. She'd need to keep close to the existing pattern so as not to trigger some alarm bells. That would mean paying his invoice in instalments. She'd explain that when she saw him in the park. Could Tim's emergency be connected to the recent appearance of Glynis? Surely not. Juliette sat up.

'Come on, Zig, time for your supper. What's that bloody woman going to do? Think she's dangerous? Ironic twist of fate as per usual. I'm beginning to think I'm in the clear with the cops, then next minute there's a posse of fucking vigilantes on my arse. You don't have to look quite so relaxed about it.'

*

The creature was clawing at her ankles, slicing into her legs as it dragged itself towards her, its black eyes leering, its barbed tongue flicking from smiling bloody lips, the claws stabbing her thighs apart and the tongue thrusting into her, ripping the sides of her vagina. She recognised the scream as her own as she hurled the duvet away and was shocked to see no blood. Steve's voice: 'Just a dream, Jules. Just a bad dream. It's natural after what you've been through. I'm here. You're safe now.'

Natural. Only natural. Safe. *Oh good. Steve'll keep us all safe. That's all right then. Problem solved.*

*

Juliette and Caroline were sitting opposite each other at the kitchen table. Steve had left for the shop. The sound of a children's cartoon was audible from the sitting room. The calming aroma of coffee hung in the air. Juliette was eating an organic granola with zero-fat Greek yoghurt and soya milk. Caroline was eating toast and marmalade, and saying, 'Darling, it's perfectly natural after an experience like that. You're going to have mood swings and flashbacks. You just have to be patient. Time will heal. Do you think it might help if you saw someone?'

Juliette looked up. Her mother was smiling. *Focus on that*, she forced herself to think. *Get rid of the image of the man's face, the messy hole, the piece of it flying off, the red spray.* She put another spoonful of cereal in her mouth and looked at her mother. 'Mum, I'm so sorry. I keep thinking of me. I want to get back into my routine. I think that'd be best for me. I've got lessons most of the day, ones I had to cancel last week. I'll probably want to rest a bit this afternoon, with my leg.'

'Jazzy loved Jimmy's Farm the last time we went. Don't you think Lulu's ready for that now? I could take them – give you a break. I'm so glad you're getting more mobile now.'

'Jimmy's Farm's a great idea.' Juliette was registering the happy look on her mother's face when her mobile, on the table beside her, emitted its jingle. She looked at the screen – new number. Might be Tim. 'Sorry, I need to take this.' She grabbed the phone, made for the door and the stairs.

'Hello.'

'Am I speaking to Mrs Walker? Mrs Juliette Walker?' A man's voice – quite a strong accent that reminded her of childhood family holidays in Malta.

'Who is that?'

'I think that must be Mrs Walker. Please forgive my intrusion when you are no doubt at this hour in the bosom of your family. I wish to invite you to join me for afternoon tea this afternoon at the Holiday Inn on the London Road, where I am currently staying. Ah, forgive me, I omitted to introduce myself. My name is Alfie – Alfie Smith. Shall we say four o'clock?'

'It's very short notice and extremely inconvenient for me, Mr, er, Smith. And yes, this is Juliette Walker. People call me Jules.'

'Then let us be friends, Jules. Please call me Alfie. I'm sure we will get along famously, when we get to know each other.'

'Why do we want to get to know each other?'

'Let us say, I was an acquaintance of your late father. Sadly, the word friend would not be appropriate in this connection, but I am, of course, sorry for your loss. You met a colleague of mine in a public house yesterday. Alas, she can be a bit difficult. I understand you two did not hit it off too well. However, there are matters of mutual interest emanating from your father's sad demise. I give you my assurance as a gentleman that neither I nor my colleague want anything that is not legitimately ours. My colleague has had a sad life, tragic even, as a result of actions taken by your father and his associates. I understand she regrettably allowed some of the bitterness she feels towards your late father to devolve on to you in person. I can assure you on my honour as a member of the Order of Saint Lazarus, that we are simple seekers of truth and justice, nothing more. So you will join me for tea this afternoon, won't you, dear Jules.'

She had to think quickly. Better accept now and assess the risk before going there. 'Well, if you put it that way, how could I refuse such an offer? The lounge, presumably, four o'clock.'

'Excellent. I have to return to London this evening, and then to my home country tomorrow morning, so take care not to be late. I look forward to meeting you so much.'

'Likewise,' Juliette said as she ended the call. *What's it all about, you pompous fart?* Was this smarmy git the swarthy little creep with the ponytail she had glimpsed in the pub? Probably. She tapped her phone to get the number of the Holiday Inn.

'Hello, Reception? Yes, may I speak to Mr Smith, please, Mr Alfred Smith, one of your residents.'

After a few seconds the receptionist replied, 'I'm sorry, there is no one by that name staying here currently.'

'Thank you, I must be mistaken.' She cut the call.

She opened the recent calls screen on her phone and tapped the mobile number that called earlier.

'Hello, my dear Jules, I trust there is nothing amiss.' The Maltese accent.

'Just that you are not staying at the Holiday Inn.'

'Oh, I assure you… Ah, I can visualise what has happened. You didn't want to entrust yourself to a man you do not know, so you made enquiries at the Holiday Inn. Am I right?'

'You sound like some kind of petty crook. Were you mixed up with my father in his disgusting activities?'

'Oh, perish the thought. But I should explain the unfortunate misunderstanding that has arisen over my name. My formal name, not the one I generally use, is Alfred Borg. I am a frequent visitor to your country and gain great enjoyment from your language and culture. It is for this reason that I adopted a popular English surname, by which I am generally known. When I first booked into the Holiday Inn, many years ago, of course they needed to see my passport, which bears the name I have almost forgotten myself, Borg. Not a pretty name; not one I am proud of; an accident of birth such a long time ago. So I hope you will forgive this confusion, dear Jules, and cast aside your misgivings. I assure you I am quite above board.'

When Juliette came back into the kitchen, her mother was still sitting, drinking coffee. Juliette was devising a reason for being out longer than she had previously said.

After confirming that Alfred Borg was indeed staying at the Holiday Inn, she had decided to chance it. 'Mum, that was a great idea you had about Jimmy's. That was an old friend from school. Isabel Sumner – do you remember her? She lives in France, but her husband has just left her. Having a bit of a crisis. She wants me to meet her for tea. It won't be much fun, but she sounds as if she needs cheering up. It might be ages before I get another chance to see her. She's at the Holiday Inn. I can go straight there after Abigail. She's the very talented one doing Grade 8 flute. Then we'll think of something else to do together on Sunday when Steve's free. How about Colchester Zoo? Although you know my feelings about caged animals.'

'My goodness. What did I say about mood swings? It's probably good for you to keep busy, and I'm so glad you'll be seeing a friend.'

'Have a lovely time at the farm. Take some photos of the kids with the animals. Tell me all about it this evening. By the look of the weather, you'll all need anoraks and wellies.'

*

Alone at last, she went up to the main bedroom and looked vacantly across the lawn towards the trees and the shed, trying to convince herself that she was doing the right thing, going to the Holiday Inn. It should be safe, as long as she took a few precautions. Glynis probably wasn't much of a danger on her own. So-called Alfie – so slippery, so pompous, so fake – had given some level of reassurance. She certainly wasn't going to trust him, but she needed to find out how much he knew. He had wanted to give the impression that he and Glynis worked together. If they really were intent on finding Richard's killer, she'd need to find a way of leading them astray. How safe was it? She understood Tim's obsession with risk management now. Easy for him, on his own, to have an escape plan.

The gun and Psycho knife should be safe buried in the copse for another few days. She had used the knife to dig the hole, taken care to wipe any fingerprints. The laptop and burners, also carefully wiped, would be redundant. She might leave the rucksack sticking out under the bench for the gardeners to find. They'd be sure to report it. She'd need to dispose of the gun. And the bullets. Soon.

She'd need to hide the cash in the rolltop desk, take it to the bank in instalments. Tim would have done his risk assessment and decided to quit and emigrate well before there was any real danger to him. It was true, what she had said to her mum. She wanted to get back into her routine. There were just these two things that had to be done first: a massive cash collection and a visit to the Holiday Inn.

She looked through the bars of the side window towards the Oakwoods' house. There was no sign of danger. She could do what she liked, behave in any way she wanted. They would say it's normal. Give it time. Don't worry. *Perhaps you should see someone.* Strange assignation in the Holiday Inn. What could be more normal?

Ziggy came into the room announcing her entrance with the usual squawk and rubbed herself against Juliette's calves. 'Careful with that one, Zig. It's still a bit sore. Big collection coming up. Wonder if Tim'll say anything. "I've never seen that much money before, you natural born killer."' Ziggy jumped onto the bed and Juliette sat beside her, stroking. 'Think you're in control, don't you, Zig. Control of your life. Relative autonomy is what I'd call it. You're stuck with us because you need to know where the next meal's coming from, where you'll find somewhere comfy to sleep, or a lap to curl up on when you feel like it. You're just as stuck as I am. Life without Steve and Jazzy and Lulu just wouldn't be worth living. That's what it comes down to.'

She dragged herself away from the cat, walked through to the music room and sat at the grand piano. She thought about phoning DS Cartwright and telling him to go to the Holiday Inn at four o'clock to arrest a greasy-looking foreigner in connection with her father's murder. Would that make it safe? No. It was a stupid idea, and she soon dismissed it. There was nothing to charge him with, and there was a risk that he might really know something about the murder.

Steve's score for his part in *Lucia* was on the music stand. Lucia – the woman who went mad and committed murder. She had promised to help him rehearse again this evening. 'I am not mad, I am not mad,' she repeated to herself as she sat on the piano stool. She played the first few bars of Liszt's '*Liebestraum*', willing herself to focus on the images of Steve, Jazzy and Lulu. *Love-dream.* Hang on to that. Don't let go. She tried, tried so hard, but her hands clenched into fists and crashed down on the keys, as their beautiful house, filled with so much love, morphed into that dark, squalid hovel in the wood. The shattered, bloody face, and now the glutinous monster that had started intruding into her dreams. All because she had taken a life? She looked at her phone – time to drive to town.

She wished she had gone to the farm with her mum and the children, wanted to hold them. She opened her phone and tapped the top number.

'Steve.'

'Shop's quite busy. How are things with you?'

'I love you.'

'I know.'

'Han Solo got turned into a slab of stuff for saying that.'

'I think you're mixing up the order of causation.'

'I'm meeting a friend. I'll probably get home after you. Can you help my mum with the children's supper?'

'Yeah, no problem.'

'It was a *post hoc ergo propter hoc*, Han Solo, and I still love you.'

'I love you too, smart arse. Always will.'

*

Driving the familiar route into town, she started thinking, there must be a way of convincing Glynis and the smarmy creep that she didn't have the money that her father had taken and didn't know anything about his crooked schemes that she hadn't already told Glynis about. She didn't buy their bad crook, good crook act. Was it revenge they were after, or just the money? Now focus – first task is to buy a shopping trolley in the department store, quite a sturdy one for all that cash.

Chapter 27

Juliette walked up the pavement from the shopping centre to Christchurch Park, the hood of her navy blue anorak over her head. Rain fell steadily. She pushed a dark red shopping trolley with four wheels, which she had just bought in the town centre. It gave her leg as much support as she needed, so she had lain the crutch across the top of it while she walked. She had decided four large Sainsbury's carrier bags would be sufficient, and these were in the trolley, loaded with, in addition to the usual boxes of tissues, a bottle of moderate Mumm champagne at £44.99 and a box of Belgian chocolates, as farewell gifts to Tim. Random acts of kindness – hoping they might be repaid in some karmic justice system.

There were fewer than usual people in the park, deterred, no doubt, by the unfriendly weather. At least she didn't have to walk too far – the third bench up from the Soane Street entrance. She took out the *Daily Telegraph* that she had also bought for Tim, assuming it would be to his taste, placed it on the wet bench and sat on it. Tim would have to manage without it. She checked her phone – no messages, five to twelve. She was glad she had allowed plenty of time. A pair of magpies flew into the chestnut tree opposite her bench. She wondered if it was really true that they decorated their nests with shiny material – discarded sweet wrappers, bits of aluminium foil. She looked at the church tower just visible behind the tree. Tried to imagine what the church would be like inside.

A small person wheeled a child's buggy with the clear plastic rain cover all clouded up. Juliette looked at the front wheels. They were both in good order. It wasn't the same one as before. She wanted to check the time, but resisted it. He would be here soon. He had never been late before. Her jeans were getting wet. She hoped the water would not drip down her leg and soak through the dressing. She was due to have it looked at by the nurse the next day. It was only for a check-up. The stitches would dissolve. She unzipped her bag and took the phone out – 12.07. He must have been delayed by the weather. She stood up, took the sports section out of the newspaper, sat down again, put the sheets of newspaper over her knees. The rain seemed to be easing slightly. The newspaper was absorbing it slowly.

She started thinking about the story of Eeyore's birthday, which she had read to the children the night before. It was Jazzy's favourite story. He was always convulsed with laughter when Eeyore was happy with the burst balloon in the empty honey pot. Was Eeyore a depressive, or a wise observer of the human condition? An adult on a yellow BMX bike that was too small for him, or her, hurtled past on the path from left to right. She checked her phone again – 12.21. What could have happened to him? Should she send a text? He'd go ballistic if she texted from her iPhone, and she hadn't brought a burner with her. She steered her mind back to Eeyore. Probably a wise observer, but not one you'd want to spend too much time with.

Did the rule apply? The twenty-minute rule that said if either of them were twenty minutes or more late for a collection the other should leave and await further communication. She gripped the handle of the trolley. Tim. What could have happened? She tried to think through the possibilities. For whatever reason, he had decided to leave early, with all the money. If that was the case, surely he would have at least sent a P number to her iPhone to indicate an explanation on one of the burners.

She looked in the chestnut tree and saw that the magpies had gone. She looked at her phone again. Half an hour late. He wasn't coming. Something had happened to him. The rain stopped as she walked back to the shopping centre.

Sitting in the Peugeot, having dumped the trolley in the boot without unloading it, she sat in the driver's seat and hurt her hands thumping the steering wheel. Her world had collapsed. No extra income from the money laundry, and no ten grand to cushion the drop. She flexed her left hand and rubbed it on her thigh, switched the phone to it and did the same with her right hand. She tried to think about what might have happened to Tim. He might have been arrested. The HMRC might have caught up with him for whatever tax fiddle it was. He might give them her name. Risk mitigation he would call it, getting a shorter sentence. She'd have her story ready. Or he had fallen foul of more serious criminals. But they would have no interest in coming after her. Surely. She felt a strange affection for him, in spite of his meanness.

She braced herself, took a deep breath, counted to ten, took out her phone and called her mum. All was well at the farm. The rain had stopped there too.

Then she thought about Tim again. He wasn't so bad really, the ace risk manager. Not someone who would ever resort to violence. Someone you could like, if you met him socially, once you had broken through the façade of public-school manners. She looked at her phone to check if there was a text she had missed. Nothing.

Three hours till she had to be at the Holiday Inn. She would go home, as planned, but without the trolley full of cash. Now she could spend some time with Ziggy, if she was around. Quick shower, change into dry, smarter clothes, a quick snack from the fridge. If she hurried, she could drive up to the copse and get the gun, ready to defend herself if Alfie proved to be dangerous. She turned the driving mirror to look at herself. *Any more crazy ideas? Shoot-out in the Holiday Inn. The cops'd love that.* Ever since that night, the night three years ago, she had hated not being in control. She stared at the strange eyes in the mirror and saw tears forming. 'I didn't mean this to happen,' she hissed.

The rape had been abstract knowledge until a few nights ago, when she had forced herself to remember. Now, sitting in her car, still looking into the eyes in the mirror, she started imagining the parts of it that must have happened while she was unconscious. Richard, the father she had once had, pushing her legs apart, on top of her, thrusting, pumping his fluid into her. The tears came and with them the image of his face as she destroyed it. In convulsions she scrabbled for a tissue out of her bag.

A man's voice through the open car window. 'Are you all right, miss? Can I help?'

'Thank you,' she managed. 'I'm just upset. I'll be fine.' After a second she looked. A man was walking away, holding a child's hand. She looked in the driving mirror again and whispered, 'You're a murderer. You know that?' She closed her eyes. Being raped, killing the rapist, the image of the face, nightmares, now Tim disappearing and God knows what happening to him. And soon going to meet these dreadful people in the Holiday Inn. She took out her phone to call Alfie and cancel the meeting. She could drive straight to Jimmy's Farm to join her mum and the kids, tell her that Isabel hadn't wanted to meet after all. Her finger hovered. Dangerous to go to the Holiday Inn and possibly dangerous not to, if Alfie and Glynis knew something she needed to know. She'd decide when she got home. She wiped her eyes, blew her nose, corrected the mirror and started the engine.

*

Back in the house, she looked in the usual places for Ziggy, but she wasn't there. Perhaps she was out hunting, looking for some small creature to play with till it died of its wounds. She sat in the kitchen, listing the options in her head. She decided to go, then tried to focus on mitigating the risk. She sent a text to Steve: *The friend I'm meeting. She's a bit distressed. If I'm not home by six-thirty, could you come over to the Holiday Inn? I might need to be rescued. J XX.* She hoped she'd pitched it right so as not to cause a false alarm, but to let him know where to start looking in case it all went wrong.

*

At about a quarter to four, crutch on left arm, bag on right shoulder, she walked up to the reception desk. 'Good afternoon. I've come to meet one of your residents, Mr Borg.'

The well-groomed young man smiled. 'I think he's in his room. He has a guest already. Shall I call him?'

'There's no need. He's going to meet me down here. Could you tell me which room he's in?'

The man looked puzzled for a second, presumably wondering why she wanted to know the room number. She gave him her best smile and he decided to comply. 'He's in room 211. I'd be happy to call him for you.'

'Please don't. I'll wait down here. He's expecting me, but I'm early.' There was a scattering of people in the lounge. She chose a table in a corner away from the reception desk – a low table with three cream-coloured easy chairs. She sat in the one in the corner, facing into the room, propping the crutch against an ancient oak beam that formed part of an open screen constructed with similar beams across the otherwise clear space. Creating a sense of cosiness – something old and familiar. But fake. She hated fake things nearly as much as Steve did. The afternoon sun was slanting through the large windows from her left. The chair breathed out as she sank into it, and she tried to guess whether it was real leather or a good imitation. On the table, there were the day's *Financial Times*, an *Economist* and the current *Elle* magazine. She chose *Elle* and tried to look calm. She was wearing plum-coloured flared trousers, quite cool, and which fitted over the dressing, her wedge-heeled sandals and a light blue silk blouse, her dark shaggy hair hanging nearly to her shoulders. *Not too bad*, she smiled inwardly, comparing herself to the images in the magazine. She took out her phone and checked her emails. There was one from an address she didn't recognise.

It had an invoice attached, 106,000 euros, from what looked like an antique shop in Barcelona. Poor old Tim. Knowing him he would have created the Spanish company, registered it for VAT, made his bolthole as legal as it could be, years ago. What a waste. That was one she wouldn't be paying, but it gave her an idea. She created a text to DS Cartwright: *Most urgent. I'm a prisoner in the holiday inn room 211. They might be armed. Need help now.* Ready to send if the need should arise. Stupid – there would be serious shit if they made her hand her phone over and they saw the text, so she deleted it, saw the time was 3.58, closed the phone and returned it to her bag. Any moment now. Relax. Breathe.

*

She recognised the woman first – Glynis. The man approaching beside her was shorter, and a shade darker. The man in the pub. He was wearing dark grey trousers that probably belonged to a suit, a white shirt and a tie with red and yellow diagonal stripes that could be something to do with cricket. Glynis was wearing a knee-length summer dress with a floral pattern.

'Ah, dear Jules, how nice to meet you in person at last.' The man smiled, revealing unexpectedly white teeth, as he reached down a hand. She put the magazine back on the table and reached up to shake hands in one movement.

'Good afternoon, Mr Borg.' She put on her best welcoming smile, which she extended to Glynis, but didn't shake her hand. The man had long dark brown hair tied in a ponytail and smelled of a rather fruity aftershave in spite of his neatly trimmed stubble.

'Ah, let us not be formal. Please call me Alfie. Jules,' he bent forward conspiratorially, 'we have confidential matters to discuss, and it would be so much more convenient to hold these discussions in my room. Would you like to join us there? We will have English tea and cakes. We can, of course, use the elevator because of your unfortunate incapacity.'

'Yes, room 211, no problem,' Juliette said as she levered herself out of the chair. As she stood up, she saw that Alfie Borg was nearly a foot shorter than her, and his beige scalp was visible through the strands of hair stretched along the top of his head.

'Ah, you are well prepared. I can tell we will get on famously. This way.'

Juliette put the crutch on her right arm and exaggerated her limp as they headed towards the lift. Once inside it, and heading to the second floor, Alfie said, 'I understand perfectly your reason for mentioning room 211. You want me to be aware that other people know you might be in room 211 and will come and rescue you if the need arises. But let me say, in an effort—' The lift doors opened, putting a temporary stop to Alfie's speech. A short way along a brightly lit corridor, he swiped a card and opened the door. 'Less spacious, but more private,' he said, ushering them in, closing the door and waving them towards a circular table in the corner of the room, near a large window, with three upholstered upright chairs. 'Now, Glynis, dear, please could you do the honours and phone room service. Jules, dear, what would you like to drink? And, Glynis, please ask for a selection of their little cakes and a plate of biscuits. And a jug of iced water.'

Juliette asked for Earl Grey and made a performance of getting from a standing position to sitting in the chair with its back to the wall, leaning the crutch in the corner. Alfie sat on one of the other chairs.

'As I was saying, my dear, in an effort to improve the trust between us, if I had any ill intention towards you, I would arrange to take you to a different room. They know me well here. I have been coming regularly for many years. So here we are in room 211, and as safe as houses. I expect you have questions. Please go ahead.'

There were so many questions. She thought quickly. The big ones about his connection with Richard, and what he knew about his death had better wait, in case they caused Alfie to put up barriers. She would start indirectly, but needing to be assertive, not let him think he could fool her easily. 'You told me your name was Smith. Why did you try to deceive me about your name?'

'My goodness, I feel as if I have been inserted into a bottle of formaldehyde and the lid screwed down, sealing me in as a specimen for inspection. I have been spread out on a board and pins pierced through my extremities, like a frog for dissection. But, my dear, did you not accept my explanation on the telephone? Smith is the surname I use all the time in this country. Borg is merely an historical formality.'

Juliette heard the phone near the bed being replaced on its cradle. Glynis came and sat in the remaining chair, speaking at last. 'Let's talk business. We haven't got all day.'

'Ah yes,' Alfie looked at Juliette, 'as always, Glynis is right. She is the practical one.' Then he put a flat hand at the side of his mouth and spoke behind it to Juliette in a stage whisper, 'If a little stern at times.'

'I'd like to cut out the small talk too,' Juliette said.

'I see. Cut to the chase. That is the ticket. Well, first there is a point of information that I should impart, in an effort to be helpful. Mr Harrington has experienced a hostile takeover. He is no longer in business. This was nothing to do with me. It is simply information that I have, and it is possible that you will be approached by his business successors requesting services similar to those that you performed for him. Good, that is out of the way.'

Juliette's mind whirled. So Alfie knew Tim and about her involvement in the money laundering. Did that mean there was a connection she didn't know about? *Hostile takeover* – what the hell did that mean? She decided not to give away her concern for Tim. 'Thank you so much for letting me know. Were you a business associate of Mr Harrington?'

Alfie shifted in his seat. 'Let us say, an associate of an associate. But there is no breach of security on my account, I do assure you. I should tell you, also, in the interests of openness and transparency, that the money your father stole, substantial though it was, is no longer of importance to us. My sources have confirmed its whereabouts – not, I should add, in this country. The portion of it that belonged to your mother is, alas, unlikely to be restored to her. I am not at liberty to give you further details.' He raised his hands in an apparent gesture of helplessness. 'Our quest,' he waved a hand towards Glynis, while keeping his eyes on Juliette, 'is entirely humanitarian, not mercenary.'

Chapter 28

'Now, Glynis, dear, I think the next thing is to explain to Jules where you fit into the picture. Do you want to tell her, or shall I?'

'You tell her. Keep it short.' Glynis was in one of her stern moods.

'This is a most tragic story, which I shall recount as briefly as possible, while seeking to do it justice. Glynis had a daughter, Miranda, a most beautiful girl, intelligent, sensitive – a girl with a life ahead of her full of promise. But Miranda, through no fault of her own, fell in with the wrong crowd. We will never know the details, but a situation arose in which a group of men were supplying Miranda and her friends with narcotic substances, which these men had purposely caused the girls to become addicted to. Miranda dropped out of school at the age of seventeen, before taking her A-levels. She also became alienated from her mother, Glynis here, who, I should add, had been struggling as a single mother for the previous ten years, after her husband, an alcoholic, had absconded, but that is another story.'

'Your father was the pimp who got her on the game,' Glynis interjected.

'Most tragically, Miranda was put in a position in which she had no choice but to become a lady of the night. Then, in the year 2006 two of Miranda's colleagues tragically met their ends in what became known vulgarly as the Ipswich prostitute murders. This circumstance struck terror in Miranda's heart, causing her to lose control of her drug habit, and, in due course, to succumb to an overdose.'

Juliette looked at Glynis, whose tearless eyes were concentrating on something she could see through the window, and said, 'My daughter, as I'm sure you know, is two years old, but if anything like that were to happen to her, when she's older, I would kill the people responsible.'

'Ah,' Alfie said. 'That brings us neatly to the question in hand. Jules, my dear, did you kill your father?'

'No.' She didn't hesitate, looked straight into Alfie's eyes without blinking.

'Oh dear, I hope we're not going to have a failure to communicate.'

Cool Hand Luke. Juliette managed to keep it to herself.

Alfie continued, 'You see, my dear, when Glynis told me you were, shall we say, less than enthusiastic about joining her in a hunt for your father's murderer, it led me to thinking. You remember, I am sure, a lady of your education and accomplishments, the famous quote from the estimable Sherlock Holmes: "Once you eliminate the impossible, whatever remains, however improbable, must be the truth." I trust I have it verbatim.' He smiled into her eyes as if seeking approval.

'It was, "no matter how improbable" not "however".'

'My goodness, what an ear for detail, but, of course, you are a musician. But you see, my enquiries have eliminated all other possibilities, so inevitably the finger of suspicion points, no matter how improbably, at you.' He pointed at her.

'If I did kill him, do you think I'd be stupid enough to admit it?' She held eye contact and heard Glynis sigh in the background. 'For all I know you might be recording this conversation. Anyway, I didn't, and I've got no idea why you're so keen to find out who did. Isn't it about time you told me?'

'They're all in it together,' Glynis said.

Alfie ignored her. 'Oh, how remiss of me. Forgive me, my dear Jules. The bond of friendship between Glynis and I arose soon after the passing of her beloved daughter. The people responsible were never brought to justice. Without entering into unnecessary detail, let me explain that I have joined Glynis in a campaign to right that wrong – to see the guilty punished for their heinous crimes. If it were not you who killed Mr Belton-Smart, then, by process of elimination, we think it must be his co-conspirators in the prostitution racket, the culprits, in other words, for the tragedy that befell Miranda.'

'I agree with that,' Juliette said, glancing at Glynis, who was looking down at the table. 'But you've just told me you've eliminated all other suspects. And why don't you give the police the information you have, and leave it to them?'

Glynis looked up. 'Told you. They won't do nothing.'

'We thought the others had been accounted for, which is why we are talking to you.' Alfie was talking again. 'If it transpires that the, as we might say, executioner was not you, then we will have to revert to the former suspects – no matter how improbable.' He paused, as if to appreciate his own cleverness. 'So you are claiming this is what happened. You went to visit your father in his hideout. He was drunk. During your conversation, you accidentally received an unpleasant knife wound to your leg. You left in high dudgeon, no doubt. You heard shots. You returned to the scene. You found the body of your departed parent. You vomited and then drove home, whereupon, in a state, no doubt of some distress, and apparent absent-mindedness, you incinerated your clothing. That is your story, I know.'

Juliette looked at Alfie, then at Glynis, then at Alfie again, and said, 'Why do you want me to know that you've got an informant in the Museum Street nick? That's all from my statement.'

'My dear, I am trying to develop trust between us. I want you to understand that my business, though I will spare you the details, is essentially a knowledge business. There is so much data in the modern world – too much. But data, when used correctly, when it is analysed and the chaff separated from the wheat, can be converted into information. And information, when processed and correlated, becomes the useful stuff we call knowledge. And knowledge, when refined and applied with the highest degree of intelligence, becomes what we strive for – wisdom.' Alfie paused, as if for applause. Juliette looked at Glynis, who looked uneasy, as if she had heard this many times before.

Alfie changed tack. 'Jules, my dear, it is cruel of me to tell you, in case you don't know, but the first shot was aimed at his nether region and left his male member hanging by shreds of skin, and exited through his anus, enlarging it somewhat. The second shot shattered his right hip and damaged his pelvis. We do not know for what duration of time his suffering was allowed to continue, until the third shot, the *coup de grace*, put an end to it. You see? An expertly conducted process: the first shot, an attack on his manhood, an obvious punishment for carnal wrongdoings; the second shot, an attack on his physical viability; then finally the third shot terminating his life on earth. Now, my very considerable and reliable sources reveal that none of the numerous people who are known to have wanted him dead, killed him, so I return to my question. Did you kill your father?'

Juliette surprised herself by having a strange feeling of being in control, but she sensed the menace under his pomposity. Would telling them the truth get them off her back? What would Tim do? She quickly dismissed that. It was a calculated risk either way – a matter of balance. They were both waiting for her to say something. 'Do you think I would have done that to my own father? I know what happened while I was in that cottage sounds ridiculous when you tell it the way you did. If I were making up a story, I could do better than that. It's always difficult to prove a negative. I might as well ask you to prove that you didn't kill him. It seems you both had motive, which I didn't.'

'Perhaps the question isn't such a useful one.' Alfie shrugged.

Juliette thought she had some kind of advantage and decided to press it further. 'My father said he was hiding from a man called John Frampton.'

'Ah.' Alfie sighed. 'And what do you know about this man Frampton?'

'Just what my father told me. He's just come out of prison and is extremely dangerous.'

'Yes.' Alfie seemed to be deep in thought.

Juliette turned to Glynis. 'I fully understand your desire for justice, but your daughter died eleven years ago. Why has it taken so long?'

Alfie put up a hand to forestall Glynis. 'Not for want of trying—'

He was interrupted by a knock on the door. He called, 'Come.' When the room service waiter had left and closed the door behind him, and the tray took up most of the table, Alfie said, 'Glynis, dear, would you be mother?'

Juliette declined anything to eat, but drank the tea as quickly as its heat would allow, alternating sips with iced water.

Alfie, between mouthfuls of chocolate cake, said, 'Jules, it has been a most perplexing and frustrating time. We reported the involvement of your father and others, all those years ago. Alas, they had already discontinued their malpractices in Ipswich. Destroyed all evidence. A few of the remaining, er, professional ladies were interviewed by the police, but were too frightened to incriminate those responsible. So we found ourselves up against a brick wall.'

Juliette was thinking what other information she could give them to gain their trust. Something they almost certainly already knew. 'My father was hiding in a brothel in Harwich that was raided. It was a terrible shock when I found out about that. And that he was involved in running it. Including trafficking the girls.'

Glynis said, 'He was the boss.'

'So you went to talk to him about it?'

She decided a little additional harmless information might also help. 'There was something else. He tried to import some drugs – heroin or cocaine, I don't know – in some antiques we imported from Belgium. He was obviously in danger from whoever he was hiding from. I wanted him to hand himself in, confess everything and get a reduced sentence.'

Alfie swallowed. 'You wanted him to give the names of his confederates?'

'I hadn't thought about that, but yes, to get a shorter sentence.'

Alfie leaned back in his chair. 'And you think, having done that, he would be safe in prison?'

Juliette didn't want to come across as naïve, but she wanted her story to be credible. She decided to try to deflect this line of questioning. 'Excuse me, but this is getting a bit like being interviewed by the police.' She sounded indignant, and she was trying to think what she needed to say to get them on side. 'It would have been his decision. What I want to say is that, although it's not what I would have chosen, I'm not sorry he's dead. Anything to do with the exploitation of women on that level is totally unacceptable, and I'll certainly do what I can to help you. My problem is, it was eleven years ago. I was at school. I know absolutely nothing about what my father was doing then.'

'Jules,' Glynis used the name for the first time, 'I just want you to know that I'm doing this for Miranda. She cannot rest in peace yet, but... those men...' Her voice cracked as she started weeping. She took a small packet of tissues out of her handbag and wiped her eyes. Then she said, 'They're still doing it,' and shook, as more tears came. 'If you can help...'

'Are you saying the people running the brothel in Harwich are the ones responsible for your daughter's death?'

Glynis spoke before Alfie could interrupt her. 'They

moved to Harwich straight after the Ipswich murders. Same bastards.'

'Surely you don't think I've got anything to do with that. I've never even been to Harwich.'

This time, Alfie got in first. 'A supporting role, shall we say. The, er, customers tend to pay in cash. Your erstwhile friend, Mr Harrington, was the money man for that and several similar establishments.'

Everything stopped. Juliette froze. She forgot where she was – just thought about the bundles, the bags full of cash she had handled. The hands it had passed through before hers. The things it had been used to pay for. She couldn't stop herself sobbing. Her hands were over her face. Then her mind refused to accept it. She put her hands down and looked at Alfie. 'Why should I believe you?'

'My dear, I can see it has come as a shock to you. You may wish to have a minute to compose yourself.'

Glynis said, 'You didn't know, did you?'

Juliette knew, deep inside, that it must be true. 'I'm so sorry,' she managed. She found herself taking deep breaths.

Alfie was looking at her intently. 'Was it always Mr Harrington who gave you the cash?'

So this was why they had asked her to come here. She nodded. 'Always him, yes, Tim.'

'Did he mention any names?'

'He isn't like that. We don't talk at all. He's virtually paranoid – extremely risk-averse.' Even with the shock of finding out where the money came from, she was trying to think about names. She had one that was still unexplained: Kenneth Almer. She could give it to them to gain more trust. But she'd have to explain how she knew it. The list. She kept silent.

Glynis said, 'Lay off, Alfie. She didn't know. You can tell.'

Juliette wanted to finish this and get out of that room. She took her phone out of the shoulder bag at her feet, and said, 'My God, is that the time? I told my mother I would be home in time to give the children their tea. Have we finished now? I need to go.'

Alfie frowned. 'Ah, we are on the verge of reaching the nub, as it were. Can you make alternative arrangements?'

'I'll have to phone her. I'll just go to the ensuite.'

'Jules, my dear, please telephone your mother here, in front of us.'

'But we all trust each other now, don't we?'

'Yes, of course we do. And if you make your telephone call here in front of us, we will know that we trust each other.' Alfie smiled as if he had demonstrated some kind of superior logic.

Juliette tapped her phone, told her mother that Isabel was extremely upset having discovered that her husband had been having it off with her best friend for the last six months, and her other friends had known about it, but hadn't told her, so her life was in ruins. Juliette needed a bit more time with her. She would get home as soon as she could.

When she had ended the call, Alfie said, 'Jules, you must guess what is going through my mind.' He raised an eyebrow. 'If you can lie to your mother so glibly, how can we be sure you are not lying to us with equal conviction?'

'You want me to tell her the truth about who I'm talking to? Come off it, Alfie. She used to be a lawyer. She's already angry with me for going to see my dad that night. Inadvertently leading the killer to him. If she knew I was talking to you she'd accuse me of joining some kind of vigilante conspiracy.'

Glynis said, 'I'm sorry I was hard on you in the pub. It was all different then. I was seeing you as, you know, like him.' She dabbed her eyes again.

Alfie said, 'Another line of inquiry has to do with the gentleman you mentioned.' He took out some A4-sized photos and put them on the table. 'Do you recognise him?' Juliette saw images of an athletic-looking man, handsome, well-groomed, various ages up to about forty. He struck her as the type that could be a Tory MP, but she didn't recognise him as an individual.

'No?' Alfie prompted. 'He is somewhat older now.'

'No, sorry.'

'He is John Frampton, former partner in crime of your late father. I am reliably informed that Mr Belton-Smart's doing a runner, in their vernacular, was a consequence of the time-honoured tradition of villains falling out. While this man had been enduring a lengthy spell as a guest of Her Majesty, your father was, it seems, as it were, making hay while the sun shone. Then our friend, I use the term loosely here,' Alfie pointed to the photos, 'was released and found, to his considerable displeasure, that all was not as had been reported to him during his incarceration.'

Glynis said, 'He must know we want to talk to 'im.'

'Indeed,' Alfie said, before Glynis could continue. 'This man is wanted by the police, for violating the terms of his probation, so he is behaving in a somewhat elusive manner. Also, I am reliably informed, the Suffolk Constabulary want him to help with their inquiries into the death of Mr Belton-Smart. And, I should add, he has a reputation of being a violent man, on a short fuse, a less than creditable representative of the human race.' Alfie helped himself to another slice of chocolate cake.

Juliette looked at Glynis. 'So, if Frampton continued to have an interest in the prostitution racket even while he was in prison, he bears some share of the blame for what happened to your daughter.'

Alfie shot a hand up and, before Glynis could answer, said, 'No, no. Well, of course there might be a suggestion of what a court of law would call guilt by association, joint enterprise perhaps. But you see, my dear, we are somewhat on the horns of a dilemma. Mr Frampton, for all his shortcomings, has paid the price, albeit for an earlier crime. The point is, while he is a dangerous man, he has information we need.'

Juliette said, 'How do you know?'

Alfie tapped the side of his head theatrically. 'As I said, dear Jules, my business is a knowledge business.' He raised a teacup to his lips without cocking his little finger. After swallowing, he said, 'Frampton is the vengeful type – unforgiving, merciless. I show you these photographs, my dear, in the hope that you would recognise him if you saw him, allowing for him now being an older man, and take suitable precautions.'

'You said you had eliminated him as a suspect for my father's killing.'

'Ah, I must plead guilty to testing you, wanting to see how you would respond to my suggestion that you might have been involved. Lack of motive is a strong defence for you, and the cruel manner of Mr Belton-Smart's, er, execution, do you not agree with me, Glynis, brings clarity to the notion that it was the work of Mr Frampton.'

'It was him all right,' Glynis agreed.

Alfie said, 'So we must proceed with extreme caution.'

'Do you think he's responsible for Tim's disappearance?'

'Time will tell, my dear. Time will tell.'

'What is the information he has, that you need?'

Alfie smiled. 'Names. Names of the men that Glynis is especially interested in.'

*

Juliette sat in the little Peugeot in the hotel car park, processing what she had witnessed in the hotel room. Tim. Should she have known about the money? Somewhere at the back of her mind, had she suspected? She had been a partner in the worst kind of exploitation of women. She hadn't known. She should have asked. No, that would have been pointless. Tim would either have told her it was in her own best interest not to know, or he would have spun her a story – some kind of tax fiddle, maybe a few added fictitious details. It wasn't surprising that Alfie and Glynis had assumed that she knew where the money was coming from.

But Alfie. Jesus, was he real? The stuff about Frampton. Was Alfie just showing off? Wanting her to know what a network of informants he had? Or wanting her to believe she was in danger from Frampton? But was she? Alfie and Glynis would be, if Frampton saw them as a threat. And she, Jules, could be in danger if he thought she was linked to them. But… But… Alfie. She couldn't figure him out. What was his relationship with Glynis? Why had he spent more than ten years trying to help her get justice for her dead daughter? And the pompous, pretentious façade – what was he hiding?

Chapter 29

The next day was another hot sunny one. Caroline was having a day at the rape crisis centre. Juliette was in the garden with the children, they in the paddling pool, she on a sun lounger, resting her leg. An opportunity for a couple of phone calls. To get anything out of Lara she'd have to offer something.

'Hi, Lara. Jules. Are you still interested in a story?'

'Personal interest? Of course. Have you got time this afternoon? An hour should be enough.'

'Sorry, busy weekend. I was thinking of Monday.' Monday was safe. They were planning a family trip to Colchester Zoo. She'd phone Lara in the morning to cancel.

'What brought about this change of heart?'

'Mutual back-scratching. Any developments with those fibres?'

'Nothing doing there. They're very generic – a common variety of denim.'

Juliette felt a surge of relief. 'Any news of Frampton?'

'He's definitely prime suspect now. They think he's on some kind of revenge mission. Your dad was first. Now there's another one. Body floating in the Orwell. Looks like Frampton's second victim. He's been identified as a Thomas Huntingdon...'

Juliette froze, seeing Tim's face. Tim-Tom. Somewhere inside she had known. Nothing else could explain Tim's sudden silence. But Lara was still talking. She'd have to process Tim's death later. 'Sorry, I missed that – signal breaking up,' she managed.

'The police have found a laptop, a load of burner phones and a stack of fake ID documents in a hole under his fridge. Some of this links him to Frampton, who's trying to buy another gun. He must have got rid of the old revolver he shot your dad with. A snout in Felixstowe said he was in some pub there negotiating for a Glock 17.'

'You mean he walks into a pub and asks if anyone can sell him a gun?'

'It's not quite like that. A pub down by the docks – the go-to place for anything dodgy. He'd have to know the right people.'

'And one of them turns out to be a police informant.'

'So it seems. That's enough for a heck of a personal interest story. What time on Monday?'

'Afternoon. I'm still juggling a few music lessons. I'll phone you in the morning to fix the time.'

Her mind switched to Tim. Thomas Huntingdon. Timothy Harrington. The poor sod probably had monogrammed cufflinks or something, needing a fake name with the same initials.

Lulu was sitting in the paddling pool playing with a boat and a duck. Jazzy was running around the lawn making aeroplane noises. Why had she been worrying about the fibres? Some sort of displacement activity? It had been a bad night. Lying sleepless, thinking about the young women whose misery she had been complicit in. She should have known where that filthy money came from. Good that the shitty place had been busted.

Current live risk. The laptop and burners. Tim would have deleted all messages, as she had, but the cops might retrieve them. Could any of it be linked to her? The one set of messages and transactions after Richard's death would be most suspect, and they'd find the decoding template on the laptop at the mansion. Up until then it would look as if it were him carrying out the money laundering. There had to be an associate carrying on the business. She had looked carefully along the road to the mansion, in both directions, and was sure there were no surveillance cameras. She had wiped everything carefully. Minimum risk – even if they found her laptop and burners.

The gun and knife buried by the gorse bush in that copse. Only a foot or so deep. Surely there was nothing with a scent that would attract a dog and get it digging. She had been careful about fingerprints. There would be traces of blood. It must be Richard's on the gun and hers on the knife. That would fit her story. But the police would know she had driven back along that road. There were cameras in Woodbridge. Moderate risk. She would need to either dispose of them or find a more secure hiding place soon.

She lay back, enjoying the sun, closed her eyes. *Lucia* intruded – the mad woman covered in blood, wielding a knife. Then a change of scene, blood, more than you could imagine coming out of one body – there in that rotting hovel. Screaming. But it sounded like a child. She opened her eyes.

Lulu was sitting in the paddling pool, yelling and pointing at Jazzy who was running around the lawn with her boat in one hand and her duck in the other.

A minute later, Lucy was wrapped in a towel, with Juliette on the lounger, which she had dragged into the shade. The child was settling, tired, falling asleep. Juliette's mind went back to risks. The bullets. The four remaining ones in the brown box. She should have taken them that night. They'd now be in the bag, underground, with the gun and knife. After loading the gun, she had left them on the shelf in the garage at the mansion. There could be a story to cover it. Richard went to that garage to use the laptop and burners. He had loaded the gun there and left the last four bullets. But he wouldn't have left them. He would have taken them.

Tim. Murdered. There was no room for doubt now. If something went wrong with his risk management, it could certainly go wrong with hers. Lucy had gone to sleep. Juliette got up and went to sit on one of the patio chairs with her phone. How much was Glynis under Alfie's thumb? But she had been friendly at the end yesterday. Hardly any risk attached to this, and she might learn something. She tapped the phone.

'Hi, Glynis, it's Jules.'

'Hello.'

'I just wanted to make sure you understood. Tim told me it was a little tax dodge – about import and export of antiques. I know it was stupid of me. It never occurred to me that the money came from prostitution, that exploitation. I had no idea. You do believe me, don't you?'

'Yeah. You was easily taken in. Quite surprising, having a dad like that.'

'I didn't know he was like that. He was always kind to me – a good father.' She winced and bit her lip.

'So are you going to help us?'

'In every way I can. Of course. I hope you don't mind my asking. Was Miranda an only child?' She could hear Glynis breathing.

'Why do you want to know?'

'Brothers and sisters often know each other better than their parents do. Tell each other things.'

There was another silence. Then, 'She used to have a sister.'

Juliette felt a spark. 'You mean you've got another daughter?'

'We're not in contact.'

'What's her name?'

'Carmen.'

Juliette rolled her eyes. 'Does she live locally?'

'Up London. Somewhere posh. She won't help. We don't talk.'

'But do you think she might know something – about what happened to Miranda? Perhaps she'd talk to me.'

'Alfie talked to her, years ago. Said she'd gone bad. She was three years older, was supposed to of looked after Miranda. Did the opposite. She was friendly with your dad. I don't want nothing to happen to her. I want to forget her. Alfie said that's for the best.'

'I could talk to her without saying I know you.'

'She sent me a Christmas card last year with a phone number. She said it was ten years and time to put bygones etcetera. I tore it up.'

Juliette wondered if it was worth continuing, then decided on one last try. 'Do you know where she lives?'

'No. Don't want to neither.'

'You said somewhere posh.'

'That's her job. Said she'd turned a corner in her life. Waitress in a swanky hotel. Royal Garden, that was it.'

Juliette ended the call, agreeing with Glynis that there was no point in trying to find Carmen, as she wouldn't help. And intending to take a trip to the Royal Garden Hotel in Kensington the next day.

*

Juliette seated herself at a small table near the huge plate glass windows at the front of the lounge bar. Probably a waste of time, but she had felt like a day out. An escape. Time to think things through. And maybe some shopping in Oxford Street before catching the train home. The air-conditioning was cooling her down after the walk from High Street Ken. There were several people milling about in the lounge. Business types – suits. A few tourists – T-shirts and shorts. A man with short grey hair, wearing a navy blue blazer, sat at a small table a few yards away. She half glimpsed his face as he turned and sat facing away from her. For a second she thought there was something familiar about him but dismissed it. She thought of Tim – ultra-cautious to the point of paranoia.

'What can I get you?' the smartly uniformed waitress asked.

'Something soft and refreshing, please. Do you have a colleague called Carmen?'

'Rasa Malaysia's popular. Lemonade with a hint of coconut.'

'That sounds good. Yes please. Do you know Carmen?'

'People move about a lot. I don't think there's a Carmen here now. I'll get your drink.'

Juliette pulled a newspaper out of her bag and spread it on the table. What had she been thinking? She was never going to find one woman called Carmen among London's floating hospitality workers.

The waitress put a tall glass on the table with pale cloudy liquid, floating fruit and ice, a straw, and the obligatory paper parasol. 'Geoff at the bar thinks it might be Carrie.'

Juliette's mind leapt. 'Is she here?'

'On her break. Are you a friend? What's it about?'

Juliette had decided, as there had been a serious falling out, not to mention she was a friend of Carmen's mother. 'We haven't met. It's about her late sister, Miranda. If it's her.'

'I'll see if she wants to talk to you.' The waitress turned and walked back to the bar.

Juliette looked at the newspaper, but couldn't focus on the words. Why did she want to talk to Carmen? Was it because of the guilt she felt about having killed Richard? Glynis had said Carmen should have been looking after her younger sister. Did that mean Carmen had also been a prostitute? Was that the only reason her mother had disowned her?

A blonde waitress, early thirties, slightly overweight, came up to her. 'Did you know my sister?'

'I know of her. Do you want to sit down?'

'I'm not allowed to. I've just got five minutes of break left. Who are you?'

'My name's Jules. I'm the daughter of Richard Belton-Smart.'

'Blimey. In Ipswich? There's a blast from the past. How is he?' The woman's face lit up.

'Did you know him well?'

'Little Richie. Yeah, you could say that. Fancy meeting his daughter. Never said he had one. I'm Carrie. No one calls me Carmen.'

'We ought to find somewhere for a proper talk. Can you take time off?'

'I'm supposed to be doing lunch. I'll see if I can swap. Usually not a problem.'

*

Half an hour later, the two women were sitting at a small table in the crowded pub on Kensington Church Street. Carrie was still wearing her tight black skirt, but had changed into a pink blouse. Juliette had ordered food and bought Carrie a pint of lager and herself a glass of mineral water.

'We often come in here after work,' Carrie said. 'So, what's Richie been up to lately?'

'I'm sorry to have to tell you he's dead.' Juliette tried to make out the changed expression on Carrie's face, in the subdued lighting.

'Oh. Your dad. Sorry. What did he die of?'

'He was murdered. Shot.'

'Oh, Jesus. I heard that bastard had been released – the one they fitted up.'

Juliette realised Carrie was the talkative type. She'd probably find out more if she didn't ask too many direct questions. 'I'm sorry if I'm bringing back unpleasant memories.'

'No, it's not that. Do they know who shot him?'

Juliette tried to make it sound light. 'I found the body, so they think it might be me. My dad was trying to hide from a man called John Frampton. Is that who you're talking about?'

'Johnny, yeah, they all hated him – Charlie, Richie and Kenny. Kenny knew someone in the same prison, Richie told me, paid him a couple of grand to go and insult Johnny, knowing he'd lose it as he always did. Bloke got in the hospital and Johnny got done for attempted murder. Been inside for yonks. Richie must have been shit-scared of him coming out.'

'You said you knew him quite well.'

'He got me out. Long story short, there was just the four of us in the house, and Charlie looking after us. He was huge – black guy. He'd say to the johns, "Nothing the girl don't agree to, right?" – kept us safe. It was fun – loads of sex and good money. A vacancy came up. Randy, three years younger than me, hated school, so I mentioned it to her. She jumped at it. It was a few months after that, Richie took a shine to me. No disrespect. Told me to stop. Got me a flat up in Westbourne – nice place – looked after me, gave me nice things.' Carrie looked up, took a sip of lager. 'I hadn't realised how dependent Randy was on me.' She pulled a tissue out of her handbag and wiped her eyes. 'We'd all snort the odd line. That was part of it. You know, sex and drugs and rock 'n' roll. Then that creep, Kenny...' She sniffed and wiped her eyes again. 'I should have told her to leave when I did. I could have helped her.'

A waiter put plates in front of them: burger and chips for Carrie, salad for Juliette.

'What did Kenny do?' Juliette said softly.

'Got her on smack. Injecting.' Carrie bit into her burger.

'Was this about the time of the murders?'

'Christ, that was scary. I told Randy she ought to get out. I was sure our mum'd have her back. She could've got a job in a shop or something. She just yelled at me. Proper smackhead by then. She obviously couldn't pay for it on shop assistant's wages. I asked Richie to help. He was fucking useless, excuse me, said it was her choice. I phoned her a few times, told her I could get her into rehab. She just yelled, told me not to come there. I still hadn't realised how far gone she was. Then Richie gave me the news. He was really upset. Told me it must have been an accident. Then there was a couple more murders and they closed the house.'

'And you were still in the flat my dad got for you?'

'He was quite a sweetie in his own way. Spent most nights with me. The girls used to call him Mr Love. Anyway, I had this falling out with my mum after Randy died, and he was quite decent, you know, supportive. Then after a while he started going on about how he wanted a son, and he'd divorce his wife – sorry, I guess that was your mum – and marry me, and I should come off the pill. So I was looking for a way out, and one day I packed a bag and got on the train to London.'

'Just like that?' Juliette was turning over the idea that Richard was Mr Love.

'An old school friend worked in a pub in Tottenham. Said I could sleep on her sofa and they'd probably give me a job in the same pub. Which they did.'

'Tell me about Kenny. What was he like?' Juliette tried to sound casual.

'Piece of shit. Tried to make out he was everyone's favourite uncle, looking after the girls. He'd keep telling us we're members of the oldest profession, an honourable one, providing an essential service, he'd make sure all our needs are catered for, all that crap. Devious, manipulative bastard.'

'I mean physically. Can you describe him?'

'Smarmy little git. Some of the girls called him The Malteser. He'd go on and on. Liked the sound of his own voice.'

Juliette stopped chewing, her mind spinning through the possibilities. Maybe Alfie knew Kenny from when they both lived in Malta. Or they could be brothers. 'You mean he's Maltese?' Another possibility was nagging at the edge of her mind. Alfie, the slippery fake, user of false names. The picture she had – Alfie helping and supporting Glynis – would be upended.

'Yeah, weird accent.' Carrie looked over Jules's shoulder, smiled broadly then smirked. 'Don't turn round. Old geezer eyeing us up.'

'Did Kenny ever use the name Alfie?'

Carrie screwed up her nose. 'Not that I ever heard. Chubby little man – trying to sound ever so English. He had this ponytail like he fancied himself as some kind of porn star. He turned up at Randy's funeral like he's a friend of the family. Fucking hypocrite. I told my mum she shouldn't have anything to do with him. She yelled at me it was all my fault Miranda, as she called her, died. That was that. I've tried to talk to her a few times.' Carrie took a gulp of lager.

Juliette was forming a whole new picture. It made sense. It would explain why Glynis and Alfie hadn't got any nearer to finding the people responsible for Miranda's death. Alfie, slippery fake, user of false names, could be the missing man on the list: Kenneth Almer. 'Tell me more about Kenny. What sort of clothes did he wear?'

'Quite smart usually, sort of dapper. He'd wear suits, always a spotless white shirt, and a tie. Seemed like he only had one. Yellow and red stripes, like some kind of club tie.'

That clinched it. The tie she'd seen Alfie wearing. It all fitted. 'So this Kenny and my dad were working it together. Do you know what they did after closing the house in Ipswich?'

'One of the girls, Simone, a right nutter, told me. They started again in Harwich. Simone went with them. She said she quite liked it for a while, until Charlie left. Then they started importing a lot of foreign girls. Teenagers she said. Kept them like prisoners. Got them hooked on smack, then gave them just enough to make them willing to do anything to get the next fix. She said it had all gone pear-shaped and she wanted out.' Carrie dipped a chip in ketchup and ate it.

'And?'

'Next time I phoned her, her phone had been discontinued. Either she'd got out, or the same thing as happened to Randy happened to her. I wasn't going to stick my nose in.'

*

In the train, on the way home, Juliette tried to analyse her new knowledge. It had to be. Alfie was Kenny, aka Kenneth Almer. She had already realised that Alfie was The Malteser, but now his role was reversed. He was up to his neck in the prostitution racket. He had befriended Glynis and pretended to help her find justice for her dead daughter. All the time he was making sure she didn't get anywhere near the truth. Why would he take the trouble? Glynis on her own wouldn't be able to do anything. But she might eventually contact Carrie. That would blow it for Alfie. And he was simply playing a game, a cruel one, manipulating and controlling. He was involved in the brothel in Harwich. It was probably he that arranged for Richard to stay in the loft. It fitted. That was how he knew that Tim was dealing with the cash, and… She, Juliette, hadn't seen it. Hadn't thought through where the money was coming from. She had been just as gullible as Glynis. But no more.

There was something nagging. Something Carrie had said that didn't seem right. Or it was the way she said it. Juliette would have to think through every detail, but now she was too tired.

Chapter 30

The following day, it was on the local news. The Suffolk police reported a male body pulled out of the Orwell the previous day. Identity was being withheld until next of kin had been informed.

Juliette was seeing Tim in his tweed coat and woollen scarf that he would wear in the winter. Alfie had said 'hostile takeover'. Not Alfie – Kenny. Cynical bastard. Tim, the risk manager, the survivor. But no longer. The images were confused. The recurring one: Richard, his cheek bursting like a tomato, the interior of his head spraying… Then Tim. All she could do was imagine. How long had he been in the water? Crabs would have been at work, probably still attached to what remained of his face and hands when he came out. He hadn't seemed like a bad man. Just got drawn in. Something had gone wrong. A flaw in his risk management. But surely he hadn't deserved what had happened – to be murdered, tossed in the river, fed to the fishes. If he hadn't got mixed up with the wrong people – Richard Bullshit, Johnny Frampton and bloody Alfie Kenny whoever he was – he might have led a decent life and lived happily to an old age.

Juliette was in the ensuite bathroom, looking at herself in the mirror. *You're not a bad person, are you, Jules? Are you? Did you get drawn in somehow? Mixed up with the wrong people?* Kenneth Almer had been on the list. It looked as if they were all accounted for now – one way or another.

She went downstairs. Another blazing day – grey-brown patches darkening on the lawn. Jazzy splashing about with boats in the paddling pool; Caroline in a patio chair, reading a story to Lulu; Steve reading *The Observer*.

'Are you okay here for a while, Mum? My leg's throbbing. I want to lie down for a bit.'

After closing the bedroom door, she got her phone out of her bag. 'Hi, Glynis, I hope you don't mind my phoning again?'

'I'm not busy.'

'Like I said, if I thought of any people connected to my dad, I'd let you know. When I was lying half-awake, I remembered my dad talking about someone called Kenny. He might have been involved in the—'

Glynis seemed to laugh, then cleared her throat. 'Oh, no. Oh, Alfie's such a character. You know what he's like with names. Well, when I first met him he said his name was Kenneth. He said his friends call him Kenny. Yeah, so it's him. Must be. I'd known him nearly a year when he told me Kenneth was his first name, but Alfred was his second name and some people called him Kenny and other people called him Alfie, and he found it confusing so now he was asking everyone to call him Alfie, or Alfred if they didn't know him so well.'

'Do you know how he met my dad?'

'That was years ago. Something to do with the removals business. I think they met in Malta. You'd have to ask him.

Once he discovered what your father was up to with the girls, he felt bad, 'specially after what happened to Miranda.'

'Thanks for clearing that up about Kenny. So now the only other person we know about is this John Frampton.'

'Yeah, but he was in prison before what happened to Miranda, so he might not have known what they did to her. But he's still, you know… Twenty-five years of his share of the profits; that's what they've been fighting about.'

'He might have killed my dad.'

'So you've got a reason to hate him as well as me. He'll get away with that too prob'ly.'

Juliette paused. There was more to 'getting away with it' than Glynis could imagine. 'It wasn't very clear to me what you and Alfie are planning to do.'

'Alfie's got a plan. He says he can coax him out of the woodwork. Talks funny, Alfie does.'

Juliette stopped herself from saying that didn't sound like much of a plan. 'I see. Thanks, Glynis. I'll let you know if I think of anything else that might be helpful.' She made it sound as if she had phoned Glynis to give her information, rather than to get it.

Carrie had known about Frampton being released from prison. That was what had been nagging. How had she known? They had swapped mobile numbers before saying goodbye. Juliette tapped her phone. It was picked up quickly. 'Hi, Carrie, it's Jules.'

No answer. Juliette listened carefully. Was that breathing? 'Carrie, can you hear me?' There was a sharp click as the call was discontinued. That was strange. Was Carrie now refusing to talk to her? Perhaps she was at work, not allowed to use her phone. But she had picked up the call, just not said anything.

She went to the Royal Garden's website, then tapped the main contact number. After listening to the formal greeting, she said, 'Is it possible to speak to a member of staff, a waitress, Carrie?'

'Are you a relative of hers?' A woman's voice with an Italian accent.

'I'm a friend. Is she available?'

'I'm very sorry. It's terrible. She was mugged on her way home last night. We are trying to trace her next of kin.'

Juliette's mind froze for a second. Could it be a coincidence? 'Was she badly hurt?'

'It's a shock. Very sad. She died. The ambulance came, but too late. Just for her little money and phone.'

Juliette gasped, then forced herself to breathe. She tried to speak, but no words came.

'Police come here talk to the manager. I have to ask your name and if you know her next of kin?'

Juliette was trying to absorb the idea of Carrie being dead. Another part of her mind quickly thought how Glynis would probably react. Her own phone number would be recorded on the hotel's system. She said, 'My name is Juliette Walker. I didn't know her well. I'm sorry, I don't know any of her relatives. Thank you for telling me. I won't take up more of your time.' She cut the call before the receptionist could reply.

Juliette felt the bile rising in her mouth. How could it possibly be a coincidence? Carrie had been murdered. The most likely reason was unbearable. Carrie was a danger to them. Them? Alfie, now Kenny, and Frampton. Somehow. Jesus.

She tapped her phone. In London local news she found the story. Murder in Shepherd's Bush. A hotel waitress died of head injuries in what appeared to be a mugging that went wrong. Her identity was being withheld until next of kin had been informed. Nothing more.

Juliette found herself weeping and shaking with anger. No, no, no. It couldn't be. But it was. She had been followed to London. The man in the hotel lounge. She had just caught a quarter-profile. Lean face, high cheekbones. It could have been him – the younger man in the photos. The man Carrie had seen looking at them in the pub. He had seen her make contact with Carrie and followed them. He must have heard some of what she was saying about Kenny. She had been a danger to them, and therefore was eliminated. Frampton and bloody Alfie working together. Her skin prickled. She had no idea why Tim had been killed, but there was only one explanation for Carrie being killed. Which meant that she, Jules, would be next. She didn't know whether it was fear or excitement that made her hands shake as she opened her laptop to study the details of a Glock 17.

*

That evening she agreed to accompany Steve rehearsing Arturo's duet with Enrico. Arturo, the man about to be murdered by Lucia.

Steve stopped singing. 'You're hitting a lot of wrong notes.'

'Sorry.' Juliette was seeing the mad woman in a white wedding dress covered in blood swinging the Psycho knife, screaming, spraying blood. 'I'm very tired.'

'Perhaps we should call it a day. Have another go tomorrow?'

'Yes.' The mad woman image had morphed into the Glenn Close character in *Fatal Attraction*, deranged, repeatedly stabbing the knife into her own leg without noticing. More blood.

*

She lay awake under the sheet. Monday, shop closed. They were planning a family trip to Colchester Zoo. All of them together would be safe. For one day. What then? Another plan started forming in her head. The sort of thing you only think of when you're half-asleep. What Tim would have called the nuclear option.

*

At breakfast, Juliette said, 'I've had a bad night. I need to rest today. You lot have a great time at the zoo.'

Fifteen minutes after they had driven off in the Volvo, she double-locked the front door and set the CCTV cameras on motion sensitive, then went out through the French doors and checked the side gate was bolted securely. Sitting in the early sunshine on one of the patio chairs, she looked at her phone for a few seconds. Then looked across the lawn at the trees shimmering in the sunlight. Did Lucia know she was going mad? Was killing Arturo something she planned? Did she see it as the only way out of her impossible situation?

The pub in London had been crowded and noisy, with people trying to make themselves heard above loud music. Frampton (she had now convinced herself that it must have been him) couldn't have heard everything that Carrie had said.

She needed to maintain Alfie's trust. For now, she had to keep thinking of him as Alfie. At present Carrie's story had the most credibility. Alfie would know that Carrie had been killed, but wouldn't know that she, Jules, knew. Alfie and Frampton were working together. They had to be. So Alfie would now know about her trip to London. She'd have to get the balance just right. She looked back at the phone. High risk, but she had decided. Whether or not she was mad didn't matter. It was the only solution. She took control of her breathing, deep and slow, then tapped the number – no turning back.

'Hello, Alfie, I hope you don't mind my calling. Is it a bad time?'

'My dear Jules, for you there is no bad time.'

'Are you planning to come to Ipswich again soon?'

'I am here! How fortuitous. My plans changed and I am right here in the Holiday Inn.'

Just as she had expected. 'Did you know Glynis has another daughter? I went to see her on Saturday. She hasn't been on speaking terms with Glynis since Miranda died. I thought she might know something that might help, you know, in our pursuit of justice.'

'My goodness, what a resourceful young lady you are. And did she?'

'I don't know. Carrie, that's Glynis's daughter, mentioned someone called Kenny, a business associate of my father's. She said he was quite friendly and supportive to the sex workers. Carrie was one of them, then became my dad's mistress, according to her. But she didn't think this Kenny was directly involved in the prostitution, more to do with my dad's other business interests. And do you know what, Alfie, I think this Kenny was you.'

'My dear, you have me pinned down on the dissection table again. But why do you think that?'

'The description fitted. Quite flattering. She liked you. And so I phoned Glynis yesterday. She told me you used the name Kenny when she first met you.' She chuckled to make sure he didn't think it was an accusation.

'I blame it on my parents for giving me two names.' He sighed theatrically.

'The thing that worries me, Alfie, is that this Johnny Frampton seems to be hunting down and killing anyone that he blames for the long time he spent in prison.'

'My dear, he has a vindictive nature, but he has been out of action for a long time.'

'I know Frampton was in prison for an unconnected crime, but are you telling me he wasn't involved in the prostitution racket?'

'I wouldn't absolve him that far. But what I can say is that after thirty years of sewing mailbags and the like, he is a changed man. Paid his debt to society, rehabilitated in the best tradition of the British justice system.'

'You mean, he didn't kill my father, and Tim?'

'It seems there are other forces at work, and Mr Frampton is innocent.'

'How do you know?'

'I have spoken to him on the telephone. I am a good judge of character.'

'I'd like to meet him.'

'My goodness. May I ask why?'

'He's made quite threatening phone calls to me. I think he still sees me as a threat, or that I've got something that he thinks belongs to him. He must know I was handling the money passed to me by Tim Harrington, and probably thinks I was an active participant in the business. If, as you say, he's been rehabilitated, I think we could have a civilised discussion and set the record straight. The sooner the better, before something bad happens.'

'You've got me thinking, my dear.'

'Can you contact him again?'

'Are you sure this is wise?'

'What I think is that the three of us should meet. You, me and Frampton. I could explain my unwitting role in the prostitution business. That I was getting commission of only five per cent, much less than I would have needed if I had known it was immoral earnings. I would be happy to go through, in detail, what Carrie told me on Saturday. I've got a good memory, as you know. I think this would be the best way to make sure I am safe from him. Have everything out in the open. I don't understand the significance of everything Carrie told me, but he might.'

'It is a most extraordinary proposition.'

'But I think, if he meets us both, in person, we can convince him that we are not responsible for what happened to him.'

'Are you worried for your mother?'

'Ah.' Juliette smiled to herself, glad that Alfie had thought of this without her having to prompt him. 'Of course, Carrie doesn't know anything about that. But if I met him, I could tell him my mother did her best as his defence barrister.' Juliette was silently pleased with herself for talking about Carrie in the present tense.

'I'm beginning to see the attraction of such a meeting. A rapprochement with Mr Frampton. Myself as facilitator and mediator. Splendid. Would you want to come here, to my room in the Holiday Inn?'

'It would be more discreet to meet here at my house. Frampton knows where it is. He was watching us at one point. Little Eastham – I'll give you directions. I think we should do it as soon as possible. This afternoon. How about three-thirty?'

'Mr Frampton is a busy man. Somewhat elusive. But I can find out if he's available. A matter of urgency, I'll tell him. We should grasp the nettle, strike while the iron is hot.'

After closing the call, Juliette tried to think through her plan. She had convinced herself that Alfie/Kenny and Frampton would see this meeting as an opportunity to get rid of her. They must see her as a threat, and she had seen how they dealt with threats. The risks were almost beyond assessment. But surely they would not kill her in her own house. They would want to make it look like something other than a premeditated murder – an accidental drowning or a mugging gone wrong. That sort of thing was more their style. If they arrived at 3.30, and things started going wrong, how long would it take? Having a random witness arrive on the scene might stop them. Timing. Everything depended on timing, but that was never going to be precise.

She tapped Lara's number. 'Hi, Lara. The story you want – grisly details of growing up with a pimp and people-trafficker. Can we do it at my house this afternoon? I've got a free hour. The family are all out. Could you come here as close as possible to 3.40? I've got music lessons till then. It should give us an hour or so before tired excited children take over my life again.'

'Great. What's your postcode?'

Chapter 31

She scanned the trees. An ash tree, she had been almost sure in the torchlight on her first visit. An ash tree with a gorse bush right beside it. A movement ahead of her. She strode forward. A black Labrador. People wouldn't be far away. The dog sniffed her leg and trotted past. A middle-aged couple came into view round a bend in the path.

'Lovely day.' She gave them a smile as they passed. And there they were: the ash tree and the gorse bush. She looked behind her. The people were out of sight. Yes – undisturbed by dogs, foxes, badgers. She had brought a garden trowel from home, and the box of bullets she had collected at the mansion on the way to the copse. Ten minutes later, the fully loaded gun was in her shoulder bag, and she was on her way home in the Peugeot. The Psycho knife and contents of the wallet were still in the carrier bag along with the three empty cartridge cases and the one remaining unused bullet, about a foot underground under the gorse bush.

*

Back in her house, she looked at the gun, which could put her in prison for life. Tim would have got rid of it, or left it at the murder scene. *Think like Tim.* There were times when you had to take a risk in order to mitigate a bigger risk.

She put the gun on the kitchen table. It all came back – the noise, the stink, the face. She had to shake it off and focus on what she had to do today. The plan. Lucia must have planned to kill Arturo. Or was it just madness? She killed a man, then died. Died of self-loathing – inability to come to terms with the dreadful thing she had done. Juliette still had her eyes closed when she felt Ziggy land on her lap. The absurdity swept through her mind. There was no one she could talk to about what she had done, except this cat. Ziggy looked into Juliette's eyes and flopped over to get her belly stroked. 'Do you have dreams, Zig? When you're lying there and you start twitching, are you chasing a mouse? Or are you being split up the middle by a terrifying monster? I hope it's a mouse.' Was she going mad? Had something in her brain snapped because of her inability to cope with what had happened? She had killed a man. Killed him instead of phoning for an ambulance.

*

At about one o'clock, Alfie phoned to confirm that Frampton had agreed to meet at Juliette's house at three-thirty.

'Will you be arriving together?'

'Alas, no. Mr Frampton has to, as it were, take precautions. To ensure he is not followed, you understand. My presence would make things much too complicated. We will be travelling separately. Jules, my dear, we can be sure that there will be no unwanted visitors, can't we. You will be alone.'

'Don't worry, Alfie. My family are having a day out. I'm still resting my leg. We won't be spied on – or interrupted.' As Juliette closed the call, she thought about Alfie's tone. Could he suspect the danger he might be in? Surely not. It was too improbable. Too risky. Too mad.

Ziggy jumped onto her lap with a '*myah, myah*'. Juliette stroked the back of her head and neck.

'Think I'm mad, Zig? You could be right. Thing is, I don't see what else I can do. I know it's not safe, but what is? Downside: I get killed; or something unthinkable is done to me before I get killed; or something else goes wrong and I spend a very long time in prison. Shit. You leave little corpses lying about. Sometimes just bits of them. Okay, okay, I know you're hardwired, a natural born killer. Oh, and you don't kill members of your own species. Well, if you ask me, as a definition of civilisation, that's setting the bar pretty low. Still, you keep getting away with it. And I love you.' Ziggy rolled over to get her tummy done. 'I never asked. That's what gets me. I should have known where the money was coming from. I just locked that possibility away somewhere safe, where it wouldn't trouble me. Convinced myself it was just some tax fiddle, near as you can get to a victimless crime. Can you imagine, Zig? That money, the actual notes I counted and carried to the bank, they were paid over by men so they could do horrible things to young women and girls who had no choice. That's what I can't forgive them for. Using me. And I can't forgive myself for letting them. So, what I'm planning is a bloody inadequate way of trying to make amends, but it's all I can think of. And it's completely insane. I know that. No one in their right mind would do anything like this. That's my best hope. They think it's impossible, so it might turn out to be rather clever. You, Ziggy, are a humble cat. We humans, having ascended somewhat further up the evolutionary ladder, have moral choices to make. Don't we just.' She looked into Ziggy's eyes to try to dispel the image of Lucia with the knife, and the blood.

*

Lunch was just a couple of rice cakes with Marmite, a few fingers of cucumber and a glass of water. *Keep it light*, she said to herself.

By two o'clock Juliette was sitting in the semi-upholstered chair which she had pulled out of the corner of the sitting room. She was aware of having shifted into a world of unreality. A world where the rules were different. Madness was the norm. In this world she could think clearly about the things she needed to do. The chair she was sitting in, and the pair of wing-back chairs, now formed a triangle round the coffee table. It looked ready for a meeting of three serious people – informal, but not too intimate. She tried to relax. What could go wrong? Thinking like Tim. Most serious risk: they could both turn up at the same time. That would require some improvisation.

She had thought in advance about Frampton wanting to search her for a weapon. The dressing on her leg was now a large adhesive plaster, so she had squeezed into her skinny black jeans, pulled on an old charcoal-grey T-shirt and black trainers – nothing to hide and nowhere to hide it.

Risks: they would kill her somehow as soon as they arrived, but they'd need to manage forensic evidence, so it was more likely that they would abduct her to kill her later in a safe place. Both men would probably need to be present for the latter.

Mitigation: she'd have to be the first to make a move.

In this world of unreality, she had thought carefully about where to place the shoulder bag, eventually deciding on the alcove near the door from the hall, on the floor. In plain sight, but not likely to arouse suspicion. At five past three she went to the study and sat in front of the CCTV screens, switching the system from Motion to Constant. Nothing yet.

The familiar furry bundle landed in her lap with a soft '*waah*'. 'How does it feel, Zig? That little bird you killed last week. I had to flush it down the loo before Jazzy and Lulu saw it. I was quite upset. It was one of the pretty ones – a goldfinch. You don't care about that, though, do you. Do you feel the power? Or is it just that that little brain of yours is hardwired? You can't help it. That's your excuse. You don't really kill your victims, though, do you. You just play them to death. Bloody lucky you don't have to worry about crime scenes. You don't get the mystery, though, do you, Zig, simple life you lead. That thing with Richard – he went from alive to dead, and I went from not killer to killer. Just like that. Turned a corner. Crossed a line. You think it's natural, don't you, your thing with birds and mice. Can't help yourself. Think you're the only one?' She looked into the cat's black eyes. Ziggy went on purring. 'It's time for you to get out of the way now.' She carried the cat to the kitchen and shut the door, before returning to the screens in the study.

At two twenty-one a tall man, with short grey hair visible under a wide-brimmed Panama hat, walked calmly around the corner of the front gate – as if he were out for an afternoon stroll. A safari-style light grey jacket, open-necked shirt, dark chinos. Juliette waited a few seconds; if there was anyone with him, they were staying out of sight. She got up and made for the hall. The entry monitor was near the door to the sitting room, about fifteen feet from the front door. The doorbell rang just before she reached the monitor.

'Who is it?' She could see the fish-eye closeup on the screen, and knew who it was from the photos.

'You're expecting me.' The deep, grating voice that she had previously heard on the phone.

'Just a second. I'll come to the door.' She moved quickly to look through the spyhole in the door. Restricted view past his head, but it looked as if he was alone. She opened the heavy oak door. 'Thank you for coming,' she said. His handshake was surprisingly limp. She guessed it was one he reserved for women. She looked at the jacket – plenty of room for a Glock in a shoulder holster. The clothes were different. The lean, hard face. It might not be the man at the next table in the hotel lounge, but it might be.

'Make it worth my while,' he said, walking through the door, looking from side to side. 'Is he here yet?' He moved with a stealthy athleticism. He must have been keeping himself in good shape in prison.

'Not yet. You're early. Come through to the sitting room.' She led him into the room and stayed by the door. 'Tea or coffee, or something stronger?' He ignored her and walked straight to the French windows, standing to one side, looking to see as much as he could of the lawn and its surroundings.

Better do it now, she said to herself, above the mounting noise in her head. She took a step to her right, reached into the shoulder bag, took out a yellow washing-up glove, slipped it on to her right hand, grabbed the service revolver, already cocked, shifted back to her left without standing up, crouching in the doorway, left elbow on left knee, dead steady, gun in both hands, left over right, finger on the trigger. Things were moving in slow motion. 'You should see this,' she said, more loudly than she had intended.

As he turned, his right hand darted towards the inside of his jacket. She squeezed the trigger. The bullet knocked him back against the French windows. She just heard the sound of shattering glass above the roar in her head. It took her a moment to stand up. This was so different from the last time. Then it had been in a filthy ruin of a cottage, fit only for sheltering animals, in a fight, a struggle for survival. Now, in her clean, well-lit sitting room furnished with expensive antiques, the sensation of firing the gun was quite different. Out of place, offensive – transgressive. And she had shot a man she did not know, even though she knew she hated him and had needed to kill him. Mitigating a risk. Trying to right a wrong.

She let out a lungful of air that she had been holding, then forced herself to breathe. She walked over to the man cautiously, the gun in her right hand pointed at his face, now partially obscured by the Panama hat which had tipped forward as he had fallen and was now resting on his nose. He was sitting on the floor with his legs out in front of him, propped up against the French windows like a drunk against a wall. Still pointing the gun, she reached down with her left hand to check for a pulse in his neck. Her hand stopped an inch short. Touching him would make it too real. She knew he was dead. Blood had spurted from his chest, making a red mess of his white shirt and leaving glistening streaks and spots on the maroon carpet. She could feel the thumping of her heart in her own chest, beating double time as if to compensate for the heart in the body on the floor, that had just stopped. She wanted to tell him she knew he killed Carrie, but it was too late.

After getting her breathing under control, she turned and put the old gun on the coffee table. She slipped off the rubber glove and dropped it behind the door. Then she went to the shoulder bag in the alcove and pulled out the other rubber glove, also a right hand. At Frampton's body, she bent over and made herself reach inside his jacket with her gloved hand to where she knew the holster must be. Just as her hand felt something hard, she looked at the body's hand on the carpet and froze. Shit. Shit. Shit. There was a jagged, dark red hole just below the knuckle of the middle finger. Fragments of shattered bone were visible, and a dark red patch was merging into the carpet from under the hand, still oozing blood. He had got his hand in the way of the bullet as he had tried to reach for his gun.

She stared at the damaged hand. She had planned this confrontation so carefully, her killer mind imagining the variations she might have to adapt to. But this wasn't one of them. As she was trying to decide what to do, she heard the doorbell. Alfie. Shit. She looked at the old gun on the coffee table; she'd have to leave it there for now. Back at the body, she reached inside Frampton's jacket to get his gun. Pulled it out in her gloved hand. God. No. No. No. It isn't a Glock. What the fuck? The doorbell rang again. Shit. She looked at the brown plastic butt of the pistol in her right hand, Sig Sauer stamped on the barrel. She had been studying Glock videos on the internet and knew exactly how to handle and fire a Glock 17. *Bloody police or that bloody reporter can't get their facts right. Maybe this Sig thing works the same.* She held the automatic in her gloved hand as she walked to the entry monitor. The familiar round, dark face, now distorted on the screen, looking up into the camera, wearing a green baseball cap.

She struggled to steady her breathing. 'Push the door, Alfie. He isn't here yet.' After pressing the button to open the front door, she ran back into the sitting room and turned right, across to the fireplace. The carriage clock on the mantelpiece told her four minutes had passed since she had shot Frampton. She looked at the strange pistol in her gloved hand. Button on the left must be the safety. She pressed it. Frampton would keep it on safe. Would he leave a round in the breach? Too late to worry about it. This shot had to be dead accurate. She pointed the gun at the doorway, left hand over right. The little gun was about half the weight of the Webley revolver. She held her breath.

From this angle, she wasn't visible from the hall. She leaned back against the mantelpiece to steady herself. The squat little man came through the door and saw the body by the French windows. He seemed rooted to the spot.

She needed him facing her. 'Hello, Kenneth,' she said.

He turned. 'What—' The bullet hit a rib just to the right of his breastbone, narrowly missing his heart. He was thrown back against the doorframe as splintered pieces of the rib assisted the soft-nosed bullet in destroying most of his right lung.

Chapter 32

Juliette looked at the small pistol in her hand. It felt like a toy. The noise and the recoil were hardly anything compared to the old revolver. She turned to the man she had just shot. He was sitting in a position strangely similar to Frampton's body, except for his legs, one of which was sticking out to the side, the other crumpled under him. His cap had come off and was in the hall behind him. His olive skin was taking on a grey pallor, his eyes staring, following Juliette as she came closer. 'Yeah, Kenny boy, thought you were going to get rid of me, didn't you. You and that corpse over there. Well, your nasty little game has just ended.'

His lips moved soundlessly as a splutter of breath came through the hole in his chest. Juliette felt her legs go and sat, just in time, on the arm of one of the wing-back chairs. She looked away, fixed her eyes on the fireplace, panting, needing more air, her breathing out of control. She needed to believe what she had just done. She felt the acid rise in her throat. The only way she could deal with the disgust she felt for herself was to turn it back on the wounded man.

She forced herself to look at him, the red froth spluttering from the hole in his chest. 'Oh, look at you. Trying to do an imitation of the Robert De Niro character at the end of *Heat*? Is that it? Not very impressive, if you don't mind my saying so. That's only air coming out of your chest, not some metaphysical life force. Cat got your tongue? Got so much to say and lost the ability to say it in your convoluted, out-of-date, cliché-ridden apology for normal communication?' She looked at the small automatic in her gloved hand, clicked the safety back on with her thumb. She was aware again of the roaring noise in her head as she walked back to Frampton's body. She bent and pressed the gun into the body's wounded hand, folded its fingers round the butt, pressed the index finger onto the trigger taking care not to get any blood from the wounded hand on the gun.

Holding the gun by its barrel, she said, 'You see what's happened here, don't you, Kenny. Bad guy was standing by the fireplace when you came into the room, and shot you. He must have found out that you killed his mate, Richie. He set up this meeting. Planned to kill me too but couldn't do that until after I'd opened the door for you. He was standing by the fireplace and shot you as you came into the room. You collapsed in a heap, just where you are now. Dying. Breathe deep, by the way. Every breath sucks more blood into what remains of your lungs. It won't be long now. You can spend your last few minutes thinking about Miranda and the other poor souls whose lives you ruined. Frampton knows that you never carry a gun, so he's walking round the room telling you what an arsehole you are, or were. But you, you cunning little bastard, are reaching behind you to get the old revolver out of your waistband.' His eyes fell, half-closed. The fingers of his left hand, on the carpet, opened and closed on nothing.

She saw blood beginning to dribble from both corners of his mouth, adding to the mess.

'Your problem, Kenny, you're stupid as well as nasty. You could have kept your head down, stayed out of Glynis's life, and mine. But you just had to play your little games, didn't you. Acting the puppet master, pulling all the strings.' She stood over him as he panted and gazed into nothing, then turned and walked back across the room. 'Now, just a few little details to get this crime scene right.'

Even as she was being so careful, following the plan, all she could feel was hatred. She had to go on directing it at the man on the floor, to deflect it from herself. 'On your way now, aren't you, Kenny. I think you've got it. Yeah, it's the gun you took from that dirty old hovel after you murdered Richard B-S with it. You manage with your last ounce of strength to raise the old revolver. You see Frampton by the French windows, you call him, because you want him to see that he's about to be killed. Bam, you shoot him through the heart, killing him instantly. But something happens that I hadn't planned for. He's gone and put his little automatic back in his shoulder holster. He tries to get it, and the bullet goes through his hand before his heart.' Juliette bent down, lifted the lapel of the safari jacket with her left hand and carefully slipped the automatic back into the holster. Then she pulled off the rubber glove and carefully rubbed it against Frampton's wounded hand, then the sleeve next to it and a bit more on the front of his jacket.

'See?' She turned back to look at the wounded man. 'Oh, you do look the worse for wear. Unable to appreciate how clever I've been? What a shame. I had planned to leave his gun on the carpet, by his body, where he dropped it when you shot him. But if that had happened, he wouldn't have got shot through the hand, so into the holster it had to go.' With a tissue in her hand, she picked the revolver up by its barrel. 'Look at this old thing. None the worse for wear after spending a week in a carrier bag buried under a gorse bush. Wouldn't guess it, would you? That's because the alternative truth is that you've had it all the time since you killed your friend Richie. What a bad boy you are.'

She had never been a cruel person. Had never wanted to inflict pain or harm on another person. But now she was in the grip of something she couldn't stop. 'Kenny, you do look sorry for yourself. Quite honestly, I'd love to put a bullet through your head, the *coup de grace* as you would say, put you out of your misery. But it wouldn't fit the scenario. It's not part of the plan. You see, I even crouched down when I shot Frampton, to get the trajectory right, to help those clever forensics officers to make a complete cock-up of the crime scene analysis.' Still holding the revolver by the barrel, she pressed the man's fingers in the right places on the butt and trigger, even remembering to press his thumb on the hammer, for when he cocked it before firing.

'You know, Kenny, with that blank look on your face, I have no idea whether you understand what's just happened – or what everyone is going to believe happened. But I'm not sure I fully trust you. So when you shot Frampton, in your weakened state you didn't have much of a grip on the old gun; the recoil caused it to fly out of your hand and land just here.' She placed the gun on the carpet about a metre away from his hand, wiping the barrel with a tissue. 'From the look of you it won't be long now, just a minute or two. Shame really – after the things you've done, I think you deserve to suffer a lot more. Anyway, if your oxygen-deprived brain is capable of thinking anything, you can die with the cosy thought that the world will be a better place without you. And let's not forget what happened when you shot Frampton.' She picked up the first glove from behind the door and wiped it over his hand, sleeve and shirt. 'Blood spatter tells them a lot, you know, Kenny, but the distribution of gunshot residue is much more random. As long as they find some where they expect to, consistent with the story, that should do the job.'

She looked at him, trying to think. She needed him to be dead for her own safety, but for the story he needed to have lived long enough after being shot, to shoot Frampton. Cause of death had to be the one bullet wound in his chest. She had to leave him, and quickly; the Oakwoods would have heard the shots.

'Sorry I can't hang about chatting any longer. I must run to the bathroom and make a phone call. Bye bye.' She picked up the other glove from the carpet. As she walked out of the room, she tore off the grey T-shirt, ran to the utility room and stuffed it in the washing machine with some other laundry. She dropped the two right-hand gloves in the sink, gave them a quick scrub with detergent and put them on the draining board with their left-hand partners. Then she ran to the front of the house and opened the front door a crack. Lara would get there in a few minutes. She was bound to let herself in when there was no answer. She'd be getting more than a personal interest story.

In the bathroom, Juliette scrubbed her hands and forearms with soap and water, wiped her face and neck with a soapy flannel, dried herself and pulled on the white T-shirt that earlier she had put ready on the side of the bath. She slid the little bolt to lock the door, then sat on the floor by the lavatory, and pulled the dirty tissues out of her left-hand jeans pocket.

Chapter 33

'Mrs Walker, are you in there?' The question jolted her back into the present moment. A man's voice. Not him.

'Mrs Walker, are you able to open the door?' She opened her mouth to say, 'Yes', but no sound came out. She moved her legs and crawled towards the door.

'Mrs Walker, can you stand well back from the door. I'm going to break it down.'

'I'll open it,' she shouted, almost sure that she had made an audible sound. Kneeling on the hard, tiled floor, she reached up and slid the bolt. She shuffled out of the way as a man in a green uniform opened the door. Past his legs she saw the fat man lying on his back, with a pad on his chest and a plastic mask with tubes over his face. A person in the same dark green uniform was crouching over him. She pointed. 'He's dangerous,' she said.

'Not at present, he isn't. He's barely alive, but we're doing what we can for him.'

'No. He's bad. He was trying to kill me. He's got a gun.'

'He can't reach the gun now. Have you any injuries?' He was on one knee in front of her, looking into her face.

'That's not the point. He was trying to kill me.' A movement on the other side of the doorway caught her attention. Now there were two green uniforms. The fat man was being lifted on to a stretcher.

'How's the woman in the driveway?' the man near her asked.

'Safe and sedated. We need to stabilise this one.' The bathroom door closed.

'Now, please can you open your eyes and look at me?' The man was talking to her in a gentle voice. He had short, dark hair – neatly trimmed stubble, wire-framed glasses. She blinked as he shone a torch into her eyes.

'Are you feeling any pain? Can you point to where it's coming from?'

She heard a siren above the other noises. 'You got here before the police.'

'You're safe now. Try to relax,' the man said. He had closed the lid of the toilet and Juliette was sitting on it. 'Stroke of luck. Man in the village with indigestion thought he was having a heart attack. We'd just finished with him when the call came.'

'Did he say anything? This man here, I mean.'

'The police are here now.'

'He's my friend. He was trying to protect me. Will he be all right?'

'Try to relax, Mrs Walker. He's got a bullet wound in the chest. We're doing everything we can for him. You just said he was trying to kill you.'

'I meant the other man. Will Alfie survive? He's my friend. He saved my life.'

'It's too early to tell. He's lost a lot of blood. They'll be doing everything possible in the ambulance. If he makes it to the hospital, I'd say he's got a better than evens chance of pulling through. There might be some brain damage. Lack of oxygen.'

Juliette was struggling to think clearly, fighting the noise in her head. She was entering a world where things had to make sense. How the hell had Alfie, or Kenny, managed to get up the stairs? He must have shot Lara when she came through the front door. Why? She had been so sure he would die where he lay in that doorway. She could just make out the sound of people shouting downstairs. 'You know the rules. You wait for us. You do not endanger the lives of your team.'

'Yeah, well when was the last time a paramedic got shot in a domestic? Bloke would have died if we'd waited for you.'

She turned and saw a tall man in thin white overalls in the doorway.

'Can you stay out of the room, please? She's my patient.'

'Is she injured?'

'No sign of physical injury. She's in shock.'

'I want you out of here. Inspector Singleton. This is a murder investigation and I need to talk to her.'

The man in the green uniform crouched in front of her and looked in her eyes. 'Do you feel well enough to talk to the police? I'll stay with you.'

'Did you say there's a woman in the driveway?' she said, her voice faltering.

'Shot in the leg. Swearing a lot. She'll be fine.'

Singleton intervened. 'Right. We need you out of the bathroom. The SOCOs have got to work in here. Help her down the stairs. Keep over to the right. Avoid the blood. Is that handgun exactly where you found it?'

'It was gripped in his right hand. I pulled his fingers back to release it. It dropped on the carpet. I didn't touch it.'

Juliette closed her eyes to the flash of a camera as they walked across the landing. She felt the paramedic's hands on her shoulders as they went down the stairs, gripping the banister on the right. She tried not to look at the blood on each step of the stair carpet. It was still wet. How could anyone lose so much blood and live?

Soon, Juliette was sitting at her kitchen table, the paramedic beside her.

'My name's Mo,' he said. 'I can give you a mild sedative, if you want it.' The label on his uniform read, Mohomet Khalid.

'My name's Jules,' she said. 'Cup of tea would be good. I want to keep alert to help the police. I'm still a bit wobbly. Teabags are in the cupboard above the kettle. Have a mug yourself.'

Singleton came into the room, as Mo was filling the kettle. 'Detectives will be here in five minutes. They've asked me not to let you out of my sight till they get here.'

Her mind was still adjusting to this different world. Where men would ask questions. A world she had been in before, where the story had to be believable. 'Did you catch the other man?' She looked at him furiously. Her anger was with herself, for not thinking to ask that earlier.

'What other man?'

'The man who shot Alfie – white hat, grey safari jacket. Tried to shoot me too.'

'You don't have to worry about him, Mrs Walker.'

'There might be more of them. Alfie's in danger. He needs to be protected.'

'Don't worry. We know our job. There's a PC in the ambulance with him.'

'He needs an armed guard. Seriously. You've seen what they're like. What they can do. They'll stop at nothing.' Got to convince them she's Alfie's friend, to explain why she let them into the house, and so they'd let her visit him in hospital, if that became necessary.

'I appreciate your concern. I assure you we'll take appropriate precautions.'

'I need to phone my husband. He's with my children. I can't have them coming here, obviously. My mother's with them too. We'll all go to her house for a few days.'

She told Steve she was fine, completely unhurt, and came close to making the mistake of telling him that Frampton was dead, but realised, just in time, that the police mustn't know that she knew who the man in the white hat was, or that he was dead. She dealt with it as briefly as possible. 'Someone fired a gun, not at me. But it's a crime scene, so the police are here. You won't be able to come in. We'll need to stay at the mansion tonight. Can you pick up something for supper – and breakfast?'

*

Fifteen minutes later, the paramedic had left after Juliette had convinced him that she was suffering no ill effects of what had happened earlier. Inspector Singleton had left the kitchen and she assumed he was looking at the work the SOCO team were still doing around the house. She was sitting at the side of the kitchen table, with DI Wentworth and DS Cartwright opposite her.

DI Wentworth said, 'So we meet again, Mrs Walker – under extraordinary circumstances.'

'Yes.'

'Micky, could you ask one of the female SOCOs to come in?'

A minute later a short, white-costumed officer introduced herself. 'PC Dixon, sir.'

'Right. Mrs Walker, I understand you have had a very frightening experience. I'm sure you would feel more comfortable in fresh clean clothes, instead of those ones which I noticed, when we came in, have a few bloodstains. So, PC Dixon here is going to accompany you to your bedroom so that you can change your clothes. PC Dixon, please bag the T-shirt, jeans, socks and trainers that Mrs Walker is currently wearing. You know what to do with them. Mrs Walker, the clothing will be returned to you when our people have carried out the necessary analysis. Before leaving today, we will give you a receipt for any items we take, and we will need you to sign an authorisation.'

Several minutes later, Juliette was back at the kitchen table wearing her baggy jeans, a light blue T-shirt and flip-flops. Cartwright had placed a notebook and pen on the table in front of him.

DI Wentworth again. 'Mrs Walker, this is an informal discussion. In due course we will need a formal statement. DS Cartwright here is going to take some notes. In the circumstances, if you wish to stop at any point, please tell us. We will stop the meeting, and plan to resume at a convenient time in the near future. You have a right to be accompanied by a solicitor, but that would only delay matters. May we proceed as we are?'

'I understand. Go on.' Juliette saw Cartwright had his head down, busy writing. She forced herself to dispel the images, the blood, the moral revulsion. She had to belong in this enclosed world of men with notebooks and questions. She had to get this exactly right and tell the same story to her mum and Steve this evening. No discrepancies.

Wentworth reached into a cardboard carton on the floor near him and brought the Webley revolver in a sealed clear plastic bag with a label on it, out onto the table. 'Do you recognise this weapon?'

Juliette examined it carefully. 'It looks like one of those old handguns from the Second World War. Like the one my father got me to hide.'

'Would you say it is the same weapon?'

'I wouldn't know one from another. I didn't look at it very carefully.'

Wentworth sighed and put the revolver back in the cardboard box.

'Can you tell us how the two men came to be in your house?'

'Alfie Borg, the one who I hope to God will recover, contacted me soon after my father was killed. He said he had known my father in the past and had various contacts who might be able to help find out who killed him. He's been very supportive – in my bereavement. He's a kind man.'

'And it didn't occur to you to tell us about this?'

'I asked him why he didn't just go to the police instead of coming to me, and he said he didn't want to because the police aren't always fair.'

'Do you know what he meant by that?'

'I assumed it was because he's from another country and he'd had a bad experience with the police there.'

'The question was, why didn't you tell us as soon as this man you call Alfie had made contact?'

'He asked me not to. He was very convincing.' She sniffed. 'I hadn't realised he was in danger.'

'What about the other man?'

'I've never seen him before. I phoned Alfie – when? – this morning; it's been a strange day. I can't believe it was only this morning. He said he had met someone who said he knew something about the Belton-Smart killing. He, Alfie, said this man wanted to tell me direct and would only do so if the three of us met at my house. I was a bit uncertain about it, whether we'd be safe with someone who was in the criminal fraternity, and Alfie told me he was confident that this man knew who had actually shot my father and would tell us. So, we agreed on three-thirty this afternoon.

'The man with the white hat arrived something like ten minutes early. He was having a look round, like to make sure there was no one else hiding in the garden or something. Then a few minutes later, Alfie arrived – still early. I'm just behind Alfie when he goes into the sitting room and then I see the other man's got a gun in his hand, and, bang, he shoots Alfie right in the doorway. I wasn't going to hang around asking him why he did it, so I just turned and ran upstairs and locked myself in the bathroom. I was sort of freaking out, and then I heard another bang and thought maybe that's him finishing Alfie off, and then he's going to come after me, and strangely up to then I didn't think to phone 999, but that was when I did it. Then there was another bang and a scream, and I realised he must have shot Lara.'

'Lara?'

For a second she tried to imagine what Lara was going

to say to her. 'I wanted her here as another witness. To make sure I was safe.' She started crying and pulled a tissue out of the box on the table.

Wentworth waited a few seconds for Cartwright to stop writing. Cartwright put down the pen and stretched the fingers of his right hand. Then Wentworth said, 'The paramedic said you thought the man you call Alfie was trying to kill you.'

'That's a misunderstanding. I thought it was the other man lying on the landing after coming up the stairs trying to get into the bathroom to kill me. I thought Alfie was lying dead in the doorway where I'd last seen him.'

'So you saw him lying in the doorway?'

'Not really. He was on his way down after being shot and I was running for the stairs, so I knew that was where he must be.' *That was close. Shit. Don't make any more mistakes like that.* The image of Alfie – Kenny – eyes glazed, blood spluttering, filled her mind. She breathed deep and slow, forcing herself back into the world of police questions.

'How could the other man be lying on the landing seriously wounded?'

So many things had happened that seemed impossible. 'It didn't make sense. Like in a dream.'

Wentworth fixed her with his eyes. 'So why did the man you say is your friend fire a shot through the bathroom door?'

Juliette put her hands over her face. 'He was barely alive. He can't have known what he was doing.'

Wentworth said that was all they needed for the present. They would contact her in the morning to arrange a formal interview.

'We'll all be at my mother's house for a while, until we've

got this sorted out. New carpets. Repaired the... repaired anything that's broken. Will I be able to visit Alfie in hospital?'

She had so nearly said, 'Repaired the French windows'. God. Focus. That could have put her in the dock.

'There are security arrangements. You'll need to ask the hospital. Assuming he lives, I don't think he'll be sitting up in bed chatting to people for quite a while. And the minute he comes round he'll be talking to us.'

Chapter 34

'Darling, I just can't understand why you let them into the house,' Caroline said.

Juliette closed her eyes. PC Dixon had helped her pack a few things for herself, Steve and the children, and feed Ziggy, before driving her to the mansion in a police car. Now she was sitting at the kitchen table. She had summarised to Steve and her mother the story she had told the police. Caroline was stirring something on the hob and Steve was scrubbing something in the sink. Steve's voice: 'She's been through a lot, Cara. This time she was actually there when a man was shot.'

Juliette heard her mother start to say something again and needed to escape. 'I'm sorry, I'm really sorry, but I'm so tired. I can't eat anything. Which room are we in?'

There, when a man was shot. It was real, but in a different world. A world where you could shoot two men, cool as you like, taking careful aim. Then sit at your kitchen table opposite two policemen, trying to make your story real. A different world, but that didn't stop the images recurring. The blood.

She was lying in a strange bed in a strange room. The chintz curtains let in too much light. *If no one knows, it didn't happen.*

But now she had to fix herself in this world. Calculate. Assess the risk. Top of the list was Alfie regaining consciousness and talking to the police. Then there were the spots of blood. It just had to be Alfie's blood on her jeans and trainers. She was trying to recapture the reality of what had happened. She had run over to Frampton immediately after shooting him. There had been a squirt of blood just after the bullet hit. More blood when she bent down to get his gun? She couldn't be sure. Then Alfie – the blood spluttering out of his chest as he tried to speak. Most of it dribbled down his shirt and onto his trousers. Then the bastard had dragged himself up the stairs and tried to shoot her through the bathroom door. But before that he had shot Lara. He must have thought she was Jules. A stroke of luck, though. It would help the police believe that Alfie shot Frampton. Surely. Juliette managed an inward smile. She had planned Lara's arrival as a safeguard in case things had gone wrong and she'd need a witness.

*

Breakfast was taken up with practical arrangements for the day. Steve would go to their house to feed Ziggy and would get Nick to cover for him in the shop. Juliette agreed to cancel her planned music lessons, and Caroline made the phone calls for her. Steve would go to the carpet shop to order new carpets. He would send Juliette photos of the samples he liked, for her to choose. He would arrange a contractor to repair the French windows and replace the bathroom door and mirror. He would also contact the insurance company.

Caroline stayed silent for a while, then said, 'But why did this terrible thing happen in your house?'

Juliette looked at her then looked away. 'I agreed to talk to them because I thought I'd find out who killed Richard. Maybe the police will be able to work it out. Do you think I would have let them in if I'd known they were going to have a fucking gunfight?'

She felt her phone vibrate. A text from Lara: *What the fuck was that? I got shot.* She had better not ignore it. Lara's experience was no doubt going to appear in the paper. She replied: *I'm sorry. So glad you weren't more seriously hurt. Police interview today. Will tell you more later.*

She went through to the sitting room where the children were watching a TV cartoon. Soon, Jason was telling her about the monkeys in the zoo and Lucy was making a variety of animal noises. Her mind drifted to the story she would have to tell. She would maintain that Alfie was her friend. With luck the cops would know better, and it would emerge that she had been deceived by him. As long as she stuck to the story, the police wouldn't be able to prove otherwise.

Risk assessment: solicitor, or no solicitor? Top risk: Kenny wakes up and tells all. Mitigation: he dies or is so brain-damaged that he can't give evidence. Either way, it was out of her hands, locked in place, as Tim would have said. Her only option was to carry on assuming Kenny was out of it. Second risk: it was Frampton's blood on her jeans. Mitigation: insist that it was impossible, demand an independent analysis, call for the solicitor. Third risk: other forensic evidence she hasn't thought of contradicts the story. Mitigation: again, that would be the point at which she calls for the solicitor.

She left the children to enjoy the cartoon and went upstairs to the guest bedroom. She tapped her phone to go to the hospital's website, then tapped the main switchboard number. 'Hello. I'm enquiring about a patient admitted yesterday. Alfred Borg.'

'Can you tell me which department?'

'It was an emergency. He's badly wounded. Gunshot.'

There were more questions about the patient's name. She said he sometimes called himself Alfie Smith. But that didn't help.

'Was anyone admitted with a gunshot wound yesterday?'

'Not according to our records. He might have been taken up to Norwich.'

Juliette closed the call. She was still thinking about what that meant, when her phone jingled.

'Hello, this is Jules Walker.'

'Mrs Walker, this is DC Andrea Gillespie. You might remember me?'

'Yes, of course. I was expecting a call from DS Cartwright.'

'He's on leave. I'm covering for him. It's about the, er, the incident at your house yesterday?'

'Is there any news about the man who was wounded?'

'Sorry. Mrs Walker, we need to carry out a formal interview to follow up the questions that DI Wentworth put to you yesterday. Would you be able to attend at the police station in Museum Street today? We can send a car for you, if that makes it easier for you.'

'Am I a suspect?'

'The technical position is that you're a witness, but we need to carry out a formal recorded interview, under caution, to eliminate you as a suspect, which means that you

are entitled to be accompanied by a solicitor, if you so wish.'
She heard Gillespie take a deep breath.

'I see. I'll need to change some arrangements for the day, but I want to help the police as much as I can. I'm sure I don't need a solicitor.'

*

Three hours later she was sitting in a police interview room. This time it was DI Wentworth with DC Gillespie. Steve had dropped her there on his way to the carpet showroom. Surely they wouldn't think she was stupid enough to create a crime scene in her own living room. Would they?

Gillespie started the recording machine and recited the statement about her right to remain silent. The early questioning repeated what she had told Wentworth in her kitchen the previous day. She was confident that there were no discrepancies in her answers. But then:

'Mrs Walker, can you explain exactly where the two men were, and where you were, when the shot was fired at the man you call Alfie?'

'It's difficult. It all seems so unreal. I had left the sitting room to open the front door for Alfie. I was more or less behind him when we went into the sitting room. The man in the white hat was standing by the fireplace so we didn't see him until we were in the room. Alfie must have turned right to go towards the man he knew.' Juliette put her hands over her face. 'Then there was the bang of the gun.' She spoke through her hands. 'I didn't know what it was at first.' She half controlled a sob. 'Alfie was knocked back against the side of the door, the doorframe. I think I must have jumped forward to avoid him crashing into me. Then I turned and looked at him, sort of sinking to the floor, and then,' she let out an uncontrolled sob, 'I saw the blood. It was coming out of his chest. Instinct must have kicked in. I just ran. I might have had to step over his legs to get out of the door.'

'Yesterday, you said you were behind the man, when he was shot.'

Juliette took her hands away from her face. 'It's very confusing. It all happened so quickly. I think I was behind him, and a bit to one side. Then the bullet knocked him back, and I jumped forwards as I've just said, so by then I must have been in front of him, otherwise I wouldn't have seen the blood coming out of his chest. I think that must be how it happened.'

'Thank you.' Wentworth looked Juliette directly in the eye. She held his gaze, determined not to blink. 'Preliminary tests show that the blood on your clothing was that of the man you call Alfie.'

'Obviously.' Relief soared through her. She did everything she could not to show it.

'Where exactly were you standing when the blood splashed on to your clothing?'

'I wasn't aware of blood splashing on to my clothing, so I can't tell you.'

'But you saw blood spraying out of his mouth?'

'There wasn't any blood coming out of his mouth. The only blood I saw was from the wound in his chest.' This was becoming difficult. He was trying to place her there for a longer time than suited her.

'After the spatter from the impact of the bullet, when you were behind him, the blood was just running down his chest. Not projecting.'

Juliette put her hands over her face again. 'Mr Wentworth, you're making me relive an extremely traumatic experience.' She put her head down, struggling to stay in this world of hard questions. 'I'm trying to help you establish exactly what happened, and you seem to be trying to catch me out.' She lifted her head, removed her hands, eyes moist. 'It all happened very quickly. There must have been a moment when I was standing in front of him as he was falling. I saw blood sort of spluttering out of his chest; maybe it was mixed up with his airways. I didn't stop to think about it. I just ran to save myself, not looking back.'

'The analyst says you must have been standing in front of the wounded man for at least one minute. How do you explain that?'

'The analyst is wrong.' She held his gaze. 'I think you should get a second opinion. I was stunned. It can't have been more than a few seconds. As soon as I realised what had happened, I got out of there, expecting a bullet in my back any moment.' A tear rolled down her cheek.

'I realise it was a shocking experience, and I appreciate your help.' Wentworth half closed his eyes, as if deep in thought. 'The paramedics told us the front door was open when they arrived. Can you explain that?'

Juliette reached down for a tissue from her bag, spent some time wiping her eyes and blowing her nose. 'It's a very old door – same age as the house, about 200 years, solid oak. It must be that Alfie didn't close it properly when he came in. It's a very heavy door. People who aren't used to it often don't realise how hard you've got to push it. I opened it from the panel. I didn't go to the door. I was in a nervous state because we'd agreed to have the meeting at three-thirty, but the man in the white hat, who I'd never seen before, turned up ten minutes early. He was… well, he wasn't at all friendly. When Alfie arrived a few minutes later, also earlier than the agreed time, I just wanted to show him in quickly, so I didn't notice the door not being closed properly.' She was suspended between two worlds. Aware that she was traumatised by what she had done the previous day, but now letting her visible distress support the story.

'Would you agree it is possible that he left the door open deliberately, to allow entry for a third man?'

Juliette fought off the black and white image of Orson Welles and the sound of a zither. 'I was locked in the bathroom, so I can't say. But I would have thought it would be possible for another man to come in, see his friend Alfie had been shot, so he managed to shoot the man in the white hat before making a speedy exit. Then Alfie regains consciousness after the shock of being shot. Then he sees someone come through the front door and in his semi-conscious state thinks it's someone else coming to attack me, so he shoots and that's how Lara got shot. Then he figures out I've probably hidden in the bathroom, struggles up the stairs to station himself outside the door to protect me. Losing all that blood – heroic…' Juliette let that word hang, and another tear rolled down her cheek.

'In which case, it was he who fired a shot through the bathroom door. Was that part of his attempt to protect you?' Wentworth appeared to be suppressing a smile.

'I imagine that must have been an accident caused by a muscle spasm as he passed out. That…' Juliette stared at Wentworth, then at Gillespie, then back at Wentworth. She had been about to say: 'That trigger's very light if you've pulled the hammer back.' *Jesus, that was a close one.*

'Yes?'

'That's the most likely explanation I can think of.'

'The man you call Alfie arranged this meeting and told you he had invited his friend to attend.'

'He didn't call him a friend.' Juliette was sure she hadn't said he had. 'He said the man was someone who could help us find my father's killer. Knew something about it.'

'So what motive could this man, who wanted to help, possibly have for wanting this man "Alfie" dead?'

'I've no idea, except for the obvious. Alfie's been poking his nose in. For all I know the man with the white hat might have killed my father. When someone asks too many questions in that world, they can end up dead. I watch films, TV.'

'But the man you call Alfie was in possession of the service revolver, which, subject to the results of ballistics tests, is likely to be the one that killed your father.'

'You showed it to me yesterday. We can only guess at explanations, can't we. Alfie was very keen to find out who killed my father. He had contacts. Maybe he acquired the gun during the course of his investigations. Was keeping it as evidence. I'm sure you'll ask him when he wakes up.'

'Mrs Walker, our technical people have completed the analysis of your mobile phone.' *An abrupt change of subject, so predictable.* He seemed to be waiting for her to say something.

'Thank you for returning it to me so promptly.'

Wentworth exhaled noisily. 'Several conversations with the reporter.'

'Lara, the woman who was shot. She approached me. I didn't tell her anything you didn't want me to. She was very insistent about wanting to come and talk to me, and I eventually gave in. I thought she might have found out something useful and might contribute to the conversation I was having with the men. And after what had happened to my father, I was nervous about this meeting and wanted a witness there.'

'I see.' Wentworth shifted in his seat, leaning forward slightly. 'And you took a particular interest in some of your father's emails – took photographs of them?'

'I wanted to find him. I was looking for clues. Only natural, isn't it? The ones I didn't understand – from anonymous senders. I wanted to think about what they might mean.'

'And you photographed documents that were just strings of numbers?'

'I was puzzled by them – thought it might be some kind of code. I was going to try to work it out if I had time.'

'And did you?'

'No.'

Another change of subject. 'Our team who searched your garden shed expected to find a roll of duct tape. Why didn't they?'

Juliette returned his gaze. 'I can't explain that. As you know, I deeply regret having been duped into hiding the old gun there. I used a roll of duct tape to attach it to the underside of the pool table. I didn't take the roll out of the shed. I'm pretty sure I would have left it on that table, or on the shelf where I found it. If it went missing, I can only assume my father took it when he took the gun. He might have thought it would be useful while he was in hiding. Just an idea.' She pursed her lips.

'It wasn't found at the scene of his death.'

'Maybe he left it somewhere else. Maybe it was all used up. I don't know.'

'Why would a man you have never met commit this murder in your house?'

'It's guesswork again as far as I'm concerned.' Juliette knew she had to remain focused, even though the questions were becoming more general. There might be a trap. 'He must have thought it was a safe place to do it. He might have guessed it would throw suspicion on me. I'd been present just before and after my father's death. If another murder is committed in my house, with me there…' She shrugged her shoulders again. 'No smoke without fire. Or it was the only place he could get Alfie and me together. Kill us both. Tidy up.'

Wentworth looked at her, as if trying to see inside her brain. She was feeling less confident than she had been. She said, 'Maybe he thought he could set it up to look as if we had killed each other.'

She saw Wentworth raise an eyebrow.

'In which case, why wouldn't he have shot you first?'

'He needed me to open the door for Alfie. Who knows? I'm just guessing. You're asking for my opinion about things. Your opinion's probably worth more than mine. You're the professional.'

Chapter 35

Steve and Juliette were sitting in the garden at the mansion. Her phone jingled. She looked at the screen – Lara. She switched it off.

'Who was that?'

'Cold call.'

Lucy was chasing Jason around the lawn. Caroline came out carrying a tray. 'Tea and home-made chocolate brownies.' She put the tray down on the wrought iron table.

'Jules, did they say who the dead man was?' Caroline whispered.

'I asked. They can't divulge that information until a formal ID has taken place. I'm sure he was Frampton. Same voice.'

'What about the man who was wounded?' Caroline glanced towards the children to check they couldn't hear.

'I phoned the hospital. They didn't know anything about him. I'm a bit worried.' *No kidding*, she said to herself. *Why can't the bastard just die?*

*

'Our reporter shot and wounded in gang gunfight.' Caroline was sitting in a chunky armchair, reading from the local paper, with a glass of white wine on the occasional table beside her. 'There's a blurry photo of your house with that crime scene tape, and one of the woman who was shot.'

Juliette was sitting with Steve on a high-backed sofa. He was holding her hand. A glass of red wine and a tumbler of elderflower cordial were in front of them.

'We'd better not let Jazzy see it.'

'They're sound asleep.'

'Two dead men,' Caroline read.

Juliette's heart leapt. 'Go on, Mum.'

'Police have not revealed the names of the two victims, but our source believes them to be John Frampton, wanted for violating the terms of his probation after release three weeks ago from Manchester prison, and to help the police with their inquiries into the murder of Richard Belton-Smart, and Axel Camilleri, a Maltese national, wanted by Italian police for people-trafficking and drug-smuggling offences.' Caroline looked up from the paper. 'You said there was a man called Alfie.'

Juliette's mind was spinning. 'Does it say any more about the Maltese man?'

'Just that he died of a gunshot wound in the ambulance and was pronounced dead on arrival at Ipswich Hospital.'

'It doesn't say anything about other false names he used?'

'No.' Caroline went on reading aloud about their intrepid reporter, Lara Salisbury, being caught in the crossfire while hot on the trail of a criminal gang, and the location of the shooting not being disclosed at the request of the police, but she couldn't pay attention. Alfie – even Kenny wasn't his real name – was dead.

Her exhilaration came to an end as she slipped back into the other world. The disgust she felt at her cruel malevolence towards the man she had mortally wounded. She ordered herself to snap out of it. Surely now she was safe. Surely. 'I'm just going upstairs. Won't be long.'

Sitting on the side of the bed in the guest bedroom, she looked at her phone and thought about Glynis. What would she tell her? Her estranged daughter Carmen had tragically died in a mugging. Her friend Alfie, on whom she had become so dependent, was no friend and had done much to ruin her life, as well as being a brutal international criminal. Her finger hovered over the phone before hitting a different number.

'Hi, Lara, how's the leg?'

'Bloody hell, Jules.'

'I had no idea they were going to be there.'

'I could have been killed.'

'So could I. What do you know about this Axel Camilleri?'

'He used the name Alfie Borg, or Smith. You choose your friends carefully, don't you?'

'He said he could help find out who killed my dad. He caught me at a vulnerable time.'

'Real piece of shit. I've had enough. I'm quitting.'

'I didn't want you to get hurt.'

'Bye.'

Juliette slipped the phone into her jeans pocket. She opened her hands in front of her, stretched the fingers to her full reach. Hands that she was sure contained the memory of so much music. And she had used them to kill three men. She flexed them, wiggled the right index finger, the one that had pulled the trigger. There must be a way of parcelling the memory up and putting it away out of reach, blocked off. The way she had survived being raped. *If no one knows, it didn't happen.*

*

'Mum, thanks for everything you're doing. Are you going to miss this house?' They were sitting in Caroline's kitchen, drinking coffee. Steve was taking another day off from the shop and was going to be at their house with the carpet fitters and other men.

'I wondered if you might want to stay here for a few days – after... what happened.'

'We need to get back to normal. For the children – well, for me as well.'

They sat in silence. Juliette drained her mug, then checked the time on her phone. 'I've got things to do in town; I'll get a cab to go and pick my car up. I'll be back here for lunch. We should be able to move back to our house this afternoon.'

'I'll give you a lift.'

'Too much hassle carting Jazzy and Lulu about. Do you mind staying here with them?'

Jason ran to her with a wriggling earthworm in his cupped hands.

'That's lovely, Jazzy. Can you put it back in the flowerbed, please? We're going home this afternoon. You're overdue a piano lesson. You can show Daddy and Granny how you can play "Ode to Joy".'

There was a protracted 'Yeah' from Jason as he ran back to the flowerbed. After having a long cuddle with each child, she left them playing in the garden with her mother. She didn't disturb them when the cab arrived. She asked the driver to wait while she walked into the open garage and reached under the workbench for the rucksack. Then she spotted the roll of duct tape that she had left on the bench.

*

The Volvo was parked behind her Peugeot, and a couple of vans took up the rest of the turning area in their driveway. After paying the driver she took the rucksack and opened the boot of the Peugeot. The shopping trolley. She had forgotten all about it. For a second she was back on that rain-soaked park bench waiting for Tim to arrive with £105,000 in used notes. Used notes. She was guilty. Had colluded in their racket, and ending the lives of three men couldn't change that. She pulled the trolley out of the boot and put the rucksack in.

She dragged the trolley across the gravel to the open front door. There were sounds of hammering and what could be an electric drill. She couldn't go in; the carpet might still be there. She called, 'Steve.'

He came through the door with a big smile, saying, 'Welcome home,' and gave her a kiss.

'How's Ziggy?'

'Fine. I've just fed her. It's a bit chaotic in here. They're just taking the carpets up.'

'I won't come in. Can you take this?' She indicated the trolley. 'Ignore the tissues. They were on special. Can you put the bottle of bubbly in the fridge for this evening, and there's a box of chocolates. Try to resist opening it till my mum and the children get here.'

'Bubbly?' He raised an eyebrow.

'I think I'll join you for a glass or two.' She smiled and kissed him. 'Can you move the Volvo to let me out?'

*

She parked in the Buttermarket car park and headed for Museum Street with her shoulder bag in her left hand and the rucksack on her back. She went into the police station and asked the uniformed officer if DS Cartwright was available.

'He's on leave today, can anyone else help?'

'DC Gillespie?'

'I'll see if she's free – your name?'

'Juliette Walker.'

'Of course – one minute.'

When Gillespie came through the door, Juliette said, 'Hi. It's probably nothing, but I found this.' She held the rucksack in front of her. 'It must have been my father's. I thought, just in case. Wanting to help – co-operate. There's a laptop and lots of cheap phones. I thought I'd better not touch them. There might be some clues. Help you catch any other gang members. It was hidden in the garage at his house.'

'Thank you. We'll need to analyse them.' Gillespie took the rucksack.

'Oh, and it's probably not relevant any longer, but DI Wentworth was interested in the duct tape.' Juliette reached into her shoulder bag and pulled out the roll of tape, wrapped in a tissue. 'This roll was in the garage too. My father must have been going there, I suppose, when he was in hiding. It might be how they caught up with him. Anyway, do you want to take this? It might be the same tape that was used before. Check it for fingerprints? I'm not sure how it's significant, but

DI Wentworth was very interested in it, so I thought I'd bring it in case it helps.'

'Thank you. Yes. I'll pass it to him,' Gillespie said.

Juliette decided it could do no harm to test a theory. 'I'm really sorry Lara got hurt.'

Gillespie beamed and flushed. 'Thanks. Goodbye for now.'

Theory proved, Juliette thought, as she turned to walk back to the car park. Lies, lies, lies. *No more*, she ordered herself. *Parcel all that up, put it away, start again.* She could take on more teaching work. The shop wasn't doing too badly. They could try more European imports, that looked like a promising new way forward. Her mum seemed to be making a new beginning. She could too. Live a good life, support Steve, be a good mum. No more lies. The police would probably go on suspecting her, but as long as they couldn't prove anything…

Her phone jingled. 'Hi, Steve.'

'The glazier's done a good job on the French windows, taken all the broken glass from the bathroom, and gone. I can fix the new mirror. The bathroom's got a new panel door, just a primer coat on it, I'll finish the painting. The carpet guys have got the old carpets out and are making good progress fitting the new ones. They'll be finished in a couple of hours.'

'How's Ziggy?'

'Fine. She's been on my lap half the time.'

'Okay. I'm going back to the mansion for lunch. We'll all come over this afternoon.'

Before she reached the car park, her phone jingled again. No caller ID. She tapped Accept.

'Mrs Juliette Walker?' A man, foreign accent, East European? Possibly Russian.

'Yes, speaking.' She continued walking towards the multi-storey.

'Mrs Walker, I have a proposition for your business, Walker's Antiques.' Russian, definitely Russian.

'In that case you should speak to my husband. He's the managing director. I just do the admin, website, that sort of thing.'

'And the financial administration and accounting, which is the subject of my proposition. A potentially lucrative one for your business, and I am aware that you possess the appropriate skills.'

Juliette stopped walking and pressed the phone to her ear a little more firmly. 'What's your name?'

'Sergei Volkov. I myself have interests in the world of antiques. I know many dealers and am known to many wealthy businessmen who have taken up residence in your country. Many of these are keen to buy antiques with which to furnish their large houses and apartments in Mayfair, Belgravia and so on. I act as a broker. My suppliers, the dealers, need a reputable company like Walker's Antiques to invoice for the goods they supply, so that they can maintain proper records for your Companies House and Her Majesty's Revenue and Customs. My customers, on the other hand, are generally shy about their financial affairs and like to pay in cash. I handle all negotiations and transportation. All I am asking you to do, on behalf of Walker's Antiques, is bank the cash my associates pass to you, issue invoices to keep your accounting records in order, and pay the corresponding invoices you receive from my suppliers through the banking system. Turnover averages between £50,000 and £100,000 per month. Transactions are weekly or at the most twice weekly, merely an hour or two of work for you. My customers are wealthy men, willing to pay top prices, so for this service I can pay your company commission of fifteen per cent.'

Acknowledgements

Thanks first to my partner, Vicky Ross, who supported me throughout my disappearances into the writing zone. A mental health professional, Vicky also gave me practical advice and told me the best books to read to understand and develop Juliette's state of mind. Thanks too to our son, Jamie Ross Evans, for additional support. And great thanks to Jamie too for designing the front cover. A reviewer at The Crime Writers' Association was particularly helpful advising me about police procedure. Thanks also to Becky via the Cornerstones Literary Consultancy for advice on story structure and for helping me to get further into Juliette's personality and mental trauma. Jessica Gregory also contributed valuable words of advice and encouragement. I ought to mention with gratitude one of our cats, Humbug, who jumped on to my lap while I was writing the first draft, and I found myself talking to her about the struggle I was having – and so Juliette's cat, Ziggy, was born. Finally, thanks to Holly Porter and the team at Troubador for making this path to publication as smooth and as enjoyable as possible. Of course, any shortcomings or mistakes are entirely my responsibility.

This book is printed on paper from sustainable sources managed under the Forest Stewardship Council (FSC) scheme.

It has been printed in the UK to reduce transportation miles and their impact upon the environment.

For every new title that Troubador publishes, we plant a tree to offset CO_2, partnering with the More Trees scheme.

For more about how Troubador offsets its environmental impact, see www.troubador.co.uk/sustainability-and-community